To

William &

Hanna Spodek
4.21.14

EPISTOLE

(A LOVE STORY IN LETTERS)

HANNA A. SAADAH

"HISTORICAL FICTION"

Hanna A. Saadah
Copyright © 2007
Tele: (405) 749-4266
ALMUALIF Publishing, LLC
4205 McAuley Boulevard # 400
Oklahoma City, Oklahoma 73120-8347
Web Site Address: www.almualif.com
or www.hannasaadah.com

Library of Congress Control Number: 2007901168
Copyright Certificate Registration Number:TXu1-342-659
Effective Copyright Certificate Registration Date:2.16.2007

ISBN 10: 0-9765448-2-2
ISBN 13: 978-0-9765448-2-1
SAN 256-467X

Saadah, Hanna Abdallah 1946—

Books by Author:
Loves and Lamentations of a Life Watcher (Poetry)
Vast Awakenings (Poetry)
Familiar Faces (Poetry)
Four and a Half Billion Years (Poetry)
The Mighty Weight Of Love (Novel)

To Order On Line:
www.almualif.com
or www.hannasaadah.com

1 2 3 4 5 6 7 8 9 10

Table Of Contents

The Fifty Letters

A Note To The Reader

When I began writing Epistole, which derives from Latin via Greek meaning letter, I found myself scattered and strewn like intercontinental clouds that go back and forth between East and West without claiming either pole as inception or destination. I had to deconstruct and reconstruct my mindset as I changed identities with each personal letter. Writing in the First Person Singular, the natural style of letter writing, I became aware that my soul was inhabited by so many others and that, like Alfred Lord Tennyson says in Ulysses, "I am a part of all that I have met."

Hence, my advice to you, the reader, is: "Please take time for contemplation and don't race through it as you would a thriller. Rather, read it as a series of letters that, among other matters, tell a love story. To be invited to peer into the secret souls of these two tormented lovers—a Western man and an Eastern woman—is a rare privilege that one seldom experiences in real life."

Poetry plays a powerful role in character development and is metaphorically splashed all over the canvas like flowers on a landscape. Strategically placed, and there is hardly a letter without its poetic quotes, it plays a redeeming role by evoking colorful vistas out of the reverent spiritual scenery that suffuses the work.

Finally, this is not a mystery novel where you must reach the end before you can find out what really happened. On the contrary, this is a soul-searching, spiritual, historical, philosophical, multi-dimensional work that wrestles with a wide range of Eastern vs. Western cultural and historical differences which beset our modern world.

Written apropos, in the formal, elegant language of the past, Epistole is there to be leisurely sipped rather than hurriedly gulped. Bon appétit.

Hanna Saadah
Oklahoma City

Disclaimer

This work is entirely fictional. Any resemblance to living people or to their lives is the product of the reader's imagination. The dates and historical happenings are accurate, but any similarities beyond these historical facts are unintended and should not be misconstrued as real. The opinions held by characters regarding religions, nations, beliefs, and social mores are intended to create tension and provoke thought—they are not to be understood as representing the author's personal views.

Prologue

I have taken it upon myself to publish these letters of a love story between two people who are most dear to me. These letters were never intended for publication because they are too personal to be shared. Nevertheless, my insistence on putting them into print is altruistic. I want the readers, who normally feed on fiction, to be able to peer into the unedited human souls of these tormented lovers and see what it feels like to be unable to un-love. I want to reveal truths about the fierce forces of love and faith as never hitherto revealed. Indeed, most writers write so that they may be published and widely read, which renders their writing cautious. John once wrote:

> *"Only children speak freely.*
> *As adults,*
> *If we were to call things as we see them,*
>   *we would offend others*
>   *and invite persecution.*
> *Hence, in order to survive,*
>   *we have learned to pretend—*
>   *and the larger our audience,*
>   *the greater is our pretense."*

This love story began at the American University of Beirut between two college sweethearts—Fatima, 18 and John, 22. Although they both grew up and went to school in Tripoli, Lebanon, they never met until 1968 when Fatima came to the AUB as a freshman and began volunteering at the coffee shop of the American University Hospital. John was a medical student at that time, and one day Fatima spilled a hot cup of Turkish coffee into his lap. That was how it all began...

They were separated in 1970 because John migrated to America and Fatima remained in Beirut. Apart, they each married and had children, but throughout a span of thirty years—years marred by personal and political turmoil that shook the East and West by their roots—they remained in contact. These lovers were not trying to write their story for posterity. They were merely trying to un-love one another by staying apart, but the harder they tried, the worse they failed, and the more of their souls they revealed in their letters.

It is most unfortunate that the letters written between 1970 and 1990 were never found. But we did find all fifty letters mailed between September 1990 and May 1999. For obvious reasons, I did take certain editorial liberties and camouflaged beyond recognition all personal facts and details of all characters.

As for the literary value of these letters, it is up to the reader to decide. Although neither of the lovers was a professional writer, it is my opinion that these letters have forged a literary genre that will be met with enthusiasm and joy by most critics and readers.

Tariq Raci
(Beirut - Wednesday, April 5, 2006)

Glossary OF Names And Families

Ahmad (M):   Married Fatima in 1974 b 1949
Amar (F):   Kamal's and Gulnar's daughter b 1988
Carla (F):   Ghassan's wife b 1973
Fatima (F):   John's college girlfriend b 10. 31. 1950
Fatima (F):   Syrian psychic at Um Al-Huda's shrine
Frida (F):   John's and Norma's daughter b 1982
Ghassan (M):   Oldest son of John and Norma b 1972
Gulnar (F):   Turkish wife of Kamal b 1950
Imad (M):   Son of Jamal and Laila b1982
Jamal (M):   Brother of Fatima b 1953
Jamie (F):   Jamal's and Mary's daughter b1993
John (M):   Immigrated to Oklahoma in 1970 b 1946
Kamal (M):   Fatima's lover, married Gulnar in 1985 b 1946
Güzide (F):   Blind Turkish student born on 10. 6. 1978
Laila (F):   Jamal's wife b 1960
Little John (M): Son of Fatima and Kamal b 1996
Mary (F):   Jamal's Australian girlfriend b 1963
Norma (F):   American wife of John b 10. 6. 1952
Nadir (M):   Second son of John and Norma b 1978
Omar (M):   Kamal's and Gulnar's son b 1986
Ramzi (M):   Son of Jamal and Laila b 1985
Tamara (F):   Daughter of Ghassan and Carla b 1995
Tariq (M):   Son of Fatima and Ahmad b 1977

Ahmad (M) (1949) + Fatima (F) (1950) = Tariq (M) (1977)

Ghassan (M) (1972) + Carla (F) (1973) = Tamara (F) (1995)

Jamal (M) (1953) + Laila (F) (1960) = Imad (M) (1982),
                                       Ramzi (M) (1985)

Jamal (M) (1953) + Mary (F) (1963) = Jamie (F) (1993)

John (M) (1946) + Norma (F) (1952)= Ghassan (M) (1972),
                                     Nadir (M) (1978),
                                     Frida (F) (1982)

Kamal (M) (1946) + Gulnar (F) (1950) = Omar (M) (1986),
                                        Amar (F) (1988)

To Judy

One

(Hints)

(Beirut - Monday, 24 September, 1990)

My Dearest John,

It depends? It depends, you say to all I ask? You will not commit, nor venture, nor take sides? Why, John? Why indeed? Are you afraid of me, of life, of crises? Or is the Americanization of your soul now so complete that you no longer share our third world passions?

John, I asked if you are coming to Lebanon this summer, if we can spend a few days together in Beirut, if you will go with me to Syria to visit the shrine of Um Al-Huda, if we can meet in Paris for a week? Four months later, your terse, laconic, letter cracked my soul: *"My dear Fatima, the answer to all your questions is—it depends."* I suppose, if I should dare ask whether you still love me, you would unabashedly answer my fawning question with, *it depends.* I am not going to ask, John. I prefer to remain shrouded in false hope. Harsh realities do not well accord with my superstitious mind. After all, I am a Muslimah from Tripoli, Lebanon's legendary city of orange blossoms, Crusades, and the faithful.

Last Sunday, I visited your father's grave on which I laid white carnations. On my father's, I laid pink roses. In life as in death, they had different tastes. My father died in bed, and on the same day, your father was executed in his jail cell, *"shot himself with a smuggled gun,"* said the newspapers!

I was eighteen then and you were twenty-two. You know, I still fear that year. I fear that 1968 might surprise us both with a second coming, might actually force us to live it all over again. Remember how you cried to me when you came to share my grief: *"Fatima, my mother is all alone. No one dares come to our home for condolences. They fear the secret service might accuse them of treason."*

On my way back from the cemetery, I stopped at your mother's for coffee. She has your photograph in the living room, attached to your brother's and your dad's in a triptych. She asked if you were still writing. When I did not answer, she gazed at the triptych and muttered, *"Being away is like being dead. In either case, the letters stop coming!"* She put the carnations I brought her in a vase next to the triptych and stood there awhile: *"Why did the sniper have to kill my son on his 19th birthday? Snipers never know how many souls they kill each time they shoot someone."*

She talked about the coup d'état of 1961, about our ongoing Lebanese Civil War, and about history as she knew it: *"Sick leaders make sick nations. Sick nations make sick leaders. Nations never rise after they fall."* She has become stooped, as if bent by the weight of memories, but her eyes are still full of dreams. On my way out, she gave me a kiss and a bottle of olive oil: *"When you write, tell John that the olive season was good this year."*

My brother Jamal is still living with me. Saddam's tribal forces took his home, his car, his bulldozers, and his bank account. It was a miracle that he and his family left Kuwait alive. He is thinking about Africa or Australia. We have cousins in both places, you know, and they could find him work. Laila and the children live in the mountains now; they are guests of Laila's parents and share their big house in Brummana. Jamal visits them every weekend, and her parents treat him with kindness and respect. On the other hand, Laila hardly eats and still refuses to speak to Jamal when he visits. He thinks she blames him for her rape. She hated living in Kuwait.

Ahmad and I are still civil with each other but mainly because of our son, Tariq, who is the joy of my life yet still too young to understand divorce. My work barely sustains us. Not enough magazines these days to keep a photographer busy. Ahmad does help with the bills, but he has become financially strained since he bought and furnished an apartment for his cute hairdresser.

Ahmad only stays with me when Tariq comes home from boarding school. He thinks Tariq does not know! I have not told him that Tariq is being teased at school. "Hairstylist," they call him, and clip at him with scissor-like fingers. He cries to me, but he is getting stronger. Yesterday, when I was driving him back to school, he told me that for last week's English assignment he had to recite a poem in class. He chose one of yours, from "Familiar Faces." I have your books next to my bed, but I do not recall reading them to him. He said the class liked his choice. Then, he turned my surprise into utter amazement when, out of memory, he recited:

> "Familiar faces, let us not pretend
> Though life may decimate and send
> Our unsuspecting souls across
> Uncharted times and unfamiliar places
> Where ever we are loved, we end."

John, do you think the kid knows about us? By the way, how is your wife these days? Are your children better now? I wish you would let me meet them one day. Oh, but if they should tell their mother, she would give you hell. Please, forget that I asked.

But, were you not the one who taught me not to be afraid to think the unthinkable, mention the unmentionable, and challenge the unchallengeable? And did you not quote Paul Valéry to me each time I became despondent:

> "What would we be without the help of what
>   does not exist...
> Myths are the very soul of our actions and of
>   our loves...
> We can act only in pursuit of a phantom...
> We can love only what we create...
>
> A difficulty is a lantern; an un-surmountable
>   difficulty is a sun."

Who knows, one day, things might change for us. Even you said it in the poem that Tariq recited in class:

"Coincidence,
She wears green shadows intertwined with
*   dreams*
Lurks unforeseen, in silence plots and
*   schemes*
At times, she hurries matters to profound
*   extremes*
Delights in rolling fortunes in reverse
Coincidence, she sways the universe. "

How can a realist write these flippant lines, John? There is a gypsy in you, a vagabond who venerates freedom, who idealizes joy, and who euphemizes fate as coincidence. Is that why you avoid me? Do I formulate you and sprawl you on a pin, like Prufrock? Do you avoid Lebanon because it stifles your prized liberties? Do you still measure all human worth with joy received and joy imparted?

Do you still believe that Shakespeare is worth more than both Muhammad and Christ because no wars were fought in his name, no violence erupted on his behalf, and because he has engendered joy without suffering and united humanity instead of separating it into feuding factions? I still remember your words: *"Fatima, leave the prophets alone and follow the God of Shakespeare. There are no Shakespearean Crusades and there is no Shakespearean Jihad—there is only Shakespearean Joy. "*

What am I to do with a mind that regards all handed down dogmas and beliefs as mental slavery and intellectual cruelty? How did you manage to blossom so far away from your ancestral roots? You were right when you said, *"The greatest distances are in the mind. "* How apart our minds are, but oh, how close our hearts? Is the severing of roots the only means of nurturing one's soul? What am I to think, John? What am I to do? Will you ever change the credo, which you sent me in your last letter—the credo, which you wrote for your upcoming forty-fifth birthday?

14

"Soon, I shall wither forty-five
While other branches of my tree
Commence their struggle to survive
I'll take my blade and painfully
Sever my roots and cut me free."

Does that mean that you are never going to write again, that you will never set foot in Lebanon again, and that we will never see each other again?

Oh, my love, I have tired myself with longing and it is past midnight. Tomorrow might be a better day, or it might not; who knows? As you say, it depends. It always depends, doesn't it?

I miss you,

Fatima

Two

(Confessions)

(Oklahoma City - Friday, 10 November, 1990)

Fatima dear,

    "Martha, Martha, thou art careful and troubled about many things." You write with lovelorn anguish; I, on the other hand, write with delight and insist on cheerfulness. I eschew worry as unnecessary and damaging to the soul. I see the speck of my personal world as a mere ephemeral spring on a longsuffering planet. You cry about the past while I find cause to celebrate the present—this rapacious, enduring state of mind that draws on the past and nibbles on the future with insatiable appetite. I had hoped to distance you with my reticent silence but you will not recant. Your inveterate relapses into atavism make it hard for us to maintain a respectable measure of cheerfulness. I honor life with joy. How do you honor life, Fatima? Must your snowflakes always tremble in the dimming light?

    My mother wants me to return and live in Lebanon where electricity, water, roads, institutions, and establishments all work to entrap the helpless Lebanese citizen. She thinks that if I return, I would be able to help uplift my birth country. She feels that it is my duty to participate in Lebanon's renaissance. No one can reverse institutional decay and social rot. Christ could not do it. Muhammad could not do it. Moses could not do it. Even Caesar could not do it.

    "I came, I saw the ice-cream men
    Inhabiting the Caesar's den
    And I could see that history
    Permits one glorious rise and then

The mighty fall they all sustain
The humbling of king and thane
Who fade in ever spreading past
And only the statues remain."

Who does she think I am, and why should I sacrifice my joy for the sake of a utopian dream that is already a nightmare? What we have in Lebanon is public slavery by archaic traditions and feudal powers. The entire family of Arab nations has grown too old, too sick, and without hope for cure. On the other hand, I choose to live a free life in a new world. This ancient tension between slavery of traditions and freedom of the soul has but one solution— the soul's self-assertive flight.

"My roots, my atavistic cage
Deprive my wings of eager flight
I am a white unwritten page
Who loves to love and reunite
And will not hate nor harm nor fight.

My roots, my harsh historic mind
They shroud about my open sight
And dull my reason; I am blind
A branch that reaches for the light
With roots that feed upon the night.

My roots, intransigent and stiff
Un-teach my meek accepting face
Presume and segregate as if
Our natures differ with our place
Our souls are slaves to our race."

Almost a thousand years ago, Rumi blatantly admonished our unconditional submission to traditions, this most irrational of our eastern traits:

"The mother and father are your attachment to beliefs and blood ties and desires and comforting habits. Don't listen to them! They seem to protect, but they imprison.

They are your worst enemies. They make you afraid of living in emptiness..."

From my now Western insight, I add to his admonition one of my own: *"When love curtails freedom or diminishes joy, it leaves the bay of peace to shipwreck on the crags of anguish."* And we are left with nothing but memories, a little wine, and fate.

My father died for a political ideology that he believed in. But, I could never reconcile his *joie-de-vivre* with his ideology's macabre consequences. He brought joy to those who knew him, while his political party troubled heaven and earth with its utopian dreams and romantic demands. On the scale of joy, his human worth is high while his party's worth remains in the red. And now, he is a dead hero and his party but an archaic political club, puppeteered by the ruling powers. Was all this wasted joy worth his while?

Love is never enough, Fatima. I loved my father, and I love my mother and you, but I will not sacrifice freedom or joy for any one's sake, nor will I suspend life for either of you. Go from me if you cannot be my freedom and my joy. *"No one can walk back into the future,"* said Joseph Hergesheimer. *"That which creates unsurpassable joy is the removal of a great evil,"* said Epicurus. I have plucked Lebanon out of my heart and in its place have planted seeds that can only bear joy. Never again will I let anyone infest my heart with melancholy. I have saved my sweetest dreams and they are mine alone.

Today, my dear Fatima, is the most important emancipation anniversary of our lives. It comes one hundred and twenty-six years after Lincoln abolished slavery on the first day of January 1864. One year ago today, on November 10, the Berlin wall fell and with it the apocalypse of communist serfdom. On this day, I celebrate freedom with my fellow humans across the mighty walls of time. I find new hope in the struggle against control and possessiveness.

Who owns anything, anyway? Everything is on loan. It all belongs to life, and from life we borrow everything.

Death liberates all possessions, and love commits suicide when it becomes possessive. Remember Gibran's *The Prophet*: *"Love gives naught but itself and takes naught but from itself. Love possesses not nor would it be possessed; For love is sufficient unto love."*

Do you remember the poem I sent you when I received your first transatlantic letter calling me a runaway fugitive, an abdicator who left his country and his girlfriend behind and moved on?

"If I can be young and wise
Strong enough to compromise
Hold you tight throughout the night
Let you fly at break of light
Watch you venture and create
Live to love and liberate."

Well, twenty years later, I have learned to love and liberate—to love you, to love my mother, to love both my countries, to love my family, to love my friends, and to liberate my soul in spite of all these trammeling loves.

Yes, Fatima, *"I have slipped the surly bonds of earth"* in my high flight and plan to dance the sky until I die. Indeed, there is a gypsy inside of me, a vagabond who is ever looking for an Elysian Plain, who has the East and West for parents—parents who were born dissonant and remain separated, as eloquently promulgated by our friend, Kipling:

"Oh, East is East, and West is West,
and never the twain shall meet,
Till Earth and Sky stand presently
at God's great Judgment Seat..."

Fatima, I feel tightly stretched between two continents, and I am about to snap. I can no longer serve two Gods. Fatima, listen to my crying song:

"Because I have two hearts
Because I straddle oceans

Because I am both banks of life
The froth, the currents in between,
The dissonant emotions
I see beyond the mighty walls of time
Beyond the eyes, the made-up lips and faces
Beyond the borrowed sentiments and faint
    laces
Because I have two hearts,
My soul is vagabond; it camps in many
    places."

Ever since her car accident, ever since her two-month-long coma, my wife continues to suffer from a progressive organic brain syndrome. As she sinks deeper and deeper into mental chaos, she becomes more and more angry and continuously brings emotional havoc to all of us who love and accommodate her. And although I understand her emotional pain, I had to inculcate the children in order to save them from her commiserating traps. I taught them that they must insist on joy, that a damaged brain must not be permitted to sicken a healthy mind, and that joy—not man, as Protagoras said—is the measure of all things.

These harsh realities are hard to comprehend in youth. What is even harder to realize is that those among us whose brains are damaged are constitutionally sentenced and have little choice in how they perceive the world and how they react to it. On the other hand, we, the well endowed with health, are held to higher standards. Indeed, we owe it to our good fortunes to help those who are less fortunate than we are. We also owe it to Joy to resist the urge to reconstitute or change them because that is not possible, and because that would inevitably lead us into misery.

We are our brains, Fatima—brains housed in train-conductors' heads and programmed to follow the rails. Lucky are those among us who do not derail. I have placed my life in savings at the bank.

I wrote a surreal poem in answer to your whim to take reprieve from your turmoil-laden world and come visit me. I imagined that I was a grieving lover, separated from my woman by capricious fate. Finding comfort in solitude, I took to the mountains to live the poetic life. When I received your letter asking me if you could come for a visit, I felt torn between the siren memories of an old love and the crushing heft of present reality. I agonized over the decision, and after sleepless speculation, *"Nostalgia On A Winter Eve"* was my solemn reply to your beckonings:

> *"The snowflakes tremble in the dimming light*
> *And it is cold and sad and very white*
> *A melancholy stillness lulls the wind to sleep*
> *And bids the setting sun goodnight.*
>
> *With memories, a little wine, and fate*
> *On winter nights like these I hibernate*
> *Away from man, my solitude and I*
> *Where peace, like death, is vast and intimate.*
>
> *I saved my sweetest dreams for you before*
> *But since I left, somehow, I dream no more*
> *Instead, I die each night, then resurrect*
> *And work by day in order to forget.*
>
> *I placed my life in savings at the bank*
> *I spend it wisely and I always thank*
> *My banker, though he gives no interest*
> *Nor does he tell me how much I have left!*
>
> *How much I hunger for your love and yearn*
> *Ignite you in my bed and with you burn*
> *But then I fear the shattering of dreams*
> *Upon a fossil past that can't return.*
>
> *So stay away, I need my memories*
> *Of all the lusty wine and dusty cheese*
> *That still I taste upon your gasping lips*
> *On cold and lonesome winter nights like*
> *   these."*

Antoine de Saint-Exupéry was the one who said, *"Truth for any man, is that which makes him a man."* Pray, Fatima, forgive my cutting honesty but I can no longer pretend to be someone else. I can only be myself and my choices are two. I can choose to be proud of who I am and what I have become; or I can chose to allow shame and guilt to infect my heart and ruin my joy. It is far nobler for us to accept our natures as gifts given to us by God, gifts that are sacred, gifts that should not be desecrated with self-deprecating emotions such as guilt and shame. I am the best that I can be, given my imperfections. Indeed, I am my imperfections.

On a softer personal scene, I have been eyeing a butterfly awhile and hope to add her colors to my tree. Every day, I hold out my branches to the sun and hope that she alights. How eagerly my soul awaits her flutters...

Poetry is a highly evolved, aesthetic form of confession. I have said enough for now. Thank you for hearing my truths.

With love,

John

Three

(Friends!)

(Beirut - Monday, 24 December, 1990)

My dear, lost love,

And you were the one who taught me that love is never lost! Why, then, do I feel that I have lost you? What happens to love when it dies? Who tells it bedtime stories? Who keeps its feet warm? Who brings it hot soup?

Do you still remember the day you wrote "Cling To Me" and read it while I drove? I parked the car by the sea, re-read the poem over and over, asked you if you really wrote it for me, and then tucked it inside my bra. When I read your last letter and discerned that you had already sistered me, marginated me to the rank of a well-loved friend, I retrieved my bra poem and read it again and again. How can you undo a poem, John? Which poem should I believe now?

In your bra poem, you asked me to cling to you, and in your snowflake poem, you ask me to stay away because you needed your memories. Am I to hold and un-hold, embrace and un-embrace, clutch and un-clutch, hope and un-hope, love and un-love? What am I to think about your new infatuation with this butterfly as you call her? Am I supposed to stand up and give her my seat? Am I to give birth to feelings, watch them grow, and then retract them back into my womb as if they were never born, as if you had never written the *"Cling-To-Me"* poem:

> *"You are my sweetest thoughts, unleashed in*
> *   playful mood*
> *My truth, elusive, solid, undisturbed*
> *   un-wooed*
> *My sense of beauty as it blends with nature's*
> *   art*

Ah, you are me in mind and soul and heart
So cling to me, like I must cling to truth
Or like when we are old, we cling to youth
Come, harvest of my dreams
Come bountiful and free
And cling to me with drowning arms
Oh, cling to me."

Of course, over the years, I had noticed that your letters had grown shorter and less passionate. But then, after each clandestine encounter, your lines would rediscover youth and blossom anew with adolescent flora.

We had natural harmony then, cycling agelessly from spring to winter with seasonal ebbs and tides. But, after receiving your snowflake epistle, I swore never to write again. I was going to fade away from your life and leave you to your awaited butterfly. I felt like a continuous fool, awaiting your letters with anguish, reading them with famish, but always ending up diminished at the finish. This last letter, however, completely incinerated me. I can still taste the ashes of your words.

Old loves default into confessional friendships, I suppose! I wonder if this would have happened were you not so far away. Nevertheless, as an Eastern woman, I must accept your terms as I accept my marriage and my life; I have little choice in matters preordained by destiny.

Why, then, am I writing to you on Christmas Eve, with Saddam roaring against Bush as if they were fighting it out in my backyard? Indeed, Saddam has just announced that in the event of war, Israel would be the first target. You know how such madness would destabilize the area?

I worry of course about myself, and about our mothers, and about our many cousins and friends. But, above all, I worry about Tariq. He is only thirteen and his chances of having a normal life might be forever ruined if political conflict should endure. This is the real reason why I am writing so soon after I had sworn that I never would.

The day might come when I might need your help in ensuring Tariq's future. He clearly prefers America to France and might choose to go to the States for his higher education. By the way, he did receive your gift, Whitman's *Leaves of Grass,* and seems to like it. He found it most amusing that anyone would sing a song to himself.

John, Tariq loves poetry. He asks about you and wonders when he will be able to meet you. However, he never mentions you to his father. I find such tacit conspiracy most revealing. It is as if we had agreed that we wouldn't speak of you except to each other. He wants to write and thank you but you know how adolescent boys are. They are more interested in butterflies and hardly have time for letters.

I have always been your friend and shall forever be. Please do not stop writing no matter how embarrassing the topic may be. I cannot see my life severed from yours. After all, was it not you who said, *"Love is never lost?"*

Please, John, let me be the keeper of our love. Let us never feel the need to hide our inner souls from one another. Indeed, let us hear each other's confessions for that would be closer than silence. Silence is the longest distance between two hearts; it is even longer than death. I cannot stand to be that far away from you.

Merry Christmas, my love,

Fatima

Four

(War)

(Oklahoma City - Wednesday, 16 January, 1991)

Fatima,

> "I am terse
> There to listen, not converse
> It's a noisy universe..."

The war has just begun. We are bombing Iraq. Watching television is self-flagellation. Of all the institutions of humanity, the media are the most predictable; they always cater to the masses. I have updated my definition of *wisdom*, which used to be: *"The ability to recognize the irrational, first in ourselves, then in all others."* Now, I have developed a much shorter version: *"Wisdom is the ability to recognize junk."*

Abba Eban once commented that *"History teaches us that men and nations behave wisely once they have exhausted all other alternatives."* Oh, how I hate war and how mercilessly it chases my fleeing years. Unless the love of humanity can rise above the love of self and country, we will never have peace. *"Love each other or perish,"* said Auden.

My altruistic mind has been repeatedly assailed by the realities of human nature, that historic engine which herds peoples into nations and hurls nations into wars. *"I keep a certain distance from the reality of things. It's the same distance between me and utter confusion,"* said Ghalib. I am so afraid for all the innocent souls who will be irrevocably damaged.

> "I am terse
> Taste the tears within my verse
> It's a bitter universe."

29

Saddam is mentally ill, shortsighted, tunnel-visioned, consumed by fear, and enthralled by one idea—power. Those who rule with fear are always afraid. All dictators are megalomaniacs. They rise, build pyramids, devastate nations, and then die, leaving a legacy of fear and destruction to transcend future generations and to pollute unborn centuries.

Whatever happened to all the innocent roses planted in the unsuspecting gardens of humanity? Forgive me, Fatima, but my heart is on fire and you are the only one who can help me put it out.

Saddam *"doth murder sleep."* I lie awake, fuming, having reached my boiling point with the first bomb. One of my dear patients, a local politician, called. He cautiously advised me not to leave home, except to go to work. He said that anti-Arab sentiments are volatile now and that I could be harmed if we were to experience heavy military losses.

> *"I am terse*
> *Fear and hate will make it worse*
> *Those who love do not coerce."*

Shall I pray that we do not experience heavy military losses? Shall I pray that victory will be ours? Shall I invoke the Lord to ensure that we prevail, all for my own safety? Who am I anyway, and why am I worth saving? Am I better than all the young men who are going die? Why should I be forewarned about protecting my own life when our youth are plunging theirs into an insatiable inferno?

I want to die, Fatima. I want to die planting peace, like Gandhi and Christ. I want to die away from war. I want to be buried in the quietude of birdsong, where the sighing earth carries gentle spring upon its tears. I want to join the nurturing soil that stretches indiscriminately across all human borders. I want to become ambrosia and nectar, sweet food for all the innocent roses planted in the unsuspecting gardens of humanity.

"Yes, I have known the peace of open spaces

The quietude, where clouds like whispers fly
Between the gray-haired earth and blue-eyed
*   sky*
Hovering like dreams with such familiar faces
In the majestic silence; only there
Is peace, where hearts are clear and truth is
*   bare. "*

Forgive my indulgence. I have only talked about myself. How is life in Beirut? Are there riots in the streets? Are you safe? Is Tariq still interested in poetry? Whence did he get that gene? Neither you nor his father have any poetry in your veins? Tell him that I will be sending him some new love poems that I have written. At thirteen, he is in that blissful stage of naïve, gullible love; he believes in poems and dreams and visions. You and I, on the other hand, have become hardened by time's ruthless realism. We look to the past while youth looks to the future.

"I am terse
I have nothing in my purse
Life will never reimburse. "

Fatima, I am tired. The night is deep into the morning, but I cannot sleep. Tell the bombs to depart from my pounding heart. Pray, tell the bombs to pay attention so that they may not fall on the innocent. Tell them to be kind to the blind, those who do not suspect that the bombs are coming. Tell them that children are earth's blossoms whose right is to fill their petals with sun. Tell them many things, but do not tell them that I am an Arab in America, an Arab-American whose soul belongs to humanity, who fights against war, fights for love, for life, for peace, and prays for all the young soldiers that they may not hear the cries of dying voices.

I feel alone. The burgeoning sunrays have already

blanched the night. I will go to work with hungry sleep behind my eyes. I will conduct myself in my calm, usual way. No one will see my melancholy mind. I shall wear my professional face, fully made-up with the subtle colors of pretense. And my heartbeats will not be audible. And I alone shall hear the pounding of the bombs.

Love,

John

Five

(Peace)

(Nicosia - Thursday, 28 February, 1991)

My dear sad poet,

We had to run away to Cyprus. The smoke from the burning oil wells of Kuwait blackened the Lebanese skies, and my asthma became intolerable. Finally, my doctor advised me to escape to Nicosia. The mood in Beirut is portentous of impending doom, and it is no longer safe to move about at night. Rumors are running rabid. Some examples for your sensitive ears: "*Saddam is dead. Bush ended the war today because he received news that a pro-American coup is in progress in Baghdad. Israel is going to invade Iraq. The Americans are going to annex Kuwait. Saudi Arabia is going to become a democracy.*"

I am too tired and too scared to really care. Tariq and I are living in a motel by the sea. There are Lebanese everywhere, but only on the Greek side of the island. They hold dinners and parties as if nothing of importance is happening back home. I cannot join the fun, nor can Tariq. All day we read the papers and listen to the news. We are exiles of the burning smoke.

Ahmad, my playboy husband, is still in Beirut living with his cute hairdresser. He calls us daily, but mainly to speak with Tariq. Two days ago, Jamal, my homeless and still unemployed brother, locked up my Beirut home and left for the mountains where the air is cleaner. He joined his wife and two boys at her parents' mountain home. Laila, still in rape rage, refuses to speak to him, which makes him feel terribly unwelcome at his in-laws.

In spite of President Bush's announcement today that the hostilities have ended, no one really believes that it is over. We all expect more social disarray and more war. Already, the Arab world is politically destabilized and inflation is increasing by the day. No one wants to use the Lebanese Lira anymore. Instead, we all use dollars for everything, but one must be careful because there is a lot of counterfeit money circulating. A severe depression is expected because the economy is in a steep decline and unemployment has reached 50 per cent.

Even Cyprus has been drawn into the conflict. The Turks have taken the American side because they fear the military might of their bordering neighbor, Iraq. The Greeks, on the other hand, are on the Arab side and are treating us as pitiful refugees.

I pray twice a day and Tariq writes poems about the war. He does not share many of them with me, but I pretend not to care lest he should feel pressured. This last poem, however, he was most eager to read aloud, and his choice of words reminded me of you.

> *"There is a beast in the East*
> *A beast that begs for war;*
> *There is a nest in the West*
> *From which birds fly to war;*
> *People who die*
> *Do not know why*
> *They die."*

I can find more work here than in Beirut because many publishing houses have moved to Nicosia to escape the Civil War. I have many good contacts, and they are eager for me to begin working on some of their projects. I may remain in Cyprus for the remainder of this year or perhaps longer. As you say, it all depends!

On a more personal note, do you feel better now that the war is over? Your melancholy letter worried me to no end. I could feel your tense depression ripping your soul apart. It is probably easier for us here than it is for you there, being so far removed from the smoke of the conflict and having to contend with your wild imagination constantly embellishing reality.

Remember, though, that our area has not known

extended peace since the dawn of history. Nothing has really changed. We have always been and will always be the children of war. I am resigned to the fact that I shall live and die in this war zone. Somehow, it does not bother me anymore. Like you, war has become my fugitive identity.

To move to a less gloomy topic, you will be happy to know that I have started meditating again, no doubt because I have more time to think. I have contemplated the states of our failed marriages—yours, my brother's, and mine—and how we have all managed to find ways to evade our painful realities. I ran away to Cyprus, Jamal is eyeing Australia, and you have lived away with your poems for years. The price of living with someone is putting up with that someone while the price of living alone is putting up with one's self.

I still do not know which option is easier or better. But, since I must live alone for now, I have resolved to reconstitute myself in order to make myself more interesting. I am reading more and having more internal monologues. Myriad ideas present themselves to my consciousness and I keep the interesting ones for internal debate.

Today's idea about marriage presented itself to me as a death analogy. The most irrational reality about marriage is that one cannot simply walk away from it when it dies. We walk away from all other personal deaths. We walk away from dead ideas, from dead countries, from dead religions, from dead parents, from dead children, from dead pets, and from dead projects. We even walk away from our own dead bodies. Why can't we walk away from dead marriages? Why do they have such an undying hold over us?

You—who believe so strongly in freedom but remain captive to your own dead marriage—are a prime example of the enthralling powers of marital contracts. Whatever happened to your call for freedom, John?

Where flies your butterfly? When her season of metamorphosis?

Don't be shy; there is nothing I cannot handle. My intuition tells me there are blanks to be filled in and untold tales to be shared... Write to me.

Love,

Fatima

Six

(Naturalism)

(New York - Saturday, 24 August, 1991)

Dearest Fatima,

I am in New York for a psychopharmacology meeting. Nowadays, emotions are mapped on the brain like nations on a globe; they have their private borders and their wars. We know that fear resides in the amygdala, that panic attacks are discharges from the locus ceruleus, that love develops deep in the limbic system, and that it can be visualized on PET scanners.

We can also target painful emotions with laboratory-designed medications. Pathological jealousy, obsessive gambling, uncontrollable anger, delusional thinking, social phobias, etc. can all be treated with unique medications that attach to specific cell receptors and produce measurable clinical effects. Indeed, whenever the perfect, intricate balance of the brain is disrupted, we become chaotic, irrational beings. Brain chemistry is the Rosetta Stone of human nature.

Watching the news in my hotel room, I realized that something pathologically similar is happening to the Soviet Union, causing it to disintegrate. The dismantling of the Berlin wall was only the first sign. Two days ago, Yeltsin, history's first elected Soviet Union president, ordered the Hammer and Sickle flag to be replaced with the pre-revolution white, blue, and red. Yesterday, Armenia declared its independence. Today, Gorbachev resigned as leader of the Communist Party, his last official act as party leader being the disbandment of the Party's Central Committee, which had ruled the Soviet Union since 1917. The Soviet Union is fragmenting back into its original ethnic states. No might can enslave freedom for long.

Fatima, from all that I have experienced during my forty-five years, I have culled enough wisdom to formulate my own philosophical hypothesis, a theory that I call Naturalism. Basically, whatever runs contrary to human nature ultimately fails. Take away freedom from any people and suppress them all you want; barring Machiavellian genocide, they will ultimately prevail. Delude them with misrepresentations and false promises, and they will find their way back to truth. Subject them to beliefs that are not their own and they will pretend until they have the power to break away and return to their own faith.

Hegel says that the progress of humanity throughout history is nothing but the march toward freedom. Without freedom, all our noble and joyful emotions surrender to our darker sides. I have stopped deluding myself since I have joined the ranks of the free. The more honest I become, the more I fathom the extent of my prior dishonesty. That is why I have meandered long around the secret I am about to share with you. My honesty frightens me, Fatima, and so will it you after I tell you all about my butterfly.

How is Cyprus treating you? Do you like your work there? Is Tariq back in school? Has Jamal made it to Australia yet? See, I am being evasive. I want to begin but I am unable to. What hollow reticence.

Tell a heart not to love. Tell hunger not to eat. Ask a couple not to touch. Tell thirst not to drink. Ask us not to be seduced by the seven deadly sins. Force a human to struggle against his own human nature, and you will ultimately fail. Naturalism is as powerful as fire.

She is in her thirties, kind, caring, careful, meek, and shy. Her husband rules with a canine bark. She fears his open jaws. I began seeing her as a patient; yes, I did, I did... Her fear and depression fed upon each other and ate her sleep and health away. She did not respond to medications. Her chemical brain map lay outside the annals of suffering humanity. Her fear of his jaws was beyond divorce. She was a hen cowered under the gaze of her mighty fox. Every week she would come and I would listen. Her emaciation weakened her spirits into utter submission. I could no longer motivate her will to live.

She would not allow me to refer her elsewhere. I watched her become a shadowless ghost.

One Sunday afternoon at the bookstore, I found her searching in the section on self-help. We talked, had coffee, talked all the way to her car, talked in her car until dark, talked holding hands.

At home, I looked at my wife, at my three children, reflected on my professional life, and contemplated vulnerable humanity. What I wanted was not permissible, not acceptable, not reasonable, but it was possible. I saw my human nature caged in by propriety, ailing from the lack of freedom. I did not sleep; I tossed between my sick wife and my sick soul. My butterfly had a Monday appointment. She was my first morning patient. I hastened the sun to rise and felt no fatigue from my insomnia.

She came in pale, more frightened than ever, even more frightened than I was. After all the talking on Sunday afternoon, we found ourselves mired in awkward silence. I flipped through her chart, avoiding her gaping eyes, trying to concentrate, hoping the chart notes would turn into lifeboats and somehow save me from imminent drowning. I said several things that neither of us heard. I pretended to check her blood pressure. I put the cuff around her frail arm. I inflated it gently. I watched the mercury fall until her pounding pulse reappeared. I then deflated the cuff, surrendered virtue to whim, and rested my forehead upon hers.

That heavy moment loomed like an unanswered question, like a held-in sigh awaiting release. It longed and lingered until I held her hand to my lips and kissed her fingertips. She said nothing, but simply held my face with her cold, sweaty palm. The eloquence of silence, the weight of destiny, the epiphany of paradise lost, enclosed us in a fateful triangle from which there was no escape. I closed my eyes and shook.

Then, in that moment's uttermost darkness, our lips found each other. We had been hungry for years, longing with desperate aspirations, hoping for the impossible. Can one kiss change life's course and redirect its gaze toward the unfathomable? We are bound to find out. Tell hunger not to eat. Tell thirst not to drink. Ask a couple not to touch. Tell nature that metamorphosis is the eighth deadly sin. Tell her not to make butterflies. Tell her not to color spring. Tell her to observe social mores.

Fatima, I will no longer be the man you know. He who falls for butterflies cannot escape his own metamorphosis. Say good-bye to your John. What I am now, I do not understand, and what I will become is not knowable. I shall eagerly await my own self-discovery. Pray for my peace and for hers. Pray that our reclaiming of life and our insistence on joy do not ultimately destroy us both. We are fugitives from the cages of propriety, victims of our own human natures, and sufferers from the freedom of our own choices.

I feel like a pilot, in a single engine airplane, circling the globe, alone between sea and sky, contemplating courage that brims on recklessness, contemplating infinity, reciting with Amelia Earhart Putnam, reciting with the lonely drone of my only engine, the one engine upon which all my life depends:

> *"Courage is the price that life exacts for*
> *granting peace.*
> *The soul that knows it not, knows no release*
> *From little things;*
> *Knows not the livid loneliness of fear,*
> *Nor mountain heights where bitter joy can*
> *hear*
> *The sound of wings."*

Fatima, my children are my life and my wife is my death. Ghassan now is 19 and goes to OU while Nadir, 13, and Frida, 9, are still at home. It is natural for a father to love his children and endeavor to give them the best possible life. It is also natural for a man to seek love and fulfillment against a stalemate of arid frustration. It is most unfortunate that in my case, if I do one, I will have to sacrifice the other. If I guard my children's feelings against disillusionment, it will have to be by suppressing my own needs. Naturalism here does not work both ways because what seems natural to me will seem unnatural to my children. But I have found a way out.

My way out is via gratitude. Gratitude teaches me to feel fortunate that I have three healthy children, that I have had a productive life, that my poor wife, my sick Norma, loved me even though, in spite of my most sincere efforts, I could not reciprocate her love. It also teaches me to be humble and not accumulate guilt each time I falter, for it is natural to weaken and naturalism is undeniable realism.

I have faltered only a few times in my life. I have, the few times I met you in Beirut and when I met you in Paris in 1976. After that last reunion, I promised myself not to capitulate to my urges. But, five years after that last promise, I have failed again. Promises are but shadows of our best wishes.

> *"I do not trust my mind*
> *It tortures and it teases*
> *And wanders where it pleases*
> *Leaving me behind;*
> *I do not trust my mind."*

It is only natural to err, and mistakes are our great teachers. They teach us to rise above guilt and, in its stead, illuminate our lives with gratitude, as the great Ghalib said:

> *"To the wise, a storm of difficulty is a school.*
> *The slaps of waves resemble the slaps of a*
> *master."*

I am a better man for having faltered, for having learned from my faults, and for having been humbled by re-faltering again and again.

As a Christian, I should say that I have sinned, that I labor under the heft of guilt, and that I should pray for forgiveness. But then, as a naturalist-realist, I say that I have achieved self-improvement through faltering and that I am grateful to God and life for having given me a guilt-free education. As Aldus Huxley says:

"Experience is not what happens to a man;
It is what a man does with what happens to
*   him."*

Fatima, I do not think that I will kiss my butterfly again. That one kiss was enough of a slap to keep my lips pursed from now on. As a doctor, I should not have become infatuated with a married female patient of mine nor should I have kissed her on the mouth. That is not only dangerous but also unethical. Oh, after this long drought, how irrational I have been rendered by my omnivorous hunger, how vulnerable has my heart become, how dry my lips, and how thirsty my soil for rain.

But what kind of kiss was it and why did I do it? It was not a sensual kiss, nor a kiss of love. Perhaps it was a kiss of compassion, a gesture of kindness, a cry of freedom against marital tyranny, an act of self-assertion against brutal circumstance, and a selfless gift of sharing unfulfilled needs.

Oh, how I long to love freely and be loved openly. But I shall not allow my hungry self its whims again. I shall dwell in the house of gratitude instead and feed on my hunger to better myself. I shall recount with the great Ghalib:

"I keep a certain distance from the reality of
*   things.*
It's the same distance between me and utter
*   confusion."*

I could say more, but I will not because I do not wish to excuse my behavior; my inexcusable behavior needs no excuse. We are all God's creatures, and everything we feel and act upon is natural and therefore, normal. And if God needed no excuse to make us the way we are, then we need no excuse to be what we are—imperfect, frail-hearted, and temptable.

It might be right to seek perfection but it remains,

nevertheless, unrealistic and unachievable. However, it is wrong to disdain imperfection its rightful place within our souls because it is inherent in our natures. Naturalism is not wrong or right; it is undeniable reality.

No, I do not wish to excuse my behavior nor need I be ashamed or embarrassed by it. What I wish for, instead, is the same thing that Solomon wished for; I wish for wisdom. That is what I need to negotiate through the narrow straits of life. I need to clearly see the four dimensions of life as described by Epictetus:

"Appearances to the mind are of four kinds.
Things either are what they appear to be;
Or they neither are, nor appear to be;
Or they are, and do not appear to be;
Or they are not, and yet appear to be.
Rightly to aim in all these cases is the wise
man's task."

Good night, Fatima. I have tired myself with philosophizing, and it is time for dreams. Remember me when you smile.

With love,

John

Seven

(Reimbursements)

(Nicosia - Wednesday, 25 December, 1991)

My Dear John,

I do not know why I am writing back. I have nothing to say. You are not my confessor. Your sick Butterfly gave me the *coup-de-grâce* last August, and since then silence has supervened between us. But it's Christmas, a time of love, and as your favorite quote from William James goes, *"In the practical use of our intellect, forgetting is as important as remembering."*

Besides, you must have heard that today, Gorbachev, formally resigned as President of the dissolved Soviet Union. That alone should cause you to celebrate the coup-de-grâce of communism. What a fitting date for opening our hearts to each other.

I would like to ask you questions, but I feel uncomfortable probing into your private life. Nevertheless, how is your Butterfly and has her depression regressed under the healing powers of your saving kisses? John, how mad of you to have a love affair with one of your own patients, how uncharacteristic of your reserve! Have you considered the respect you could lose? What would your colleagues, your children, your friends, and your patients think of you if they were to find out?

Oh, why did you entrust me with such a heavy secret? Would it not have been easier to resume your affair with me? We could visit each other periodically, just like we used to, and no one would ever know. Wasn't I enough for you, or was I just too well to need your healing hands?

I think that you have a Messiah complex. You are attracted to misery and repulsed by power. I lost you when, with your help, I triumphed over my weakness and became an independent self-assertive woman. You left me when I became strong, when I no longer needed your help. I know how fond you are of e.e.cummings' *Somewhere*, and how frequently you would quote it to me when, out of shame, I would lament my own frailties. I will never forget the line, *"Nothing which we are to perceive in this world equals the power of your intense fragility."*

Enough bickering. I am slowly accepting the loss of your love, but I do not want to lose your friendship. I know that you will always love me as a friend and that you do love Tariq because he is my son. I treasure both loves, and I will not compromise them with negative sentiments. Incidentally, Tariq loves your poems and longs to meet you one day.

Tariq is spending this Christmas vacation with me and seems to like Cypress. The island is half lit with Christmas decorations as the Greek side proudly flaunts its saturnalia against the Turkish side. Of course, when Ramadan comes around, the Muslims retaliate by flaunting their fasting and feasting against the Greek side. Hate, fear, and mistrust seem to be seasonal sentiments on this beautiful island, sentiments fueled by national and religious identities that separate Greek from Turk and prevent peaceful coexistence. Oh, how inhumane are human beliefs, how aggressively segregating, and how ridiculously childish when juxtaposed.

I am doing well living here. I go to Beirut occasionally to take care of business or family obligations, but I am always eager to return to my Cyprus. When I am away from Beirut, I miss it, but when I am in Beirut, I miss my Cyprus. Like you, I must have two hearts...

I have many friends here with whom I socialize, and I have taken a charming lover who takes good care of my needs and helps me with my chores. Kamal is a gentleman Turk who works for one of the publishing houses on the Christian side. He has fallen in love with me and wants me to divorce Ahmad and to marry him. I am not ready yet to give Tariq a stepfather nor do I love the man. I like him a lot but not enough to let the relationship grow beyond Cyprus.

We have talked and he understands that when I return to Beirut, we'll have to say good-bye. Tariq thinks that he is just one of my many friends, and they have a good time together whenever Kamal visits. I have not told Ahmad, nor do I plan to, not only because he would tell the whole of Beirut, but also because he would use Kamal as a justification to continue living with his cute hairdresser.

Spending too much time alone is not healthy; it goes against nature. I felt alone before I met Kamal, but now I feel quite fulfilled. Your theory of Naturalism has indeed hit home. *"What ever runs contrary to nature cannot endure."*

My brother Jamal has found work in Australia and writes to Laila once a month. She deposits the check that comes with each letter but never writes back, still refusing to communicate with him, still blaming him for her rape, and still blaming him for all that they lost in Kuwait. On the other hand, his boys are doing well at Brummana High School and like living with Laila's parents who are well to do and have a big home that is only ten minutes away from school.

Our air is now clean, but the Indian Sea waters are still heavily polluted from the oil that Saddam spilled into the Persian Gulf. This has caused the worth of Mediterranean fish to soar to unaffordable prices because it is highly prized in the Emirates. One sea's demise is another sea's prosperity. Isn't that what life is all about?

I received a letter from Jamal that put my mind at ease. He was very depressed before he left for Sydney because he did not want to leave his boys. Nevertheless, it seems that he not only has found good work with one of our cousins, but on a more personal note, he now has a nice live-in Australian girlfriend who takes good care of him. I feared that he might not tolerate living alone in that vast continent. As I said, spending too much time alone is not healthy.

Look at us John, the happy three, each unhappily married and each with someone else on the side to fill the emptiness. We three seem to live parallel lives, don't we? I do not know how we have succeeded in having happy children in spite of our sad marriages. In a way, adversity has reimbursed us well. God is great. *"Allahu Akbar."*

Love,

Fatima

Eight

(A One-Line Note)

(Oklahoma City - Saturday, 18 July, 1992)

Dearest Fatima,

Since your Christmas letter, much has happened to the world. While vicious fighting continues in Bosnia, delegates from more than a hundred nations met in Rio de Janeiro for the first Earth Summit. They worked on regulations for the development of an environmentally sound planet.

In Israel, Rabin declared his intentions to make the Palestinians under Israeli occupation partners and with the same national and personal rights as the Israelis. He said that as apartheid was ending in South Africa, as negotiations between factions were eminent in Northern Ireland, and as a post-communist world had emerged in Eastern Europe, it was only fitting that Israel should join this evolution toward freedom.

But I still believe in my theory of naturalism. Alas, peace is not natural to *Homo sapiens* and hence it cannot endure. I predict that all our hopes for a clean and peaceful planet will fail because we can never rise above our self-interested, animal natures. I am a realist, Fatima. It is undeniable that we are the dirtiest species planet earth has ever known and the most anachronistic, because the greater our progress, the worse is our littering and pollution. It is equally undeniable that violence is our legacy and peace, our tantalizing ideal.

I loved what you wrote about the Turkish-Greek tensions of Cyprus in your last letter: *"Oh, how inhumane are human beliefs, how aggressively segregating, and how ridiculously childish when juxtaposed."* I can add some aphorisms of my own that might displease you at first, but after reflecting upon them, you will be able to see their penetrating truths in contemporary examples that abound.

My first and most poignant aphorism is about religion. Whenever religion espouses a political ideology, it becomes deadly to itself and to its adversaries. Whenever religion becomes politicized, it falls down from the elevated realms of spirit and becomes disfigured by its lack of love.

My second aphorism is about conquerors and the conquered. When a people are conquered, they need to drop their weapons and teach their conquerors love, by loving them instead of resisting them. It is self evident that the conqueror does love the conquered, and that victory engenders hubris. Defeat, on the other hand, engenders humility, which lights up the way to love.

My third aphorism is about peace. There will never be peace unless we learn to love our enemies. Love is mightier than war because it conquers without casualties and its sovereignty lives on beyond empires.

My last aphorism is about the Jews. I know of no other people who have suffered as much suppression and persecution throughout their history, who have been starved for humanity's love and kindness for three thousand years, and who are more deserving of our compassion than they are. I think that the Arabs are in a position to be the first to embrace them with love and acceptance, and interact with them as neighbors and friends. If they could do just that, we would have lasting peace, and furthermore, everyone would feel victorious.

If my people should ever find out how I feel about Israel, they would ostracize me and crucify me as a traitor. Nevertheless, if I were ever given the chance to address the multitudes, I would preach love as the only antidote to violence. If humanity wants peace, it must learn to love. There can never be peace without love, and there can never be love without peace, for love is the healing gift of God to souls infested with cruelty and aggression.

Forgive me if I have over-philosophized, but these topics have been on my mind awhile and you are the only one who is willing to listen to the solemn cries of my soul. I know that no one else will listen to me. Who am I after all, and what do I know about world politics? I am just a physician who has come to understand, after years of study, that humanity is overwhelmingly delusional and that humanity's delusions are ineluctable, impossible to exorcise.

You inquired about my nameless butterfly! Fatima, as you suspected, I did allow myself to fall in love with one of my sickest patients. I did not hesitate nor did I allow morality to intrude upon my feelings. What started as vicarious sympathy became a platonic love.

She lives within a marital siege. Her husband does not let her out of his sight. He insists on knowing where she is every moment of the day and calls to check on her all too often. She has no time alone; she is either teaching or she is with him. Nor does she have time for me unless she has an appointment.

My one, solitary *"saving kiss"* worsened her depression, created more tension, and complicated both of our lives. I began losing my cheerfulness both at work and at home. The talons of fate had scuttled our ship; it was leaking, and we did not have enough arms to bucket our way back to harbor. Overloaded with love, we sank together and had little time for hope.

Then, she stopped coming and I could not call her without risking a confrontation. Time helped but did not heal. It was a most painful denouement.

One Sunday, the emergency room called. She had overdosed on medicines I had given her. I rushed to find her pale, frail, comatose, and on the respirator. Her husband stood next to her, his eyes muddy with disbelief. I had never met the man, so I introduced myself. He thanked me for my good care and seemed most meek and accepting of all my medical decisions. I informed him that I would be moving her to the intensive care unit and that I expected her to regain consciousness by morning.

He was grateful which made me feel even more awkward. I certainly did not expect such meekness from a wife owner. How shallow is our vision when we can only look from one angle? The heart has no brain and the brain has no heart. I went home feeling only one emotion, terror. I could have killed her with my *"saving kiss."*

The next day, I took her off the respirator and called in the husband. She was too hoarse to speak. He held her hand and sat by her side, his eyes quivering with tears. I looked at the two of them; one was sick with depression and the other sick with possessiveness.

She had no love for him and hated how he owned her. Indeed, with time, she had grown to hate almost all of him. He, on the other hand, clearly loved her in his own possessive way. Like all of us, he could not discern that he had a fated flaw in his disposition, a blind spot that eclipsed the sun. I struggled against my revered aphorism, *"a sick mind must not be permitted to sicken a healthy mind."* There she lay, sick with love and hate, her throat silenced with the swelling of suicide. And as she dozed in her limp apathy, her husband held her hand and watched over her with doleful eyes.

I felt a sincere compassion for both because neither of them could escape unscathed the formidable jaws of their personal realities. They were a pair trapped in a life-mismatch awaiting nothingness.

I returned in the evening to find her sitting in bed, her hair washed, and a half-eaten meal by her side. She smiled, held her hand out to meet mine, and whispered, *"I am sorry to have dragged you into my mess."*

"Why did you stop coming for your appointments?"

"Because they became too painful."

"Is this less painful?"

"No, I guess not."

"What are you going to do when you return home?"

"I am going to tell him."

"Tell him what?"

"That I want a divorce."

"And how do you think he will react?"

"He will get very angry and give me hell. He cannot stand to lose control, especially over me."

"Can you go through with it."

"It depends."

"It depends on what."

"It depends on you!"

"You mean..."

"Yes..."

"So, if I divorce my sick wife, you will divorce your sick husband?"

"Yes."

I went home dizzy with dissonance. A short conversation had shattered my shell. I had naked thoughts that I feared my children and wife would be able to discern because I did not know how to camouflage them; I wore them over my face like a death mask. How did this come about so swiftly and why is it so believable to my heart yet so deniable to my mind? I was in the melee of a bitter battle of the wills, sailing with the winds of imagination, away from my harbor, toward uncharted seas.

When relationships first explode, love and knowledge inversely regulate each other; the less we know the wilder we love. Later on, when passions plateau, love is pruned by knowledge and becomes more reasonable. I knew I was in the throes of a relationship that could not endure and that would ultimately prove destructive, but these realizations did not seem to dissuade me at the time. Somehow, the allure of the unknown interlaced with the passion for liberty seduced me beyond reason. I was a passenger on rails, traveling in life's train, destination unknown.

If I let this beehive grow, if I insist on honey, I will have to sting my wife, my children, her husband, and so many others who would not understand why they were assailed by honeybees. Again, I repeated to myself my agonizing aphorism, *"A sick mind must not be permitted to sicken a healthy mind."*

Perhaps she was reaching with her drowning arms, hoping to hold on to my neck, hoping that I would either save her or drown with her. Perhaps I should choose not to drown. I cannot wrestle anyone out of the jaws of destiny. Reality is harsh, Fatima, nature is ruthless, and the poor get poorer. Nietzsche was right: *"A living thing seeks above all to discharge its strength – life itself is will to power; self-preservation is only one of the indirect and most frequent results."* I resolved to make my deadly decision after a good night's sleep.

The next morning I awoke angry, restless as if before a battle upon which many lives depended. First, I made rounds on all my other hospital patients, and then I went to her room. She was alone. I held her hand and inquired: *"Are you feeling better? Would you like me to discharge you?"*

She was quick to repartee: *"Would you like to discharge me home, or to discharge me out of your heart."*

"I would like to discharge you back to your psychiatrist because, instead of helping you, I have unwittingly hurt you. I am no longer fit to be your doctor, but I can still be your friend."

She lowered her gaze and mumbled: *"I guess, good lovers should give one another the freedom to walk away whenever they so resolve. You must feel that it is time for us to say good-bye."*

I released her hand, stood up, and before I left her bedside, softly muttered: *"Let us become each other's memories instead of each other's undertakers."*

Hearing that, she stared at me as if I were a total stranger, and with a brisk brush of the hand said a silent good-bye, then turned her head away toward the window.

Fatima, saying adieu to my frail butterfly was like a gentle drowning into the night. Unlike Dylan Thomas, we did not *"rage against the dying of the light."* I was again at peace, ready to view my personal realities with a renewed measure of wisdom, ready to reclaim my lost *joie de vivre,* ready to go forth unarmed, unprotected, and unafraid.

A week later, my nurse asked me if I had seen the paper. On my desk lay *The Oklahoman* with a red circle around her picture in the obituaries.

I called her husband. He said that she left a one-line note telling him that she loved him. He sounded like an echo lost in tenebrous emptiness. All he had left in his meaningless world was her one-line note.

Did I kill her or did she kill me? Surely, time will

tell. Meanwhile, I have more to live for than to die for. I must cling to my aphorism, *"a sick mind must not be permitted to sicken a healthy mind,"* and somehow find it in me to continue to insist on joy.

Please give my best to your son and to your lover. Oh, no, please forgive what I have just said, and instead, give my love to Tariq and Kamal because they both love you. Tell them that, perhaps one day, I might get to meet them.

And, Fatima, do not forget to pray for me.

All my love,

John

Nine

(Two Secrets)

(Beirut - Tuesday, 18 August, 1992)

My dear, sad John,

Your butterfly tragedy cried in my heart. I cannot tell you how sorry I am. I wish there were something I could do. How are you faring after the quake? How long will it take you to recover?

Suicide continues to hurt for years. I remember how we all felt when my cousin Jafar shot himself after his wife left him for another man. This was 17 years ago and it still hurts to talk about it. May Allah hold your heart in his hands and ease your suffering. I know what a sensitive man you are and how you nearly die each time one of your patients dies.

John, the same thing almost happened to me when you sent me your rejection letter after our Paris meeting in December 1976. I did not want to live without hoping for our reunion. I almost did it one dark, stormy night, sitting alone in my Beirut apartment, exiled from my world. Out of despair, I almost used Ahmad's gun, which is not a woman's first choice because women like to look good, even when dead.

The only thing that saved me that day was your poetry. I read the sonnet you wrote to your father after you learned of his jail execution, a sonnet so positive in its outlook to contrast with his unjust demise. I was touched by the permeating love that held the sonnet together in one undying ode. But what really saved my life was the last crying couplet:

"So long as we can love, death can not be
So then, forever, shall you be with me."

I will always love you, John, and no matter how far away you stray, parts of our lives together will forever grow within me.

I am spending August in Beirut. I found a remote beach that I frequent during the hot hours of the afternoon. It is as peaceful as it is primitive. I sit in the shade of a handmade straw umbrella, listening to the sounds of the sea. My gentleman Turk, Kamal, calls me from Cyprus every morning, and we have trans-Mediterranean coffee together. He is becoming too attached and that worries me. I would hate to hurt him, but I will have to when my time comes to leave his beloved island.

Not surprisingly, I started to have feelings for him, feelings that bordered on love, feelings that frightened me. That is why I chose to spend August in Lebanon and why I began seeing another charming man. Having two lovers is the best way to dilute emotions before they become strong enough to overwhelm me.

At this point in my life, I cannot allow myself to fall in love again. When one is not emotionally ready, love grows rotten fruits. I can either have love or peace. At present, I need the tranquility of peace much more than the turmoil of love. Forgive me, John; I did not mean to rub it in. I'm sorry if I have spurred on your pain.

Two important happenings are about to change our 20-year political stalemate. We are resuming parliamentary elections and that will give a facelift to our geriatric parliament. Thanks to our Civil War, we have been unable to hold elections since 1972. Now that the war is almost over, political life is sprouting back in the country.

But do not think the elections will be democratic and fair. Syria has made sure that no one gets elected unless sanctioned by Assad. So, as expected, all the candidates have been awarded their *"BTD"* degrees. They have Been To Damascus, each in his private turn attempting to win the favors of the Syrian Sultan.

What we are about to have is a perfunctory democracy, hailed by our newspapers as the new face of post-war Lebanon. Indeed, it is a new face, a young face, a submissive face, a vacuous face without heart or conscience. Like you used to say, *"The poor can never be free."*

The other major change comes from your noble president, Mr. George Hubert Bush. Yesterday, he amended the prohibition of all transportation services to Lebanon enacted by Congress on July 1, 1985. With this amendment, the transport of U.S. cargo to Lebanon is now permitted but only by foreign carriers. All the other prohibitions including the prohibition of U.S. air carriers or passengers from flying into Lebanon remain in effect since the June 15, 1985 incident that cost the whole of Lebanon its solvency.

As you recall, two Shiite gunmen hijacked TWA flight 847 from Athens to Beirut, held more than 100 American citizens hostage, and shot one passenger dead after a brutal beating. They demanded the release of Arab prisoners held by Israel. I am sure that those who committed this most cruel crime had no idea what its repercussions would be. They probably thought it was a brave thing to do. Isn't that how all terrorists think, and didn't you tell me once that, *"Terrorism is distorted altruism?"*

You have always said that the two best counter measures against terrorism are the elimination of poverty and the enlightenment of ignorance. This amendment by President Bush should help boost the economy and resuscitate our destitute country. People are hopeful but do not seem to understand that economic recovery takes many years and requires peace in the region, a peace that I do not see as forthcoming soon.

Enough with politics; now let me delve into the confessional part of my letter. It is such an inopportune time for you to commiserate with me. The bitter taste of your own tragedy must still linger in your mouth. But you are the only one I can open my heart to, a heart that has two secrets it needs to unload—two deep and personal secrets that have overburdened my soul and drained away all my peace.

The more serious one has to do with my brother Jamal and his live-in Australian girlfriend. They are no longer on speaking terms since she became pregnant because he wants her to have an abortion and she is refusing. She has already moved out and is living with her parents who, being devout Christians, want her to carry the baby to term and are willing to help her raise it.

Jamal is back alone and feels abandoned. Both his wife and his girlfriend refuse to speak to him. He calls me daily, and I can feel him sink deeper and deeper into depression. John, I am very worried because he is the kind of man who cannot survive alone and who desperately needs a woman to share his life. As farcical as it may sound, is there any way you can help him? Can you call him and feel him out? Perhaps you can convince him to see a psychiatrist. He respects your opinion and is more apt to take medical advice from you than from me. That is why I have appended his contact information on a separate page.

The other matter is less unpleasant. My Tariq, who will be fifteen this month, is madly in love with one of his Brummana High School classmates. He opened his heart to me last weekend when we were all spending the day together at the beach. He spoke of Issam, his boyfriend, with such passion that he made me cry because he reminded me of you when you were my young, mischievous lover. You should see how the two hold hands under the table and kiss on the lips when they think that no one is watching—just like you and I did and with the same nonchalant attitude.

During our discussion, he said some things to me that caused me to suspect that he's not only reading your poems but also your letters, which I keep under lock in a drawer inside my closet. I did not confront him because it would have hurt his pride, but some words that he used are definitely yours. For example, when I asked him if he was sure about his homosexual feelings, he said that he felt naturally drawn to boys instead of girls and added: *"there is no shame in nature and naturalism always wins."* These were your exact words to me; do you remember?

Tell me John, how could a fifteen-year-old boy think like that? Then, to make things worse, when I asked him if it were possible for him to find happiness living his life as a homosexual in our conservative society, he answered with sincere confidence that regardless of our societal mores, he was going to *"insist on joy!"* You see, my son is not only using your words in his conversation, he also believes in them. Oh, what am I to do with him now that he has adopted your own concepts of freedom?

John, this is Lebanon, not Paris. My family would die if they should find out, and they most certainly will find out because these two foolish boys are not at all discrete. They take their homosexuality much too lightly and think of girls as stupid, giggly creatures. Such handsome boys... Oh, what a waste!

But, I must accept reality, which is what you have always taught me. I still remember our conversations about reality and what to do with it when it becomes too unpleasant. Your answer was always the same, *"Learn to enjoy all things inevitable; it is a far nobler solution than any other."* And do you remember, when I asked you if this philosophy applied even to death and illness, how you looked at me with amazement and said, *"If you cannot enjoy your own illness and death, you will die miserably instead. Is that what you really want to do?"*

Do homosexuals change their minds later on in life? Is there hope for me to have a grandchild? Oh, John. What am I to do? What would you do if he were your son? This is my only child. Wait until his father finds out, and then may God help us all.

Life is a confusing mystery. I am confused and so are you, and so is Jamal. Didn't I tell you that we three seem to live our lives in parallel?   Tomorrow, I shall go to Syria. I want to visit the holy shrine of Um Al-Huda and pray for all of us. I shall ask her to make Tariq sexually normal so that, one day, he would be willing to marry and give me a grandchild. I shall ask her to influence Jamal to return to us and find work in Lebanon so that he can be reunited with his boys. I shall ask her to give you back to me because we belong together, and no other woman will ever love you as much as I do.

Um Al-Huda has always answered my prayers.

Beware, John, I am about to invoke deity.

With love,

Fatima

Jamal Muhsin Al Sharaf
53 Bruce St.
Nedlands,
Western Australia
Zip Code: 6009

From the U.S., dial 011-61-8-9-329-1954

This is his home, and the best time to call him is on Fridays or Saturdays. Remember that at this time of year Western Australia is 13 hours ahead of the U.S. and so if you call him at 8pm your time, it will be 9am the next day in Nedlands, and you will be able to catch him having his morning coffee. I have told him that you might call, and he seemed pleased.

Thanks again, John,

Fatima

Ten

(Adieu In September)

(Oklahoma City- Friday, 18 September, 1992)

My dearest Fatima,

I read your letter several times before I was able to digest it all. It left me bewildered and overwhelmed with helplessness. Your two secrets smoldered under my ribs; no sigh was large enough to put the fire out. We have much to ponder, you and I.

My butterfly left an emptiness that I have tried to fill with books and exercise, to no avail. Her pale, frail face haunts me, her drowning arms still cling to my neck, I hear her cries at night, and on my desk her unfinished chart still awaits my pen.

Her husband came in as a new patient. He was starved for compassion, lost without love, flattened with loneliness, subdued with loss, and depressed to the point of capitulation. He came to me not knowing that I had loved his wife and kissed her on the very same examination table he sat upon. He trusted me with his life as he had trusted me with his wife.

I felt compassion for both of us, victims of her suicide, victims of her love. We quickly became friends and began feeling sorry for each other. I felt sorry for his loss and he for my guilt about her failed treatment and subsequent suicide. Such a preposterous reversal of sentiments confused me until I deciphered the meanings underneath all the unsaid. I could not feel his guilt because he had none; like all possessive, controlling husbands, he merely thought of himself as very caring. But he could feel my guilt because I could not hide it; it permeated all our encounters as thinly veiled, compassionate melancholy.

We became comrades in pain and partners in

emptiness. I do not know how long it will take us to surface back into the sunshine. In case you are still wondering, I only kissed her once, and after that first kiss, we never touched again. In a way, I am glad we had this one solitary intimacy. Somehow, although that lone kiss became my fountain of guilt, it also eased my grief because a part of her still hovers between my lips each time I breath. A love kiss is a mighty mystery, Fatima. I wish we only kissed those whom we did not love. With love, a saving kiss can sometimes become the kiss of death.

Now, Fatima, before I respond to your secrets, I am going to ask you to attempt the most difficult task in the world—a task most formidable especially for the mighty, the learned, and the intelligent—a task that can only be realized at the expense of painful soul searching. This task is worthy of the liberated few, those noble few with emancipated minds. It is a task beyond the intellects of most ethnic, religious, military, and national leaders. Fatima, I am going to ask you to *think*.

Thinking is easy when we think with our closed eyes, with our locked brains, and with our ramifying biases. What is even more lamentable is that we are our biases. This means that to think with crystal fairness, with lucid clarity, we must migrate away from our dogmatized selves, extricate our minds from the stifling mud of our cultures, and free ourselves from the sanctimonious commandments of our mores.

I'm fond of a quote attributed to William James, a thorny quote that stings us all: *"Most people who think that they are thinking are merely rearranging their prejudices."* Now, Fatima, let us think unfettered, not as man or woman, not as parent or friend, not as Arab or American, not as Muslim or Christian, for all of these are but shackles of the mind. Let us think as highly evolved, open-minded *Homo sapiens* who were liberated by love, long before they were enthralled by deity.

Your only son, your Tariq, is living his own biological truth. He feels free expressing his unique individuality. He is homosexual because that is how he was constituted. He not only cannot help who he is, but also, he should not be asked to behave contrary to his nature, especially by you. Subjugating him to the pressures of cultural mores will create tension and guilt in his heart that could destroy his innocence and mire the creativity whence his poetry emanates.

What shall you do? Do nothing. Let him never suspect that you have ever noticed. Share his enthusiasm. Think of his welfare. In short, love him, love him for what he is, love this miracle of creation you call your son, and do not blame him or his Maker for your jagged cultural biases.

Regarding Jamal, I shall call and offer him my help, although I tend to side with his Australian girlfriend and vote for life. I can understand an abortion if the welfare of the mother is in danger, or if the child is sentenced to a life of hopeless, joyless misery by genetic, circumstantial, or environmental coincidences. But this child will be well loved, well cared for, and should have the unconditional support rather than the unconcerned repudiation of its father.

When I call Jamal and tell him what I think, he will become more angered than pacified. I will not succeed in liberating him from his un-thinking state unless, during his short stay in Australia, he has learned to become more receptive to enlightenment. *"You can only receive what you already have,"* said Ben Okri. As a Muslim, it would be nobler for Jamal to have two wives and father a new hope than to kill a womb or return to an excommunicating wife. Life is a chance, Fatima, a chance to flee the inanimate, a chance to feel and grow and make an impact, a chance at free expression before returning to dust.

Fatima, August burned us all, but September has brought a cool mist and is busy powdering the red Oklahoma cheeks. The mums are wearing sly lipstick, and my mint smells like the mountains where I grew up. My children are in the garden playing with friends, a gentle afternoon saunters underneath an umbrella of clouds, my wife is napping, and I am sitting at the porch writing to you. I have just completed a long poem, *Adieu In September*. It came to me partly because of your worries, and partly because August almost desiccated the land with its angry sun.

> *"It will not happen soon*
> *Do not worry*
> *Let us watch the silken morning stretch*
> *Into the afternoon and tarry*
> *Weaving light into a cotton blush*
> *Upon the lips of evening."*

It came to me because I do not feel sorry about anything anymore, because I have become pregnant with gratitude, and because I have come to love my fate, my nature, my naturalism, the surprises of my life, its puzzles, and all its mysteries. I love being imperfect, incarnate, animated, vitalized, and spiritualized. I love being so far removed from dust, from sin, and from worry.

> *"Do not worry*
> *Like a cat the gentle moon*
> *Suddenly, gets eerie-eyed and wild*
> *Flirts around at night till full with child*
> *Then, on a pink-eyed unsuspecting morn*
> *The stilling, silent, sighing mist is born*
> *Lunar fresh, like dreams, with milky echoes*
> *Pronouncing September."*

It came to me because pain is more delicious than death, and worry more delicious than apathy, and anger more delicious than surrender, and sorrow more delicious than pretense, and loss more delicious than caution.

> *"Come September, let us not pretend*
> *You have been my savior and my friend*
> *And we have much to tell before the end*
> *Of timid times in suntanned Oklahoma*
> *Where August rises up from hell*
> *And summers fry*
> *And lips of tulips cleft and dry*
> *And poems, pierced with arrows*
> *Bleed and die*

Without a cry, without a friend
So let us not pretend."

Tell Tariq to write a poem about free love. Tell him that freedom promotes spiritual growth while atavistic traditions stifle the soul. Tell him to be proud of being God's unique creation. Tell him that his own conscience holds all the pure truths of humanity while the collective conscience of all cultures breed sanctimony.

Tell him to be true to his soul before being true to any culture or creed, and to be fearless and uncompromising in playing the role that God has cast for him. Tell him that when he listens to his own conscience, he listens to God, but when he listens to the collective conscience of fanatics, he listens to a mob.

Tell him that counter-naturalism is ephemeral antinomy (from nomos, the Greek word for law); it cannot endure because it runs against nature's laws. Tell him that every idea, belief, and ideology that splits humanity into fierce factions is a denounced anathema (curse). Tell him that whosoever harshly judges another judges not with compassion or empathy but rather with hubris, which is the downfall of humanity.

Tell him that I am proud of him for being proud of what he is. Tell him that I love him.

With love,

John

Eleven

(Swords)

(Jeddah- Friday, 22 January, 1993)

Dear John,

I am in Saudi Arabia working on a book project for Al Emir Fadil. He is a great collector of ancient Arabian swords and wants us to photograph each sword, help chronicle its history, and tell its story. Every sword has its own set of manuscripts upon which we are to base our research. Verses from the Koran are etched in beautiful calligraphy on many of the curved blades. The prince, my editor, and I work together from morning till noon. Then, after a lunch siesta, we resume work until dark.

There is a 1400 year-old sword, which might have belonged to the Caliph Omar, but it is impossible to be certain. The Emir pressured us to say that it did, but we have succeeded in convincing him that it would be more truthful to merely suggest that it could have belonged to the Caliph Omar, thus leaving the question of authenticity open for future historians.

Our only free day is Friday, which I spend indoors. Being a woman, I am neither allowed to drive nor to wear short sleeves, which makes coming and going during the days' heat most inconvenient. At the rate we're plowing, the project will take about two more months to complete. In the evenings we are usually invited to the homes of Lebanese friends who live and work here. The mood is somber because the threat of Saddam at the border is still very real.

Last Friday in Paris, 120 nations including the U.S. and Russia signed an agreement banning chemical weapons. What a relief! The day after, the U.S. bombed strategic sites near Baghdad because Saddam placed surface-to-air missiles in the No-Fly Zone that had been declared in southern Iraq. Of course, this has caused fear and rumors to flourish in spite of President Clinton's reassuring inaugural address two days ago. I wish wars were still fought with swords. I have come to appreciate the dignity inherent in a curved blade; it cuts but does not stab.

Jamal is leaving Australia. He has found work in Kuwait. Your telephone call did no good, just as you predicted, but thank you for the effort. He wants to leave before his child is born. His girlfriend, Mary, has called me several times asking me to plead with him. She is carrying a girl, due in early May. I promised to stay in touch with her.

She wants to name the girl Jamie, after her father, which has angered Jamal even more. He thinks that running away will make the child disappear. He lives a grand denial, which I hope time will shatter. I tried to tell him that a fish cannot fly away from its waters, but he remains stubborn.

Mary promised to send me pictures, which I plan to use to soften Jamal's stubbornness. If I have to, I will even show the pictures to his wife and boys. Like you said, *"Children are earth's blossoms and it is their right to fill their petals with sun."*

Tariq is back in school after the Christmas break. I let him read your last letter, and he got upset with me for talking to you about him behind his back. But even while he was upset with me, I could tell that he was very proud of what you said.

The other day, he called me to say that it is snowing in Brummana. The weekend before I left Lebanon, he gave me this poem and asked me to share it with you. As you can see, my son is utterly shameless.

"My love and I
My friend and I
Went to the cinema
In the dark, together
We touched each other
And never saw the film;
But oh, what pleasure...

On the way back to school
We laughed and laughed
Because cinema
Rhymes with enema..."

Are you shocked or are you laughing? I laughed and cried when he read it to me. I am glad he thought that my tears were caused by laughter. John, do you still think that he is normal? Doesn't he have any sense of propriety? I am very worried about him, but he has no idea that I disapprove. I heeded your advice and did not let him notice that I was perturbed.

I hope your Mr. Clinton will bring us peace. He is bright, educated, young, handsome, and seems to prefer women to war. We have to hang our hopes on America because only America can bring lasting stability to our war-torn Arab world.

Meanwhile, with Syrian troops in Lebanon, we have a false security, or a *Pax Romana*. But if the Syrians were to leave, the Civil War would erupt again because none of the peace requirements have been satisfied. We still have horrible inequality and a weak democracy. Our national economy is near bankruptcy because our main natural resource, tourism, has been devastated by the long Civil War. I might not leave Cyprus after all, which would please Kamal immensely. I am trying my best not to get attached to him, but it is becoming harder and harder especially because my Lebanese lover, as charming as he is, does not measure up to Kamal. The Ottomans ruled our people with force for eight centuries, and now one of their descendants is attempting to rule me with simple kindness. I may not have a choice but to return the favor.

John, tell me about you, your life, your wife, your grief, your children, and your work. How is the economy in Oklahoma, and what do the Americans think of us feuding Arabs? Do they still believe that we are all Bedouins who live in tents and stride across the desert atop our camels waging tribal wars?

From where I stand now, with one eye on Iraq and the other on Saudi Arabia, this image seems not too far from the truth. You may have done the right thing after all; you chose to emigrate and you did, without ever looking back. Perhaps I should have done the same thing?

Love,

Fatima

Twelve

(Symposium)

(Washington D.C.- Monday, 13 September, 1993)

Dear Fatima,

I am in Washington D.C. at a medical meeting. The city is bursting with emotion, and all the TV stations are at the White House. Today, while I was attending a symposium on migraines, President Clinton witnessed the signing of the Declaration of Principles by Arafat and Rabin, where both the PLO and Israel recognized each other and announced their willingness to negotiate a peaceful settlement and to put an end to violence and terrorism.

It sounds too good, doesn't it? Well, I am neither gullible nor hopeful. Both sides are too fanatic about their beliefs, too blinded by their own ways of thinking, too stubborn in their attitudes as traditional enemies, too shortsighted in their outlooks. I detect no sincere flow of kindness, forgiveness, readiness for change, or respect for each other's way of life.

Reason is always wasted on those who have already made up their minds. It will take many generations before fired passions mellow down into meaningful tolerance, before poverty is redeemed, and before ignorance is enlightened. In the meantime, we shall continue to suffer the consequences of man-made beliefs that separate humanity into dissonant factions. I believe that Hobbs was right when he said, *"Violence is not a primitive, irrational urge, nor is it a pathology. It is a near-inevitable outcome of the dynamics of self-interested, rational social organisms."*

Fatima, I want to change *Homo sapiens* from a warring to a loving race. Do you think that I will be able to do so in my speck-of-life? Do you think that I will be able to overcome our genetic code, the same code that promoted our survival, and that now is promoting our demise? I wish I had the brains of Socrates and Christ inside my skull, the two teacher geniuses of humanity who never wrote a word.

My life is stable, and the children are well. My wife continues to struggle with her post-traumatic organic brain syndrome. She does her best to remain functional, and we do our best to support her. Her tragedy unites the family, and for that I am thankful. I do feel an emotional void, however, a vacancy that love once filled, and an emptiness that has become more painful since my butterfly fluttered off to the other bank of life. I am trying to fill this vacuum with intellectual matter; I read, I write, and I think, but the emptiness remains overwhelming. It gasps for emotion, a very specific emotion; it gasps for the love of a woman, which is the only music missing from my soul.

As for sexual satisfaction, I have none. Instead of satisfaction, I harbor fear; fear that one day my hunger will fatigue me into dishonor. I have resisted many an urge, which has both ennobled me and impoverished me. I feel strong in will, but I also feel deprived in intimacy. I need the courage to accept my humanity, to accept that finding a kind lover is better than languishing in deprivation. But my soul wants to love before it consumes, for it has not learned to separate love from intimacy.

I wish I could learn from you how to separate these two passions. You can love, you can have lovers, or you can combine the two into a *grand amour*. I believe that, according to my theory of naturalism, you are living in accordance with natural law while I am living antinomy.

Whatever flows contrary to nature ultimately fails. It is not natural to abstain, and I fear that through abstaining I might diminish myself into a one-eyed moralist, one of the cruel moralists prefigured by Bertrand Russell's frightening aphorism, *"The infliction of cruelty with a good conscience is a delight to moralists—that is why they invented hell."*

You have always believed that it is cruel to deny sexuality its proper place. I do not deny it its place, Fatima; I am just unable to elevate myself enough to reach it. Perhaps I am rationalizing? Remember Jeff

Goldblum's reflections in *The Big Chill? "Rationalization is more important than sex. Have you ever gone a week without rationalization?"*

I loved Tariq's poem; it made me laugh but, unlike you, it did not make me cry. Why are you so worried about his sexual freedom? It can only lead him to intellectual freedom, and the reverse is also true. When sexual freedom is denied, intellectual freedom suffers. Think of my own self-denial and how vulnerable it has made me and then thank your God for Tariq's enviable state of mind. He has achieved in youth what would take vernacular wisdom decades to accomplish. I congratulate him to you, and you lament him to me. How distanced we have become.

Please, give this little book, *Plato's Symposium,* to Tariq and tell him that I am sending it in response to his delightful poem. I have underlined the last statement of Socrates, his final declaration at the end of his own speech: *"I declare that it is the duty of every man to honor Love, and I honor and practice the mysteries of Love in an especial degree myself, and recommend the same to others, and I praise the power and valor of Love to the best of my ability both now and always."*

At his age, he should find the speech of Aristophanes the most endearing. In it, Aristophanes explains that in our natural condition we were complete beings, but then our wickedness caused us to be halved by Zeus. Ever since that time, we spend our lives looking for our missing halves because, *"Love is simply the name for the desire and pursuit of the whole."*

Fatima, did Mary have a healthy baby girl, and is she still living with her parents in Nedlands? Were you able to soften Jamal's stubbornness with Jamie's pictures? Would you be so kind as send me one picture of Mary with Jamie so that I can conjure their images when you relate their stories to me.

Has Laila softened her stance, or does she still blame Jamal for her rape? Is she still refusing to speak to him? How are conditions in Kuwait after Saddam? Susan Sontag said, *"The only interesting answers are those which destroy the questions."*

Please, be careful with the swords.

Love,

John

Thirteen

(Cedars And Snow)

(The Cedars - Friday, 31 December, 1993)

My Dear John,

We are spending New Year's Eve among the holy Cedars of Lebanon. Our dear friends, the Barakats, invited Tariq and me to spend a few days with them at their Bisharri home. We have been here since Wednesday enjoying the calm scenery of these ancient Northern Mountains that you once believed were yours. Do you remember that Saturday in the spring of 1969 when you had just finished your pediatrics rotation and felt hungry for your North?

We took off in your little white Datsun and stopped in your little village long enough for me to meet your grandmother and to be blessed by her. She blessed me by dipping her little finger in olive oil from your orchards and then signing the cross on my Muslim forehead.

From Amioun we drove up to Bisharri where we spent the morning visiting Gibran's shrine. At lunch you surprised me with a copy of *The Prophet* that you had managed to purchase on site without my noticing. Do you remember your inscription? *"Fatima, you are my Almitra and I am your Almustafa?"*

I did not understand what you meant until I began reading the book and discovered that it was Almitra who had first asked the departing Almustafa to speak to the gathered people of Orphalese. *"Then said Almitra, Speak to us of Love."*

I remember reading the prologue and wondering if you were telling me that you were going to leave me? *"Almustafa had waited twelve years in the city of Orphalese for his ship that was to return and bear him back to the isle of his birth."* Two years later, you left to the States, left me without a promise, left me with the blessed oil still on my forehead, left me with *The Prophet*, left and never returned.

Each morning Tariq and I take long walks in the snow and have heart-to-heart talks. Then, when the cold rattles our bones, we hurry back to the Barakat's large pine-burning fireplace where we have hot tea and toast. Tariq wanted me to take him to Gibran's shrine but I resisted. The only time I had ever been there was when we saw it together. Somehow, I was afraid to return to the spot that marked your valediction, and I did not wish to explain my fear to my adolescent son.

After much insistence, the Barakats volunteered to take him, and I took advantage of this private time alone to drop you a few lines. They should be back soon, and I will tell you more after they return. Tonight, we are going to welcome the New Year at The Cedars under the 4500 year-old-tree by the roadside, where a crowd always gathers, where kabob is grilled on hot coals, and where snow-cooled champagne is consumed in large quantities.

One of the local entrepreneurs has built a wooden temple in the plaza behind the tree, which he says is modeled after King Solomon's Temple. He tried to build it out of dead cedar wood from the floor of the forest, but the authorities would not let him carry off even the smallest twig. It was a good try, but he should have known, being a native of Bisharri, that he would never be permitted to desecrate The Cedars with commercial ventures.

I will tell you more tomorrow when I get some time to finish my letter. For now, I will occupy myself with reading *The Prophet* that I brought with me for the memory.

Happy New Year,

Fatima

(Saturday, 1 January, 1994)

John, the sun is making diamonds out of the snow. We have just returned from our walk. Tariq could not stop talking about Gibran and bought several of his books. He has already found the passage on children and quoted it to me during our walk. *"Your children are not your children..."* I think this kid is telling me to leave him alone and is doing it in your own grand style. I must be over-mothering him. But, I do not know how else to love him. I think I need some help in that regard.

He was with us when we toasted the New Year under the 4500 year-old cedar-tree. I thought that he would have much to say afterwards, but he did not. He must not have been impressed. All he wanted to talk about was Gibran's shrine, Gibran's paintings, and Gibran's books. He must have identified with Gibran in some occult, adolescent way.

Perhaps he aspires to become a writer. He continues to surprise me with his writing abilities. I fear that with his wide and sundry readings, he might soon begin fathering me, which might indeed put an end to my over-mothering him. Do you find my excogitations strange? Well, I do.

You inquired about Jamal and Laila. You will not believe what happened. Jamal fell ill while in Kuwait and had to be hospitalized. He developed some sort of *"hemorrhagic fever"* and came near death because his kidneys shut down. When Laila found out, she left the children with her parents and flew to Kuwait. She slept in his hospital room for 18 days, and when he was discharged, she went home with him and took care of him until he was fully recovered.

When he was ready to return to work, he told her to go back to the children, but she refused. She has been with him ever since, a model wife, much to everyone's surprise. He says that their relationship has never been better and that they live as newlyweds with much joy and love. God's work is great, John, and so is Um Al-Huda's.

No one knows this but when I found out that he was unconscious in the hospital, I went to the shrine of Um Al-Huda and cried to her to save him and his marriage. When I returned to Beirut, I was told that Laila had flown to Kuwait that very same morning. The next day, without telling anyone, I went back to Um Al-Huda's and laid pink roses at her shrine.

Mary has stayed in touch with me because I am her only connection with Jamal. He still repudiates her and his beautiful daughter, who is six months old now. I get monthly pictures from Mary, but I am afraid to mail them to him with his wife around. Who knows how she would take it? They need to stay together because they have two boys to raise.

I relay to Mary his news each time we talk, and have asked her not to communicate with him as long as his wife is there. So far, she has been most noble and accommodating, but I do not know how much longer she will be able to keep her distance.

Jamie is his responsibility and, according to your theory of naturalism, anything that goes against nature must ultimately fail. Sooner or later then, Mary will have to confront him with his paternal responsibilities, and I will help her do so. When that time comes, she and I will act as a team.

Poor man, he has no idea that we are tacitly plotting against him.

I plan to return to Cyprus the week Tariq goes back to school. I stopped seeing my Lebanese lover after I laid pink roses on Um Al-Huda's shrine. I did not understand why, but I did feel that it was the right thing to do. When Um Al-Huda speaks to my soul, I always obey, even though I seldom understand her wisdom.

I miss Kamal, and he is waiting for me. After all, weren't you the one who said:

"Familiar faces, let us not pretend
Though life may decimate and send
Our unsuspecting souls across
Uncharted times and unfamiliar places,
Wherever we are loved we end."

The book, *Ancient Arabian Swords* by Al Emir Fadil turned out beautifully. It was printed in Beirut, and a thousand copies were shipped to Jeddah just two weeks ago. The prince was so pleased that he is planning a grand reception to launch the book and wants me to attend, all expenses paid. I will have to comply no matter how inconvenient that might prove to be. But of course, as you had intimated in your last letter, I shall be careful with the swords.

Love,

Fatima

Fourteen

(Mountains And Stages)

(Denver- Friday, 13 May, 1994)

Dear Fatima,

Your last letter revived my mountain nostalgia and fired my soul with longing. I remember that day when my grandmother anointed your forehead, but do you still remember what she said afterwards? She had you stand in the middle of the room and turn around one full circle. Then, after carefully inspecting your figure, she said: *"You have a fecund pelvis, my child, and you are very pretty; may you bring forth many children."* You blushed, stuttered a muffled reply, and quickly sat down as if by sitting you could conceal your hips from her circumspect eyes. How shy you were at eighteen.

My grandmother died two years later, the year I came to the States. I remember going to see her the day before I left. She knew I had come to say good-bye and would not let me say it. She put her finger across my lips when I tried to kiss her farewell and said: *"America takes our best youth and leaves us with the rejects. You will come back to see me every summer, won't you? I cannot let America keep my grandson away from me."* How painful are the good-byes that last forever.

I am in Colorado at a cardiovascular disease meeting. After your cedar tree letter, I craved mountains. When I found out that our Infectious Disease Society was meeting in Denver, I immediately signed up. Fatima, here as in Lebanon, the mountains have facial expressions and affable personalities. They smile, they cry, they gossip, they have trouble keeping secrets, and they tell funny stories. I gaze at their haughty aspects, at their snowy countenances, at their majestic smiles in the sun, at their brows unperturbed by marauding clouds and wallowing winds, and I feel poems quicken behind my eyes:

"I stood, and stared, and stared, and gazed,
And gazed, and could not stop
Devouring each darting slant
And every haughty top.

These never-ending chains of crowns,
Lips and faces, smiles and frowns
Engulfed me in their magic maze
I could not help but gaze.

Here evolution stoops and dies
Such perfect beauty could not rise
From nature, nor could time alone
Have carved these faces out of stone.

This is the master's masterpiece
An ode to man and earth
A tribute to the might of love
And miracle of birth."

I want to go hiking now, before the sunset hides their smiles and before I lose my lust for prayer. The temple of nature is my dome and I shall worship all alone beneath the safety of its hovering, mighty shoulders. As Ralph Waldo Emerson said, *"Happy is the man who can learn from nature the lesson of worship."*

(Denver- Saturday, 14 May, 1994)

Fatima, having joined the mountains, I feel a youthful newness, an incomprehensible alacrity to meet life at its own terms. I now believe that it is not the situation but rather the spirit that determines our mood. With an elevated spirit one can make light of the direst situation, as Christians made light of lions in the Coliseum. The reverse is even more striking when good fortunes are wasted on miserable souls. We are either enriched or impoverished by our own spirits, for in the end, it is only through the spirit that we can acquire joy.

I do miss Lebanon, Fatima, but I am not yet ready to visit again. There are no *Cedrus libani* in Colorado and no tree is 4500 years old; but there is mighty freedom, mountains of sunshine, domes of quietude, and skies of peace—and that is where I belong. I have weaned myself from the milky breast of my motherland:

> *"Motherland,*
> *If only I can hold you hand*
> *And stand upon your shore*
> *Behold your hoary mountains dive*
> *Into the sea and snore*
> *With mystifying grace*
> *Implore the endless waves*
> *To wash your ancient face."*

Fatima, last month, multiracial elections were held in South Africa, ending 342 years of white rule, and now Mandela is president. When a Palestinian president is elected in Israel and a black president is elected in the U.S., you and I will be long dead. But this has to come because suppression is incompatible with life. It is primitive to destroy your enemy's pride—all you do is plant anger seeds that fester at a later time into acts of terrorism perceived as acts of martyrdom.

How unfortunate we are because, as a race, we can only think from within the confines of our own times. Somehow, we are unable to think from outside our centuries, unable to see our situation from a lunar stance. If we could, we would make Humanism our creed.

"History is life
Viewed from a distance;
Wisdom is seeing
Ourselves from the stars."

It is clear that we are slowly destroying our little planet and that there will come a time when, unless we work together under one global rule, we will add our bones to the dinosaurs. Nonetheless, we continue to behave as if nations, religions, borders, and beliefs are veritable differences that constitute our separate identities. W e do not wish to hear that what we are willing to kill for or die for today will become irrational in the near future. It will become irrational because the survival of our species will depend upon global cooperation and desegregation of the myriad *Homo sapiens* tribes that homestead this planet, tribes that inhale the same air, drink the same water, and multiply under the only sky dome they will ever have.

I loved Tariq's fascination with Gibran. It takes a certain degree of refinement to recognize quality, for the appreciation of quality is an acquired skill. Let him sensitize his taste buds now so that he can learn to savor life rather than become disgruntled with it. Let him nourish his spirit in youth so that it will not be starved by age.

"Do not worry about the little river
It will always find its way to the sea."

I would like to help you out with Jamal's denial of Mary and Jamie, but I do not think that direct intervention would do much good. We are cyclic beings; our moods and resolutions orbit around us, causing ebbs and tides, rendering us seasonal. Constancy is not a human attribute; there are no human constants; there is only change.

If one is afflicted with a certain mood, all one has to do is wait and another mood will soon come to the rescue. If one is faced with a bad situation and waits it out, it will pass into a better state. If you want to believe in something eternal, omnipresent, omnipotent, believe in change and the endless motion of the universe that engenders it.

Jamal will find his heart one day; he will find it on his own and without anyone's help. He will exit his denial stage and see with bitter clarity the dire consequences of his actions.

Fatima, just as we cannot exit our centuries, also, we cannot exit our stages of consciousness. Every emotional or mental state must run its course, in stages. Grief, loss, illness, belief, passion, intuition, rebellion, anger, denial, and so many other states of mind, in order to run their course from beginning to end, must pass through their particular stages.

First, the stage of newness or shock must live its infancy. Then, the stage of incomprehension or distortion must live its adolescence. Then, the stage of resolve or confrontation must live its adulthood. Then, the stage of depth perception or insight must live its maturity. Then, the stage of resignation and peaceful capitulation must live its wisdom.

These stages may be short or long, fast or slow, and may vary depending on the situation or person, but giving each stage its own time remains a useful generalization. If we can just wait for each stage to pass, we will change our perceptions and decisions with each passage, and move in the direction of inner peace.

You have not sent me a picture of Mary and Jamie. If the prince would not mind, could you also please send me a copy of *Ancient Arabian Swords*? Are you still resisting falling in love with your gentleman Turk, or has your passion already passed from the stage of denial into the stage of peaceful capitulation? Please do not go to the shrine of Um Al-Huda and ask her to make Kamal disappear; on the contrary, if you should go again, ask her to help you fall in love with him as he has with you. And ask her to find me a new love, for I have exited the stages of loss, grief, emptiness, and despair; I am now ready to venture out again with rejuvenated anima, thanks to these Rocky Mountains and the blissful passing of time.

Have a glass of wine on your way to Jeddah because, in Saudi Arabia, alcohol is verboten. Ask the Emir to kindly sign my copy of *Ancient Arabian Swords*. Give my love to Tariq, and ask him if they plan to have Internet access at Brummana High School. Encourage him to use the computer. The Internet is coming.

Love,

John

Fifteen

(A Procreative Mess)

(Nicosia - Tuesday, 5 August, 1994)

My Dear John,

My heart is broken, and there is much to tell. I have resisted writing lest I contaminate your soul with my pen. But my agony has become so unbearable that I have decided to share my grief with you. They say that sharing sorrow halves it while sharing joy doubles it; pray help me then by accepting half my pain. Please bear with me and listen to the story of my Kamal, my gentleman Turk who worships me, and whose love has sustained me through these most difficult of times.

After Tariq returned to school in January, I returned to Cyprus expecting to find Kamal waiting for me at the Larnaca airport, as we had agreed when we talked the night before. I waited one hour and called his apartment repeatedly to no avail. Finally, I took a taxi to my place hoping to find a note, given that I had left spare keys with him when I went to Beirut. When I entered my apartment, I saw that all my plants looked healthy with freshly watered soil, but there was no note anywhere, which frightened me to no end.

I called his Lebanese boss, Naji Karam, who owns and operates the publishing house where Kamal works. His wife answered the phone, and I heard her calling him with hesitant whispers, *"She's back; do you want me to tell her you're asleep?"* *"No,"* he answered, *"tell her to come over."* In the taxi, I wrestled with my wild imagination and tried to calm myself down, but I must not have succeeded because my appearance startled both Naji and Nada. The first thing Naji said was, *"Do not worry; he's fine, but he's in jail. The police arrested him this morning. They came to the print shop where he works and took him away, and no one seems to know why."*

The next day, I called everybody I knew to find out where he was and to find out if I could visit him. After some of my friends called some of their friends who called some of theirs, I was told that he was held for questioning and that no one was allowed to communicate with him. Six months passed without a word from him, and during these six months I kept everyone busy with my irrational requests and emotional visits.

This morning, his boss Naji called to say that Kamal had been accused of spying, and that he will remain in solitary confinement until his trial at an unknown date. Then Naji proceeded to inform me that Kamal was an illegal resident, that he had flown into Cyprus from London with a false passport, that he has a wife and two children who live on the Turkish side of the island, that he will most likely serve a stiff jail sentence unless they decide to exchange him for some Greek Cypriot prisoner on the Turkish side, and that, only if he is exchanged, will he be able to communicate with me.

At noon today, the police visited me. They were extremely polite and only asked me general questions about Kamal, and how we met, and what we talked about, and what he told me about his origins. They wanted to know if he had commissioned me to do anything for him such as deliver any letters, carry any money, or make contact with any person when I went to Beirut or Saudi Arabia. I answered all their questions, but they never answered any of mine. They seemed pleased when they left. When I asked Naji why the police waited six months to question me, he said that they probably wanted to watch my activities awhile before confronting me.

John, I do not know why this is happening to me. I should have known since we live our lives in parallel, you and I. I should have known that because bad things had happened to your butterfly, that bad things were going to happen to my sweet Kamal. When I told the police that Kamal came to Cyprus to find work, they laughed but said nothing, which made me feel very stupid. When I told them that he was a printer for a Lebanese publishing house, inspector Kakos smiled and asked me if I had ever seen ink under his fingernails.

I called Jamal to see if he could find me work in Kuwait. I want to leave Cyprus, and I don't want to go back to Beirut. Jamal said that the local economy is closed for any kind of creative photography and that I would have a hard time finding work. When I asked him about Laila, he hesitated a bit then informed me that she is pregnant.

John, can you believe this polygamous procreative mess? Jamal is 41, Laila is 34, and their two boys are 8 and 12. Also, Jamal has a fifteen-month-old daughter in Australia whom he still refuses to acknowledge.

I hate the position I am in as guardian of my family's secrets. I hate not telling Mary about Laila's forthcoming child for fear that she might get angry enough to fly to Kuwait and show up at Jamal's door. I also hate not telling Mary that, in contrast to her own pregnancy, Jamal is not suggesting an abortion to Laila but, Instead, he is looking forward to their coming baby and thinks that it will strengthen their marriage. The fact that he never asks me about Mary or Jamie even though he knows that we stay in touch shows that he has chosen denial as his major coping strategy.

Soon, I shall have to go to Um Al-Huda's shrine to ask that she guard Laila's unexpected pregnancy and that she preserve the health and peace of mind of Mary and Jamie. I know you think that I am superstitious, but we three do live our lives in parallel, and since you and I have been hit so hard, I am afraid that Jamal is next in line. I wish to prevent disaster with faith. Um Al-Huda is the only one who always comes to my aid.

Tariq is on summer break, and he is spending it with his father in our Beirut apartment. They are having a good time going to the beach and socializing. Ahmad's cute hairdresser continues to live in the apartment that Ahmad bought and furnished for her. He will not let Tariq meet her and continues to pretend that Tariq has no knowledge of the situation.

Tariq plays along and acts as if our life as a family

is undisturbed. However, he wants to come to Cyprus at the end of the month and I know that he expects to see Kamal. How do I tell this unsuspecting kid that Kamal, his friend and his mother's friend, is a married man with two children of his own and is also in jail for spying?

How do I tell him the truth without breaking his heart? How do I tell him a lie without breaking his heart? Sometimes, truths and lies are equally offensive. Sometimes, I think that I should remain silent and say nothing. I know what you would prefer, however. You would prefer that I tell him the truth and let him deal with it. *"Good training for life,"* you would say. I wish I had your calm resolve.

John, can you believe that next summer Tariq will graduate from high school? He wants to go to the American University of Beirut but he is also thinking about the U.S. He says that he wants to major in philosophy. How can he make a living as a philosopher?

His choices always drive me crazy. He may be writing and asking you to help him out with his college choices. His poems are getting better and more serious, and he still has the same boyfriend. I do not think that he will choose the U.S. if his boyfriend decides to stay in Beirut. As they say, insanity is hereditary; you get it from your children. This is his latest poem, which he shared with me with hopes that I would share with you:

> *"One thing I love*
> *More than life*
> *More than any lover*
> *More than my father*
> *More than my mother;*
>
> *The one thing I adore*
> *More and more and more*
> *Is what all good feelings are made of*
> *The one thing, the one thing I most love*
> *Is Love."*

I hate to admit it, but it would have been easier to live with the idea that Kamal is dead, or that he is a spy, than it is to live with the fact that he is married and has two children. Knowing that, I harbor no hope of recovery. I feel betrayed. I feel that my heart has been shot full of holes and will never be able to hold another man's love again. I feel like a sailing ship that has lost its anchor and its rudder, a ship wrecked by the rough winds of life, a ship that no longer has control of its destination.

I feel dizzy with the swirls of time. I feel lost, purposeless, and disillusioned. I feel intoxicated with anger. I feel choked as if my neck is in the fist of fate. I know that I must go to Um Al-Huda's shrine and pray with all my might that she grant me back my controls.

Faith is my only stabilizing force and Tariq, the only love that I am certain will never betray me. As you said, I should have been careful with the swords.

Love,

Fatima

Sixteen

(Simplicity)

(Boston - Thursday, 10 November, 1994)

My Dearest Fatima,

Your last letter set my thoughts aflame. Your love must have meteored when Kamal was taken away from you; it burned high and bright then hovered up in a cloud of hot ashes. With love we concur, but in love we surrender. At least your Kamal is alive. Oh, how I wish my butterfly had had the same fate. It is more difficult to write letters to the dead. Have you written Kamal yet? Surely, they will allow him open letters from an innocent lover.

As for your disillusionment about a wife and two children on the other side of the island, please reconsider your opinion. Again, I must ask you to think freely, think purely, and think only with your reason. Avoid thinking with your traditional biases, with your archaic beliefs, and with your handed-down dogmas. Do not forget that you loved him while you were married, and I loved my butterfly while she was married.

How can marriages overcome feelings? How can distance, deprivation, and loneliness control the passionate surges of necessity? Remember that, although we are the captains of our ships, feelings are our weather, the climate upon which we have no control. The winds and storms of emotions can wreck our best-built ships whereas sunshine and propitious winds can lead them to safe harbor across the most dangerous of seas. Remember naturalism: *"Everything that runs contrary to nature ultimately fails."*

Now, if you will try to think from Kamal's perspective, if you were Kamal himself, what would you have done? Would you have told the woman you are madly in love with that you are a spy and exposed her to the danger of becoming a tacit accomplice? Would you have told her that you are married and exposed her to inspector Kakos's intuitive suspicion regarding her involvement? Is it not more believable that a woman with a failed marriage is more apt to fall in love with a single man, keeping the relationship's future hopeful, rather than with a married man where the relationship's future is, at best, precarious?

Fatima, by not telling you anything, Kamal was protecting you. Indeed, your utter ignorance was your best alibi because it allowed you to behave normally and respond innocently and convincingly to inspector Kakos's interrogations.

Fatima, your intoxication with anger diminishes your soul. Anger, which arises from feelings of injustice, is nurtured by vilification and sustained by negative perception. To dissipate anger and rid yourself of its painful pangs, all you have to do is rediscover the positives in Kamal and the negatives in yourself. This balancing of positives and negatives, this vicarious transposition of viewpoints, opens wide your tunneled vision and defuses your charged emotions.

Fatima, like the sides of a coin, every truth has two faces, but we can only see one face at a time. With luck we might meet the same face a few times in a row, but with enough flips of the coin, the laws of chance will finally force us to see the other side with equal clarity. If we wait long enough, truth will change its face. Please, give the tumbling coin a chance and let me paraphrase for you what Robert Frost once said: *"Why abandon a belief because it ceases to be true? Cling to it and it might turn true again. Is it not true that most of the change we see in life is due to truths being in and out of favor?"*

Now, Fatima, I am going to suggest a tranquilizing antidote to your emotional storm. I am going to ask you to find and visit Kamal's wife on the Turkish side of the island. She could be grilling on the skewer of worry after her husband's disappearance and may be without income or support.

Go to her and help her find peace. Tell her as much as you think she wants to know. Get to know her children.

Befriend her if she is capable of friendship. Let inspector Kakos help you find her. Let him give you Kamal's true name and address. Bring back some news to Kamal, who must be mad with guilt.

You have a humanitarian mission which only you can accomplish. As a non-Greek Muslim, you will be welcomed on the Turkish side. Do not tell me that you have no time for this venture; passion makes time. Love does not have to be reasonable, but it has to be meaningful. Unanchored love leads to spiritual drift. Go to her before you visit Um Al-Huda's shrine and you will astonish the Gods.

Boston in November is cold, but Harvard is always in bloom. I am attending a one-week course on pain management that began on Monday. Ghassan, my oldest son who goes to college in Cambridge, brought his Carla to meet me. I had surmised that he had fallen in love because his grades had suffered a lamentable defeat on the battlefield of emotion.

We went to a local fish restaurant, and for the first time I was able to observe the subtleties of their interactions. Carla, being Bostonian, helped Ghassan with his food order and discoursed with ease on the merits of certain fish selections. When I asked her to help me with my order, the gleam in her eyes brought about a tender blush to Ghassan's cheeks.

During dinner, their hands spent more time under the table than at their plates. The rapid sputters of giggled phrases and speculative gazes allowed for little intrusion by their awaiting food. Their plates—in spite of the obvious consternation of our waiter who frequently asked us if the fish were cooked to our liking—remained unattended.

Everything I said sounded funny to them, and before long I added my frivolous laughter to theirs, all this without a drop of alcohol. We were inebriated with the newness of our love triangle—I, watching youth lay its claim to life, and they, watching age approve of their reckless folly.

I did not bring up the subject of grades to Ghassan, even when Carla went to the restroom. Rather than feeling dismayed, I was indeed happy that he is learning his love lessons first. School can wait but love never does. When Carla returned, I managed to capture their imagination by discoursing on the less appreciated attributes of love.

Indeed, I shocked them when I said that every love carries hate upon its back; that I love you also means that I hate losing you; that I love freedom also means that I hate captivity; and that there are times when hate even precedes love. Could you, Fatima, have loved or even appreciated peace as much as you do now and would you not have found it boring were it not for war, and the hate of war, which have created in you a love and a longing for peace?

I hope that Ghassan will learn all he can about women before choosing his life-mate because that will be the most important decision for his future. Without a good wife, life brings less joy and suffers more strife than necessary. I hope that, at the frail age of twenty-two, he will begin to realize that a woman's love is liberating when not infested with jealousy or, as Lawrence Durrell put it, *"It is not love that is blind, but jealousy."* As a good-bye gift, I gave Ghassan *The Alexandria Quartet* by Durrell and dedicated it to him by highlighting the following lines in the novel, *"There are only three things to be done with a woman; you can love her, suffer for her, or turn her into literature."*

In addition to love, I also hope that he will suffer and write, because by so doing he will complete his human experience.

Hand in hand, I watched them fade into the cold Bostonian night, unaware that I was following them with my blurring eyes.

> *"Let us wander to the tavern at the corner of*
> *the street*
> *Share a jug of frothy spirit, something warm*
> *to eat*
> *Watch the many faces of a lazy afternoon*

Exit together in the dimming light
And then pretending we shall be together
soon
Depart on separate ways into the night. "

Fatima, I love my children with all my life, and I love the fact that as long as I am useful, they will continue to use me. But, gratitude is short lived. They will migrate away to their own wives and lives and, in their turn, so will their own children. Such is nature's ruthless wisdom.

Unlike you, I am unwilling to dilute the tragedies of my life with faith; I want to feel them deep into my soul, all the way down to my marrow.

Fatima, sometimes humor is the only sane strategy against adversity. Please humor your plight and remember that in spite of life's injustices and inequalities, two things equalize us all—joy and death.

Unlike death, joy is not of the flesh but of the spirit—our simple, unadulterated, most primal spirit. Therefore, the more we simplify, the greater are our funds of joy.

As for death, the ultimate equalizer, it is not at our command, and therefore, it is needless to spend time worrying about it. Nevertheless, we may want to pray for a good death so that our good life would not end on a bad note.

Fatima, let us simplify all the complexities of our lives down to our personal levels of meaningfulness. Oftentimes, thinking is painful whereas simplicity is joyful. When you go to Um Al-Huda's shrine, please do pray for our simplicity.

Love,

John

Seventeen

(Triangulated)

(Kyrenia - Saturday, 31 December, 1994)

My Dear John,

On New Year's Eve last year, I wrote to you from the Cedars of Lebanon. We drank champagne under the 4500 year-old hoary cedar of the Lord. This year, I am alone in a seaside motel, apart from Tariq, who is celebrating the New Year in Beirut, with his father. John, get out the map of Cyprus and look up Kyrenia. Yes, I am on the Turkish side.

After I received your antinomian letter asking me to find and visit Kamal's wife and children, I wondered if you had lost your mind. Why should I put myself in this meddlesome jeopardy? I decided that it would be better to forget Kamal and return to Beirut, which I did without much regret. Soon after I removed to Beirut, I went to visit the shrine of Um Al-Huda.

The weather was angry, the skies tenebrous, the clouds wore frowning faces, and the rainstorms swept the land with fierce showers. Still, I couldn't help but yield to my urge to go. Like a mad woman, I drove through muddy roads and shoving winds, all the time asking myself why am I in such a hurry and why couldn't I wait for better weather? I was mad with emotional turmoil and needed to find peace. Like you suggested, I needed to simplify in order to find joy.

I arrived before dark and immediately began to pray. I asked her for peace, cried, and listened to my inner thoughts, but no revelation descended upon me. Disillusioned and exhausted, I found a nearby motel, checked in for the night, and instantly fell sleep.

At night, Um Al-Huda visited my dreams. She wore

a long black robe, a white shawl covered her head and shoulders, her eyes were pale blue, and her skin luxurious white. Smiling, she stroked my forehead, then held my hand and whispered, *"Follow your heart wherever it may lead you, otherwise you will be left heartless."* I awoke with a throbbing migraine behind my eyes, sat in bed, and listened to my galloping heart. It was early morning, and the storm had passed.

I tried to go back to sleep but couldn't because I was overcome by shaking chills and cold sweats. I could feel something happening inside of me—deep in my pelvis— a swelling, growing, causing pressure, and straining my breath like a sudden pregnancy. It was a frightening, suffocating feeling that was also wonderful because it announced Her presence inside my body.

Drenched and motionless, I waited until the painful fullness slowly delivered itself out of me, leaving a show of blood between my legs, leaving resounding cries of rebirth in my ears, leaving a calm sense of peace within my soul. I got up, washed, dressed, and returned to Beirut a changed woman, intent on finding Kamal's wife.

Inspector Kakos was kind and did give me Kamal's address in Kyrenia. I did not hesitate at all; I took a Greek taxi to the border, and then a Turkish taxi to his home in Kyrenia. I had no idea what I was going to say or how I was going to introduce myself. I felt driven by some implacable force and could not stop myself long enough to think.

When she opened the door, I said, *"Hello; I am a friend of Kamal,"* and asked her if she spoke English or French. She smiled and said in perfect English, *"I have been expecting you. Come in please. My name is Gulnar, and you must be Fatima."*

John, she wore a long black robe, a white shawl covered her head and shoulders, her eyes were pale blue, and her skin, luxurious white. Shaken and cold, I froze in my place and tried to look calm. My pelvis began to swell, just like it did when Um Al-Huda visited my dreams. I placed my purse over my abdomen, followed her into the living room, and collapsed into the nearest seat.

Her two kids watched me cautiously; the boy is

about eight, and the girl about six years old. After all this travel, I found that I had nothing to say to this kind, hospitable woman. I felt like a student in the principal's office, awaiting his verdict. Thank God, it was she who broke the silence by saying, *"The boy is Omar, and the girl is Amar, and they do not understand English."* She then prepared Turkish coffee, and we spent the entire afternoon talking.

She said that Kamal was her first cousin and that they had an arranged marriage in 1984. They were both born in Turkey and grew up next door to each other in Ankara. As an officer, Kamal took part in the Turkish invasion of Cyprus in 1974 and was thereafter stationed in Kyrenia with the military intelligence section. That was how, after their marriage, Kyrenia became their home and the birthplace of their two children. Four years ago, they sent him to the Greek side of the island and would not allow him home visits lest he be found out. His five-year-mission was to end next July after which he was to return home for good.

They could only communicate through letters, which they forwarded to a domestic address in London. They used no names; he addressed her as dear mother and she, as dear son. The letters were written in camouflaged English, and hers were screened before they were dispatched. Each was allowed six letters a year, and the intervals between letters were kept irregular by the military intelligence.

Then her tone became grave and the discussion switched from Kamal to me. She held my hand, looked me straight in the eyes, and said: *"Thank you for being Kamal's friend. Before you came into his life, he lived alone, isolated, and very depressed. But every good man needs a good woman by his side; Allah made it so, may he be praised. I would not have minded if he had married you because, as a Muslim woman, I was raised to accept the God-given rights of men, as taught by our Prophet Muhammad, God's prayers and peace upon him."*

At that point, she broke down and began crying, saying that she may never see him again, that the children could grow up without even remembering their father, and that she is planning to return to Ankara to live close to her parents where they would have more love and support. This time I was the one who held her hand and tried to reassure her by saying that, someday, he will be exchanged for a Greek-Cypriot prisoner and they will be reunited, God willing. I was also pleased to find out that she had been awarded Kamal's salary for the rest of her life.

At the door, our good-bye lasted almost an hour. She would make up conversation just to keep me tethered, as if she did not want me to leave her yet, as if she had one more thing to say, but could not formulate the words or bring herself to say it.

Then, all of a sudden, she turned pale as she stammered: *"There is one more thing you should know. During his early years in Kyrenia, Kamal had a relationship with a Turkish schoolteacher, the daughter of a very rich and powerful Istanbul merchant. She became pregnant with Kamal's child, but her father would not let them marry because he disapproved of Kamal's poor background and military career. Instead, he arranged for his daughter to have an abortion in Cairo and sent her away to Egypt accompanied by her mother, a faithful Muslimah who was against abortions.*

In spite of the father's irate insistence, she carried the baby to term and gave birth to a girl. Before long, it became apparent that the newborn was hopelessly blind because of underdeveloped eyes. This angered the father even more, and he vowed never to let his daughter or her newborn set foot in his Istanbul home. Moreover, fearing that his daughter might choose to return to Cyprus with her out-of-wedlock child, be reunited with Kamal, and, in the process, bring shame to the family name, he promised to support her and the baby as long as they remained in Egypt.

This broke Kamal's heart, especially since, because of military reasons, he was not allowed to travel to Egypt during that period. If you remember, 1979 was the year when Sadat signed a unilateral peace treaty with Israel, angering the rest of the Arab world.

They communicated by phone and letters until 1981

when Sadat was assassinated. During the ensuing chaos of that horrific day, the mother was hit and killed by a speeding car while crossing the street back to her home with a birthday cake in her arms. It was her daughter's third birthday.

Ever since that day, Kamal lost all contact with his daughter. He believes that she was raised by the grandmother, who took her back to Istanbul after her mother's death. He presumed that her angry grandfather must have mellowed down after his daughter's death and allowed his granddaughter back into his home on condition that she would have no contact with her father.

Kamal has never told me their names. I know that he must have his reasons, and because of that, I have refrained from asking him to tell me more. I was most relieved, though, when my children were born with normal eyes because Kamal's older brother was also born blind with underdeveloped eyes. You see, Kamal's mother and father were also first cousins."

When she finished her story, Gulnar wiped her tears and went back into the house without saying good-bye. I returned to my hotel just before dark with a storm in my heart. I regretted that I had promised Gulnar to drop by for morning coffee, before returning to Nicosia.

John, I need you next to me so you could tell me how I should feel. I cannot wait three months for your letter. I need some clarity now. I need a deep analytical mind like yours to translate my emotions into intelligible words. It is maddening for an emotional storm to sweep through my soul, swirl me into dizziness, fling me into the winds of confusion, strip me of my self-control, and suspend me in a dimension of unfamiliar sentiments.

Should I feel redeemed or angered? Should I feel delivered or defeated? Should I capitulate to my echoing emptiness, or should I fill up my soul with nebulous aspirations? Should I choose hope, or should I adopt resignation as my keynote? And if I should choose hope, what then should I hope for? Should I hope that Kamal return to his family or to me? Oh, why do I choke? Why do I feel confined? Why did I allow love to triangulate me within its sharp confining angles?

Confusion is far worse than grief. I know how to grieve, but I do not know how to be confused. Confusion is even worse than hate because there are times when hate is emancipating. Confusion is much worse than anger because anger slowly dissipates while confusion continues to grow the more one tries to unravel it. Confusion is madness, but with the awareness that one is mad. How did that Tennyson poem go? You used to quote it to me when I would become frustrated. Oh, yes, I remember it now; I remember it in spite of my confusion:

"So runs my dream: but what am I?
An infant crying in the night:
An infant crying for the light:
And with no language but a cry."

I have ordered room service because the hotel dining room is noisy with New-Year's-Eve, and I am not in a festive mood. I am going to eat, have a glass of wine, take a sleeping pill, and with it try to silence the noise within and without. When I awaken, the storm will have passed, I hope, and I will return to Nicosia.

I do not wish to see Gulnar again, nor do I wish to be re-enthralled by her pale blue eyes and luxurious, white skin. But, I have to live up to my promise. Perhaps I could buy toys for Omar and Amar and concentrate on them instead of Gulnar's eyes and skin.

Oh, John, why on earth did you ask me to do this, and why did I obey? I am going back to Beirut, to my friends, to my son, and to my charming Lebanese lover who will be delighted to take me back. I am leaving this suffocating island. I need a new faith. I need a new self. I need a new distance. I need to forget Kamal and Kamal's blind daughter and Gulnar and her two noisy children.

I need to wash Um Al-Huda out of my soul. I need to cleanse my heart of love and all its intimate feelings. I need to do my laundry by hand and dry out my memories on a long clothesline under the burning sun.

I need to sever my spiritual bonds so that I will become love free and free to never love again.

John, please write soon.

Love,

Fatima

Eighteen

(Renaissance)

(Oklahoma City - Saturday, 28 January, 1995)

My Dearest Fatima,

I am answering your crying letter with anguished haste because I know how reckless you become when disillusioned, and I fear that in your recklessness you might resort to your irrevocable guillotine. Indeed, I worry that in your thrashing despair you might, unwittingly, sever your own bonds of hope and drown your soul in a pit of emptiness *"from whose bourn no traveler returns."* Forbear, my dearest, and wait for this gloomy cloud to pass. Tomorrow, your thoughts will awaken to a different tune and your heart to a different beat. Do not burn your ships on foreign shores lest you lose the freedom to sail back home. From here, from my transatlantic pulpit, I have much to say. Pray, do not disdain my preaching, not until you have heard the last word.

Fatima, I feel your pain in spite of my distance and sense your confusion with vicarious clarity. I do not need to think for you, my dearest, for you have already done your own thinking and seem resolved to disassociate yourself from your deity. I fear, however, that in so doing, you will deny your soul its habitual refuge. Do not get angry with the gods, Fatima, and do not get angry with me because neither of us is blameworthy. Let fate dictate, and like good stoics, let us obey for there is more dignity in humility than in hubris and more wisdom in acceptance than in rejection.

Forget the villanelle we much loved in youth; we were sanguine then, and romantically rebellious. Instead, accept your realities, *go gentle into that good night,* and *do not rage against the dying of the light.*

Youth, Fatima, is the fuel of revolutions and age, the cradle of wisdom. It is a most lamentable reality that, while wisdom always recognizes folly, folly seldom recognizes wisdom. Do I need to remind you that you are forty-five and I am forty-nine, and that we no longer can pretend that we can escape our lives?

For believers like you, the supernatural is more important than the natural, because faith dilutes the burdens of reality. In *Justine*, Lawrence Durrell says that *"We are all looking for reasons to believe in the absurd."* Pray, do not lose your faith for Kamal's sake or for mine. Apostasy is a much worse punishment than any tangible loss. Remember Antoine De Saint – Exupéry and what the Fox said to the *Little Prince*? *"Only with the heart, can we clearly see; the essentials are invisible to the eyes."*

Fatima, love is the suckling of faith and faith, its mother. Without faith, love cannot feed, and without love, the nipple of faith goes dry. Indeed, when starved for faith, love dies and faith dries. Fatima, listen to this quote from *The Brothers Karamazov,* by Fyodor Dostoevsky and try to recall the day I first read it to you. *"Life is paradise... and hell... the suffering of being no longer able to love."*

Remember the date in 1968 when we first made love? It was on the same date, January 28, but it was a Sunday. You were an eighteen year-old freshman and I, a twenty-two year-old second-year medical student, and we were both virgins. We went up to Brummana, where now Tariq goes to school, and spent the night alone at the mountain home of my father's friends, the Habibs.

They were so kind to me after my father was executed, and offered me their mountain home so that I could study on weekends. Remember how afraid we were, and how we could not sleep after we consummated our love? To help dry your tears, I read to you certain passages from the Brothers Karamazov, passages that I had underlined. When I read to you this part from the talks and homilies of the Elder Zosima, you gleamed and with smiling words said, *"So, now that we are in heaven, let us stay in it; let us never leave it like Adam and Eve did. What fools they were."* I laughed and never told you that you had committed antinomy and that you had secularized the teachings of the church with your reverse creationism.

Now, twenty-seven years later, you dare complain that love triangulated you; you dare say that you wish to cleanse your soul of love; and you dare proclaim that you will not allow yourself to ever love again. Are you eager to shroud your soul in a loveless void?

Love is never lost, Fatima. We are the ones who feel lost when we can love no more. If you cannot love Kamal, love your memories instead, love your pain, love your life, love your body, love your future, love your fate, love your faith, and never run away into emptiness because nothing returns from its bourns except despair.

Fatima, you do give up too easily. Do not forget Winston Churchill's famous one-line speech delivered to the 1964 graduating class of Harrow School, his alma mater. It was his last public speech, and he died a year after. Be a Churchill, dearest, and *"Never give up, never, never, never."*

On a more euphoric note, Ghassan called today. He talked and talked about nothing at all for a quite a long while, which is not his nature. I gave him all the time he needed, but he wouldn't say it. Unfinished and frustrated, he said good-bye and I waited. Minutes later, he called again, but this time I helped him out. I asked him if Carla was well. He paused awhile then stuttered almost unintelligibly, *"Well Dad...Carla is...she just found out she's...she's just found out that she's...that she's..."* To ease his awkward embarrassment I screamed at the top of my voice, *"Well done, well done, CONGRATUALTIONS son, CONGRATULATIONS. Thanks to Carla and you, I will soon become a grandfather."*

He was quite relieved when he received my enthusiasm. You should have seen his mother's speechless eyes when she heard my screams. Her face danced, her eyebrows jumped up and down, and she swirled round and round like a whirling dervish. Then the four of us got on the phone and talked all afternoon. They want to get married during spring break. They have already rented a little old house in Cambridge and have begun decorating it. I cannot wait to visit their first nest.

When the quadralogue ended, I had a Jack Daniels and Norma had a glass of wine, which was absolutely verboten by her physicians because it speeds up her dementia. Then we celebrated by taking the family out to dinner. Norma, who is starting to have problems with speech, smiled continuously but said little. She kept arranging and rearranging her hair and, throughout dinner, maintained an elevated aspect most becoming of the mother of the groom.

In contrast, Nadir and Frida chattered, giggled, and gleamed shamelessly. I heard Frida (twelve) whisper to Nadir (sixteen), *"They did it before getting married— OOOPS—can you believe that?"* Nadir whispered back through a paper napkin behind which he concealed a wry smile, *"Too bad. It looks like I'm gonna become an uncle before I get a chance to have sex."* Throughout dinner, they fidgeted like a pair of mating squirrels, poked at each other underneath the table, and their eyes twinkled with adolescent mischief.

Driving back home, we all fell silent as if overcome by the significance of this annunciation. What joy lurks in the cries of birth, I thought. One more child to love, one more torch to light hope into the future, one more family to homestead on the un-trodden meadows of tomorrow, meadows green with expectation, meadows which—as Gibran says—I cannot visit, not even in my dreams.

Don't fall out of love, Fatima. Hold on to your dreams, especially the ones that are impossible. *"For with God nothing shall be impossible,"* says the Gospel according to Saint Luke. The impossible is our best defense against reality. Remember how Napoleon answered general Lemarois: *"You write to me that it's impossible; the word is not French."*

Please give my love to Tariq, and ask him for me: *"What would you like for a graduation gift?"* If my memory still serves me correctly, I believe that in Brummana High School the valedictorian is chosen by his classmates and not by the administration. Being such a free spirit, I wonder if Tariq might be chosen to be this year's valedictorian? Unless there are other free-spirit contenders among his classmates, he might be the only one who is actually capable of saying what everyone else is afraid to say.

It would be most revealing to witness a freethinking adolescent undress his soul in front of an eclectic audience made up of multiple religious cultures. May God have mercy upon those who are not ready to hear other truths except the ones they grew up believing in. For as my philosopher friend, Dr. T. S. taught me—to live without questioning is to live without thinking; to live without thinking is to live without consciousness; and to live without consciousness is not to live at all.

All my love,

John

Nineteen

(Parallels)

(Beirut - Saturday, 4 March, 1995)

My Dear John,

Your letter from the pulpit took away my breath. I understood all you said and agreed with your thoughts, but I could not force my feelings to obey my mind. Feelings are unschooled, illiterate sentiments; they speak no foreign tongue, and trying to sway them with reason is a wasteful endeavor. I spent days contemplating what you had written, but I could not make myself feel any better. I am still unable to accept the dictates of my fate and the confines of my life. The truth is that I do miss Kamal; I miss his kindness and his unfaltering dedication to me, but at the same time, I feel angered and betrayed. I also feel empathy for his wife and children, but I am glad to have distanced myself from their inner lives. Before I left Kyrenia, I did not buy his children toys, as I had intended to, nor did I stop to bid Gulnar good-bye. I simply left for Nicosia without looking back. Within one week, I had relocated to Beirut and said adieu to my Cyprus saga. Was I a bad girl to have run away from pain? Do you still respect me or have you changed your mind about your first sweetheart?

I am still not on speaking terms with Um Al-Huda. At night, I sleep with the Koran underneath my pillow, hoping to prevent her from visiting my dreams. One night, I fell asleep on the couch watching television, and as I slept, she reappeared in her black robe, white shawl, and pale blue eyes. She said nothing at all and did not even try to touch me. She simply gazed at my chest, causing it to rise and fall with long laboring sighs.

I awoke startled, air hungry with sore breasts and

a bad headache. Immediately, I ran to my bed, held the Koran to my chest, closed my eyes, and this time, I kept the lights on. I am afraid that she no longer likes me and that she might even try to hurt me, but I felt less afraid when I went to bed with the lights on and Koran underneath my pillow. John, I am now afraid of the invisibles and can no longer trust my dreams. Something dark and dangerous shrouds me; I can feel it in the air I breathe, especially at night. I pray and pray but it will not dissipate. Something is going to happen, something bad, very bad, very soon, I know it.

Tomorrow, I am going to visit Tabrize, my old psychic. She is the one who, fifteen years ago, told me that you were going to leave me, immigrate to America, marry an American woman, and live an unhappy marriage. If anyone could save me, she would have to be the one. I have no one else to whom I can turn.

Goodnight my idealist prince, my refined intellectual, my lover in absentia. The Koran is underneath my pillow. I need to sleep now. I am having a chill. I will have to finish your letter tomorrow. I always wake up with a clear head after a good night's sleep.

Love,

Fatima

John, a whole week has passed, a most eventful week. I went to Tabrize, my psychic, and she recognized me before I said a word. She motioned to me to sit next to her on the carpet, gazed into my eyes, smiled, and inquired, *"He did not marry you, did he?"*

She then asked about your American wife, *"What happened to her after the she came out of the coma?"* She then said that lovers never lose each other; they are merely flung apart by angered love, flung into separate orbits that intercept each other repeatedly throughout life.

When I told her about Kamal, she looked at me with worried eyes and said, *"Poor girl, poor girl..."* and would say no more. *Then when I asked her what am I to do, she held my hand and whispered in my ear, "Go back to Um Al-Huda..."*

I left her apartment more disturbed than reassured. I came to her hoping she would give me peace, and instead she gave me back to Um Al-Huda. I felt that I had to obey her wishes because if I did not, I knew that something bad would happen. I did not sleep that night; I drove straight to the shrine of Um Al-Huda amidst another vile storm. I prayed, cried, apologized, asked her forgiveness, and asked her for help. She did not respond, but I knew that she was appeased because my belly remained flat and I suddenly felt hungry.

I went to a nearby restaurant and ate a hearty fava-bean breakfast with bread, green onions, and olives. Then, I turned back and drove home feeling no fatigue from the trip and the sleepless night.

I had hardly gotten into my house when the phone rang; it was my brother, Jamal, from Kuwait. He told me in interrupted phrases that Laila had gone into labor and delivered a baby girl. He then paused a long while, panted audibly, then repeated, *"A baby girl...yes...a baby girl... Laila is fine...very fine...she does not know...they have not told her...they only told me...not even our friends know... nobody knows...nobody."* I was afraid to ask him, but he finally told me that the baby was so deformed that they did not expect it to live. The doctors said that they had seen several similar cases, all born to mothers who had been exposed to the gases and radiation during the Gulf War.

The baby died the next day, and they buried her in Kuwait. Laila plans to leave Jamal and return to her parent's home as soon as she is able to travel. Now she is blaming Jamal not only for her rape but also for her deformed baby, and she is refusing to speak to him, just as she did when they first ran away from Kuwait. I am afraid that their brief honeymoon has already turned to vinegar.

And now, the *pièce de résistance* is that the baby's death begot a cruel renaissance. Jamal, on his own, called Australia, cried like a child, told Mary that he loved her, and that he wanted to be a good father to Jamie. He then asked her to join him in Kuwait, marry him, and make Kuwait their home.

Mary called me, frantic with joy, laughing bitter tears, confused like a bee trying to fly through glass. She said that Jamal asked her to be his second wife. She also said that he was not planning to divorce Laila because she is the mother of his two boys; however, he wanted to stay away from her for the rest of his life. He planned to tell Laila about Mary and Jamie but only after he and Mary were married. By then, she would be at her parent's mountain home in Brummana, too far away to do harm.

The way he plans to tell Laila is typical of Jamal's evasive nature. He wants his boys (Imad 13, and Ramzi 10) to visit him in Kuwait as soon as school is over at the end of May. He will surprise them with his new wife and their new half-sister, and they will all live together throughout the month of June. When they return to their mother, they will carry a letter telling the whole story.

All this planning was done tacitly, behind my back, and Jamal still thinks that I do not know. He has no idea that Mary and I have become good long-distance friends and that we communicate regularly. I cannot wait to meet her and Jamie; can you believe that Jamie will be two years old in May? I think that I will startle Jamal with a surprise visit to Kuwait in June. He will need me to prevent his chaotic family mélange from boiling over.

Now I know what my psychic meant when she said, *"Go back to Um Al-Huda."* Um Al-Huda remains the guardian of our parallel lives and insurer of our fates. I see it now; I see it well and I understand its full meaning. Can you see it, John? Can you? Just think along with me. Jamal has two kids and a wife; he wants to marry Mary as his second wife. An adversity has occurred, the death of a deformed child. Mary is away in Australia, but soon she will be joining Jamal.

Kamal has two kids and a wife; he wants to marry me as his second wife. An adversity has occurred; Kamal was incarcerated for spying. Kamal is away in Cyprus just like Mary is away in Australia. This can only mean that Kamal will soon be joining me, and asking me to become his second wife. Gulnar did tell me, when I visited her, that she would not mind if we were to get married.

John, all of a sudden, I have lost all my anger and have hope instead. I shall stay in Beirut and work patiently until Kamal returns to me. Tomorrow, I am going to lay pink roses on the shrine of Um Al-Huda and thank her for not forsaking me. I can see clearly now; the future is no longer a blur. And now that Jamal and I are to be married for the second time, it is your turn to find a wife, and soon you might, but not before an adversity occurs. Oh, John, please be careful.

Tariq graduates this June and wants a laptop computer for his graduation gift. He has heeded your advice and wants to take a computer course during the summer, which may help him get accepted at the AUB where his boyfriend is planning to go. I doubt, however, that his classmates will choose him to be the valedictorian, but one never knows? As you always say, *"it all depends,"* doesn't it?

Love,

Fatima

Twenty

(Adversity)

(Oklahoma City – Saturday, 29 April, 1995)

Oh, My Sweet Fatima,

I am now convinced that peace will not come to earth until humanity expires. To believe in an ideology is to close one's mind to all other competing ideas, to spurn all debate, and to forge a group identity that separates one herd from the rest of humanity. Our human orchestra, even under the baton of the most philharmonic conductor, is destined to produce nothing but dissonance. Oh, I feel so alone in my quest for world harmony.

> *"Humanity's delusional*
> *The rational, unusual*
> *They roam and roam*
> *But find no home."*

On April 20, I awoke a disillusioned man with three new realizations. First, the rational are few. Second, passions supplant reason. Third, the passionate have closed minds; they believe that they are always right, and their convictions swell in direct proportion to their passions. Fatima, I have become a lonely, homeless orphan because I refuse to belong to any particular human club—I only belong to humanity. I refuse to Faust my soul to Mephistophelian bribes that apartheid humanity. I will remain an outsider, an open-minded fugitive, a rational pacifist, and a passionate lover of peace.

Fatima, by now you will have heard of our tragedy. You predicted, since we do live our lives in parallel, that I was about to have my own adversity and indeed I did. A fertilizer bomb shattered our sun-washed, wind-swept city, bringing down the Federal Building, killing 168 innocent adults and children, shattering our tranquil quietude, and violating a brooding peace under whose white wings we had hatched and prospered. The shocked expressions have made indelible furrows in the faces of those whose loved ones went to work and never returned. Fragments of bodies, still looking for their names, continue to bleed out of the wounded dust. In the rubble lies the shattered soul of Oklahoma.

> *"It was an act of love*
> *The way we raised our wounds*
> *Up, up to the sky*
> *And licked them high*
> *Nor bowed our brows;*
> *This pride, our cross*
> *Borne with giant hearts*
> *So Oklahoma*
> *Would never heed*
> *The mighty weight of love."*

Nadir and some of his classmates are still involved in the rescue efforts. Each day after school, they go to the bombing site to join the volunteer clean-up crew. At seventeen, Nadir is consumed by trying to understand why a few angry men could justify inflicting so much suffering on so many innocent members of their own society. After many a late-night discussion, I believe that I have inseminated his eager, impressionable mind with my own ideology.

The other day, I heard him explaining to his mother that a logical mind cannot understand a sick mind's logic, that sick minds reason correctly but from the wrong precepts, that terrorists strongly believe in what they do, and that all violence is a form of terrorism. It pleased me to hear Norma's response, *"You think just like your dad."*

Her mind, at times, clears enough to comprehend simple, abstract thinking, but her balance is becoming more and more precarious, which is causing her to fall frequently, especially while cleaning house. Our cleaning lady comes twice a week and is most willing to come more often, but Norma will not let her and insists on taking care of the house the rest of the days. To remain functional is her primary struggle, and she asserts her functionality by doing her housework, unaided. Alas, her dementia is progressing in spite of our dedicated support. She laughed when she first heard about the bombing, which made the rest of us cry.

Yesterday, Nadir came home with a big block of granite, a souvenir from the rubble of the Federal Building. He knew that it was illegal to carry off anything from the bombing site, but he did it anyway. I did not ask him to return it because I felt that he needed something tangible to cling to, something to commemorate his civic efforts and emotional bloodletting. He put it atop his bookshelves, opposite a picture of his class rescue team, and keeps a burning candle in between the two. My son, my sensitive Nadir, has been baptized in the bloodbath of futile suffering and has erected a shrine in his room to preserve the memory. He is far too young to realize that he will be spending the rest of his life washing his soul from the clots of this bloody crime against humanity.

The casualties that reached my hospital had minor injuries and were all released the same day. There are other casualties, however, casualties that I am beginning to see at my office, casualties who were not at the bombing site. They are the loving extensions of the dead, friends and relatives of those who were trapped in layers of suddenness. I am now seeing the victims of incomprehensible loss, those who are suffering from anxiety, panic, depression, insomnia, somnambulism, nightmares, night terrors, inconsolable grief, and implacable shock.

> *"Quiet pain is harsh*
> *I heard the dusty dead whisper*
> *Trapped in layers of suddenness*
> *Not a child could scream."*

Fatima, even though you predicted my adversity, you forgot that I am a Christian living in America, where polygamy is against my creed and against the law of the land. Islamic law, which allows Jamal and Kamal to marry more than one woman, is not recognized here. Please, take me out of your parallelogram; your theory of parallel lives frightens me. Moreover, please make no further predictions about my life, and no more visits to your morbid psychic; I do not want nefarious thoughts broadcasted into my already troubled mind.

I need peace to replace fear, restful sleep to replace insomnia, and a miraculous resurrection of my cheerfulness to replace depression. I miss flowers, blushing sunsets, and smiling eyes. This year, April did not color Oklahoma with its impressionist brushstrokes. Instead, it transformed the Federal Building site into a wasteland. It was, indeed, the cruelest month, the month of 168 innocent deaths by a bombing squad of sick minds intoxicated with lethal ideas.

No society in history has ever developed a successful solution for mentally deranged individuals, or groups of individuals, who inflict harm through acts of violence. Instead of preventive strategies, we use punishment as our main antidote, as if punishment has ever reduced the incidence of violence in the world.

> *"Unite or die, no other humankind*
> *Will have another chance to realize*
> *The greatest distances are in the mind*
> *How far apart we are when we are blind."*

On a more pleasant note, a friend of mine, Farouk Saba, is traveling to Beirut this coming June. He will be carrying with him a graduation present for Tariq, an Apple laptop computer, which Tariq will put to good use throughout his college years. It also has an internal modem, which will allow him Internet access whenever that becomes available to him. I am still hopeful that he might be chosen as the class valedictorian and that I will receive a copy of his valediction.

You still have not sent me pictures of Mary and Jamie. Perhaps, when you surprise "Kuwait" with your well-meaning visit, you would remember to capture some shots of Jamal's bi-continental family and forward them to me. I wonder how Jamal's boys will feel about an Australian second wife and a Christian half-sister, all simmering in the same family pot?

Oh, Fatima, my mind is so real and yours, so surreal. How could we possibly live parallel lives? Please offer my respects to Um Al-Huda the next time you visit her shrine and promise her that you will not visit Tabrize, your morbid psychic, ever again.   Um   Al-Huda holds your peace and freedom in her heart while Tabrize holds you captive to her portentous madness. Reason is the only antidote to the absurd. Hold on to your mind, Fatima; hold on and never let go of your thinking soul. Let me reiterate to you what William James once said:

"Belief is desecrated when given to unproved and unquestioned statements for the solace and private pleasure of the believer..."

Outside rationality superstitions lurk, and around the gravity of reality delusions orbit. Do not suffocate your precious intellectual breaths with unexamined thoughts, nor flood your heart with untenable beliefs.

Please, Fatima, stay with me; stay on *Terra Firma.*

Love,

John

Twenty-One

(Graduation)

(Brummana – Saturday, 17 June, 1995)

My Dear John,

I have so much to tell you, and it is close to midnight. The party is over, and everyone went home. Tariq and I are staying the night with Laila's parents, the Malouf's. They have been most hospitable to us, and as generous as Hatim Tai.

John, something wonderful has happened to us all. The Malouf's heard from Laila that I was going to hold Tariq's graduation party in our small Beirut apartment. Her mother called and offered to hold it at their large Brummana home. She argued that it made more sense to have the party close to Tariq's high school, where most of his friends are, and where the air is dry and cool unlike June-humid Beirut. This would also spare many guests the drive to Beirut and back. She was absolutely right. We had the party on their large veranda overlooking Beirut, which shimmered like the Milky Way with its bay full of bright-eyed yachts and massive ships burning with neon.

Tariq beamed with the glory of achievement but was most kind and attentive to his guests, his father, and his nephews—Laila's and Jamal's boys who go to the same school. He made me feel so proud not only because he was chosen as the class valedictorian but also because he never lost the *"human touch."* That was from Kipling's *IF*, which I still remember because you made me recite it over and over until I memorized it?

Even Laila was gracious and kind. She and I had a polite conversation about the weather, our children, and life in Lebanon. We were both cautious, avoiding unpleasant topics such as Kuwait, her dead baby, and her resolve to blame Jamal for it all. She seemed sad, as if in grief, and had no clue that Mary and Jamie existed, let alone that they will be joining her husband in Kuwait next week.

I felt like a spy who knew too much but pretended not to know anything at all. I was tempted, however, to break the news to her because I did not agree with Jamal's plan of telling her by letter, after the fact. I did not, of course; I kept all these secrets shackled behind my pursed lips. You should be proud of me because I acted contrary to my native nature; I acted with reason and stood my *Terra Firma.*

Ahmad came alone, thank God; it would have been an affront to all had he brought his cute hairdresser with him. He and I interacted normally, and Tariq pretended that everything was fine between us. Ahmad still thinks that Tariq does not know. I thought of telling him, but it would have spoiled his evening. Instead, I inquired about the health of his concubine and wished them well.
He was most touched by my spiritual generosity, and his eyes brimmed with withheld tears during our long, tedious conversation. I felt compelled to tell him about Kamal. He was not surprised and seemed concerned and supportive. When I mentioned that Kamal wanted to marry me, he promised to give me a divorce should Kamal get out of jail and propose. He said that things should become easier after Tariq goes to college. He even asked about you and wondered if we were still writing. Then he said something painfully odd; he said that when Tariq delivered his valediction, he reminded him of you when, many years ago, he heard you read your poetry to a group of students at the AUB.

You know that he has never forgiven you for having deflowered me, and he often behaved, during our lives together, as though he were in competition with you. Even now, it would destroy him if he should find out that you and I had a clandestine reunion in Paris two years after he and I were married. Oh John, how mad and foolish we were, how intoxicated with passion for each other, how well we loved, and how impossible it is to rewind life for a second look.

Now, I have to tell you about Tariq's speech. You were right, my dear psychic; he won his classmate's majority vote, and when he showed his speech to the graduation committee, they hardly changed a word. He stood like a precocious sage and delivered it with masterful ease as if he were a professional orator. He made us all so proud, and many of his classmates and their parents congratulated us (I and Ahmad sat together during the ceremony) and expressed amazement at his perceptive depth and wisdom.

I overheard several people say that he could not have written such a profound work unaided, or that some adult must have written it for him. To put it humbly, the kid was a sensation, and a lot of parents asked for copies of his speech. Some, however, were a bit miffed because not once did he mention Allah or quote from the wisdom of the Holy Books.

Other remarks that I overheard disturbed me greatly because they seemed to imply that he was a nonbeliever. There was one mother who walked up to me and, without shaking my hand, firmly said: *"I hope your son is not an atheist."* Then, before I had a chance to respond to her aspersion, she turned her back to me and walked away.

When the party was over, Tariq surprised me with a sealed envelope that contained a copy of the speech and a personal letter, which he asked me to mail to you. Then, as though he could read my thoughts, he smiled and embraced me as if to reassure me that sealing the envelope did not imply that he no longer trusted me.

Oh John, I am suffocating with curiosity. Please share with me what he wrote. After all, I am his only mother.

Love,

Fatima

Twenty-Two

(Valediction)

(Brummana – Saturday, 17 June, 1995)

Dear Dr. John,

I rose at 6:00 a.m. to write this letter. Thank you so much, I love my laptop. I love how you and mother love each other. She has your picture in her wallet. I am not supposed to know that, but I do. I found it one day when she asked me to fetch her purse. It fell out of my hand, and the wallet opened to your picture. You were together, holding hands, standing under the big cedar tree, where she and I had champagne two Christmases ago.

I know a lot more about you than you think because I have read all your poetry books. My mother keeps them next to her bed and reads a poem a day. She may not remember this, but when I was a child, she would occasionally read to me one of your poems instead of a bedtime story. That was how I became enthralled with poetry. I want to become a poet like you. I only know you from your picture because we have never met. But, my mother talks about you a lot, and this makes me think that I already know you.

To write my graduation speech, I used your books and paraphrased some of your verses. I also used your letters, which mother locks in a cabinet drawer and hides the key in the empty vase that sits on top of the cabinet. Between the end of school and graduation, I spent a lot of time alone at home while mother was at work. My mother does not know this but I have read all your letters and used the ideas that I liked to compose my speech.

By the time I finished writing the valediction, it sounded like one of your letters, which pleased me. You will see what I mean when you read it. I have not told a soul about my references and hope that you will not tell my mother. She would kill me if she were to find out that I know all about you and her, Kamal and her, you and your butterfly, my uncle and his Australian baby, my father and his cute hairdresser, and all the other secret discussions about my homosexuality.

Anyway, everyone liked what I said, and they clapped so hard it embarrassed me. I cannot wait to meet you. Mother says that you refuse to come to Lebanon. Why? Perhaps, one day, I will come to America to meet you. Anyway, here is my speech, which I wrote on the laptop you sent me. Thank you for being our friend.

With love,

Tariq

Ladies and Gentlemen:

I am not going to pretend to address everyone else gathered here. I can only address my classmates because they speak my language and understand my feelings. If I were to address the rest of you grownups, I would have to pretend and that would bother my conscience. Please accept my apology beforehand, and think of yourselves as my classmates when you listen to what I am about to say.

My Dear Classmates:

I promised myself when I was writing this speech that I would say nothing from this podium except what I believe to be the truth. That made writing a lot easier because it allowed me to avoid emotional language and all the topics that I do not know enough about. Well, if one leaves emotions out, that cuts the speech in half. Then, if one only talks about what one knows to be true, that cuts the other half of the speech out. Therefore, my speech should be a very brief one indeed. I should say to you, *"Thank you for choosing me to speak. What do I know? I have nothing to say. Good luck, good-bye, and farewell."*

But then, I had another idea. What if I limited my speech to words of wisdom? We all like to listen to wise sayings because we believe that they can teach us to live better lives. But since I am too young to be wise, I had to go to other sources in order to find adages that I considered useful for us at this time in our lives.

As far as my own thoughts are concerned, all I know is that I love life, I love all of you, and I will miss you terribly when we separate. I also know that we cannot grow and prosper unless we leave this nest. This means that the pain of separation is necessary for our maturity. I would like to think, therefore, that as we grow apart, we would also grow stronger and more independent. That as we separate, we will become better citizens, citizens who have set high standards for themselves, citizens who do their best to improve their own lives and the lives of all those who depend upon them.

I hereby promise you that I will live the best possible life I am capable of living, that I will bring as much joy into the world as I possibly can, and that I will reduce suffering whenever I have the ability to do so.

As far as my choices of wise adages are concerned, a friend of mine whom I have never met but who is always with me, has inspired me to put together this credo of collected wisdom as my good-bye song to all of you:

Insist on love but love all of humanity. Do not allow your love to become selective because that would diminish its holiness.

Insist on joy but not at the expense of other peoples' suffering for that would transform joy into a cruel thrill.

Insist on life but not at the expense of dignity for without dignity, we become exploiters and usurpers.

Insist on play but not at the expense of harm to your health because without health, we burden our souls and tax those who love us.

Insist on rest but not at the expense of duty lest we become parasites to our families and societies.

Insist on doing your best and on using your time efficiently but not at the expense of rest, play, and kind attention to others.

Insist on thinking for yourselves, especially when it comes to private matters and personal beliefs.

Insist on peace but not at the expense of defending human rights.

Insist on kindness but only when it leads to the betterment of others and do not bestow it on those who abuse it.

Insist on power when it leads to freedom and do not relinquish it to those who favor slavery.

Do not spend your valuable time trying to be what you are not. Insist on being what you are, liking what you are, and do that regardless of the vernacular opinions of your times and places.

Insist on passion because it is our prime mover, but harness it with reason lest it lead you astray.

Insist on fighting fear with faith, for without faith life becomes hopeless and desperate.

Honor life by living it well and remember that everything is on loan and nothing lasts.

Be generous; for unlike your outer wealth, your inner wealth grows in proportion to how much you give.

Always set your standards higher than others set them for you. Compete with yourselves instead of competing with others and be the best you can be instead of trying to be the best among others.

There is no shame in nature or in you if you live according to your own conscience instead of the collective conscience of others.

Let us go to work and take our chances.

Let us not complain or run away for these are signs of weakness. Instead, let us confront life with our will to prevail.

Let us not postpone living but, rather, let us live the present and insist on joy for that is the only way to honor life and express our gratitude to it.

Let us tickle the world into a smile because we are only here a while.

I love you all,

Tariq

Twenty-Three

(Tamara)

(Boston – Tuesday, 11 August, 1995)

Dear Fatima,

Tamara is beautiful. She has big, black, intelligent eyes, auburn hair, and spends most of her time sleeping, feeding, and groping her brave new world. Carla is a natural mother and wants to breast-feed my granddaughter for at least a year. Ghassan is transmuted to a new reality, seeing life anew with enthralled paternal eyes, and harvesting feelings nature had sown for him millions of years ago. They have a small cottage in old Cambridge, charmingly arrayed with youthful colors, and furnished with well-saved, garage-sale items. Norma smiles and scatters tears like a summer shower, nodding her head with speechless amazement. We let her hold Tamara only when she is sitting. Her balance has become so ataxic that it is no longer safe for her to walk while carrying a child.

What a day, what a month, what a year. Today, fifty years ago, on August 11 of 1945, we dropped the atomic bomb on Nagasaki. Today, President Clinton announced that the United States would no longer carry out nuclear tests—a decision that should pull the world back from the nuclear precipice. Today, for the first time in the history of humanity and the history of the entire universe, I carried my first grandchild in my arms. We have traveled, over fifty years, from devastation to peace and from death to rebirth.

What a historical cyclone of events epicenters around August 11. August, which derives its name for Augustus (Latin for venerable), was the title given in 27 BC to the first Roman emperor, Octavian, adopted son of the great Julius Caesar. With the Oklahoma City bombing, April became the cruelest month and the Federal Building site, our wasteland. Now, with the birth of Tamara, August, the hot month of atomic bombs and Roman dictators, has mellowed into the kindest month, the venerable month, the month of renaissance.

Fatima, forgive my digression; I had to yield to irresistible grandfatherly whims. I did not even tell you about their April wedding, which was overshadowed by the Oklahoma City bombing. They had a subdued ceremony, elegant in its simplicity, profound in its sincerity, spring-like in its emotional colors, bright with the primal smiles of youthful love. We met Carla's parents for the first time—traditional, stoic, and honorable, but disinclined to dance, drink, or play. I do not know whence Carla's playfulness came, but I am glad of it. Reared by Carla and Ghassan, Tamara should grow up to be a cheerful, confident princess.

I loved Tariq's valediction and was astonished by its poignant profundity. I wish you and I were as mature when we were his age. I am most eager to meet your fine stripling, and I might do so sooner than you think. His letter to me was a most honest exposé, a translucent self-portrait, and he asked me not to reveal any of its details to you. I can say, however, that if you were to read his letter, you would begin by feeling surprised, exasperated, and perhaps a bit embarrassed, but you would end feeling ennobled by your rearing achievements.

Fatima, your son is a free thinker who will grow up to be a happy man. Thanks to his upbringing, he will not have to spend his adulthood jettisoning from his brain stifling bits of dogma with which he was inculcated during his childhood. He will become a man of letters, a spot of joy upon the frowning face of earth, and a blithe spirit who will perfect the noble art of living and loving to the betterment of all those who chance to know him.

Your story of Laila is most proverbial. On the surface, she blames her husband for all mishaps and punishes him with silent estrangement, a puerile abdication of personal responsibility and a most primitive retaliation against natural misfortunes that are not within human control.

She must not love him enough to endure with him the stormy seasons of life, but she seems quite capable of loving him as long as the lilacs are in bloom. Otherwise, it could be that she simply is not strong enough to deal with that level of stress? If strength comes to us from God, who are we to judge?

She made me re-ponder the types of love between couples. The least passionate of such loves is also the most superficial kind, which loves only during the days of wine and roses and runs away when love becomes a struggle. Then there is the dutiful kind, which loves during both the good and bad days of life but does it with a measure of passion barely enough to sustain the relationship. Then comes the sacrificial kind, where passion rises in proportion to hardship and declines in proportion to good fortune. The last is the noble kind, where two souls happen to collide and startle each other into a higher orbit, far brighter than its origins. This is the love that we all want but seem unable to find except in chivalrous tales and romantic books.

I wonder how much fairy tales contribute to our disillusionments. Could that be the reason why mature love is so rare or why natural love no longer exists? Would we recognize love fomenting deep within our souls if the word *love* were not part of our repertoire? If we could not name a feeling, could it exist? Can you, Fatima, describe a feeling that you have experienced but that has no name? Isn't this what art is about, the expression of emotions that lie beyond words, or as the German painter Max Leiberman once said, *"To make visible the invisible: that is what we call art."* Which kind of love did we once share, Fatima?

I am quite impressed with Ahmad's noble acceptance of your situation. He seems to have become less possessive of you, especially now that he has built his own private love nest in a far off tree. I am shocked to know that he has never forgiven me for having been your first lover. Is it possible that after all these years he ended up leaving you for a younger woman because he never felt that you truly loved him? Could your having had a love life before him represent an emotional watershed that he could never traverse? Or could he have an innate character flaw or a cultural blind spot that impaired his ability to forgive, forget, and go on? It's all in the wiring, isn't it?

Why do some of us have a need to possess the pasts and presents of those we profess to love? What makes such loves possessive to the point of death? How can possessive love manage the mental tortures of reality? I blame fairy tales for the unreasonable aspirations of lovers.

Is first love really better than second, third, or fourth love? Is love forever better than love for a while? Is not love, at any time and for any length of time, better than no love at all? Is not giving better than possessing? I blame the fairy tales for most of our romantic, unrealistic concepts of love. I blame the fairy tales for the *"and they lived happily ever after"* concept. One loves not to be happy but to be alive. There is more suffering in love than there is joy, but there is also more truth and more life in love than out of it.

In one of her sonnets, Edna St. Vincent Millay says that many a man makes friends with death for lack of love alone. We love to live, Fatima, and when love becomes possessive, it dies and we die with it. Gandhi said that wherever there is love, there is life; he never said that wherever there is life there is love.

> *"If I can be young and wise*
> *Strong enough to compromise*
> *Hold you tight into the night*
> *Let you fly at break of light*
> *Feel you more when out of sight*
> *Watch you venture and create*
> *Learn to love and liberate."*

Some secrets are better left buried, Fatima, because if they were ever exhumed, they could only do harm. Love secrets are the earliest forms of biological warfare. It is best to censure damaging broadcasts aired toward our tender souls lest they infect our precarious emotional minds with dormant historical spores.

Having said that, I will remain a champion of the freedom of expression, but not when its only possible consequence is personal pain. I would protect the personal feelings of a fellow human being at the expense of my own freedom to reveal a private truth. A secret is private property where trespassing is not allowed.

Fatima, have you heard from Kamal or his wife? Have you written to tell him that you still love him, that you are awaiting him, that you are willing to become his second wife, and that your husband is willing to give you a divorce?

A letter from you might help him better cope with his solitary confinement, might refresh his wilted spirits with needed hope, might brighten his loneliness by firing his imagination, and might usher spring into his prison cell.

Send your letter to inspector Kakos, and he will give it to Kamal. Do not leave love unattended in the arid garden of time.

Love,

John

P.S. Please reassure Tariq that I will answer his letter as soon as I get back to Oklahoma City. Do not worry; there were no secrets in his letter. He merely related the happenings of graduation from his own perspective and expressed his desire to meet me.

Twenty-Four

(Humanism)

(Oklahoma City – Saturday, 2 September, 1995)

Dear Tariq,

Your kind confessional helped me re-visualize your new world with my old eyes. It reminded me that once ago, like you, I too had an unrestrained measure of youth's wisdom, that fearless wisdom which abounds with passion and is caution free. Then, I wanted to believe that adulthood, which is naught but the cautious child of youth, is not merely a resigned state of mind tamed by accruing experience. I wanted to believe that adulthood could remain passion green, rust resistant, and un-awed by the mighty winds of time.

I wanted to waltz through life with romantic strides and graceful swirls. I wanted all the noble impossibilities of dreams, especially peace, to materialize for me because I could not see how they could possibly resist my forceful stream of optimism. Indeed, all that I wanted in youth, I still want now, and shall want more the older I grow. People do not really grow up, my dear Tariq; they merely grow older and, with age, come to deny their inner youthfulness. Oscar Wilde said it best: *"The tragedy of aging is not that one is old, but that one is young."*

Your valediction speech was a manifesto of your precautious humanism. I liked how you developed your themes, from doubts to certainties, as if you were paraphrasing Francis Bacon: *"If a man will begin with certainties, he shall end in doubts; but if he will be content to begin with doubts, he shall end in certainties."*

I can even feel how your words must have touched your audience because wisdom has a cold, penetrating cruelty about it, regardless of who utters it. It awakens the soul out of its dormant trance by slowly soaking through its many levels, layer by layer, until it wets its core wherein lies the moral seed of humanity.

But humanism has its opponents, too; people who think with their faiths and follow heteronomous rather than autonomous philosophies. Heteronomy sits at the opposite pole of autonomy and is more native to human nature. Consequently, it will always be the religion of the people while autonomy will ever remain the religion of the cognitive elite.

I hereby welcome you to the cognitive camp and declare you one of the thinking few, the cheerful few who do not camouflage reality and insecurity with mighty myths.

What is most dangerous about myth is that it becomes indelible with time; the older it gets, the more sacred it becomes to our belief systems and we believe it to the letter in spite of overwhelming evidence to the contrary. Here is what Charlotte Brontë once said about this subject: *"Prejudices, it is well known, are most difficult to eradicate from the heart whose soil has never been loosened or fertilized by education; they grow there, firm as weeds among rocks."*

As far as security is concerned, I love what Helen Keller had to say about it: *"Security is mostly a superstition. It does not exist in nature... Life is either a daring adventure or nothing."*

Your being called an atheist after such a noble valediction does not surprise me. The lady who posed this rhetorical question to your mother represents the voice of those who cannot get in touch with their spirituality except through religion. To criticize religion is to criticize humanity, which I will not do because religions came into being long before reason and science penetrated the human mind. Consequently, our religious roots are far deeper than our intellectual tentacles.

I do not think that religions corrupted humanity, but on the contrary, I believe that humanity invented and corrupted religions. As a race, we are innately superstitious, believers in the supernatural, and strong holders of faiths that are impenetrable to reason. Religions grow and take hold of us because of these innate tendencies. As long as they serve humanity, I consider them a noble necessity in response to life's mysteries. But when, instead of emancipating, they enslave humanity, I then take issue with them. *"Whenever religion espouses a political ideology, it becomes deadly to itself and to its adversaries. Whenever religion becomes politicized, it falls down from the elevated realms of spirit and becomes disfigured by its lack of love."*

At this point, let me introduce you to how William James, the great American religious philosopher, summarily dismissed the issue of religious corruption: *"A survey of history shows us that, as a rule, religious geniuses attract disciples and produce groups of sympathizers. When these groups get strong enough to "organize" themselves, they become ecclesiastical institutions with corporate ambitions of their own."*

Reason and open-minded enlightenment are exceptional and always will be, in spite of all the accruing scientific weight in their favor. The innermost identities of each race lie in its regional myths and beliefs, which are supported by faith alone and not by reason. To make reason the new religion of humanity is to erase all religious and national borders in favor of Humanism, a universal ideology that is too elevated for our state of development. Abba Eban once commented that *"History teaches us that men and nations behave wisely only when they have exhausted all other alternatives."*

Indeed, when humankind has exhausted all other possibilities of peaceful coexistence and when the survival of the race is no longer tenable without sincere global cooperation, then at that point, reason might reunite humanity into one race again. Until then, religions, cultures, nationalities, affiliations, and beliefs will continue to separate us into ferocious factions. War is the main reason I avoid my beloved Lebanon and is probably why I will not get to meet you unless you come to America where, as C. Vann Woodward put it, we have *"unfettered freedom and the right to think the unthinkable, mention the unmentionable, and challenge the unchallengeable."*

Your mother mentioned that you wish to study philosophy. I hope that while pursuing a liberal education, you will also develop your gift for creative writing. Please do share your writings with me, and I will share some of mine with you. Let us maintain an epistolary friendship based on the mutual exchange of ideas, for free thought is the most solid bridge across the formidable gaps created by age and cultural differences. I would like to see my old world anew with your fresh incredulous eyes.

> *"The greatest distances are in the mind*
> *The sun and stars seem near to open eyes*
> *But oh, how far they are when eyes are blind."*

To end, I would like to reciprocate with some of my own personal aphorisms, just as you shared some of yours with me. These are aphorisms that I hold to be true at this point in my life, aphorisms that are not indelible but represent my present state of mind, aphorisms that expose my cultivated soul beyond what my poems and letters have already revealed to you:

Science and irrefutable evidence are two inescapable realities that should be upheld rather than resisted. Unfortunately, while evidence is what moves science, emotions continue to be the prime movers of humanity.

Those who will not or who cannot entertain themselves deserve to be entertained by their entertainers.

Those who possess humility are the ones who learn continuously, and learn from everything.

> *"Only the humble paint with hearts ablaze*
> *Live life as if it were a lusty dance*
> *Hear the seductive tunes whistled by God's*
> *Meek, moist, fecund, smiling, musical lips*
> *Commanding us to play, to pray, to burn*
> *Only the humble learn..."*

Our wise open-mindedness is inversely proportional to the intensity of our beliefs and the tenacity with which we resist opinions that are contrary to ours. Alfred North Whitehead once proclaimed that *"knowledge shrinks as wisdom grows."*

Solitude provokes our thoughts but society and nature spark our creativity.

Beware of today's ideas; just like yesterday's, they cannot endure. Those who believe in the stability of their ideas do not progress with change. So many thinkers have commented about this issue:

Henry Bergson said: *"...for a conscious being, t o exist is to change, to change is to mature, to mature is to go on creating oneself endlessly."*

William Blake said: *"The man who never alters his opinion is like standing water, and breeds reptiles of the mind."*

Gandhi said: *"It is unwise to be too sure of one's own wisdom. It is healthy to be reminded that the strongest might weaken and the wisest   might err."*

I admire your open mindedness, your willingness to think freely, and your courage to share your thoughts. As Seneca the Younger said: *"No man ever became wise by chance."* I hope that you will constantly apply yourself to the betterment of your soul. Excellence in anything always comes at the price of long, hard labor. Or as Nietzsche better put it: *"Not the intensity but the duration of high feelings, makes high men."*

Congratulations Tariq. Insist on joy, and let us stay in touch.

With love,

John

Twenty-Five

(Coincidence)

(Kuwait City - Saturday, 30 September, 1995)

Dear John,

I am still in Kuwait because the turn of events has frustrated my efforts to return to Beirut. I miss my apartment; I miss Tariq; I miss my friends and my extended family. The winds of fate have not been propitious in this oil-spattered desert.

One week after Tariq's graduation, I accompanied Jamal's two boys to Kuwait, which pleased Laila because she did not want them to travel unattended. They were delightful company, and they did not even bicker throughout the four-hour flight. Ramzi, now ten, and Imad, thirteen, kept me entertained with their mirthful tales until they saw their father waving to them, with a blond little girl on his arm and a young red-headed woman by his side.

The children gasped with surprise as they surveyed the scene. I gave them a moment to internalize the stark contrast between their father's forty-two year-old Lebanese features and Mary's thirty-two year-old Australian countenance. Then, I eased them out of their breathless trance and lead them gently toward their sudden family.

It seems that Jamal and Mary decided to marry before the children arrived so as to spare them the awkward discomfort of their nuptial ceremony. To Jamal's unsettled mind, that must have seemed both wise and merciful, but to my apprehensive eyes it was a startling cold shower in Kuwait's smoldering desert. The children had no time to become inured to their father's new state.

"Ramzi, Imad, this is Mary, my new wife, and Jamie, your new sister." That is what he said as he embraced

them both with his free arm. Mary was clearly troubled; she said a British hello to each of them while incessantly patting Jamie, perched on Jamal's arm like a doll.

Jamie, on the other hand, looked upon her brothers with bright-eyed curiosity, which did indeed soften the encounter. She leaned forward, dismounted off her father's arm, walked toward her incredulous brothers, and gave one hand to each as she situated herself between them. Thank God they both spoke English, because it afforded them the opportunity to form a play triangle, which carried them off on its oblivious wings from airport to home and throughout all the days of their sojourn in Kuwait. Jamie, Imad, and Ramzi became well insulated from the awkward troubles of their parents by the elevated state of mind they engendered with their newfound love for each other.

Mary and I had already become allies through numerous letters and telephone calls. Friendship flowered comfortably between us as soon as we had some intimate times alone, and we spent many hours in discussion while Jamal was at work. We prepared meals, took the kids on outings, shopped the magnificent malls rebuilt after the sack of Kuwait, and shared ideas about love, faith, and religion from our opposite poles. I told her our love story and read to her some of your old poems; you do know, of course, that I carry your books with me wherever I go. Of all the poems I read to her, her favorite was this stanza from *Cling To Me:*

> *"You are my sweetest dreams unleashed in*
> *playful mood*
> *My truth—elusive, solid, undisturbed, un-*
> *wooed*
> *My sense of beauty as it blends with nature's*
> *art*
> *Ah, you are me in mind and soul and heart*
> *So cling to me like I must cling to truth*
> *Or like, when we are old, we cling to youth*

*Come, harvest of my dreams, come bountiful
and free
And cling to me with drowning arms; oh, cling
to me."*

We talked about Tariq and Ahmad, Jamal and Laila, and Kamal and me. We realized that we had similar life situations, I with Kamal, and she with Jamal, and how improbable our liaisons seemed at their inception. I was not envious that she had forged her way into a new life across some deep international canyons. She, on the other hand, prayed that I would have the same fortune. I prayed too, prayed to Um Al-Huda, but my Kamal remained immured behind fateful circumstances like an echo crying in the distance.

The contrast between Mary and Laila was noticeable. Mary was innately cheerful, playful, and eager to please. She quickly befriended the children and treated them as if they were her very own. She delighted at their acceptance of Jamie and organized family games that kept us all entertained. She and I took turns at cooking, alternating Australian and Lebanese cuisines, which delighted the kids and Jamal. In spite of our strained spirits, we managed to have fun by avoiding the issue of Laila until it was time for the children to return to Brummana High School, where classes resumed on the first Monday of September.

About a week before the children left, Jamal began writing the fateful letter to Laila. He would write and rewrite and then whisper it to us while the kids were asleep. Mary and I were afraid to make serious suggestions, but we did help him with editing and word choices. The day before the children left, he was satisfied enough to seal the letter, which he handed to Imad at the airport saying: *"Please give this letter to your mother; it is very important; do not lose it."* That was all he said, leaving the boys burdened with Mary and Jamie's secrets and giving them no instructions on what or what not to say.

Departure was especially touching when the children and Jamie said good-bye. Jamie cried and pleaded with them to stay. They tried to look brave but failed miserably in suppressing their tears. Even Mary's eyes brimmed as she pulled Jamie away from her brothers and held her back in spite of Jamie's incessant kicking and screaming. As I watched Jamal and Mary hold Jamie between them and walk back toward their car, I realized that I was no longer needed and decided to leave Kuwait as soon as I could get a flight out.

Next morning, after Jamal went to work, I called the Middle East Airlines and made my reservations. It felt good to leave Jamal's new family to their new life. Jamie, at two-years-four-months, was too young for school but needed playmates, who were readily available thanks to Jamal's many eager friends. Mary and Jamal, on the other hand, were newlyweds who needed time alone, and that was also readily available, thanks to the isolating effects of the desert.

The evening before I was to leave, I received a call from Tariq. He said that Kamal had left several messages on my Beirut phone, including a telephone number where he could be reached. I was swept by a sudden hot flush that traveled along my spine, all the way from my face down to my knees, leaving me vacuous, startled, overwhelmed with expectation. Nevertheless, I managed to take down the number and ask Tariq whether Kamal sounded well or seemed distressed. *"Mother, stop worrying and call the poor man. He sounded more and more distressed each time he called and could not find you."*

I sat long enough to calm down and then looked at the number in my hand. The country code was neither Turkey nor Cyprus; it was Kuwait. My legs trembled as I ran to tell Mary, who was in the kitchen preparing dinner. She seemed alarmed when she first saw my face but was delighted when I told her the news.

Oh, John, can you believe this? Not only you and I live parallel lives; it seems that Mary and I have parallel lives as well. Mary and I held hands and prayed together to Um Al-Huda. At first, I thought that she went along so as not to disappoint me, but I soon realized that she was a true believer. Oh, John, do we really run our lives, or are they run for us? My faith tells me that they are conducted by divine powers, but you do not believe me. I am letting go of my reins. I am letting Um Al-Huda be the puppeteer at least when it comes to Kamal and me. But then, tell me, John, how come that, in spite of my faith, I remain fretful and you remain fearless? Love is a mighty mystery indeed!

I know that you are dying to find out what happened to my Kamal and me. Well, after praying with Mary, I took the phone and called him. He gasped when he heard my voice and began to sob like a child. *"Where are you? Where are you?"* He kept asking the same question without giving me time to respond, until I interrupted him with a sudden loud shriek: *"Kamal, Kamal, Kamal; please stop crying; I am here in Kuwait; I am here close to you; just tell me where you are, and I will come to you; please stop crying; please."*

I called a taxi and went to the Sheraton. I found him waiting for me in the lobby, wearing his military uniform, part of a delegation to Kuwait regarding security issues between the two countries and their neighbor Iraq. As we had hoped, he was released in exchange for a Greek Cypriot spy on the Turkish side of the island.

It seems that such clandestine exchanges are fairly common these days. He said that inspector Kakos drove him in his private car to the Turkish border and, while in transit, gave him the three letters I had written to him while he was in captivity. He told me how he arrived home and surprised his wife and children, who were getting ready for dinner. That very night, Gulnar told him that I had visited them and that she and the children liked me.

He said that Gulnar knew that he was planning to contact me and seemed resigned to the idea that he might marry me. Her only request was that he take me on as his second legal wife. She argued that a divorce was not necessary because we lived in two different countries and he could divide his time between us without obvious friction. He told me all that before he even proposed to me or listened to any of my suggestions.

He spoke as if I were not a married woman, as if Ahmad had already divorced me, as if I did not have a life of my own and a son who was my *raison d'être*. I had never seen the man so overwhelmed, so vulnerable to loud bursts of tears, so lovingly irrational.

I had to leave Kuwait the next day and so did he. We went up to his room and, like a pair of cyclones, groaned and moaned the night away. Then after the storm, hand-in-hand and drenched, we solemnly watched the arid desert lips pronounce the crimson sun.

I saw him off at the airport, and in the four hours remaining until my flight, I wrote this letter. John, am I a fool in love, about to become a second wife, in parallel with my brother and Mary? I have to trust in the wisdom of Um Al-Huda and let her strings puppeteer my future. John, I feel like a happy dog, restlessly licking at life, stunned by coincidence. I still remember the words you wrote to me when we teenaged like a pair of honey bees through the fragrant, Beirut summer nights:

> "Coincidence –
> She wears green shadows intertwined with dreams
> Lurks unforeseen, in silence, plots and schemes
> At times, she hurries matters to profound extremes
> Delights at rolling fortunes in reverse
> Coincidence, she sways the universe."

Please John, forgive me for leaving my congratulations to the end but my mind is on furlough with Kamal. I am glad that Tamara is beautiful and healthy. I am even gladder that you have become a grandfather. Nowhere in your poems, however, do I find a single seed of grandfather-hood. I wonder what poems you will write next, now that you have been touched by this new love.

New love is like an epiphany, a holy revelation, a personal message from God. Your new love is a new child whose future contains all the unfulfilled hopes of humanity. My new love is a new hope, which contains the future dimensions of a new marriage and the higher orbit of a new freedom, the freedom to be what we are and not what we ought to be, the freedom bestowed upon us by our spouses, because both Gulnar and Ahamd have already sanctioned the union between Kamal and me.

God is great, John. He has, indeed, shown us that, as Elder Zosima had said in *The Brothers Karamazov*, *"life without love is hell, and heaven is in every one of us."*

With love,

Fatima

Twenty-Six

(Free Associations)

(Oklahoma City - Sunday, 19 November, 1995)

Dear Fatima,

This year's lusty fall—having delivered us from August, shamelessly disrobed the trees, and quilted earth with rustling love letters—is about to relinquish us to the white teeth of winter. Home alone, eleven days before Thanksgiving, my head is a tempest of thoughts and stormy ideas. Forgive me Fatima, for I write extemporaneously. I need to vent my soul in all directions, but its torrents seem to blow only eastward, only toward you.

Two weeks ago, Yitzhak Rabin was shot in the back at a Tel Aviv peace rally while singing *The Song of Peace*, murdered by a twenty-seven-year-old religious law student opposed to Palestinian self-rule. How did the Arab world react to such horror? Did anyone renounce this ideological murder? Why did humanity find it necessary to murder Socrates, Christ, Gandhi, and the many other ambassadors of peace who have tried to swerve it away from violence?

Do you know, Fatima, how Socrates replied when his mournful jailor handed him the hemlock saying that the Athenian Senate had sentenced him to death? *"And nature, they"* replied Socrates, as he drank the hemlock and resignedly died in the arms of his weeping disciples. I wonder if those who find it necessary to murder the peaceful ever realize that they, too, have been sentenced by nature, and that the fore killing of others will not mitigate their death sentences. Oh, how easy is violence, how difficult is kindness, and how rare is wisdom. Like John Donne, I feel personally responsible for all the murders of humanity: *"...any man's death diminishes me because I*

*am involved in humankind; ...therefore, never send to know
for whom the bell tolls; It tolls for thee."*

Remember, Fatima, May of 1970, when the pre-
Civil War riots broke out in Beirut and an angry mob
came charging toward the AUB? Remember how you and
I merged with the mob and, while chanting anti-American
slogans, swayed the mob leader away from the AUB by
reminding him that the AUB had a lot more Arab students
than American professors. Remember what you said
to me after the mob dissipated and we sat, hoarse and
exhausted, on a rock by the sea? *"John, we are both mad;
we could have been shredded by the mob."* That night, I
wrote *"The Fool"* and read it to you the next day in the AUB
milk bar.

I have not changed, Fatima. I am still an
extemporaneous fool, a itinerant citizen of this volcanic
world, still trying to find an antidote for violence, still
trying to water with my poems the neglected spirit gardens
of humanity. So much more will have to happen to our
humankind before it becomes extinct. My only wish is
that other intelligent beings, which might succeed us on
this planet, will become the merciful interpreters of our
legacy. Life is a poem, Fatima, a poem that comes alive
only when it is recited. Life is nothing but the awareness
of life, it is all in the mind, and whatever lives and is not
aware of life is but a plant, as Shakespeare says:

> *"The summer's flower is to the summer sweet
> But to itself, it only live and die;"*

There was peace on earth before humans came. Oh,
Fatima, sing this verse with me, sing this verse about our
brutal race, the race which has contaminated this green,
peaceful planet with its premeditated violence:

> *"Sometimes I wonder
> Will the Homo sapiens brute
> Decline, destruct, or evolute
> Into a nobler institute than we
> Where love might be a little less dilute*

And where there is a place for fools like me
Fools who are simple, nonetheless diverse
Who with compassion for their universe
Reach out to mend the future with a verse
Untouched by fashioned thoughts or views
Inclined to meditate and muse
  Who seldom read the press or watch the
news."

Now, relieved and soul-vented, I return to my
personal life with its pepper and salt. Ghassan, Carla, and
Tamara are coming from Boston for the long Thanksgiving
weekend. Nadir and Frida will get to see their three
month-old niece for the first time. On the Oklahoma
front, because too many fathers seem to relinquish their
paternal responsibilities, a law has just gone into effect, a
compassionate law that allows the suspension of driver's
licenses for failure to pay child support. Indeed, this
November is a kind month for many Oklahoma children
because it is the month of gratitude to life and to her
innocent blossoms.

Norma fell off the porch yesterday and broke her
femur. Her balance has slowly deteriorated to the point of
dangerous uncertainty. The children and I took her to the
emergency room, and she was operated on this morning.
The doctor said that she could leave the hospital next week,
but that she will need to spend some time in rehabilitation
before she could return home. In short, Norma will not
be home for Thanksgiving, which means that the children
and I will have to be the hosting chefs. I was trying to
explain all this to her this afternoon, but she was still too
sedated to comprehend her new reality. I shall try again
tomorrow, but given her progressing dementia, she might
not understand the situation any better and that would be
merciful, indeed.

I was thrilled about Kamal's release and your
sunrise reunion. You winged your words with such joy
that I felt their flutters upon my face. However, the desert
marriage of Jamal and Mary parched my throat and
must have caused Laila's to become forever hoarse. Her

irate soul could not have softened up enough to mitigate such an affront. Having already estranged herself from Jamal, blamed him for her rape, the baby's death, and their marital demise, what else could she do to punish him further? In our turn-the-other-cheek society, such a wife could divorce her husband, take half the marital assets, and take custody of the children as well. On the other hand, in Muslim societies under Al-Shariah law, if she were to ask for divorce, she would have to forfeit both her promised prenuptial settlement and the custody of her children.

I only hope that her anger at the way her life has unfolded will not contaminate Imad and Ramzi, who are at a most impressionable age. Instead, I wish her peace and acceptance because implacable anger, given enough time, burns holes through the souls and drains them of all their joys.

I am happy for you, Fatima, happy that you have found meaning and significance through love. As a spiritual exercise from someone who has loved and lost, insist on finding beauty in everything, especially in what at first impression may seem unbeautiful. Insist on finding beauty through gratitude, even in the ugly, lest you should think as most people do, that the ugly is bad and the beautiful is good. If you do not fall prey to this common confusion, you will be able to insist on joy, to fill your days with wonder, and to spare yourself the disillusionments of nature. In nature, beauty is distance and hunger dependant; too much of anything makes it less beautiful and viewing it too closely reveals its imperfections. But, beautiful or not, nature is always a wonder, a mystery, a love letter from God, and should thus be received and accepted with gratitude and joy. Fill up your coffers with joy during the seasons of joy that this joy may sustain you during the seasons of joyless famine.

As for me, I remain loveless since the suicide of my butterfly. I watch Norma drown into a fog of oblivion, blissfully unaware of her fading world. Nevertheless, I persevere in my insistence upon joy as my spiritual calling, for from joy flows all that is good. I constantly exercise my soul to mistrust my vulnerable mind and its seductive reasoning. I fully realize that I am most gullible when I am ill—ill with loss, ill with deprivation, or ill with despair. I hope to love again before I die. I hope to love just one more time and, unlike Norma, I hope to die aware that I am in love. Norma is at peace, dying unaware. I want to be love-aware as I die so that I *"do not go gentle into that good night."*

We all live at the mercy of our unconscious mind. It is the source of our most spontaneous thoughts—thoughts that stir our emotions, actions, impulses, ideas, and creativity. It is the soil that incubates our experiences and cultivates them for us into flora—varied in beauty, fruits, thorns, and poisons. How merciless my unconscious mind has been, today...

Fatima, why do I feel this need to unfurl my morbid mind before your blithe eyes? Do I feel more alone, now that you are no longer alone? Is my joy for you tainted with a smear of envy? Do I seem more aware of reality's guillotine and its sharp blade, which falls upon our necks when least expected?

I do need to keep a more accurate record of my inaccuracies, an endeavor most nurturing to my humility. Forgive me, Fatima, but my mind is a howling wind, strewn with dissonant sounds; it babbles unaware. However, unlike Macbeth, I hope to rise better after a good night's sleep.

> *"...the innocent sleep,*
> *Sleep, that knits up the raveled sleeve of care,*
> *The death of each day's life, sore labors bath*
> *Balm of hurt minds, great nature's second course,*
> *Chief nourisher in life's feast."*

Goodnight, my sweet Fatima.

With love,

John

Twenty-Seven

(A Sign At The Shrine)

(Istanbul - Thursday, 4 January, 1996)

Dear John,

Your last letter arrived just in time to save my sanity. I read and re-read your poignant lines: *"Insist on finding beauty in everything, especially in what at first impression may seem unbeautiful. Insist on finding beauty through gratitude, even in the ugly, lest you should think as most people do, that the ugly is bad and the beautiful is good. Fill up your coffers with joy during the seasons of joy that this joy may sustain you during the seasons of joyless famine."* Oh, John, where should I begin?

I flew from Kuwait to Beirut on the last day of September, looking forward to a new life with my freed Kamal, hoping to iron out our marriage details before the end of the year. Kamal was most attentive. He called me daily from wherever his military itinerary took him, and we made plans to meet in Beirut by the end of October.

I began preparing my family and friends for the inevitable outcome. Tariq and I worked out the arrangements for a small reception at my apartment where we would announce our engagement, and I tried to get as much of my work done before Kamal's arrival so that I could dedicate my entire time to him during his stay in Beirut. All was proceeding with alacrity, and the excitement proved contagious because my friends and extended family decided that we should prepare all the food ourselves, avoiding caterers even for the engagement cake. There was a discernable glow that seemed to crown these jubilant moments, and indeed, it was a season of Joy.

I commissioned Tariq to talk his father into giving me a divorce, which he had promised to do upon my asking. Of course, he made sure that I forfeit my prenuptial agreement before he thrice announced, *"I divorce thee,"* in the presence of the Shaikh, signed the divorce contract, and set me free. It was most sensitive of Ahmad to be so accepting of my reality, and his sensibility well suited his cute hairdresser's designs because she made a point of calling me, congratulating me, and wishing me happiness in my new life.

We held the reception on a glorious Sunday, November 12, in beautiful weather; the sky shone like a chandelier over the crowded veranda, and my apartment was like a beehive, buzzing with myriad landings and takeoffs. After giving me the engagement ring and cutting the cake, Kamal was kissed by so many men and women throughout the evening that he grew weary and retired to the bedroom in order to avoid further assaults. We drank, sang, and danced till sunrise. A famous jeweler in Istanbul designed my engagement ring—on the inside were inscribed Kamal's well-meaning words: *"Cyprus is not just an island."*

When we were finally alone, and the sun was high in the sky, we sat exhausted and turned on the TV to catch the news. It was then that we saw the pictures and learned about the bombing of the U.S. Military Complex in Riyadh, Saudi Arabia: *"A powerful car bomb ripped through a building occupied by American military trainers in Riyadh, killing seven people—including five Americans—and wounding 60 others."*

We did not bother to go to bed. Kamal made one call and informed me that he had to leave on the first flight to Turkey. He said that such a bold attack in the heart of Saudi Arabia signified a dangerous destabilization throughout the area brought about by an escalation of fundamentalist passions. He was indeed correct because a few days later, claims of responsibility were issued from three groups: the Islamic Movement for Change, the previously unheard-of Tigers of the Gulf, and the Combatant Partisans of God. John, how can anyone hope for a normal life when the whole Near East boils inside this hot pan of terrorism? Perhaps, you were right in leaving us to our woes.

Kamal left that very afternoon, and I insulated myself with layers of work. The newspapers of Beirut spewed political fears, and nightlife became unsafe, which worsened the economic depression by discouraging Saudi Arabian and Gulf Emirate tourism. People began to wonder if the Civil War was going to reignite, sparked by this growing social unrest. I became concerned for Tariq's safety because the student body at the AUB fractured into jagged political factions, a reflection of the volatile political milieu that supervened.

One evening after dinner, I asked him if he would like to leave the AUB at the end of the semester and finish his education in America. He seemed eager and required no further persuasion. We decided to make a quick trip to the American embassy in Damascus in order to start the tedious process of obtaining a student visa. You remember, of course, that since the Beirut American embassy was bombed in 1983, we have had no American representation in Lebanon.

We left Beirut at nine on Thursday night, and at 2:00 a.m. that Friday morning we stood in line at the embassy door in Damascus. There were about forty people ahead of us, equipped with sleeping bags and umbrellas, awaiting the embassy door to open. We were told that thirty to forty persons were processed daily between 8:00 a.m. and 2:00 p.m., while those who were left behind had to spend another day in line before they got a second chance. This meant that if we did not make it, we would have to stand in line until the coming Monday because the embassy closes its doors on weekends.

We waited patiently, visited with those ahead and behind us, listened to their desperate stories, and when the conversations quieted down, I prayed to Um Al-Huda. It was cold in spite of our heavy coats because the Oldest City in the World sleeps at the edge of a desert and, in winter, wraps itself with the desert's cold night air. When the first call to prayer announced the morning, vendors selling hot Arabic coffee and foods seduced the long, limp line; they sold their high-priced products to unprepared people like us who came without rations.

When the embassy door opened, the liners stood up, groomed their sleepy faces, tidied up their attires, and hoped. For a while, time loitered like morning fog but the closer it got to closing time, the faster it sped. When the door closed at 2:00 p.m., there were five ahead of us and about seventy behind us. The empty disillusioned faces stared at the closed door awhile, gazed at each other with weathered, capitulated looks, picked up their stiff legs, their wet gear, their yawning children, and left their precious positions to those Monday hopefuls who decided to hold the line throughout the weekend.

Before returning home, I visited Um Al-Huda's shrine and prayed while Tariq waited in the car. As I prayed, I became aware of a deep, strange nausea that stayed with me all the way back to Beirut. It stayed with me throughout that weekend and all through the next week. Like a fool, I went to my doctor, waited my turn, and after he examined me, he asked:

"How old are you, Fatima?"

"I am forty-five."

"Forty-five!"

"What is it, doctor?"

"You are pregnant."

The memory of that last night in Kuwait thundered through my soul and bolted out my eyes. Dr. Haidar took me into his arms and let me sob. When I regained my composure, I thanked him, went home, and called Kamal.

"Come to Istanbul, Fatima."

"No, you come to Beirut."

"Abortions are easier in Istanbul, and no one will find out."

"Abortions! Who wants an abortion?"

I hung up the phone, darted out of the house, walked all the way to the AUB, and waited for Tariq to come out of class. We walked by the sea and considered options. Dr. Haidar said that at my age, the chances of Down's syndrome were rather high, especially that I am a heavy smoker. Intuitively, I realized that a baby at my age would reshuffle all my priorities and strain the rest of my life.

But there was a sequence of events that haunted me—the bombing of the American complex in Saudi Arabia, which caused me to consider sending Tariq away to America, which caused the trip to Damascus followed by a visit to Um Al-Huda's shrine, where while I was praying, my nausea first manifested itself. At the end of our walk, a deep calm pervaded me as I told Tariq that I was not going to have an abortion.

After a long pause, he nodded approvingly, held my hand, and told me that he felt rejuvenated at the prospect of having a sibling. But when I told Kamal of my decision, he hung up on me, and we have not spoken since. That is why I am in Istanbul today. I am in Istanbul because that is where Kamal lives and because I need to confront him with our baby in my belly just like Mary confronted Jamal with Jamie in her arms. You see, John, we do live parallel lives.

I am writing to you from the Istanbul Sheraton, overlooking the Bosphorus glimmering with galaxies of seafaring vessels, smelling of the deep scent of history. Tomorrow, after the Friday Morning Prayer at the Blue Mosque, which is located next to Hagia Sophia Museum (or the Aya Sophia Byzantine Church completed in 537 AD, converted to a mosque in 1453, and to a museum in 1935) I plan to walk into Kamal's office and surprise him.

I have no fear because Um Al-Huda has given me the sign to launch my life into a new direction, a direction beyond my reason, beyond my comprehension, beyond my assets, and beyond my capabilities. That is why I need Kamal; I need him because I cannot do it alone. Pray for me, John; pray for us, and pray for our unborn.

Love,

Fatima

Twenty-Eight

(Morning Love)

(Rochester - Thursday, 15 February, 1996)

Dear Fatima,

My mind is a pendulum vacillating between you and Norma. Your letter startled me out of complacency; it sounded like a rendezvous with fate, a duel in inclement weather between the mighty vessels of love and freedom. Remember, Fatima, nature always wins and naturalism is life's own prized philosophy. Whatever runs contrary to nature hurries toward its own death. In your case, however, it is as natural for a mother to fight for her unborn as it is for a father to flee such sudden responsibility.

Throughout the animal kingdom, fathers abandon their newborns with merciless ease, and as I mentioned in my previous letter, child support is a duty so often abdicated by fathers that protective laws enforcing children's rights had to be enacted. I fear that Kamal will prove resistant to your maternal pleas, and I await your next letter with trepidation.

Now, bear with me, Fatima, and try to understand, in spite of your anguish, the timeliness of what I am about to say. Remember December of 1976, when you and I had our clandestine reunion in Paris... Well, midair on my way back to Oklahoma, I became convinced, as if by epiphany, that it would be best if we would never see each other again. Then, a while after you and I had gone back to our different continents, to our different countries, to our different lives, and to our indifferent spouses, I sent you my good-bye letter in which I wrote that a mismatched love is more apt to sunder families apart than effect a peaceful reunion between long-estranged lovers. I wanted us to fly asunder, to flee each other, and to free each other for old love's sake. Let me reiterate one stanza from the poem that accompanied the letter:

"If I can be young and wise
Strong enough to compromise
Hold you tight into the night
Let you fly at break of light
Feel you more when out of sight
Watch you venture and create
Learn to love and liberate."

You resented both the letter and the poem and retaliated with tearful consternation. We finally agreed that we would avoid all forms of direct contact, including telephones, but that we could continue to communicate through letters. Well, now that the Internet is an accomplished fact, I want us to extend our promise to exclude e-mails because they are almost as direct as telephones and can be equally evocative. Let us maintain our handwritten tradition and leave spaces between our communications so that our letters will continue to unburden and support rather than oblige and overload.

Forgive me, Fatima, for bringing this up at such an inopportune time, but this idea has worried me ever since it intruded upon my consciousness. This restriction, of course, does not extend to Tariq. Tell him that I will answer his e-mails without fail, especially if he uses the laptop I sent him.

Norma's condition, after her hip fracture, deteriorated quite unexpectedly while she was still in rehabilitation. She developed clots, which detached from the veins of her broken leg and went to her lungs. That put her back in the hospital during Thanksgiving and caused great anguish for the children and me. As a family, however, we still managed to muster enough gratitude to life to afford us a measure of joy in spite of her illnesses. After she was released to come home, it became quite obvious to me that she was no longer capable of caring for herself. I hired an aide to stay with her during the day, and then Nadir, Frida, and I take over her care in the evening. Nevertheless, in spite of good care and support, her condition deteriorated to such an extent that one of my colleagues, a very good neurologist, suggested that I take her to the Mayo Clinic for a second opinion. That is why I am writing to you from Rochester, Minnesota, where the deadly cold makes even the white snow seem tenebrous and bleak.

Her doctors have confirmed the diagnosis of post-traumatic dementia and, surprised at her fast deterioration, have concluded that her prognosis is poor. I was afraid to ask how long... The words clung and refused to leave my lips. Tomorrow, we return to Oklahoma to await the verdicts of destiny. My imagination, unleashed, runs wild and errant. I see the children and me visiting her at her nursing home. I see her blank stare as she looks at our blurred faces. I see our disappointed aspects as we look at one another and tacitly ask the same question—why are we here if she can't recognize that we are here? A poem, which I had written years ago for one of my demented patients—unsuspecting that I was also writing it for myself—continues to un-scroll before my eyes. I titled it Visitation:

> "Everywhere sighed blue
> The fallen skies
> Her setting eyes
> The fingertips with azure nails
> The sprawling veins which swarmed her
> thighs
> Her skin worn thin with seasons
> The hollowed smiles that lost their pink
> The frothy words that drooled before her
> tongue could think
> Her stoop uncertained by implacable gravity
> The plastic nosegay, dust pallid and wan, next
>   to her bed.
> There was a time her breath was green
> And she would stride across the room
> To fill my arms

But elegance at first took leave
Then names and nouns
Expression next eloped with poise
Left her face ajar
A home forlorn, laughing echoes through the
halls
With grass reclaiming at the walls."

On the news today, I heard that the Turkish Cypriots condemned the Greek Cypriot parliamentary declaration, which according to the Turks, sabotages the chances for peace on the island. How would that affect Kamal's family and your liaison with him? Another news item declared that the British Arms-to-Iraq report has finally been published regarding embarrassing arm sales in the 1980s and containing strong criticisms of the ministers involved.

What happens to honest citizens on both banks of conflict? What happens to us all when political factions gain momentum by jettisoning wisdom? Why are governments incapable of learning from history? And why is it that historic laws, regardless of time's sway, remain ever poignant?

Great leaders, who are the architects of history, lead unsuspecting humanity through a series of violent competitions towards alleged glory when, in reality, greatness and glory are mere euphemisms for that kind of joyless power, which can only be acquired through cruelty. Unlike me, Hobbs was not disenchanted when he said: *"Violence is not a primitive, irrational urge, nor is it a pathology. It is a near-inevitable outcome of the dynamics of self-interested, rational social organisms."* Perhaps, like Hobbs, I should become resigned to the notion that our inveterate human nature is what actually spells doom for humanity.

I am sad, Fatima, sad when I need not be, sad for you and sad for me, and sad in spite of many blessings. Indeed, today, I violated one of my most precious precepts because I failed to insist on joy. Joy is like faith, easy to uphold when blessings, crowned with gratitude, are the keynotes of our lives. But when tragedies overwhelm our spirits, we can easily become disenchanted with faith and, in retaliation, repudiate it with angry disbelief. Similarly, I repudiated joy when, under the heft of reality, I lost my faith in life. However, I managed to regain my peace and find my lost joy through poetry. I recited and re-recited a sonnet I had written to you a long time ago. It was on that day when we awakened in each other's arms and watched the sun gloriously climb up the sky dome from behind the snow-capped mountains. You were the one who titled it *Morning love:*

> "I watch the birth, far at the edge of earth
> A gladdened shimmering without a cry
> And then the flapping, golden clouds of mirth
> Before the fireball redeems the sky.
>
> At splendid morns like these, I find your eyes
> In quiet clouds that lash upon the skies,
> In vast awakenings that reunite
> The depth of darkness and the laughs of light.
>
> The mighty kindness of the morning sun,
> The Maker's daily gift for everyone
> A giving love, condition-less and free
> Is for the ruthless, frightened world to see.
>
> I love you so, just like the mornings do,
> And find the morning joys in loving you."

This bleak climate must have dampened my spirits. Nevertheless, life is too short for melancholy and too bright for gloom. Tomorrow I shall flee these murky Minnesota climes. I shall return to my Oklahoma, to my sunny skies, to my home, to my children, and to my work. But before I say goodnight, let me reignite your joy with a kindling spark from Helen Keller's profoundly deaf-and-blind insight: *"Security is mostly a superstition. It does not exist in nature... Life is either a daring adventure or nothing."*

With love,

John

Twenty-Nine

(Happy Birthday)

(Beirut - Saturday, 27 April, 1996)

Dear John,

Three months ago, I wrote to you from Istanbul with a baby in my belly and hope in my heart. I was vibrant with expectation as I plowed my way through the congested Istanbul streets, after the Friday morning prayer, all the way to Kamal's office at the Ministry of Defense. I was attired like a bride, my pink dress smiling from underneath my black coat, and my crimson lipstick a confident sunrise. In Istanbul, the fifth of January was cold in spite of the clear, sunny skies.

I wandered through the Ministry until I found Kamal's section. Thanks to Ataturk, the Turkish language is now written with English letters, which made it easier for me to find his office. The guard at the door spoke only Turkish, and I had trouble telling him who I was. I kept repeating, *"Kamal Bey, Kamal Bey,"* while pointing to the closed door behind him. He answered by holding up his big, cold palm to my face. I was becoming rather exacerbated at this inter-lingual stalemate when I felt a hand tap my shoulder, and a surprised voice exclaim: *"Fatima! What are you doing here?"*

It was Gulnar with her son and daughter, Omar and Amar. I had prepared myself for all sorts of surprises, but I did not expect to run into Kamal's family, here in Istanbul. I felt naked, transparent, and flushed with sudden anxiety; not even my crimson lipstick could hide my consternation. And to render matters more embarrassing than they already were at that very odd moment, the door opened and Kamal walked out with two folder-carrying subordinates.

Omar and Amar jumped into his welcoming arms as he surveyed the scene. When he saw me, arrayed in bridal pink, his face focused a furious frown. He stared at me as if I were a meddlesome stranger and, without saying a word, marched back into his office with Gulnar at his tail and slammed the door.

I was left outside in the dumb company of his guard and the two folder-carrying men, who looked equally stunned by my sudden awkwardness. I gazed at my pink dress smiling beneath my black coat, at the guard standing at attention and looking through me with a stern, oblivious gaze, at the folder-men scurrying away into the long, cold hall, and said to myself, *"Do not cry, Fatima. Do not cry. Remember that the Ottomans ruled our people for 800 years. Drive this Turk out of your heart. Fight for your independence."* I held my tears until I reached my hotel room. Not a Turk saw me cry.

I returned to Beirut that very afternoon, indignant, quickening with wrath at the souvenir Kamal left inside of me. Kamal never called, nor did I. My Mediterranean *grand amour* with a Turkish spy, which was engendered in Cyprus, and conceived in Kuwait, was egregiously repudiated in Istanbul. And yes, in your last letter, you did remind me that in the animal kingdom, fathers devour their newborns and men abandon their children. Too bad, my darling; your letter was written after the Istanbul rejection and arrived a month too late.

This is my destiny from which you cannot save me. And do not think, that had I received your letter before the rejection, I would have changed my mind about Kamal. No. Not, indeed. My blind love was beyond insight, beyond redemption, beyond reality.

Do you know what the first thing I did was after I arrived in Beirut? No, I did not call Tariq, nor did I call my cousins who helped me with my engagement party. Instead, I drove my car in foul weather all the way back to Um Al-Huda's shrine. I arrived at midnight, weather-beaten and exhausted. I spent the night next to the shrine, in my car, hoping for a clear morning.

The sun awakened me from my cold, stiff sleep at

about the same time that a preadolescent vendor knocked at my window with a hot cup of coffee in his hand. I drank it with relish and went directly into the shrine. There was no one around, which relieved me because I addressed her with a loud, crying voice: *"Why are you doing this to me? I am tired. I am forty-six years old. What am I to do with an unplanned baby at my age?"*

At that point, like womb water, my tears broke; I sobbed aloud and waited for a sign. Many visitors came and left while I stayed at my knees and prayed. Then, on my way out, the same preadolescent vendor came up to me with another cup of coffee and a sandwich. *"You pray hard but eat nothing?"* He had deep blue eyes, a sweet face and, for the second time, he refused payment. *"You pray too hard. I remember seeing you here before. You always come alone. I do not accept money from the devout friends of Um Al-Huda. You have a husband?"*

"How old are you, my son, and what is your name?"

"I am ten years old."

"You did not tell me your name?"

"My name?"

"Yes, your name."

"My name is Kamal."

I spilled the cup of coffee, and the sandwich fell out of my hand; I sat down on the steps and began to shudder. He ran to his little car and came back with another cup of coffee and another sandwich. "My father said that you need to rest at our home."

"Who is your father?"

"He is the custodian of the shrine."

"What is his name?"

"His name is Al Hajj Tariq."

"Tariq? Al Hajj Tariq?"

"Yes ma'am and he is the custodian here."

The father emerged from the little car, helped me to my feet, and the two of them led me to their nearby home. At the door, his wife appeared with a big smile on her face, as if expecting me: *"Welcome, welcome to our home; my name is Fatima."* That was all I could bear—first

Kamal, then Tariq, and now Fatima—I collapsed at the threshold.

They dragged me in, laid me on a sofa, and went back to their little car, leaving me in the care of mother Fatima who prepared a cup of tea and covered me with a blanket. When the shivers died down and I was able to sit up, I placed my hands on my bulging belly and asked her, *"Does Um Al-Huda help women in distress?"*

She looked at me, sighed, and replied, *"Um Al-Huda will not allow abortions."*

"Why are we talking about abortions?"

"Because you are pregnant and your man has left you."

"How do you know that my man has left me?"

"Because you are here."

I began to feel faint again. She helped me lie down, covered me with the blanket, and whispered, *"You need to sleep now. When you wake up, we can talk."*

I must have slept like a child. When I woke up, it was noon, and I could hear the call-for-prayer, resounding from the nearby Minaret. She had lunch ready and insisted that I eat before I began the long drive back to Beirut. I told her my story, and when I cried, she also had tears in her eyes. Before I left, she confided in me saying, *"Al Hajj Tariq almost divorced me because, for ten years after we were married, I could not get pregnant. But, Um Al-Huda came to me in a dream; she told me to wake up my husband and lie with him before sunrise. That was how I became pregnant with Kamal. I wish I could have another child, but Um Al-Huda did not visit my dreams again, not until last night."*

"Last night! You mean she visited you last night? And what did she say? What? Please, tell me."

Fatima smiled, held my hand, and continued: *"She told me that a child will be coming my way, and that I should name him John."*

"You're not talking about my child, are you?"

"Yes I am."

"But John is not a Muslim name? And how do you know it's going to be a boy?"

She nodded knowingly and whispered, *"We cannot change what is fated. Name him John and I will raise him for you."*

"Raise him for me? Why? You don't think that I can raise him by myself? And what if I don't name him John?"

"It is fated that I should help you. You are a busy woman. I have time. Think about it."

When I left, I was not at peace; my thoughts were focused on my future, my fate, and on Um Al-Huda's new messengers—Kamal, Al Hajj Tariq, and Fatima, whose faces became fixed behind my eyes. I saw them wherever I looked, and they were always smiling. Driving back, I entertained myself by imagining Al Hajj Tariq and my son Tariq standing side by side. The images became animated, shook hands, and began to pantomime as if they were talking. When I tried to visualize my own image, standing side by side with Fatima's, I was unable to see us together. Instead, she always appeared alone with her back to me and stood as if she were holding something to her chest, something I could not see. But, whenever I tried to see the two Kamals together, I could only see Fatima's boy. No matter how hard I tried, I could not bring the image of my baby's father into focus. I felt as if it was never in my memory.

John, I know that you don't believe in such omens, and I remember how you used to knock on my forehead and say, *"Stay cognitive, Fatima. Resist the urge to find personal meanings in meaningless coincidences."* But, what if you are wrong? How can you be really certain that our lives are not fated? Weren't you the one who wrote:

> *"We travel life upon a charted course*
> *A microcosmic replica, of course*
> *Humbled by illness, poverty and age*
> *Maddened by youth, by sense, by love, by rage*
> *So endocrine, so biological*
> *Predictable, yet so irrational!"*

Muslims believe that their lives are predestined and their life stories are prewritten in heaven long before they are born. My encounters with Um Al-Huda have always been meaningful. In proof, my ultrasound revealed that I was carrying a boy, just as Fatima predicted. There must be another dimension to life besides reality. I can feel it with my heart, which always sees better than my eyes. Isn't that one of your favorite quotes from Saint-Exupéry's Little Prince: *"We don't see well except with our hearts; the essentials are invisible to the eyes."*

My gynecologist wants me to stop smoking, but I don't think I can. I am an inveterate smoker, and I have no desire to stop. Nevertheless, he says that the pregnancy is progressing well, and he has scheduled my Caesarian section for Friday, June 7, a medical necessity since Tariq was delivered by Caesarian section nineteen years earlier. Nineteen years between siblings is a bit too long, but this is my fate.

All my friends and family are a bit perturbed about the name. They prefer a Muslim name like Ali or Omar, but I am going to name him John, and they will have to get used to it. Of course, everyone thinks that I am naming him John after you, which is not really true. Six weeks before my delivery date, I am too overwhelmed to care about what anyone thinks. I have gained a lot of weight, my legs are swollen, I'm having bad headaches, and at forty-six, I don't feel all that great. Nevertheless, I loved the Helen Keller quote with which you ended your letter: *"Security is mostly a superstition. It does not exist in nature... Life is either a daring adventure or nothing."*

When a deaf-blind woman says these words, how can I complain? My life has always been a daring adventure. Being overwhelmed is far better than being bored. And being single, middle-aged, and about to have the baby of a man who rejected me is still better than being barren. I feel fertile and young. John is coming back into my life. I have no time for silly details.

I am sorry about your wife's illness and equally sorry about your decision not to use e-mails. But if this is indeed our fate, then I will accept it as I have accepted everything else. Letter writing, as slow and tedious as it may seem, is still better than nothing.

The Arab world is boiling with anger at the Qana Massacre. Surely, the incident was carried by your media, camouflaged no doubt in some sanitized garb to make it acceptable to decent Americans. But, that you may hear both sides of the story, let me also relate what happened. On April 18, 155 mm Israeli shells—donated by the U.S.— rained down on Lebanese men, women, and children taking refuge in a UN peacekeeping compound in Qana, southern Lebanon. These civilians went to the UN compound to escape Israeli air, sea, and land bombardment of their towns and villages. As a result, the bodies of 102 Arab civilians were shattered to pieces.

Leading up to the Qana massacre, 17 villages had been flattened, over a half million people had been rendered homeless, more than 200 had been killed, and hundreds were wounded. Israeli Prime Minister Peres, who was granted the Nobel Prize for Peace, ordered the bombing blitz. The entire world, with the exception of the White House, condemned this attack against defenseless civilians. The refugees have flooded our cities, causing horrible socioeconomic problems that have no solutions.

Now, John, do not get upset with me because I insinuated that the U.S. sanctions the shameless cruelties of Israel. The Arab nations, Israel, and the U.S. have all been unjust, immoral, and cruel. There is no side of this war triangle that is better than another, and I am equally ashamed of our own as I am of the other two sides. Do you remember what you wrote to me when our Civil War broke out? *"Fatima, there are no moral wars and no moral nations. Even among individuals, a moral being is a rare phenomenon because we all have our breaking points. Violence and cruelty are native and natural to humanity, while kindness and compassion are hard-to-learn behaviors."* I was so angry with you for having said that, but now, after twenty years of war and violence, I have come to agree with your point of view. Oh, how I hate admitting this to you.

Tariq sends you his best regards, and we both wish you a happy fiftieth birthday. I need to sleep now; I've had a long day, and my feet are like balloons. My mother said that she would take care of the baby when I return to work. Good-bye social life as I had known it. Too bad you cannot be with me to witness my fatherless birth.

Remember, John, that you and I live parallel lives. I have already lost my Kamal, and as you had indicated in your sad letter, you are slowly losing your Norma. Later on, when propriety permits, do I dare ask if you and I might have a second chance? My abandoned baby needs a father and, as we age, I will need more security. Oh, how painfully your Keller quote throbs in my heart, *"Security is mostly a superstition. It does not exist in nature."* But I cannot allow myself to believe her adage, in spite of my unrequited *grand amour* with Kamal. I want to believe that love, deep love, dedicated love, remains our best security.

Do you remember what you told me when we visited your father's grave, just before you left to the U.S., that dry summer day in 1970? Standing in front of his tomb, you held my hand and whispered: *"Fatima, love is the anchor of our souls; each time the anchor is hoisted, we drift away from shore."*

Yes indeed, it is very clear to me that as we age, I will need more security and you will need more attention. No one will ever pay more attention to you than I will, and no one can ever love your poetry more than I do. Am I being too blunt, too inappropriate? Or am I being a Helen Keller, adventurous and daring? Wish me well, John, and please forgive my forwardness.

The baby is coming. I will send you pictures. Oh, my head is killing me. I must sleep now. I kiss you good night.

Love,

Fatima

Thirty

(After All The Prophets Died)

(London - Friday, 7 June, 1996)

Dear Fatima,

After all the prophets died, you and I were left alone with the rest of humanity, still lost, still unable to learn how to love our enemies. If we could love them then we could forgive them; and if we could forgive them then we might have peace on earth. The poor prophets, they all came and died in vain. No one can reform humanity except God. Only God could will that we die twice. Only then, when we will have come around a second time, we might learn from Mother Wisdom how not to live in the shadows of fear and delusion. We fight and die for ideas, that if we were to come around a second time, we would neither fight nor die for.

My dear Fatima, all-consuming beliefs—when untempered by reason and humanitarian compassion—are dangerous to humanity because they close our minds to free thought and to the legitimate rights and perceptions of others. Indeed, fierce passions lurking within unexamined beliefs carry the seeds of destruction to the individual and to society. By inviting tragedy upon believers, passionate beliefs also render believers insensitive to the tragedies of their opponents. Indeed, those who have been punished because of their passionate beliefs find it easier to punish others for theirs and do it with a degree of cruelty proportional to the passion with which their beliefs are held.

"Had I a thousand years
The detail smothered scenes of everyday and
place
The narrowed streets that creep and froth
with chatter
The brewing feuds, the subterranean race
All ephemeral, would no longer matter."

Your last letter about Kamal's rejection, about the Qana massacre, and about your perceived insecurity with a fatherless child cracked my soul's shell. I do know, however, that I cannot be your savior. I am not the solution, Fatima; I am the problem. I feel helpless because I cannot come to your aid. Indeed, life betrays those who live dangerously.

I write on the day of your Caesarean section, on the day when Little John is to be born, on the day when another innocent soul will join our indifferent universe and plunge into the rough waters of our complex world, an ocean of worries and insecurities. On this day, the first two of Um Al-Huda's predictions will come true; you will have a son, and you will name him John.

I hope that the rest of her predictions will not materialize and that you will be the one who will mother your newborn into fruitful adulthood. Sometimes, especially after reading your letters, I hearken to the surreal intimation that, although all the prophets have died, Um Al-Huda lives on in your heart and takes good care of you. I have to admit that I do not know if there is another dimension to life besides reality. I further admit that not knowing is not proof of nonexistence. Perhaps I have become so frightened and so disenchanted with beliefs that, like Socrates, the only thing I am certain about is that I do not know anything.

Today was the last day of the International Headache Society meeting; I have spent an entire week in London's tenebrous climes. Tomorrow, however, I shall return to my Oklahoma where the sun is reliable and the days are long and bright but where Norma is fading away into the murky smog of her own mind, wasting the long, bright Oklahoma days in oblivious sleep. She does not seem unhappy or even disturbed; on the contrary, she seems suspended in beautiful indifference, this merciful state of mind where the family takes on all the suffering of their seemingly happy but sick beloved. The children are being very brave coping with their mother's childlike state. She no longer knows who they are and smiles inappropriately when they attempt to converse with her. As for me, I still want to believe, with all the powers of my wishful thinking, that she still recognizes me as her husband and the father of her children. Perhaps, I am not yet ready to face the facts. Perhaps, drowning twenty-five years of marriage into the river Lethe, that river in Hades whose water made those who drank it forget their past, still strikes me as impossible. What did her mind do with those precious twenty-five years? How can the memories of loving, raising children, caring for a household, and hosting so many significant occasions vanish into mere oblivion? How can a full life fade away without a trace?

Indeed, the subterfuges of reality render us most vulnerable. I do need more attention, as you insinuated. I do, but I cannot allow myself to reach for it, not yet that is. I must harness my thoughts. I must put my mind on leash. I must curtail my emotional needs and bury my primal passions underneath my skin. The only measure I will not take is the censorship of my imagination. It must run wild, limitless, rebellious, and unconcerned with propriety. Fatima, at this time in my life, imagination is my grand outlet, the blue ink that pens all my poems, and the mighty force that protects my sanity and controls my behavior.

Uninvited thoughts are seldom noble; they arise from the animal savage inside of us and are not within our control. Actions, however, which are within our control, are our only means to ennoble the savage within us. I may be tortured by my unfulfilled needs, but I remain in control of my actions, and I shall keep them elevated. Living in shame is like living in hell, the hell that also consumes all those who love us.

Speaking of poetry, I had an interesting encounter with a lady poet during our monthly poetry gathering. She is a pharmaceutical representative who periodically visits my office. Like most others, I sign her slips and she leaves us samples of the medications she carries. This time, she picked up one of my poetry books and browsed through it while waiting her turn. After I signed her slip, she informed me that she, too, writes poetry and wondered if I knew of a poetry group where she could read her work and get some feedback.

I ignored the deep undulating blush that swept over her pretty face and, nonchalantly, invited her to our gathering, which is always held at our home on the last Friday of each month. She is a married woman in her forties, elegant, attractive, articulate, meek, and helplessly shy. When Friday came, not knowing her name, I asked her to introduce herself to the group. With the same deep blush blotching her neck and face, she told the group that her name was Juliana Settembrini, that she has a son and a daughter ages 16 and 18, that she is a "closet poet," and that she has never shared her work with anyone, not even her own family. When it was time for her to read, she read this simple poem:

"Before the prophets died
And I was not alone
I prayed to them and cried
Asked them to save my throne.

But now, they all are dead
I have nowhere to pray
I pen poems instead
And drown in work by day."

The group fell silent as they watched her tremulous hands fold the poem, put it back in her purse, and gaze at the floor avoiding eye contact. To direct attention away from her, I asked other members to read and watched the merciless blush reluctantly relinquish her face. She never said another word. I walked her to her car when the meeting was over, watched her fumble for her keys, get in, and from behind the closed window nod in appreciation and drive off into the night.

Behind every poem lies a story, I thought, as I walked back into the house. What did she mean by, "*Before the prophets died and I was not alone?*" Did she mean that when she had her faith she was not alone? And could the death of the prophets signify the loss of her faith? Or was she talking about her faith in marriage, which she might have lost? She must have read Elizabeth Barrett Browning's sonnets because there is a similar line in Sonnet Forty-Three: "*I love thee with a love I seemed to lose With my lost saints, ...*"

Indeed, Juliana Settembrini left me musing about all the stories that hid behind her blush. As I tried to sleep, the name Settembrini kept intruding upon my mind. I knew that I had heard or seen that name before, but where? After an hour of supine restlessness, I got out of bed and went into my study. By happenstance, my eyes were drawn to *The Magic Mountain* by Thomas Mann, a novel I had read in 1968 while I was still in Beirut. I sat down in my big leather chair, opened to page 152 and began reading. The first line of the first paragraph began with: "*But to the cousins Ludovico Settembrini talked of himself and his early life...*" My startled eyes then jumped to the second paragraph where the first line began with: "*Settembrini spoke of his grandfather...*" I read a paragraph here and a line there until I felt sleepy. Settembrini was my favorite character in that book; he was the Italian thinker who stunned the pages with his mordant wit and acrid satire. I vividly remembered his motto:

"*A fouler, bald, in me you see*
Forever, laughing merrily."

Before I fell asleep, I remembered your words: "*How can you be really certain that our lives are not fated? There must be another dimension to life besides reality.*" I mused and mused on your lines until I became confused and fell asleep in exasperation, uncertain if I were musing about Juliana, the blushing poet, or Settembrini, her literary name, or serendipity, which guided me to *The Magic Mountain*. Perhaps I was merely touched by her unambiguous honesty:

> *"Before the prophets died*
> *And I was not alone."*

Perhaps we have something in common since both of us are married and alone? Forgive me for dwelling on this incident, Fatima. This is not a good time to unburden my old heart, not a good time at all, especially since yours is already overburdened with a new life. This is not a good time to venture into so many disparate whys:

> *"And why and why?*
> *There are so many whys in all the eyes I greet:*
> *Whys with ever changing answers,*
> *Whys who plead and cry,*
> *Whys and whys, how oft' there lies*
> *The answer in a why!"*

Incidentally, on the BBC today, a British reporter from inside Kabul described the prevailing mood in the capital as that of fear and despair. The feeble communist government, left in power after the Russian withdrawal, seems to be losing the battle to the besieging Taliban Islamic militia—whose main aim is the imposition of a strict Islamic regime. When the Taliban forces succeed in overrunning Kabul, which seems eminent by all indicators, one of the most important casualties of their Islamic Law will be the education of women, which thereafter, will be strictly forbidden.

How can that many believers become that irrational, all at the same time? How did the Taliban leaders manage to use the Koran to justify their mediocre misogyny? How can preventing education be good for any community? But then, why am I surprised when history is full of religious passions that transmute into political disasters? Think of the Crusades and all the other religious wars across time.

Religious zealots will never learn to *"Render therefore unto Caesar the things which are Caesar's; and unto God the things that are God's."* As I said earlier, *"all-consuming beliefs—when un-tempered by reason and humanitarian compassion—are dangerous to humanity because they close our minds to free thought and to the legitimate rights and perceptions of others."*

Remember my theory of naturalism: anything that runs contrary to nature hurries toward its own death. It is not natural to deny women equal rights. Look at how nature treats the females of all species and then examine the history of humanity with respect to women. Men have so much to be ashamed of. Indeed, the Taliban men now are where humanity used to be one or two hundred years ago. These ancient walls of social injustice will ultimately crumble. I am sad for humanity and ashamed of the past and present blunders of my gender. Life must move forward, Fatima. Regression is deadly. As Joseph Hergesheimer said, *"No one can walk back into the future."*

I cannot wait to hear about Little John; spare me no details, please, and do not forget to send pictures. I wish you well, Fatima, and I am certain that your faith will guide and protect you because, unlike me, you have not lost your saints and your prophets are still alive.

Love,

John

Thirty-One

(Family Affairs)

(Beirut - Thursday, 26 September, 1996)
<**Tariqraci@hotmail.com**>

Dear Dr. John,

My mother does not know that I am writing to you. Please keep this letter a secret between the two of us. The library at the AUB has new computer facilities and computer instructors who teach students how to use the Internet. I have just learned how to use my laptop to send e-mails. I have so much to tell you.

Little John was born on June 7, as planned. He is beautiful with big black eyes, but he cries a lot. My mother is having trouble taking care of him because she had a little stroke right after the C-section. The doctor said that the stroke was caused by many years of cigarette smoking.

Instead of taking the doctor's advice seriously, my mother began bragging to everyone that she has not smoked in the house ever since Little John was born. But what's the use? Every time she feels like a cigarette, she steps out on the veranda and lights up. Her right hand is still a bit weak and her speech is not always clear, but she is much better than when it first happened.

My grandmother has moved in with her and helps her with the house chores and with Little John. The doctor thinks that she will not be able to return to work before next year. The whole family is worried about her.

Last weekend, I overheard her talking to one of her cousins about you. They were in the kitchen whispering, as women tend to do when excited by gossip. My mother said that she was not going to write to you until her right hand fully recovers so that you would not detect from her handwriting that something is wrong. But she is also worried that if she doesn't write soon, you will know that something went wrong anyway. Her cousin wanted her to call you or e-mail you, but my mother said that you would get very upset if she did. She would not tell her cousin why.

Two weeks ago I witnessed an embarrassing family scene. When Uncle Jamal (my mother's brother who lives in Kuwait) found out about mother's stroke, he sent his new Australian wife, Mary, to help my mother take care of Little John. Of course, Mary brought their three year-old daughter Jamie with her.

We were all sitting in the living room when the doorbell rang. It was Aunt Laila (uncle Jamal's first wife) with her two boys, Imad and Ramzi. I was thrilled to see my young cousins and welcomed them in, forgetting all about Aunt Laila. When little Jamie saw them, she let out a loud cry and ran into their arms. They seemed overjoyed with surprise, but that was not the case for Aunt Laila. She and Mary eyed each other like two wild cats, while my mother and grandmother froze with astonishment.
The ice took a long time to melt. Then, Mary walked up to Aunt Laila and extended her hand saying *"I am Mary; you must be Laila."* In response, Aunt Laila turned her back to Mary and without saying a word, pulled Imad and Ramzi away from Jamie and walked out with them leaving us all speechless. Jamie followed them to the door crying loud tears while Imad and Ramzi looked back at her with longing eyes.

After Aunt Laila slammed the door and marched away, my mother took Mary into the kitchen and spent a long time calming her down. It did not work because Mary took Jamie and went back to Kuwait the following day. Aunt Laila has not visited my mother ever since that incident, and my mother thinks that she will never visit her again. Aunt Laila must be consumed by hate and anger. I do not know why she is like that, and my mother will not talk to me about her. What a waste of life and love. What a sorry state of mind.

Here is another secret for you. Two weeks ago, Kamal came to see me. He waited for me at the dormitory, and we went for a walk by the sea. I have no idea how he was able to find me, but spies know everything, I suppose. He knew about the C-section, about the stroke, and even knew that my mother named the baby John. Incidentally, everyone, including Kamal, thinks that John is named after you.

During our walk, Kamal said that he was very sorry about the way he treated mother after he found out that she was pregnant and wanted me to take him to see her and the baby. I didn't know what to do but couldn't say no to him because he was so good to us when we were in Cyprus. I was afraid that the shock would hurt my mother, but he reassured me that it would be for the best. We made plans to visit her after dinner.

When I rang the bell, my grandmother opened and was shocked to see Kamal with me. She was so surprised that she stood and stared at us without saying a word. Then, my mother called to her and asked who was at the door. Still, she stood there and said nothing, while Kamal and I stood facing her not knowing what to do. Finally, after several calls, my mother came to the door and saw us.

She turned pale, and her lips began to quiver. Then, as she fainted, Kamal caught her in his strong arms and carried her inside. They fought for a long time, but when my mother began to cry he held her in his arms and she let him smooth her hair and wipe off her tears. Then, they went into the kitchen and had a drink together.

Grandmother and I remained in the living room, and we could hear them giggling. Then she took him by the hand and led him into the baby's room, where they stayed a very long time. When they came out, they were both crying. They kissed at the door, and Kamal walked me back to the dormitory.

On the way, he told me that he and my mother were going to get back together but did not say that they were going to get married. He spoke at length of the many complications they would have to overcome. He seemed disturbed and overwhelmed as if he had lost his peace of mind, and he smoked one cigarette after the other.

The next day, he visited my mother again and took her shopping while grandmother watched Little John. When they returned home, he held Little John in his arms for the longest time. That same night, he flew back to Istanbul.

I am starting my sophomore year, and I have chosen the humanities as my major. I want to take courses in literature, psychology, and philosophy. I find the sciences boring, and my mother is worried that I may not be able to make a living as a man of letters. In spite of the deteriorating political situation, life at the AUB is not so bad and I have many friends.

As for lovers, I have many choices, but not one of them is loyal and that bothers me. Somehow, I connect intimacy with commitment, but they seldom come together anymore. Rather than risk any more disappointments in new relationships, I am devoting more time to reading and writing. I wrote a short poem about my new, little brother. Please tell me if it is good enough to publish in the AUB student magazine:

> "Little brother
> You come too late
> To take away my throne.
>
> My poor mother
> Is it her fate
> To raise you all alone?"

I guess that now you know my true feelings, feelings that I have hidden from everyone else, especially my mother. It is so hard to like what is going on. Without the pregnancy, my mother would not have had a stroke. Nineteen years from now, when Little John reaches my age, she will be sixty-five, and he will have a grandmother for a mother. This makes no sense at all.

Kamal will never marry my mother. The most he will do is send her some money and see her occasionally. His loyalty will always be to his own wife and their two children. My mother pretends to be happy, but she is not.

Sometimes she cries more than the baby does. She can no longer afford to send me to America, and my father spends all his money on his cute hairdresser whom he married as soon as he and my mother got divorced.

I feel trapped in Beirut, and no one seems to pay attention to me anymore. Everything seems to revolve around Little John and my mother's medical condition.

On the Lebanese political front, the parliamentary elections have ended with Hariri victorious, his supporters winning 14 out of 17 seats. But in reality, it was Syria that decided who was to win. All the elected deputies made pilgrimages to Damascus and obtained Assad's approval. Lebanon is not a democracy; it's an annexed Syrian state with a democratic mask. We have no freedom of speech like you do in America. No one dares say anything negative about Syria, not even the private citizen and especially not the media. Syria is a presidential autocracy that rules the Lebanese with its own interests in mind. Nothing significant can happen without Syrian approval. The Syrian generals in Lebanon have gotten rich; they own palaces and drive Mercedes cars.

Our philosophy professor told us in class that throughout history, all occupying powers become kleptocracies. After class, I looked up the definition of kleptocracy and realized that he was talking about the Syrians. Studying philosophy helps me understand many things that are happening to us, but I continue to feel trapped. Like you, I have lost my loyalty to my own country. I wish I could run away to freedom as you did.

Dr. John, my mother still loves you. Please do not stop writing to her even though she is unable to write back. She keeps all your letters and reads them over and over. After your last letter arrived, she went into a bad mood and would not tell us why. But we all knew that you told her something that she did not like to hear. Then, after she came out of her blue mood, she had me go to the bookstore and get her a copy of *The Magic Mountain* by Thomas Mann. The book seemed to help her feel better, and she spent a lot of time reading it. One time, I overheard her tell a friend that Settembrini reminded her of you. Who the hell is this Settembrini, anyway? Do I have to read the book to find out?

Incidentally, as I told you in my graduation letter, I have always been able to read your letters to my mother because I know where she hides them. But, since she had her stroke, she has not left the house long enough for me to find and read your most recent letter. That is why I do not know who the hell is Settembrini. But after my mother returns to work, I plan to resume reading your letters, not only because I am curious but also because I learn from them. I especially like your theory of Naturalism and your views about the East and West.

On the radio today, the WHO announced that smallpox had been eradicated from the world. My friends are not so sure that this is true. They think that Saddam Hussein has the virus and plans to use it as a biological weapon should he be threatened again. As you must know, the student body at the AUB is littered with rumors and divided into multiple political clubs. I do not know what to believe anymore.

Another friend told me that the UN announced that Bill Gates is the richest man in the world today. How could he be richer than king Fahd of Saudi Arabia and the Sultan of Brunei? Is that really true? But then, the Microsoft program in the laptop you sent me works very nicely and is user friendly. In fact, I know that Microsoft helps a lot more people than does King Fahd's oil and because of that, I am glad that Bill Gates is the richest man alive. I hear that he is a generous philanthropist. Perhaps I should apply to him for a scholarship?

Let me share one final incident with you. My last lover was Mongolian, and he and I got drunk on June 30 because his country voted to bring down seventy-five years of Communist rule. He wanted to celebrate the new Mongolian freedom and, indeed, we did. Then, as we were relaxing in bed, he asked me what I thought of freedom. Without much reflection, I said that freedom is like spring; it suddenly sprouts after a dark winter, blooms gloriously for a while, and then is browned by summer. He became angered and asked me if I meant that freedom does not last. I said that freedom, like youth, has a short lifespan after which it gradually ages and decays. He spit in my face, got out of bed, put on his clothes, and left without saying good-bye. My truth must have murdered his dreams. He has not spoken to me since. I think that the study of philosophy is hard on relationships.

Doctor John, will you be my friend? May I e-mail you when I feel the need to share my emotions? Do you have time for one more responsibility? Do you still love my mother? Do I ask too many embarrassing questions? What will happen to us if my mother couldn't return to work? Who would take care of Little John if my mother has another stroke? Could you influence my mother to stop smoking before something bad happens to her? Every time I voice my fears, she answers me with smug confidence that God and Um Al-Huda will always take care of us.

This seems to be her answer to everything. I am so tired of hearing her proclaim that God and Um Al-Huda will take care of all our tragedies, and that God and Um Al-Huda do not need our help to do their good work. Sometimes, I think that faith can be an easy way out, an escape from reality into fatalism, or just another excuse for lazy thinking. I cannot wait to discuss faith in our philosophy class.

I have so much on my mind these days. But, thank God, I am still young, and youth solves most problems by laughing at them. Personally, I find that laughter is the best response to the pressing questions of life because it's nature's way. Nature, I have learned in my philosophy classes, takes nothing seriously. Nothing really matters to Mother Nature because she thrives unconcerned. Therefore, as a natural being, I look at my family, at myself, at Little John, at my mother, at Kamal, at Um Al-Huda, and I laugh. From a natural point of view, all our tragedies are ridiculously funny and transient. I was touched by this quote from Hamlet: *"There is nothing either good or bad, but thinking makes it so."* I can even add to Shakespeare's insight that also feelings make it so—especially, those feelings that are not within our control.

Speaking of Shakespeare, I have one more story to tell you. Professor Hammoud wanted us to write an essay about the universality of Macbeth and discuss why it still speaks to audiences today. I read it three times, and with each reading, I gained deeper insights and discovered that a lot of its wisdom hides between the lines. I could feel the thrill of understanding a complex work travel into my arteries all the way up to my brain. My heart sank under the weight of its universal truths; it was a most awesome feeling. In this feverish excitement, I wrote a three-page essay about the unchanging traits of human nature that are featured in the play and ended it with this quote from your poem, *Impressions Of A Fading Generation:*

> *"Yes, I have known the gentle peace of death,*
> *The pain and sleepless anguish of Macbeth,*
> *Have loved and hated, even leased my soul*
> *With perfect logic, softened to comply*
> *With inner whims that do not yield or die*
> *Until they find expression; this is I...*
> *There hardly is a process that I could not*
> *justify."*

The teacher asked to see your book and has not returned it yet. Mother is getting anxious because she wants her book back. I may have to ask him for it before long.

Oh, I've said too much. Like drinking alcohol, writing e-mails is a dangerous thing; it loosens inhibitions and invites confessions with reckless ease. Mother must neither find out that I secretly read her letters nor that I find humor in tragedies and things she holds sacred. Perhaps, the old Arabic adage is really true: *"The worst of woes are those that provoke laughter."* Indeed, we do live in a funny world.

Please say hello to your children. Perhaps I will get to meet them some day?

With all my love,

Tariq

Thirty-Two

(Paternal Advice)

(Oklahoma City - Sunday, 10 November, 1996)

My Dear Tariq,

Your letter astonished me with news of your mother's little stroke. In our medical world, the term little stroke is as meaningful as little pregnancy. The realization that something serious has happened to your mother has left me feeling lost, like a homeless drifter. Unconsciously, I must have viewed your mother's friendship as my primal home. Such are the dictates of human nature—no matter how far away we stray from our primal home, we can never become detached from it. Indeed, our memories dwell in the suburbs of distance, on the outskirts of time, and seem little influenced by their meddlesome parameters. Instead, they are tethered to love, the love that first startled us into life and then shocked us into puberty. Therefore, you need not wonder if I still love your mother. We can never forget our epiphanies. Indelible are the memories of love.

Although you are merely nineteen, your liberal writing, your transparent honesty, and your precautious prudence have titillated my heart. From this moment onward, although we do live on the opposite banks of life, I shall write to you as my equal with total freedom to explore personal thoughts that I could never share with your mother. Friendships that inspire freethinking and equalize souls are rare phenomena. Indeed, outside of true friendship, which is a form of love, equality is an illusion or a pretense. Ultimately, only two things equalize us all, Joy and Death. Love equalizes with Joy, and Life with Death. Let me then be the one who launches this dialectic by responding to certain matters that you have related to me.

My dear Tariq, why don't you want your mother to know about your letter? My own insights into human behavior reveal that we often censor our private thoughts and camouflage our true opinions by giving voice to contrary views. In that regard, I believe that your mother would rather have someone else spare her the agony of telling me the truth. Withholding truth to postpone the hurt may ultimately end up causing more harm. Do not worry; she will be pleased that you told me.

I am thrilled that you chose the humanities as your major, but I also understand why your mother is against it. For women, security is the foremost priority, whereas adventure is the priority for men. Like most mothers, your mother wishes you to choose a more secure profession. But mother's wishes aside, I know that if you will follow your own passions, you will have a better chance at success in life. Myriad opportunities present themselves to men of letters, opportunities that you cannot possibly foresee from your youthful vantage point. Moreover, meticulous planning for the future is either a wild presumption or a calculated gamble because today can never hold the reins of tomorrow. Therefore, follow the sirens of your own calling and you will end up with fewer pretenses that you will have to live with. Courage is having faith in your own abilities. Have the courage to be yourself because only then can you reach your best.

As far as your poem, it is Dickinsonian in structure but childlike in substance. I do not recommend it for the student magazine. I presume that it was your way of discharging negative emotions about your family situation, and in that regard, it did serve its purpose. Remember, however, that there is neither shame nor anger in nature. Indeed, all opinions, reactions, and judgments are but the dissonant noises of our biased perceptions. Try to find some peace by recounting the revered Islamic adage: *"Hate naught for it might hold some good for you."* Have faith in coincidence, but always fear and avoid the irrational. Rejoice in the knowledge that nothing happens for a reason but that everything happens because of myriad reasons. There is more peace in accepting fate, more turmoil in resisting it, and more joy in sharing its pains. Here again, it is joy that equalizes us all.

I understand your feeling trapped in Lebanon and your wanting to run away to freedom, like I did. When the time comes to make that move, I shall help you. Dictatorships stifle creativity and excellence, and by so doing, they interfere with peoples' *joie de vivre*. I can have no loyalty to a country that usurps freedoms, and I am glad that you feel the same way. However, as far as the Syrian presence in Lebanon is concerned, I have a different perception than yours. Natural laws always side with the strong against the weak, and historical laws are not any different because they derive from human nature. Tiny countries that cannot protect nor support themselves die an historic death. Think of earth as a large pond with little and big fish swimming side by side and you will no longer be surprised when big countries devour little ones. It has little to do with justice, which is an altruistic human concept. It's nature's way; there is no justice in nature, and there is no kindness in the pond:

> *"I have lived with fishes of the pond*
> *Have watched them all*
> *The colors that bewilder and the sizes,*
> *Large and small*
> *The marvelous disguises that elude*
> *Have watched the fittest and the shrewd*
> *Selected by endowment, thrive*
> *Not everyone can stay alive*
> *The mover is the hunger drive*
> *It goes beyond the human bond*
> *I find no kindness in the pond."*

Shopping for a better country has become the *modus operandi* of modern *Homo sapiens*. It is natural to belong to earth, to owe your loyalty to humanity, and just like earth's fauna, to migrate to the most suitable land with total disregard to national borders. There are no national borders. There is only humanity in constant flux, and there are natural boundaries, climes, and resources that shape its history. Like flora and fauna, different regions grow different people. If we could learn to think in terms of centuries instead of years, most of earth's unjust happenings would seem natural to our historic eyes. But, instead, we are tiny creatures with miniscule life spans, incapable of perceiving global phenomena with our myopic visions. Consequently, we spend our lives denying the mundane reality that what is natural is indeed normal and cannot be suppressed.

Now, to return to your question, *"Do you still love my mother?"* The answer is not simple. Yes, I do love your mother, but I love her with my memories, not with my passions. To me she is like Lebanon; although I ran away from her, she continues to be a part of me. I wrote this poem when I painfully realized that I will never return to Lebanon, and it may help you understand my true feelings about your mother:

> *"Because I have two hearts*
> *Because I straddle oceans*
> *Because I am both banks of life*
> *The froth, the currents in between,*
> *The dissonant emotions*
> *I see beyond the mighty walls of time*
> *Beyond the eyes, the made-up lips, and faces*
> *Beyond the borrowed sentiments and faint*
> *laces*
> *Because I have two hearts*
> *My soul is vagabond*
> *It camps in many places."*

On the other hand, your mother still loves me with her passions and is not willing to let go. I have become her obsession instead of her memory, and although she also has two hearts, she is unable to see beyond the mighty walls of time.

As for the character Settembrini in Thomas Mann's *The Magic Mountain*, my advice is that you should read this excellent novel. I am even pleased that Settembrini reminds your mother of me. But, that is not what the name is about. I have met a woman, and Settembrini is her married name. Your mother must have surmised, given her acute feminine instinct and penetrating insight, that I was drawn to Mrs. Settembrini. She is a most interesting woman who is also a poet. We meet occasionally at my office because she is a pharmaceutical representative, and she also comes to our monthly poetry group meetings. My feelings are most vulnerable at this stage as I watch my wife drown deeper into dementia. I have a strong urge to find love with another woman, but I am resisting this most pressing natural need.

Now, I am not sure that I should be telling you this because it is about an embarrassingly personal matter. But, given my proclivity for telling the truth, I am going to tell it to you regardless of consequences. Sometime ago, I slipped and had a fleeting, platonic romance with one of my married patients, an innocent romance that ended with her suicide. I do not believe that I was the cause of her suicide; instead, I prefer to think that she was unhappily married and must have realized that our relationship was not going to save either of us. Like Lazarus, this left me with the bitter taste of death in my mouth and caused me to resolve never to allow myself to be involved with another woman while my wife is still alive. And now, even though my wife no longer knows who I am and reacts to me as if I were a total stranger, I still feel ethically bound by my resolution.

Nonetheless, Mrs. Settembrini and I have had much to say to each other, but all of it has been strictly indirect and metaphorical. The attraction between us is fierce, and she has repeatedly indicated that her marriage is failing. I have no idea how long we will be able to withstand this mounting tension, and I do confess that I think about her quite often. Imagination has become my therapy and my agony.

Only hard work keeps me sane. There are no vacuums in nature. I do not know how long I will be able to hold my vacuum in check. The fact that I am allowing myself to relate to you the conflict between my human nature and my conscience is in itself revealing. Indeed, sharing troubles dilutes their bitterness.

You seem surprised that Bill Gates is the richest man alive? This is how market forces work in nature. If you were to distribute the current human wealth equally among the living, it would not take long before market forces redistribute the wealth creating a rich class, a middle class, and a poor class. And within each class, the wealth would have a pyramidal distribution, with one person at the top of each pyramid. At present, Bill Gates is at the top of the rich class. There were others before him, and others will come after him to occupy the cupola. Capitalism is nature's way. Socialism and communism are not natural and, when forced upon a country, seem to lead it to ruin. History is full of such examples. Pick up a copy of *The Wealth Of Nations* by Adam Smith and browse through it.

To me, the richest person is the one who is wealthiest in joy and who has the wisdom to say no to material wealth after his sensible needs are met. Wealth beyond reasonable needs complicates life and ruins life's quality. Indeed, we are equalized by joy for there is more joy where there is less worry, and there is less worry where there is less wealth.

The story of your Mongolian friend intrigued me. Indeed, when we are most hungry, we are also blinded by hunger. His hunger for freedom must have been so strong after years of suppression that he was incapable of seeing the truth in your words. What else did you learn in your philosophy classes? Did you also learn that, like human beings, all human institutions rise with pioneer passions, ripen into a golden age, and then fall prey to gradual decay? Such are the laws of nature, and what applies to the individual also applies to all groups made out of individuals such as congregations, institutions, peoples, and nations. Nothing escapes time's enzymes. Everything will be digested in time's eternal belly. Indeed, it is this finiteness of life that is the fountain of our joy. Can you imagine how sad and meaningless life would become if it were trouble-free and endless. What gives worth to life is the fact that it is ephemeral. What dies is more precious than what does not die because, outside life, nothing is valuable.

Death touches us with its finality and makes us appreciate life's glittering bubbles rather than lament their transient sparkles ere they burst into nothing. It has taken me all my years to learn that instead of fleeing from death, I should make use of it. Wallace Stevens said it best when he said that death is the mother of beauty and from death alone shall come the fulfillment to our dreams and our desires. Even love, the noblest human emotion, is most valuable because it is most frail. It invariably dies with our own death or else it dies before we die, leaving us alone and loveless in a life that becomes meaningless:

> *"Yes, I am well aware*
> *That nothing lasts beyond the moment's edge*
> *That love at first will crawl*
> *Then springs like roses, marvelous and tall*
> *Then browns and all the petals fall*
> *And scatter through the air*
> *Only the thorns remain*
> *On branches, pleading, bare*
> *With every thorn a pain*
> *Yes, I am well aware."*

As for your frustration with your mother's fatalism, be patient and remember that you belong to the future and she, to the past. To her, indeed, God and Um Al-Huda will take care of everything because they always have. Your mother's faith is strong, and it sustains her against despair. If you were to take her faith away from her, she would fall into despair and feel helplessly alone. Proven or not, faith is a vital force and a prime mover in the history of humanity. It is an integral part of our imagination— through it we reach the sublime realms of bliss, and with it we dull the prickly thorns of reality. Faith is not a choice; it is a need because, as T. S. Eliot said, *"humankind cannot bear very much reality."*

Throughout my career, I have taken care of so many dying patients, and many of them were agnostics. Nevertheless, at dying time, they all became believers and regretted their atheism. Faith is not an abstract notion or an imaginary force; it is a necessity because we need it to negotiate the wry currents of life.

Philosophers repudiate religions as unproven doctrines that bribe humanity with heavenly immortality. My simple answer to such intellectual dogmatism is an even simpler question. Why ridicule a sentiment that has stood the historic test of time and remains indelibly etched in the human psyche? Would it not be more fruitful to study the reality of faith, come to a better understanding of its nature, and accept its fantastic hold on humanity. Because faith is an inseparable part of human nature, it must be natural. And my theory of naturalism proclaims that whatever runs contrary to nature hurries toward its own death. Well then, all the philosophers are either dead or dying while faith lives on, unscathed by philosophy, and continues to light up with hope the tenebrous alleys of life. On the grand scales of joy, hope is heftier than reality, and faith is just another word for hope, and faithlessness, another word for hopelessness.

Joy, my dear Tariq is the measure of all things. If a belief conjures joy, then it is good. If a leader brings joy to his people, then his leadership is good. If a person inseminates others with joy, then what that person does is good. If an idea increases joy then it must be good. And if life is joyful, then it is a good life.

Moreover, the reverse is also true; whoever increases the suffering in this world does something bad. Insist on joy, therefore, and you can do no harm. Insist on joy, and you will beget love. Insist on joy, and you will make beauty. Insist on joy, and you will increase peace and reduce violence and suffering. Insist on joy, and you will find truth because nothing joyful is false. Let your gratitude to life—in spite of all its surprises—light up your way to inner joy.

However, to have joy, you must have love, and to have love, you must have peace, and to have peace, you must have God. Without God, there can be no faith and without faith there can be no peace or love or joy. I like how Meister Eckhart phrased it for us all: *"For you will have peace to the extent that you have God. Anything that is at peace has God in it to the extent that it is at peace. Thus you may measure your progress with God by measuring your peace or the lack of it."*

On our political front, Clinton was re-elected for a second term, and many are hopeful that world peace will become a reality under his leadership. Of course, I cannot see how one man or one administration can achieve something so unnatural to societies or nations. Peace is a personal attribute, which is diluted whenever the identity of the individual dissolves into that of the group. All groups, sooner or later, become adversarial, feud, split, and go to war. The sizes of groups determine the sizes of their wars, and the only trustworthy unit in society is the individual who has a cultivated conscience.

In the history of humanity, there has never been peace on earth because it is more natural to fight than to surrender the other cheek. Outside the human soul, there is nothing in the entire universe that is at peace with itself. All the atoms, moons, planets, stars, galaxies, black holes, outer spaces, and living things are sustained in a state of cosmic tension.

Outside our God-given souls, peace is another word for inertia and inertia, another word for death. Life is another word for struggle, and struggle is another word for war. We are always fighting, fighting for so many sundry things, fighting as individuals, fighting as groups, and fighting as nations. We live, we fight, we die, and that will never change.

My dear Tariq, I hope that I have not overstated my ethos or overstrained your pathos. Your letter must have unlocked my festering unconscious mind and allowed me to drain some long-held tensions that have overburdened my mind. Friendships that unburden and lighten our loads are some of the kindest blessings of love. I thank you for becoming my friend and for being the one to first reach out with your innocent heart.

Age needs youth as much as youth needs age. Nature discourages dependence but encourages interdependence. Since you and I have become symbiotic, I hope that we will continue to write to one another whenever we feel the need to speak freely. Humility lights the way to inner peace.

"I feel my life unscroll and role
A tale of thrills and ills and ails
And endless winding trip on rails
A tour of moments lit with dreams
An ebb and tide betwixt extremes
A test I neither pass nor fail
I'm just a passenger on rail."

Please tell your mother that I know about her stroke and that I am still awaiting her reply to my letter. Let her type it if her handwriting is illegible. Let her dictate it to you if she is unable to type. Writing is an assertion that everything in us is still alive. I need to see for myself how alive she is by reading her thoughts.

Tell her that, between friends, silence is a retreat from friendship's dynamic life and that friendships do not grow without dialogue. Tell her that if she would write a line each time she smoked a cigarette, she would have a long letter ready to mail in just a few days.

With love,

John

Thirty-Three

(Recovery)

(Beirut - Sunday, 29 December, 1996)

Dear John,

When I first received your letter, I was incensed at your forwardness in relating the Settembrini episode. Knowing you, I knew that you were setting up again your own tragic conquest by another woman. You are not a man who can ever conquer love with reason; rather, you are a man who revels in love's agony. You actually believe that love is the fulfillment of your destiny, and you think that not being in love is synonymous to not being in life.

I know you too well John, too well to trivialize your casual remarks. And yes, I am jealous, jealous of Mrs. Settembrini who seems meek and healthy while I still slur my speech and struggle with my right body as if it were a toddler. You have always been vulnerable to meek women, let alone a meek woman who writes poetry. Unfortunately, I am not a meek poet; I am a single, struggling mother with a child named after you, a child whose father is a Turkish military spy and whose mother is a tobacco-addicted media photographer.

If Kamal and I were still in love, your letter would have bothered me much less. But, instead of being a couple in love, we are now a couple in trouble. We can no longer avoid each other nor can we have peace and joy together. Our child rattles like a chain between our necks, a chain that tethers our lives but not our souls.

Kamal calls, of course, and pretends to care, but his calls sound like sighs. He asks how I'm doing and then asks about Little John. I ask him how he is doing and then I ask about his wife and two children. We both say the right things but are most careful not to speak a word more than necessary lest we plunge the conversation into deeper shades of discomfort. He asks me if I need money and I, being proud and fiercely independent, say no. He does not insist on doing his share, like a man should, which diminishes his worth in my eyes. While Little John grows bigger with time, Kamal seems to grow smaller. I am not even hopeful that he will return to visit Little John again.

Last week, I had Tariq drive Little John and me to the shrine of Um Al-Huda. I prayed for a long time then we went to the house of Fatima. She met us with wide-open arms and welcomed Tariq and Little John as if she already knew them. She then took Little John into her arms, looked into his eyes for the longest time and said: *"You will have two mothers and two fathers."* Then tears took away her smile as she handed him back to me saying: *"Keep him as long as you can; I'll be here when you need me."*

At that very moment—as if by deliberate synchronicity—her son, Kamal, and her husband, Al Hajj Tariq, both came in for lunch. Of course, they insisted that we join them, and after some polite resistance, we broke bread together. On the way back, Tariq asked so many questions that I could not answer. He was not amused that we have similar names (Fatima, Tariq, Kamal) and called Fatima a witch. When I inquired if he meant that she was a bitch, he said: *"No, Fatima is a witch, and her son Kamal is a devil, and her husband Al Hajj Tariq is a religious fool."*

I have never understood why he formed such antagonistic emotions against this family who has been so kind to me and whom he had just met. Something has gone awry in his mind; he seems angry with me and more taciturn than usual. He did tell me, however, that he had written to you about my stroke and that you had written him back. When I asked him to share your letter with me, he said that I was a spy, like Kamal, and refused to talk to me for several days. My heart is too full of anguish, John, and I do not know what to do with this rebellious stripling.

Perhaps a letter from you would help calm him down?

For reasons that I cannot understand, I always seem to write to you at the end of each year. This year almost brought my end with the birth of Little John and my little stroke. I had to relearn to speak, to write, and, most importantly, I had to struggle in order to become independent again. My mother who has been living with me since I left the hospital babies me like a child, which drives me crazy.

I plan to begin work this coming January, and I have no other reliable babysitter except her. It is too cold to transport Little John between our homes, which means that she will have to stay with me for another long while. In the meantime, I have no privacy in my own house and the situation is getting more and more awkward for my friends. I have to admit that the idea of letting Fatima keep Little John, while I try to get my health and work back in order, nags constantly at my mind. It is a good way to get my mother out of my hair, but I do not think that I can live without Little John. Whenever I leave him with mother to go out a while, I return famished for him. At middle age, this new motherhood has become my *raison d'etre.*

As for my health, I know that Tariq told you that I am still smoking. John, I cannot stop no matter how hard I try. Aside from Little John, cigarettes provide me with momentary relief and keep open the communications between Kamal and me. You see, Kamal calls me once a week to inquire about our Little John and about my health. Then, twice a month, he sends me a package in which I find a short perfunctory letter and two cartons of delicious Turkish cigarettes. His letters always end with the cautious words, *"Give my love and kisses to Little John."* We no longer profess to love each other, but I cannot allow the father of my son to gradually drift away. Any bond, any tradition, any form of regular communication gives me hope that if something should happen to me, Kamal would be there for Little John.

As for my stroke, it has left very little damage besides slowness. I can now do almost anything I could do before the stroke, but I do it slower, and my reflexes are not as crisp. It is taking me longer to write, to bathe, to dress, and to move. I continue to improve but at a slower pace than before. I have been driving a little, but only in Beirut, and only after traffic dies down. I will have to drive myself to work and back starting next week, and I am hoping that this will not prove dangerous. I do not need the challenge of another traumatic event.

Due to my precarious health, I have become acutely aware of my age, something I hardly noticed before the stroke. At forty-six, I find myself reading more poetry. One of the poems that touched my soul was the one you had written on aging when you were only thirty-five. How did you gain these wise insights at such a youthful age? Do all poets see beyond the mighty walls of time?

"But now the black retreats away
Defeated by advancing gray
That slowly drowns my youthful zeal
A sentence I cannot appeal
For youth was never meant to stay

So love me that I may not feel
The march of years upon my heel
That makes me slow and wise and weak
With failing eyes and bones that creak
And wounds that do not seem to heal."

Now, I have some interesting family news for you. It seems that everyone has taken to using Little John as the preferred nickname of my child. This way, when they gossip about you and me, they do not need to qualify. Indeed, they are convinced that the reason Kamal left me is because I named his son after you and because, after all this time, I am still in love with you. No one believes me when I say that it was Um Al-Huda who really chose his name for reasons that we cannot understand, for reasons that, perhaps, may have something to do with his future.

Another family news fragment has to do with Laila,

the wife of my brother Jamal. Tariq related to you how she behaved when she ran into Mary and Jamie at my home last September. Well, since that time, she has refused to let Jamal visit his boys unless he comes alone. She says that it is not fair to expose the boys to Jamal's Australian wife and child because it would confuse their emotions. Of course, Laila knows how much Mary and Jamie became attached to her boys during their visit to Kuwait last summer. Indeed, she witnessed first hand Ramzi and Imad's joy when they were surprised by their half sister at my home three months ago.

Anyway, not to bore you with more details, Jamal and his new family have come to Beirut this Christmas season so that Jamie will experience the marvelous lights and festivities that bedeck the city. They did have a small Catholic church in Kuwait, but it was sacked and destroyed by Saddam's troops. Mary is very religious and wants to raise Jamie as a Christian, which further annoys Laila and feeds her claim that this will add spiritual confusion to the boys' emotional state. Consequently, when Mary takes Jamie to Mass, Jamal goes up to Brummana to visit his boys, who still live at their grandparents' home.

Mixing religions within the same family requires that all parties keep an open mind, which is seldom the case. I hope that time will soften Laila's heart and that she will come to accept her new reality. I asked Um Al-Huda, when I visited her last week, to help me bring peace into Laila's heart. She will guide me when the time comes.

Beirut is alive again, bustling with new business. Hariri is investing a lot of money in rebuilding the downtown, which was totally destroyed by the Civil War. They are using the rubble from fallen and condemned buildings to claim more land from the sea, and they are renovating the salvageable buildings to their prewar beauty.

The excavations have yielded a lot of buried Roman ruins, which has caused problems. The archeologists have lobbied the historically minded and are asking for delays so that the buried treasures could be properly removed to the museum. The investors, on the other hand, are against delay because it increases cost and postpones revenues. From the way things are moving, it looks like the investors are going to have their way. And for similar reasons, they have also killed the idea of a Beirut subway because underneath our Beirut, several ancient Phoenician and Roman cities are buried, one on top of another, dating back to 5000 BC. These lost opportunities are being grieved by the entire archeological world.

This New Year's eve, I'm invited to a dance at the Bristol Hotel. The gentleman is a middle-aged widower whom I have known for a long time because he owns one of the largest bookstores in Beirut. He is quite charming, and Beirut is full of single women, which makes me wonder what he wants with me? I am a middle-aged woman who has a six-month-old child born out of wedlock. Moreover, I smoke, I have had a stroke, and in spite of my best efforts, my figure is no longer perfect.

He, on the other hand, is an athlete in perfect form and is much admired by women. I was so intrigued by his invitation that I accepted without hesitation. It cannot be about romance or sex because, for that, he has many better choices. I wonder if he wants me to create a picture catalogue for his bookstore?

Nevertheless, I did feel flattered by his invitation to the extent that I went shopping and bought a new dress for the occasion. It's a long black soiree with a gray fox collar. The lady helping me said that I looked dazzling in it, and I willingly believed her. My ego defenses must still be good because, otherwise, I would have fallen prey to Tariq's comments: *"Mom, get rid of this silly dress. Everyone knows that you are a peasant. You're not going to fool anyone by looking like a princess."* Instead of crying, I laughed and took his acrid remark as an adolescent compliment in the guise of an insult. What would become of us without our formidable ego defenses? Is it not easier to assume that the entire world is wrong than to accept our own errors?

I am sorry that your wife is doing so poorly. But, as you know, life must go on for you and for me. Please take care and beware.

I will let you know how the party went when I write again.

Love,

Fatima

Thirty-Four

(Homo barbarus)

(Oklahoma City - Sunday, 4 May, 1997)

Dear Fatima,

For a change, I awoke from sleep and found my spirits soaring aloft my realities. Surprised by my pleasant temperament, I decided to spend this Sunday morning writing to you. But, instead of seizing the moment, I read the paper and listened to the news—two things that I have an aversion to and staunchly abjure. This must have caused my blithe spirits to plummet from their lofty skies down to the murky realities of planet Earth.

Indeed, as I held my fountain pen, I realized that my native cheerfulness had slipped out of my fingers. I could no longer insist on joy, nor could I uphold the precept that few things are worth a tear and fewer still, a frown. Listen then to my extemporaneous pronouncements and my apocalyptic barrage. Though writing does lend credence to gossip, pray read but do not judge. Pray read me with pathos for I am about to birth my credo, in breech presentation, after a painful labor.

This world is seduced by myth and rocked by unexamined beliefs. Our spirits are sirened by mythos, not by logos. Reason is relegated to justify our sentimental inclines rather than free our shackled minds from enthralling atavisms. Conflicts condense into tugs of war between self-interested parties. We would rather die than risk a change in our traditional beliefs. Peace, the harmony between reason and soul, is undermined by tacit tensions between the north and south poles of human nature. Strummed by leading players, humanity is a grand guitar that resonates with dissonance. Forgive me Fatima, but I do not think that the *Homo sapiens'* guitar will make lasting music.

This pervasive pessimism of mine has been reaffirmed after reading reports about Rwanda and South Africa, Tutsis and Hutus, apartheid and antiapartheid, etc... etc... Mass pleasure killings no longer satisfy our famished anger; torturing victims then burying them alive seems to have become the *modus operandi* that best surfeits our vengeful appetites. The nomenclature of our species, *sapiens*, is a misnomer. We are not wise; we are not *Homo sapiens*. We are cruel barbarians; we are *Homo barbarus*.

Indeed, even though there are other natural creatures that are deliberately cruel, as far as we are concerned, cruelty is our thumbprint, our signature, and our legacy. I am even ashamed to tell you why we are a cruel race. We are cruel because, in order to survive, we were specifically wired for that end, evolved that way, and got much better at it with time. In a group, cruelty is the quickest way to achieve order, and when that was necessary for group survival, it was the natural thing to do. But now, in our present world, when we have witnessed the short-lived effects and backlashes of cruelty, those who still resort to it, which includes most of us, must suffer from poverty of insight. They cannot contemplate an alternate solution to crises nor can they await the healing wisdom of patient time, and hence they regress to their fundamental animal instincts. Cruelty is animalism at its basest level. A civilized individual should resist the urge to be cruel, but nations are another story. All nations are cruel regardless of their level of enlightenment, and everything military is based on cruelty. Indeed, military glory is nothing but a euphemism for cruelty. As Nietzsche said in *Beyond Good and Evil, "Almost everything we call higher culture is based on the spiritualization of cruelty, on its becoming more profound. In all desire to know, there is a drop of cruelty."*

I fume with shame, and my fumes contaminate your already polluted atmosphere. I should have chosen a less distasteful entrée, my dear; do excuse me if I have spoiled your appetite.

But, on the other hand, there is progress in England, which after seventeen years of Conservative rule has elected Labor's Tony Blair who is willing to talk to the IRA. Moreover, Israel's Netanyahu has transferred 80% of Hebron to the Palestinian Authority under Yassir Arafat. These traditional enemies have finally learned the proverbial historical lesson that violence spawns violence and that the embryos of violence can only hatch by cracking the shells of peace. Enough, enough of this gloomy political discourse; I have said too much, and now I turn to you.

Your last letter brought me warm feelings. Having vanquished your stroke, I saw you back on life's map, reclaiming your lost territories. You spoke of returning to work, of going to a dance, of Little John, of Kamal, and of Tariq. Indeed, you spoke with such refreshing alacrity, which convinced me that you are well—ready to mount the saddle of life and gallop into the future.

I was a bit dismayed, however, at your blind but truthful assessment of Mrs. Settembrini. In fact, your veracious perception startled my unconscious mind. After twenty years apart, you still know me better than I care to know myself. I am, as you said, ever ready for romance, ever needy of love. Even if I could change these frailties of mine, I would choose not to. I like my vulnerable romanticism because it is my veritable identity. I am a romantic fool, Fatima; I specialize in love, and I do not discriminate. I love all who will let me love them and even those who won't. Love is my nocturnal aroma, my seasonal flowering, and my *raison d'être.*

As you have surmised, Mrs. Settembrini and I have become friends, but our friendship has not extended beyond the Poetry Group. I do admit, however, that when I walk her to her car after our monthly meetings, the night air seems to titillate the sky and excite the stars into sparkling gossip. We have never touched, of course, but we have commiserated in iambic meter about our wounded marriages.

I find her interesting not only because of her poignant poetry but also because she has some peculiar fascinations that intrigue me. For example, she has a strong fascination for heights and knows all there is to know about the highest skyscrapers and mountains all over the world. However, in spite of this fascination, she is afraid of heights to the point of phobia and has never ridden in an elevator. Perhaps it is her strangeness that particularly attracted me. Or perhaps because everything strange is new but not everything new is strange, I tend to find her newness doubly inspiring?

I read this poem *(Were She Aware)* at our last gathering, and it was met with much interest, especially from her. I did not tell her so, but her fascination with heights was what gave me the inspiration to transform certain dry facts into aesthetic concepts:

"How tall, she stands
Among the morning hymns
All hat, whispering colors;

Her hands like veils
So delicately veined
With nails, too sharp for lovers;

Aback, I step
Beauty must have its distance
Nothing too near is perfect.

Were she aware
How beautiful she is
It wouldn't be sad;

Were she aware
Without my eyes to see
My heart to skip and gasp,

My soul to shout:
How beautiful you are
What pretty hat you wear;

Were she aware
That if I weren't there
She'd only be a rose."

Do not worry, I will not make the same mistake twice, Fatima. You remember the story of my pale, nameless butterfly and how tragically it ended. I still have not recovered from the guilt of having contributed to the suicide of one of my own patients. Falling in love with a married woman was an insensate sin that I could have averted had I wished. But I was too hungry to resist such an overpowering urge. I was too alone with a fading-away wife to resist the numinous society of love. I could see agonizing regret looming behind the sunset, but it did not deter me from drowning into her arms.

I will not make the same mistake twice, even though I desperately want to. I am a sailor in mid- ocean, at high noon, without water, without wind, holding a cup of sea in my parched hands, delirious with thirst but having just enough awareness to know not to drink.

No, I will not make the same mistake twice; instead, I will write longing poems that tell the ancient stories of humanity, stories that repeat like seasons, stories about all the men and women who were vouchsafed a morsel of time ephemeral but were forbidden to love.

I will not ask, *"why me?"* Life gives no answers so why bother to ask. Instead, I shall kiss fate with lips of gratitude:

"Come now into my quivering lips
Into my archaic cave of passions and poems
You will see throbbing on the walls, your
*   name*
Inscribed with tedious care to suffer centuries
To tell our phoenix tale afresh, anew
A timeless epic that regenerates
And dares declare that life is naught but love
That all that seems important might be trivial
And all that seems trivial might be important

And that we live our lives in the reverse, from
young to wise
And make mistakes to suffer pain
The livid pain of love
Love unattained."

I write longing poems to fill my limbic void with affective echoes. My poor Norma, the wife whom I could not love enough, my wife of twenty-six years, no longer recognizes me, or our three children. Her post-traumatic, organic dementia has progressed to the degree that she can no longer take care of herself; even her bodily functions have escaped control. Keeping her at home, in spite of excellent day help, has become a dreaded burden for the children and me. We have even discussed the possibility of a nursing home, but we continue to procrastinate and refuse to make the agonizing decision. We are prisoners of frothy waters, struggling between the banks of guilt and the shores of exhaustion, relentlessly flowing down delirious currents toward a tenebrous sea.

Ghassan called last week and informed us that they would not be coming home this July because Tamara is in her terrible twos and Carla is having trouble controlling her. Nadir wants to spend his junior year abroad and has already been accepted at the American University of Beirut this coming September. This is possible now because the U.S. has resolved to lift its ban on travel to Lebanon by the end of July, a ban which had been in effect for U.S. nationals since 1985. Frida, who is now fifteen, is talking about going to an out-of-state college. Indeed, all my three children are tacitly trying to escape our painful home reality, and I have not discouraged them from so doing. The kind of emotional shredding that they have had to endure, unless tempered by distance, will scar their transparent souls worse than physical torture.

Soon, you and Tariq will meet my Nadir. Before he leaves, I will tell him that you and I were college lovers and have kept in touch through the years. Yes, I would rather be the first to tell him of our romantic saga. You must have surmised by now that Tariq has read many of my letters to you, and if he does not tell Nadir, other well-meaning friends, when they find out who Nadir's father is, would delight in telling him our story. Indeed, fate has again surprised us and coincidence has reaffirmed that secrets wash back upon life's shores no matter how deeply they are buried.

Again, bear with me Fatima, but I cannot seem to get the news out of my mind. I feel compelled to reveal my thoughts and feelings even at the risk of overburdening you—you, who for twenty years have watched the beautiful face of Beirut become poxed with bombs while Oklahoma City groomed its unsuspecting cheeks. On our national news front, the question, *"Should Timothy McVeigh die for his role in the Oklahoma City bombing?"* went before the jury in Denver, Colorado. Judge Matsch told the jury: *"You are the conscience of the community, and the decision you make here must be a moral judgment, not a decision that will be reliant on emotion."*

Then prosecutor Patrick Ryan, who is the U.S. attorney in Oklahoma City, addressed the jury by saying: *"You know, we are obligated to present some information here to you about the people who are the victims and survivors of this crime. It's going to be difficult for us to present, and it's going to be painful for you to hear, but you have a duty to hear it and to make a decision."* He then explained that of the 168 deaths, there were nineteen children, none of whom was over six years old. By the time Patrick Ryan finished his opening statement, half the jurors were sobbing. And although Judge Matsch did ask the jurors not to make an emotional decision, emotion cannot be denied access to court.

"Quiet pain is harsh
I heard the dusty dead whisper
Trapped in layers of suddenness
Not even one could stir.

Little feet couldn't run
Mother's hands couldn't hold;
When the deep noise drowned
Death surfaced high."

Indeed, if we were to judge only with our reason, we would not even have a trial. We would simply conclude that McVeigh is a dangerous, mentally deranged man with impaired judgment, and we would relegate him to the mental institutions for life. In fact, Timothy McVeigh is not the one on trial; rather it is our collective emotional pain that went on trial in order to vote for its own catharsis through the verdicts of punishment. Human societies, which have always been infested with the mentally dangerous, will forever be vulnerable to the macabre devastation of warped minds.

This was not a cheerful letter, Fatima, and you know how much that goes against my personal ethos. I would rather spend my creative energy finding cheerful meanings in life's tragedies. I want to be able to find joy beneath sadness, beauty within ugliness, gentleness underneath violence, reason beyond madness, and peace behind war. I want to insist on joy by viewing life as the ephemeral gift of awareness before we are recycled back to atoms. I want the bad to be as normal as the good, equally expected, equally deserved, and equally revered. I want to venerate life with gratitude because that is the only attitude worthy of wisdom, worthy of *Homo sapiens*. If joy were everyone's calling, it would leave little room for pain.

In that regard, my mother is looking with joy to Nadir's year at the AUB. He has already written to her and promised to visit her often while he is in Lebanon. Unlike his father, he is a homebody who does not like to stray away from family and friends. I plan to introduce him to Tariq at the same time that I tell him about you and me. He is a spirited stripling, cheerful in affect, altruistic in intellect, with a deep concern for humanity that propels him toward becoming a *citizen of the world*. He dreams of peace and of prosperity on earth and longs to devote his life to these ideals. He is too young to see that such goals are unattainable, not even in dreams. Indeed, he wants to brighten up the dark side of the moon because it is unjust that the other side gets all the sun.

We have discussed numerous issues, he and I. We have discussed global, moral, humanitarian, historical, and philosophical issues, but we have never discussed personal issues. He is more interested in global inequities than in sexy women, which is preposterous at his age and a bit disconcerting. On weekends, instead of going out on dates, he volunteers at nursing homes as a reader for the blind. He intends to join the Peace Corps upon graduation and hopes to be stationed in Africa. His *joie de vivre* is contagious and his philanthropy is genuine. His favorite quote is from Nietzsche: *"Love of one is a barbarism; for it is exercised at the expense of all others. Love of God too."*

As far as my dear mother is concerned, I am forever in trouble because I refuse to visit her in Lebanon. Every year, ever since my father's death, I have sent her an open airline ticket to come visit us. She always returns the ticket and answers my plea with these words, *"I am too old to travel to America. Instead of subjecting me to this hardship, it would be much simpler if you would use the ticket to come and visit me."* In vein, I have tried to argue that by coming to America, she would be able to share our life as we live it, see our home which she has never seen, interact with the children as a live-in grandmother, and experience the American culture first hand. These arguments, as rational as they sound, do not seem to move her at all. She is intransigent in her position and the older she gets, the firmer she clings to her old-world notions.

The reason I am relating all this to you now is because of Nadir who, come summer, will be traveling back to us and would be delighted to bring my mother back with him. Of course, if she will let him, he can make her trip so much easier, and I have already asked him to try to convince her to come along.

What I need from you is to support Nadir in his efforts and help him break her deadlock, which is entirely a state mind. Semitic mothers, old world mothers, and Jewish mothers all behave in a stereotyped way. They are accomplished in the art of reproaching and use guilt as an effective tool to gain their ends. Moreover, they insist on wearing the mask of grief as their persona and seem more comfortable with melancholy than with joy. They even resist laughter, act as though a smile would belie their true identity, and cover their faces with their hands if they should succumb to humor. Because they seem more comfortable with this morose, self-inflicted state of mind, it might be wrong or unwise to try to force a change upon them. Therefore, please try to help Nadir understand this concept so that he will not be contaminated by his grandmother's grief. I could not possibly tell him what I have just told you because it would sound uncouth coming from me.

With our boys together at the AUB, we stand to learn a lot more about life this year. Please stop smoking, take good care of yourself, and, now that you are well, keep your eyes on the boys.

With love,

John

Thirty-Five

(Children)

(Beirut – Friday, 5 September, 1997)

Dear John,

You must be anxious to hear our news, and I have much to tell you. First, let me talk about myself because I know that you and Nadir are in touch by phone and e-mail—means of communication you have denied me—and that he has told you all about his trip and welcoming parties.

In brief, your eighty-one-year-old mother met Nadir at the airport and insisted on taking him in her own car to the AUB dormitory. Tariq and I followed them, made sure that he was settled, and then took him out to dinner at a nearby restaurant. We invited your mother, but because it was getting late, she declined and had her driver take her back to Tripoli.

Nadir and Tariq hit it off immediately and Tariq has already introduced Nadir to many of his friends. Nadir's plane was four hours late because Heathrow Airport was in a state of chaos last Sunday morning due to Princess Diana's death, which had occurred a few hours earlier and sent shock waves that caused multiple delays. Even in Beirut, the grief was unanimous and sincere. She was every woman's heroine and every man's Helen.

My work is getting busier by the day, and my health has improved enough to meet the new demands put upon me. Little John is beautiful, but I see him only on weekends. The idea that my mother should stay with me and take care of him did not work out. She got on my nerves with her constant nagging until I could not stand it any longer. On Saturday, 7 June, I took him to Um

Al-Huda's shrine where I prayed and prayed until I could hear her voice whisper to my heart: *"Take him to Fatima; she will take good care of him for you."*

I obeyed and went to Fatima's door. I did not have to knock; she opened when she heard my footsteps and, as if she had been waiting for me, did not act at all surprised. When she opened her arms, Little John went to her with a warm smile. Her first words were to him, not to me; she held him close to her chest and whispered in his ear, *"Happy Birthday, Little John. Welcome home."*

I almost suffocated with astonishment. How did she know that I was coming to leave my son with her on his first birthday? John, God has a plan for us, prewritten long before we were ever born. Um Al-Huda is my guardian angel, and because of her I have lost all my fears. Why worry; whatever will be, will be.

At Fatima's home we had tea and talked about children and fathers. She showed me where Little John would sleep; she had a crib ready next to her bed with a blue bead hanging over his pillow to protect him from the evil eye. She must have known ahead of time that I would be bringing Little John to her and was prepared for me when I showed up. Before I left, she told me that someday Little John would move to Turkey to live with his sister. That pronouncement frightened me to no end because it could mean so many different things; nevertheless, I did not ask her to explain because I knew that she couldn't. Just like an oracle, she says things as they come to her, even though she may not be able to explain them.

I know what you are thinking, John; I can even see your smirk as you read my letter. You are a man of science, and I am a woman of faith. You have your logos, and I have my mythos. How does your logos help you deal with your wife's dementia? You should try some of my mythos for a change. You might find that blind faith would dilute your suffering as it has mine.

Remember when you used to tell me that imagination is far more hopeful than reality. Well, ever since Kamal dumped me after finding out that I was pregnant with his child, I have resorted to Imagination as my savior. You have no idea what I am capable of imagining, especially about you and me. As for Mrs. Settembrini, both Fatima and I agree that she will, through her efforts to win you, lead you back to me. Yes, Fatima knows all about you; she even knows things that I have never told her. This woman can see through time and space with the eyes of a prophet. She has given me hope about us, hope I had lost *"with my lost saints."* Do not act shocked; Elizabeth Browning has already forgiven me for plagiarizing her expression.

Kamal has stopped calling me to inquire about Little John and no longer sends me delicious Turkish cigarettes. He lives with his wife and two children at their home in Istanbul and considers Little John and me to be impertinent intruders upon his life. His last package of cigarettes arrived in early June with a $100 note, Little John's birthday gift, and a recent picture of Kamal in military uniform. On the back of the picture was an inscription, handwritten in Turkish, which when I had it translated read: *"Happy Birthday, son. I am sad that our lives have been separated by fate and that I shall not be able to enjoy watching you grow up. Always remember, even though we may never meet, that I love you and know in my heart that you will have a wonderful future."*

With the picture was an apologetic note asking me not to contact him again because Gulnar was getting jealous of his attention to us ever since he told her about Little John. At the bottom of the note, as an afterthought, he added that if I ever needed to contact him, I could mail my letters to a certain Mr. Ahmet Arslan, Ticarethane Sokak 19, Sultanahmet Istanbul 34420.

To me this sounded like the last good-bye, and I do think that the real reason he gave me this secret address was because he wanted me to continue to send him pictures of Little John, which in the past I had sent to his work. I expect no help from this man; he has gone back to his life, and I have reclaimed mine. But what shall I tell Little John when he comes of age? Like you told Nadir about us, I want to be the first to tell him before some officious fool blurts it out to his unsuspecting face.

Fatima has already told me that Kamal would take

care of Little John if Little John should need his help. I did not dare ask her what she meant by that portentous assertion. She says many things that I cannot understand but things that, somehow, make sense to my inner being. I can see you smile as you read this, but do not lose sight of the fact that I can see through my faith truths that are opaque to your mind.

My entire family thinks that I have gone mad because I have placed my child in the custody of a strange woman that I barely know. My mother feels personally offended because I chose Fatima over her. But Um Al-Huda was the one who sent me to Fatima, and Little John loves her and is doing much better with her than he ever did with my mother. I go with my heart, John, with my faith, with my spiritual dimension. Reason is too primitive to aid me in my quest for God's will.

Jamal and Mary are still in Kuwait and doing very well. In May they celebrated Jamie's fourth birthday. Laila still does not allow Mary or Jamie into her Brummana home and refuses to let her boys see their half sister that they are crazy about. She will not even let them go to Kuwait to see their father and his new family. When Jamal comes to Beirut, he has to leave Mary and Jamie with me and go up to Brummana alone in order to see Imad and Ramzi, now fifteen and twelve. This curfew cannot last much longer because the children are becoming more assertive with age. Time has failed to pickle Laila's hate; it is still as bitter as fresh, green olives. Fatima says that *"Laila's hate is Laila's punishment,"* another portentous assertion that I did not dare question.

As for Mr. Shukri Baroudi, the bookstore owner who invited me to the New Year's dance at the Bristol Hotel, my intuitions proved correct. Unlike most men, he was not after my body or my company; he was after my abilities. A most charming man, he lavished me with attention all through the dance. Many women approached him with wry, knowing eyes and made contact with us just to scrutinize and taunt me. Women do not play chess, you know; they make their instinctive moves without considering their opponent's response. Of course, the more they eyed me, the more adoringly I gazed into Baroudi's eyes. They must have been women whom he had slept with along his way to other conquests. I wanted to tell them that I am not sleeping with him, but they would not have believed me; he has a reputation, if you know what I mean.

When the dance was over, and the New Year was a few hours old, he took me home in his Jaguar, walked me to my door on the third floor, kissed my hand and asked if he could meet with me at his office to discuss a business matter. Of course, for a woman who has not been kissed for over a year, I felt a bit rejected. Not that I wanted sex with him, although the idea did cross my mind, but rather I wanted to be the one to say no to the anticipated move, the move which he did not make.   Indeed, it insulted my feminine sense of worth to be sought after for my photographic abilities rather than for my sex appeal. Don't be shocked, John; most women think exactly like me, especially when they get close to fifty. That night, as late as it already was, I could not sleep. My mother and Little John slept soundly while I chain smoked one cigarette after the other and managed to look back at my life as a chain of one rejection after another. All of a sudden, I started to laugh at the obvious parody; I am a chain smoker who cannot break the habit and my life is a chain of rejections, which I cannot break. All this because a rich and charming man was more interested in my mind than in my body. Oh, how the scent of fifty in my nostrils nauseates me. I need a good man before I turn, someone who could break my unlucky chain.

When Mr. Baroudi and I met at his office, he showed me a copy of the book, which I had produced for Al Emir Fadil of Saudi Arabia in 1993. The book was about his collection of ancient swords, with each sword photographed and its story chronicled. He had received his copy as a gift from the Emir during a book fair about the pre-Islamic (aljahiliah) Arabs, which was held in Jeddah in 1994. It was obvious to me that he liked the book, which made me think that perhaps he wanted me to help him with a similar project. However, he seemed over-cautious when he asked me if I would be interested in doing something similar for him. I read his caution, and knowing that he himself was not a sword collector, I answered with a favorite phrase of yours, *"It depends."*

He then showed me pictures of children—children emaciated, gaunt, and malnourished—children in streets, in hospitals, in shrouds, in graves, and curled in their mother's laps. Each photograph came with a story; this child died of typhoid fever because antibiotics could not be found; this one died of diarrhea because intravenous fluids were not available; this one of appendicitis because the operating room had run out of anesthetics; and this one bled to death because the blood bank ran out of intravenous tubes and blood sacks. There were lots of pictures and lots of stories, every story a heartbreaker that brought me closer to tears.

Finally, when I could no longer stand it because, for some unholy reason, several of the dead children resembled my Little John, I closed the folder and asked with a moist quivering voice: *"Where the hell is this taking place."* He pointed to the title of the folder, which I presumed would be the working title of the book, *Consequences of the Iraq Embargo/Children Paying the Price.*

I froze with fear because I did not wish to be involved in political anti-Western propaganda. The message of the book was stark; the U.S. and its European allies were not punishing Saddam with their trade embargo, they were punishing the Iraqi children who were suffering and dying because of the lack of milk, food, and medicines. The reporter was an Iraqi journalist who managed to smuggle the folder to Mr. Baroudi just before he was arrested and tortured to death in a Baghdad jail. Apparently, using the pseudonym of Jaber Al-Kharasan, he had written an article for the Lebanese newspaper, *Al Nahar,* about the plight of the Iraqi children who were suffering from the lack of essential foods and medical supplies while Saddam lived lavishly in his palaces, oblivious to the needs of his people.

I told Mr. Baroudi that I needed time to consider the offer and went home in a very disturbed state of mind. If I produce the book, which is the right thing to do, I would become forever labeled as an anti-American political activist. This would not only limit my ability to obtain travel visas to the U.S., England, and France, it would also limit my ability to attract and produce pro-Western photography. I am an unwed mother with a child; I do not need to invite more problems into my life. But, I am also a mother whose heart cries out to all the suffering children on this planet. After a sleepless night, I went back to Mr. Baroudi and politely declined. He understood but was unable to conceal his disillusionment. We parted with a handshake, and I have not heard from him since. He will find someone to produce the book, if he pays enough; I am sure of it.

I am also certain that the book will have no impact on Western policies because it will not be allowed to reach the Western public, especially in America. As we all know, no one can censor the American media; however, the American media routinely censors unfavorable news especially when it pertains to unjust American foreign policies, Israeli cruelties, and futile military operations. Democracies, the best forms of government that history has cultivated, harbor many dictatorships within their city walls. Your Jesus said it best when he announced that the poor get poorer and the rich, richer. Such are the inbred traits of *Homo sapiens*, our human race that you renamed *Homo barbarus* in your last letter.

Don't get me wrong, John. I have no anti- American sentiments; I am merely stating that the collective behavior of human beings, under similar circumstances, is remarkably similar and predictable. There are no superior or chosen races. Just like William Wordsworth stated that *"the child is father of the man,"* so do I state that nations are the children of their circumstances.

On the news today, Hamas masterminded a triple suicide bombing against Israel, killing seven and wounding 172. Netanyahu blamed Arafat for not controlling the Palestinians. Contrary to what you said, these traditional enemies have not yet learned the proverbial historical lesson that violence breeds violence. What a slow-learning world we live in! *"Love your enemies,"* said your Jesus.

"Love each other or perish," said your Auden. It must be easier to hate than to love, to fight than to love, and to die than to love; otherwise, why do we continue to perish?

John, think of me when you are alone. Think of the way we were when you need uplifting memories. Try not to get involved any deeper with Mrs. Settembrini; remember that she is married and I am single. Do you know what Fatima said to me when I read her your last letter? She said, *"Women who fear heights are deadliest when they are closest to the heights they most fear."* I have no idea what she meant by this arcane, abstruse pronouncement, and of course, I was afraid to ask. Please, John, be careful and try to avoid unnecessary heights.

Perhaps, one day when you are free, you will come to visit us or I will come to visit you. Perhaps love is immortal and never really dies. Perhaps there are coals still glowing underneath our ashes. Perhaps what Fatima told me will come true. She told me, when I entrusted Little John into her care, that my two Johns will be united one day. I, being a Muslimah, believe in fate, believe that it has been predestined that you and I will be reunited.

Of course, you think that I am silly. For now, think what you wish and believe what your logical reason sanctions. But, in the meanwhile, do keep your hands off Mrs. Settembrini and I will, in my turn, keep my eyes upon our two college boys.

Please write soon. Write when you feel alone. Write when you feel afraid. Write when you are delirious with thirst. Write anytime you need anything; I am always waiting.

Love,

Fatima

Thirty-Six

(American University Of Beirut)

(Beirut – Tuesday, 28 October, 1997)

Dear Dad,

I can't wait to tell you about my exciting new life at the AUB. I'm studying very hard but still find time to enjoy myself, and I think that Beirut—in spite of its swarming crowds, chaotic traffic, and tooting cars—is cool. Every day brings its peculiar surprises, and there is no day that hasn't surprised me yet. For example, late yesterday a bomb was thrown inside the AUB campus, breaking windows and causing a wall to collapse. I was studying in my room when I heard the explosion. The whole dorm became excited, and many of us ran to the site. The damage was slight, and no one got hurt. The bomb must've been small compared to the one that brought down College Hall a few years ago.

What shocked me the most was the calm with which student life continued. We all returned to our dorms and were back in class the next morning as if nothing had happened. Violence doesn't seem to bother the life of the Lebanese anymore; they must've gotten used to it. Did you know that during the Civil War the AUB president, Malcolm Kerr, was assassinated and still the AUB kept its doors open? Ten days ago, we saw and heard the Israeli warplanes bombard Palestinian positions in the south of Beirut, but life still went on as usual. You should change your mind, Dad, and come visit Grandma. The war is over, and it is no longer as dangerous as you think—just a few bombs here and there that don't seem to have an impact on daily life.

You should see how the Hariri government is renovating downtown Beirut after it was totally destroyed by the war. They are dumping the rubble into the sea to create more land and salvaging the old buildings to preserve the traditional character of the area. I will send you some pictures that will surprise you and perhaps entice you to visit some day.

I visited the site with Tariq and found it awesome. There were vendors all around selling Roman coins that were unearthed with the rubble. When I tried to buy a coin from one of the vendors, Tariq pulled me aside saying that they're all fake. The vendor heard him and swore that he had dug them out of the rubble with his own bare hands. But when Tariq explained to him that I was a student, not a tourist, the vendor changed his tone and complained that it was getting harder to make a living and that there was no work to be found. I bought the coin anyway, and the vendor blessed me. He said, *"May God grant you what your heart desires because you believe the poor even when others think that they are lying."* Tariq wanted me to show the coin to a friend of his who works at the AUB Museum. I refused because I didn't want to risk finding out that this poor old man was, indeed, lying.

Last weekend I visited Grandma at her home in Tripoli. She was so happy to see me and, in the same breath, griped to me about you because you won't come to visit her. *"Does he think that I will live forever? I am already 81 and may not have too many tomorrows left. Tell your American father that the Civil War is over and that, today, Beirut is safer than New York City."* She's happy that you call her once a week but would like you to write more often. *"Letters have staying power, and I can read and re-read them as often as I wish, while telephone voices begin to fade as soon as they are heard."* These were her exact words as we sat for lunch and ate fresh fried fish with homemade hummos-bi-tihini. We went together to the fresh fish market in Mina and bought a kilogram of small, red fish called Sultan Ibraheem. Grandmother said that this was the best-tasting Mediterranean fish and the one you liked the best when you were growing up.

The fruits here are not always as perfect in appearance as they are in the U.S., but they do have stronger aromas and are far more delicious. After lunch, unlike us, the Lebanese eat fruits instead of desserts. But what use is this healthy Mediterranean diet; everyone smokes and they smoke everywhere, even in class. I've developed a cough because of all the second-hand smoke I'm inhaling. I admire Tariq for not picking up the habit even though his mother chain-smokes and coughs constantly.

Our teachers are excellent, and many of them are American. Our social life is too busy, thanks to Tariq who has introduced me to all his friends. We spend a lot of our free time together. He is such a funny guy, and many think that we're brothers. Indeed, some even say that we look alike. Fatima has us for lunch at least once a week. She is such a good cook and cooks things I have never heard of, green slimy things like Mulukhiyeh, which look bad but taste good.

One day, Tariq asked me if I was interested in girls? I said that I was but not now while I am trying to get settled in a new country. Girlfriends require a lot of time, I said, time that I'd rather devote to other activities. He laughed and said that perhaps American girlfriends require a lot more time than Lebanese girls. He then introduced me to the sister of his boyfriend, a pretty girl named Suha. We all had lunch together and took a long walk along the Corniche. She is pretty enough but isn't at all interested in humanitarian issues. She said that she grew up during the war and saw too much suffering for too many years. This has caused her to want to spend the rest of her life as far away from suffering as possible.

I told her that I understood her way of thinking but didn't agree with it. She seemed surprised by my answer and became rather quiet. I tried to explain that, to my mind, those who have suffered should become more sympathetic to the suffering of others. She seemed offended by my explanation and retorted by saying that, obviously, I had not suffered enough for me to think the way I did. We walked in silence the rest of the way while Tariq and Sami continued to laugh and carry on ahead of us, totally unaware of our stalemate.

Later on that night, I thought a lot about what

Suha had said and realized that, indeed, I've not suffered enough. Unlike the old developing world, we do have peace and prosperity in America and abundant opportunities for those who are willing to work hard. However, I still disagreed with her assumption because, as the Bible teaches us, suffering should purify our souls instead of make them more selfish.

Dad, did you know that they don't have nursing homes in Beirut? When I told Tariq that I liked to volunteer at nursing homes and read for the blind, he laughed and said that I'd have to go back to the States for that. With a few exceptions, most families take care of their own elderly at home, which is most kind, just like you take care of Mom at home.

I hate to ask, but how's Mom doing? Sometimes, I feel guilty for having chosen a university so far away from home, but being far away makes me feel free, and this I like. I miss you and my brother and sister, and I miss Mom in spite of the fact that she no longer recognizes me. I miss the mom she used to be, the mom who brought us up and was always happy to see us when we came home from school. Sometimes, when I'm alone in my room, I look at her picture and cry. I want to do something to help her, but I know deep in my heart that Mom has already left us and that there's nothing anyone can do to bring her back.

While in the U.S., whenever I would read for the blind in nursing homes, I would feel that I was helping Mom. That's why I'd like to do something similar in Beirut, but I haven't found my niche yet. Tariq tells me that there are several blind students who take classes at the AUB and that they'd be delighted if they could find someone to read to them. Yesterday, I went to the AUB library and volunteered as a reader for the blind. The librarian thanked me and said that they would contact me when the time comes. She further explained that blind Lebanese students usually have plenty of support from family and friends whereas the blind international students are the ones who need a lot of help when they first arrive. She also said that my services might not be needed till the next semester when the new batch of students come in. I was a bit disappointed, but I'm sure that my disappointment won't last long because, in the meantime, I plan to make myself useful in other ways.

In our goings and comings by car, I've had to get used to roadblocks and checkpoints by the peacekeeping Syrian military forces. There are standards and etiquettes that are necessary for a smooth passing. The driver must lower his window and salute the guard with a friendly phrase. The guard then visually inspects the passengers and, if none of them arouses his suspicion, motions for the driver to pass. If the driver doesn't lower his window, it's a sign of disrespect, which might infuriate the guard who could use it as an excuse to search the car and detain the passengers.

One time, while Tariq and I were passing a checkpoint in Fatima's car, the guard noticed my OU sweatshirt, pointed to me, and asked my name. As soon as I spoke, he could tell from my accent that I wasn't a native. This aroused his curiosity even more, and he asked if I was American. I answered in broken Arabic that I was American but that my father was born and raised in Lebanon. He paused awhile and then with a smirk asked if my father was Armenian? His remark caused Fatima and Tariq to burst into laughter. The guard grinned and playfully waved us on.

When I asked Fatima and Tariq what was so funny, they explained that Lebanon has a large population of naturalized Armenians who fled from the Turks during the First World War to escape internecine conflicts. Apparently, even second and third generation Armenian Lebanese still prefer their own language and don't take Arabic seriously. Consequently, they speak broken Arabic with distinct Armenian inflictions. Regrettably, I must've sounded Armenian when I spoke Arabic with my American accent.

Of course, you know all about Armenians because you grew up among them and half the AUB nurses were Armenian when you were in medical school. I don't know why I am trying to tell you things you already know?

Perhaps it's because I've only known you as an American that I tend to forget that you are also Lebanese. Anyway, because of this incident, I've resolved to learn proper Arabic and have made plans to take beginner's classes with other foreign students. I'm going to speak Arabic with all my Lebanese friends in spite of their snickers. I promise that I'll not sound like an Armenian very long. Who knows, one day I might be able to write you a letter in Arabic. I may even decide to stay and work in Lebanon until I acquire the language. You wouldn't mind if I graduate from your Alma Mater, would you?

Dad, please don't take me seriously. As you know, I tend to change my mind with the seasons. Still, it has felt good to share my thoughts with you, especially since you've always encouraged us to plan our own lives without help from well meaning, significant others. Well, Dad, I'm planning my own life, and my plan is to go to wherever I am most needed. I have no idea where I'll end up, but I know that I'll spend my life wherever I can make a difference in the service of humanity.

Please take care of yourself and give my love to Frida, Ghassan, Carla, and Tamara. Kiss Mom for me and whisper in her ear that I miss her, that I pray for her everyday, and that I keep her picture next to my bed. I'll write again when I get some free time. Goodnight for now; I have an early class tomorrow and lots of homework *"and miles to go before I sleep."* I thought you'd like this Frost finale because I remember that this particular poem is one of your favorites.

Oh, I almost forgot something really important. I wrote a limerick about the noisy car jams and the crowds of people that swarm Beirut. Tariq memorized it and recited it to all his friends. I know that you'd appreciate reading it and sharing it with my sister and brother. I also know that I've taken liberties with the format and that you might object to my calling it a limerick. Well, call it a little rhyme if you wish; it doesn't really matter. It's my first overseas poem, and here's how it goes:

"Cars and smokers in Beirut
From opposing ends pollute
Unlike people, you will find
Vehicles smoke from behind
And from their front ends they toot."

I love you dad,

Nadir

Thirty-Seven

(Confessions)

(Oklahoma City – Sunday, December 28, 1997)

Dear Fatima,

This time, I am the one who is writing to you as the year prepares to shed its writhing tail. Christmas Eve died quietly in its sleep—a good death that we all wish for. Frida wanted to stay home, but I sent her away to a Santa party at one of her friends. I sat by Norma's bed while she gazed into her arcane void, unaware that the children were not home. I read to her from *One Hundred Love Sonnets* by Pablo Neruda. She listened with a smile when I read and became restless when I stopped. I read and read until she fell asleep, the smile still on her face.

Poetry must penetrate into Norma's trapped soul like a fervent prayer. How little we know about the crying echoes of dementia. What does a soul feel, buried beneath six feet of unawareness? Do smiles and frowns grow in the same soul garden or do they thrive in different climes? Does time grow in the garden of dementia?

I wish I knew how to unlock Norma's gaze to see what vistas she spies with her infinite eyes. Pablo Neruda said it for me in one of his *Hundred Love Sonnets*; let me paraphrase it out of memory:

> *"To love you, I need two loves;*
> *One to love you with when I don't love you*
> *One to love with you when I do."*

That is how I feel, Fatima. I feel like a famished tongue groping for a sweet taste, smacking between the fire of love and the ice of hunger, but never finding its warm cup of tea.

I no longer understand how I feel about my fading-away wife. I am in an emotional storm that blows cold on one cheek and hot on the other, rendering one side blue and the other red. I sweat in my flushes, and I shiver in my sweat. The whirlwind of destiny has confounded me, and I cannot find my way out of its tempest. I pray you then, be my priest, hear my confession, and hold my hand from behind the blind curtain; perhaps through confession I might find my way back to peace.

Fatima, when I left Lebanon in 1970, I left to run away, to run away from you. I loved you but could not marry you because I knew that we would set each other on fire because of our dissonant, social backgrounds and unforgiving, religious identities. Our love was not a peaceful love; it was a volcano stirring with lava. My passions for you overwhelmed my mind, spun it out of orbit, and rendered it vertiginous. To regain control, I had to strangle love in my throat before it choked me.

I said good-bye to your moist, incredulous eyes and disappeared into the New World hoping that the vast transatlantic distance I traversed would, in time, fade you out of my soul. It did not, Fatima, and you continued to colonize my thoughts with your omnipresence until I met Norma, who quietly displaced you.

I was so relieved at having regained my spiritual independence, so eager to maintain it, that I married her with absolute alacrity and reassured myself that, indeed, her beginning was your end. When, at the end of 1971, Norma and I toasted the New Year, I felt that marriage had redeemed my freedom and I was ready to love again, to love without dissonance, to love with abandon, and to live a life of love instead of a life of longing.

You remember how I refused to answer your letters, the letters you sent to the hospital so that they would not fall into Norma's hands. Year after year, your letters came and I hid them, unopened. I was afraid to open them and afraid to shred them so I locked them up, a symbolic gesture no doubt that Freud would have prompted me to interpret if I were lying on his Viennese couch: *"Do you think that locking her letters unopened would lock Fatima out of your heart, and that opening them would let her back in?"*

Our inscrutable *Homo sapiens'* unconscious mind wields a formidable force, Fatima. There is more philosophy in living language than in dead books. I kept your letters alive under lock-and-key, and each time I thought of them, I felt ashamed. I tried to love Norma. I tried to love her when she smiled like you, when she smelled like you, when she felt like you. I tried to love her when our firstborn said his first word and took his first step. I tried, but all I saw was you, and I think her heart knew it, but she never said a word. She was a most dedicated mother and wife whose face was always laced with a trace of melancholy, a tacit sadness that I could not erase.

One weekend, in the summer of 1976, I had the house to myself. I was studying for my boards, and Norma took the occasion to visit her parents in Tulsa. She said that her parents had not seen Ghassan for a while, which was her excuse for giving me space whenever she read tension in my face. As soon as they left, I felt a strong urge to do it. I unlocked your letters and read them all. I read and reread them until night overcame that burning day.

I could not study. I could not sleep. I did not eat. I sat outside my body and took pity upon my captive soul, which after six tenebrous years had set your letters free. That was when I called you and we agreed to have a clandestine reunion in Paris, away from our loving, unrequited spouses. On the way back from that December reunion, midair between Paris and Oklahoma, I resolved never to see you again. Ever since that time, I have been a tortured man, struggling against a love whose endless waves thrash incessantly upon my shore.

I was relieved when Kamal came along and, for a while, unburdened me. I needed you to love him, to marry him, to become entirely his, because that could have liberated me. My one-kiss affair with the pale butterfly, my tragic patient, was another attempt to escape love's enthrallment by transference to another. My present infatuation with Mrs. Settembrini provides me with a most tantalizing distraction.

I feel like Tantalus in Hades, standing in a pool of water up to my chin, beneath fruit-laden boughs, and each time I attempt to eat or drink, the fruits and water recede out of my reach. Tantalus, however, angered the Gods by divulging their secrets, stealing their nectar and ambrosia, and offering them his son, Pelops, boiled and sliced. That was why Zeus enfamished Tantalus, his ill-behaved son, with insatiable hunger and thirst before throwing him in Tartarus, the lowest region of Hades.

On the other hand, all I did was run away from you, from my violent old world, from my archaic life. I ran away to a peaceful New World that afforded me a fresh start. Can you imagine my implacable disillusionment when after a while, I realized that in spite of a vast, oblivion-fostering distance, in spite of twenty-seven years of abdication, in spite of dedicating my life to my family and work, I remained incapable of loving another woman? I wanted to love Norma, but the harder I tried to reach her fruit-laden boughs, the farther away they receded. My poor Norma, dedicated wife and mother, who lived twenty-six years with unrequited love, is now drowning away in the River Lithe, oblivious, unreachable, and unaware of my relentless efforts to love her.

What is this love, Fatima? What is this indelible numen? What is this transmuting, anachronistic phoenix? What is this puppeteering, merciless, obsessive God who programs change into everything living or dead, born or unborn, real or imagined, but exempts this love from self-destructive attrition, a universal phenomenon that biologists call apoptosis? Is this intransigent love privately revealing to us that it is unchanging because it is descended from God, the never-changing spirit of our ever-changing universe?

Humanity has always been paranoid about its inexplicable mysteries, and I am no exception. Love's mystery is, indeed, my solipsism, my epiphany, my paranoia, and my Cartesian *I love therefore I am,* or *"amo ergo sum."*

Fatima, I do not wish to love you, to be Siamesed to you, to taste your breath with my lips each time I inhale. I feel that I have been pre-programmed to fall into your love, to fall so profoundly into an abyss from whose dark depth I can no longer find the rays that light the window through which I have fallen. Help me detach into a different orbit; I need a new sky with another sun, a milky way without my Fatima.

> *"I rub my eyes and beg a color hither never*
> *seen*
> *No shades of white that rainbow on my screen*
> *A stardust color, bare before my eyes*
> *Deep, penetrating, panoramic, wise*
> *Adrift aloft my tumbling time and space*
> *A cosmic breath, a smile without a face.*
>
> *Where are my wings?*
> *Have I become what I was hatched to be*
> *A wingless bird perched on an ancient tree*
> *Poised high enough to fall*
> *But never high enough to see?"*

After our last poetry gathering, and quite unexpectedly, Mrs. Settembrini whispered that she might be getting a divorce. We were standing by her car when she said: *"I think that I shall file for divorce this coming January."* I said nothing in return as cold silence permeated the moment. Looking through her, I thought, how insensitive she is, and at the same time, how sensitive. Indeed, she could have but did not follow her liberating invitation with: *"By the time your wife dies, I shall be free and we can become a couple."*

The silence grew colder when she surmised that she had, unwittingly, offended me. In return, I paraphrased a doleful quote from Robert Frost's *Home Burial:*

"From the time when one falls ill
Until the time one dies
One grows more and more alone.
Friends pretend compassion
But their minds quickly re-focus
On life and the living
Instead of death and the dying."

She left without a word, and I walked back into the house angry at my anger, angry because I could not sympathize with my own theory of naturalism. Indeed, it was most natural of her to tell me of her intentions. A woman has to look after herself in this man-dominated world, and she was merely doing that. There was nothing unnatural about her self-preserving, forthright honesty, and I should have accepted it as normal behavior. Regrettably, I did not because it lacked sensitivity.
Unfortunately, whether natural or unnatural, one wrong word at the wrong time can irreversibly damage goodwill in a burgeoning relationship. I am sure that Mrs. Settembrini will absent herself from future poetry gatherings, and I am equally sure that she will try to redeem her status at Norma's funeral. Rest assured, Fatima, I shall not make the same mistake twice. I shall keep my hands away from Mrs. Settembrini, and instead of touch, I shall write longing adolescent love poems:

"Heartless wings can never fly
But hearts, un-winged, fly high
Yes, all they need is love
And they will tame the sky.
With love, hearts fly apart
With love, hearts oft return
With love, hearts flame and burn
To ashes then revive;
Love keeps our hearts alive."

I was pleased to hear that on Christmas Eve, Carlos, the terrorist, was convicted in Paris for killing two

French police agents and a Lebanese informant, no doubt a small fraction of his total kills. During the war, he took refuge in Amioun and was treated well by my little town's people because, at first, everyone thought that he was a war hero. Gibran, one of my closest friends, spent a lot of time with him and learned to fear and revere him. He could tell that Carlos was ruthless but was also very loyal to his friends. Nevertheless, the town sighed in relief when Carlos moved out and was later on captured by the Interpol. They followed the news of his apprehension and trial with great interest, unmindful of the notoriety that Amioun received for having unwittingly given refuge to a world-class terrorist. I cannot wait to receive Gibran's next letter with all the town's new gossip in it. When you see my mother again, you should ask her, in jest of course, about Carlos's stay in Amioun and listen to her say: *"What shame this man has brought us, what onerous shame!"*

How are Tariq and Nadir doing? Neither of them has written in awhile, which does not surprise me. They are young and busy with life, discharging their passions. As Nietzsche said: *"A living thing seeks above all to discharge its strength—life itself is will to power; self-preservation is only one of the indirect and most frequent results."*

Thank you for keeping an eye on Nadir and for hosting him periodically at your culinary table. Nothing warms the immigrant heart like a home-cooked meal, *"even if it is made of slimy green weeds that look bad and taste good."* These were Nadir's words, in his last letter, describing your Mulukhieh.

How is Little John, and has Nadir met him yet? Are you still smoking? Do you hear from Kamal? Please take care of yourself. I love you.

John

Thirty-Eight

(Mélange)

(Beirut – Saturday, February 14, 1998)

Dear John,

Your last letter shook my bones like malaria, and each time I re-read it, I chilled again until my whole body ached from emotional rheumatism. Still, I could not stop myself from re-reading and re-chilling until sleep rescued me at dawn. The last voice I heard was the Adan from the nearby minaret calling the faithful to prayer: *"Allahu Akbar, Allahu Akbar."* Indeed, my love, God is great.

Oh, darling, darling. You have, in your own circumventive way, given me hope again. You have, after a twenty-eight year flight, boomeranged back to where you had started. Oh, darling, let me not say anymore; I do not want to become your second Mrs. Settembrini.

Darling, darling, oh please, let me call you so. I need to hear my heart resound with your name and to feel my chest resonate with your memory. Call me a fool, and I will be overjoyed. Laugh at my adolescence, and I will blush with teenaged cheeks. Take your time writing back, and I will wait with a Mona Lisa smile, for only I know the secret that no one else knows, not even you. I smile like La Gioconda because I know that you are coming back to me. Oh, I have said too much again. Forgive me, darling, and blame it all on Um Al-Huda.

The weekend before I received your letter, I went to see Little John and stopped by the shrine for a short prayer. For a long time, Um Al-Huda had been talking to me, indirectly, through Fatima. This time, however, when I finished my prayer and was ready to rise to my feet, she whispered: *"Pray some more, child, pray; Allahu Akbar."* Seven times I prayed, and seven times she commanded me to pray again. When I prayed the eighth she was gone. When I asked Fatima what was all that about, she merely said that the first seven prayers covered our twenty-eight years apart, a prayer for each four years. When I seemed puzzled at her answer, she added, *"He will see you in the next four years."*

On the way back, I had time to meditate because the drive to Beirut took me three and a half hours. I saw myself in a boat drifting down a river. I had no power to change my direction, so I did the only thing I could do—I went with the flow and marveled at nature. One gray dove kept me company, flying along the bank, waiting in the trees for my boat to pass, and then flying downstream again to wait for me. When I arrived at the delta where the river meets the sea, the dove stood eyeing me, perched on a nearby tree.

When I reached home, I felt a deep sense of peace and fell asleep without eating dinner. The next day, your letter arrived, and it was then that I understood the meaning of the dove.

You don't have to believe in my fairy tales; however, you must realize that even though you are East-born, and even though you have chosen to become a West-grown man of science, it only takes one believer for things to happen. It is belief, darling, that has kept us alive all these twenty-eight years apart. I pray to Um Al-Huda, and your mother goes to church twice a week and lights a candle for you. The last time I saw her, she told me that when you were in medical school, she would say a prayer and light a candle for you before each major examination. Well, you passed all your examinations, didn't you? You even passed your most difficult exams when you and I stayed up all night playing instead of studying. I should say no more; forgive my fabulous mind, my excited, silly mind, and my female mind so full of Eastern fables.

Nadir is doing what he wants to do, studying hard and reading for the blind. With the new semester, he was assigned two blind students; one is Iranian and the other, Turkish. He told me that three times a week, he reads to them their humanities assignments, whereas Tariq helps them with their social calendars. I feel particularly sorry for the Turkish student because there is current resentment toward Turkey. You must have heard that Turkey is being accused of committing genocide against the Kurdish populations in the Kurdistan Mountains of Turkey. That is all these poor Kurds need, Saddam attacking them from one side and Turkey restraining them from the other.

Boatloads of Kurdish refugees are leaving to Italy, which is putting a strain on the Italian government, while Greece is refusing to allow any refugees to disembark. The International Human-Rights Committee at the UN is making lots of noise but to no avail; both Turkey and Iraq have denied any human rights violations. No one can police the world, not even your omnipotent, omnipresent, democratic America.

Incidentally, you will not believe what I am about to tell you. Kamal sent me a postcard wishing Little John and me a Happy New Year. The stamps on the card are from the Kurdistan region of Turkey, which means that the Turkish military intelligence is involved in the Kurdish crisis. Of course, the postcard arrived unaccompanied by money or cigarettes. What am I to tell Little John about his father, who seems to have totally abandoned us? Why am I surprised at Kamal's lack of support? Perhaps, I wanted to believe that the father of my child was a better man than he truly is?

Who needs him anyway? I am doing fine now and have enough work to cover my expenses and put some aside for Little John. Ahmad, thank God, in spite of the protestations of his cute hairdresser wife, is still covering all of Tariq's expenses. Ahmad is a good man, which is why I married him even though I knew and he knew that I could never love him. I cannot blame him for straying away. A man cannot live by food and sex alone. A man needs a home, and what makes a home is love. And yes, just like your experience with Norma, I tried to love Ahmad, but the more I tried, the worse I failed. Oh, how we live our lives in parallel, you and I. Praise God who, in his infinite wisdom, planned our lives for us. *Allahu Akbar.* God is great.

To make things even worse for the Turkish students at the AUB, Israel has been helping Turkey rebuild its fighter-jet fleet and Turkey has been flying these armed jets over Cyprus and Greece, both of which have filed complaints with the UN. Nadir told me that the Turkish students are feeling uncomfortable because they can sense the hostile tensions in the student body and many of them are planning to leave the AUB at the semester's end. adir, who is violently opposed to discrimination, has befriended many of the Turkish students who are friends of the blind student assigned to him. This has been good for Tariq who, along with Nadir, is doing his part to reduce these inter-student tensions. Next weekend, I am having Tariq, Nadir, and the two blind students for lunch. I am eager for Nadir to finally meet Little John. A most interesting mélange of American, Lebanese, Turkish, and Iranian students will gather around my table next Saturday; I am looking forward to enlightening discussions representing multiple points of view. Remember what you used to say to me each time violence broke out? Your exact words, darling: *"As long as debate is kept alive, violence remains dormant."*

John, I am still coughing, but my chest x-rays are normal. My doctor says that my cigarettes are the cause of my cough and that I should stop smoking. I try, and I don't try. I cannot imagine life in Beirut without cigarettes. Perhaps danger makes us reckless—we justify and tend to find cigarettes innocuous compared to bombs. All armies smoke, and in Lebanon there is an army of civilians that smokes incessantly and gives the activity little thought. I am, my darling, an unarmed smoking soldier in the defeated Lebanese civilian army.

I do not smoke, however, in the presence of Little John, and I promise you that when I see you again, I will stop smoking forever. Please do not look at my promise as a form of emotional blackmail. Just think of it as black smoke, smoldering black smoke that symbolizes the fire within our souls. Oh, I have said too much again, but surely you understand that I am too excited to be quiet.

Speaking of boomerangs, Jamal and Mary are going to Australia for their third anniversary, and of course, they are taking Jamie with them to see her grandparents who have not seen her since Mary brought her to Kuwait. They plan to spend the month, from mid-September to mid-October, in the Continent Under. No one has told Laila yet because we are afraid of what she might do. Even Imad and Ramzi have kept their mouth shut to avoid their mother's irrational wrath.

Oh darling, my Little John is adorable and very bright. He has his father's black piercing eyes, handsome looks, and his chin dimples when he smiles, just like Kamal's. He spends most weekends with me and most weekdays with Fatima. Unless my work schedule prevents it, I pick him up from Fatima on Thursday evenings and return him to her on Sunday afternoons. He is always happy to see me and always happy to return to her. The child has two mothers, I suppose, instead of a mother and a father.

I wrote to you last year what Fatima had said to me on Little John's first birthday; do you still remember? She said that, someday, Little John would end up moving to Turkey to live with his sister. You know what that means, of course. It means that Kamal would never visit us again and that Little John would grow up not knowing his own father except in pictures. A child cannot move to Turkey to live with his sister unless all four of us die—Kamal, Gulnar, Fatima, and I—and there is no other woman left to take care of him except his half sister, Amar, who turns ten this year. I suppose that we will have about ten or more years together before Amar, who should have married by then, takes on the responsibility of raising her ten year-old half brother.

Perhaps, after being raised by three women, Little John would grow up to be more sensitive than most men and more loyal to his own woman. Oh, what did I just say! Forgive me; I did not mean it the way it sounded. Again, I have said too much. Perhaps I am still too excited about your letter. Perhaps I need to shut up. Forgive me, John; you know how I babble when I am afraid.

I am very afraid that I am going to die and lose both of my boys and you. I am afraid of Fatima's thoughts and of my own thoughts. I am afraid for Little John having to become Turkish after spending his first ten or more years as a Lebanese. I am afraid of my smoking. I am afraid of Beirut. I am afraid of the next four years that should bring you back to me, after twenty-eight years of separation. I am afraid of waiting. I am afraid of that heavy secret, which I have never revealed to you or anyone else because I wanted to protect you. I am afraid that you will, out of loneliness, rebound to Mrs. Settembrini.

I am going to stop writing now and have a good cry. Then, I am going to have a glass of wine and go to bed. I will finish this letter when I am in a better mood. Like you say, I must insist on joy—insist in spite of life's wars and catastrophes.

Good night my love,

Fatima

(Beirut – Saturday, February 21, 1998)

It took me a whole week to get back to you, but the wait was well worth it. They have just left, and I have so much to tell you about the wonderful mélange that discoursed around my lunch table. It turns out that the blind students were both women, and neither removed her veil, even while eating, because there were men (Tariq and Nadir) among us. They were both shy, polite, and ate very carefully without spilling. Tariq helped the Iranian girl, Shamira, with cutting her meat, and Nadir did the same with the Turkish girl, Güzide.

Little John and Nadir played a while, and then the Turkish girl, Güzide, asked Little John to come to her. As soon as she put him in her lap, they bonded and she even let him play with her veil and peep underneath it with no resistance or embarrassment. Little John was the only one among us who was allowed to see Güzide's face and the only one who cried when she said good-bye. He clung to her and wouldn't let her leave, much like Jamie clung to Ramzi and Imad when Laila dragged them out of my house that awful night. It was a most heart-wrenching scene, and I believe that Güzide was crying underneath her veil because, twice, she wiped her cheeks while going down the stairs.

As you can imagine, the elevator has been out of commission since the war and the owner of the building refuses to repair it because Lebanese laws, which prohibit rent increases in spite of inflation, have made the owners' revenues so meager that owners of buildings can no longer afford to keep up their properties.

These are very bright girls, John, and very brave to be at the AUB competing with sighted students. I was the one who broke the conversation icecap by asking the Iranian, Shamira, to tell us about the current conditions in Iran and what her people think of America. With a shy voice, Shamira first apologized to Nadir for what she was about to say and then explained that, being a political science major, she fully understood that nations cannot be held to the same moral standards as individuals because individuals are held to higher standards by the human conscience within them. She supported her opinion by paraphrasing Kant: *"Two things fill the mind with wonder and awe, the starry heavens above us and the moral laws within us."* Consequently, she argued, individuals can only judge nations with their own individual consciences and from their own personal points of view. She then explained that Iranians cannot forget that democratic America allied itself with the Shah, a ruthless dictator who usurped the country's oil resources and brutally suppressed its people. And, to make things even worse, after Khomeini came to power, America allied itself with Saddam, an equally ruthless dictator, and sanctioned his horrible war against Iran.

Nadir protested the fact that Shamira was blaming the American people instead of the American government and defended his position by saying that most Americans are moral, peace-loving people who want to befriend all nations that will accept their friendship. Shamira agreed that Iranians are lumping the American government and the American people together and that it was wrong to do so. She then lamented the fact that human nature is such that most people are spontaneous lumpers and not calculating splitters.

When Nadir then asked her what she foresees as the solution to the current crisis, she muttered from underneath her black veil, *"God is the only solution,"* and much to Nadir's surprise, paraphrased St. Augustine's dictum, *"If you can love God enough, you can do no wrong."* When Nadir asked her if what she meant was that people believe in God while governments believe in national power, she nodded and said with a sigh: *"That is why peace will always remain tantalizing."*

Throughout this entire conversation, Güzide held Little John in her lap, stroked his head, and did not participate in the heated discussion. She seemed perfectly content to concentrate on Little John who, like a kitten, purred in her lap until Tariq served her the hot question: *"How does Turkey justify the occupation of Cyprus?"*

She continued to stroke Little John as she answered, unabashed, *"The same way Europe justified the occupation of America and Israel, the occupation of Palestine. The powerful dominate because they can, especially when natives are unable to defend their rights."* Then, quite nonchalantly, she continued her discourse by saying that in the dictionary of human history, the winners, invariably, redefine justice and the masses accept these definitions as self-evident truths. She then concluded that ruthless leaders, those who do not value the human rights of others, justify, in the name of national glory, the creation of ephemeral empires and in the process, cause widespread devastation.

Seizing the momentary silence, Nadir inquired if she was including the Persian and Ottoman empires in her generalization to which she answered, still with downcast head, *"All empires are ruthless human rights usurpers, including the Persian, Hellenic, Roman, Islamic, Ottoman, and British."* Then she paraphrased Hegel saying that human passions are the prime movers of history and that human nature is what fuels these passions. She then explained with a resigned voice that the human passion for justice can be easily supplanted by other more primitive passions and supported her argument by quoting from Nietzsche: *"A living thing seeks above all to discharge its strength—life itself is will to power."*

At that point, Nadir asked her if, as a philosophy major, she believed that what Nietzsche had said applied mainly to individuals or to nations. *"It applies more to individuals than to groups,"* she answered, *"because the larger the group the more dilute becomes the individual's conscience and the more it is subjugated by group ideologies and behaviors; we cannot be true to ourselves in a group."*

Nadir seemed intrigued by her comfortable delivery and, after a polite pause, asked: *"When, then, are we the most true to ourselves, Güzide?"* Still stroking Little John's hair, she answered with downcast head: *"We are truest to ourselves when we are alone, when we are born sightless, and when we are dying because in all these three situations we do not pretend."*

At that point, in order to diffuse the tacit tensions accrued, I fetched your book and read:

> *"Yes, I have known the gentle peace of death,*
> *The pain, and sleepless anguish of Macbeth,*
> *Have loved, and hated, even leased my soul*
> *With perfect logic, softened to comply*
> *With inner whims that do not yield, nor die,*
> *Until they find expression; this is I—*
> *There hardly is a process that I could not*
> > *justify!"*

Nadir reached for the book, took it out of my hand, and opened to the dedication page where you had written: *"Happy Birthday Fatima. With Love, John 10.31.87."* That was your gift on my thirty-seventh birthday; do you still remember? Nadir did not comment when he gave me back the book, but I could tell that he was surprised—surprised that I had it and even more surprised that I was able to quote from it as if I knew it by heart. He must have noticed my apprehension when I surrendered the book to him, and my obvious relief when he gave it back to me.

On the way out, he smiled as he took a long look at the book, which I still held in my hand. Then gave me a long, warm embrace as if to say, I know ... I understand ... and it's OK. He then held Güzide by the elbow and led her down the stairs, a few steps ahead of Tariq and Shamira.

What a kind, perceptive gentleman you have loaned us, John! What a pleasure it is to have him around, and what a joy to watch him influence Tariq, among other things, with his sincere concern for the less privileged strata of humanity.

John, it is past my bedtime, and I must say goodnight. I am sure that Nadir will write to you in more detail about his life in Beirut. Tariq sends you his love and so does Little John. Please write soon.

Love,

Fatima

Thirty-Nine

(Touching Hands)

(Beirut – Saturday, May 30, 1998)

Dear Dad,

I am sorry for not writing sooner, but you know how busy student life is, especially now that finals are near. But Dad, I also have so much to tell you that cannot be told on the phone, which is another reason for writing this letter. First, hear me out, please; you can make your decisions later.

To begin, how is mother doing, and do I really need to come home this summer, or may I stay in Beirut and study Arabic? I find Beirut invigorating, and there is so much I could do here that I couldn't do in Oklahoma including practicing my Arabic and going to the beach. The AUB beach is where most students hang out, and I get to speak and listen to Arabic all the time.

But, there is another reason that makes me want to stay, and that is my work with the blind students, mainly Güzide who would like to take two summer courses if I could continue to be her reader. She is so bright and motivated, and I would love to help her out if you could extend my stay. As I told you on the phone, the six of us have become very good friends. We call our group the LAITH club: L for Lebanese (Fatima, Tariq, and Little John), A for American (me), I for Iranian (Shamira), T for Turkish (Güzide), and the H to indicate that Little John is also half Turkish and that I am half Lebanese. ` Tariq was the one who coined the acronym because in Arabic, the word *"LAITH"* means lion. In other words, the Lion's club meets at Fatima's home almost every weekend for lunch, and to solve the problems of humanity with our deep discussions.

Don't get any ideas about what else is going on; nothing is, Dad. Shamira loves Tariq because, being homosexual, he poses no threat to her conservative mind. Güzide and I love to have discussions and take long walks along the Corniche. I have never seen her face because she keeps her veil on all the times we are together. But, sometimes, when we walk facing the sun, I can glimpse her hazy features through the veil. Except for her eyes, which are recessed and closed, she has a peaceful, pretty face.

I have never seen her smile however, because each time anyone says something funny, she turns away and tilts her head down to laugh. Also, she never talks about herself or her family and gives vague answers whenever she is asked anything personal. But, in spite of all that, everyone likes her because she is so smart and speaks her mind without hesitation.

Onc day, while walking together along the Corniche, she asked me if I had a girlfriend in the States. I was rather shocked because she had never asked me a personal question before. Her question put me in a teasing mood, and so instead of giving her a simple answer, I served her a repartee: *"What kind of girlfriend are you talking about?"* For the first time since I have known her, she was at a loss for words and mumbled under her veil before she could come back with: *"I didn't know that there were different kinds of girlfriends!"* Teasingly, I replied that in the United States of America we have five basic types of girlfriends. *"Five,"* she exclaimed with a sudden gasp? *"Indeed,"* I seriously affirmed, *"because America is quite different from Turkey."* *"Tell me the five types then. You're kidding, aren't you? I don't believe a word you're saying."*

"Well," I began, trying not to laugh, *"the types in order of intimacy are: type 1 - steady girlfriends with sex, type 2 - steady girlfriends without sex, type 3 - shared girlfriends with sex, type 4 - shared girlfriends without sex, and type 5 - faceless girlfriends, the kind you talk with but never see."* Immediately she turned away, tilted her head down and began to laugh. A whiff of sea breeze lifted her veil up enough for me to see her chin, contorted with laughter, dimpled like that of Kirk Douglas.

I must have hurt her feelings because she said very little after that, but when I took her back to her dorm, she put her hand out for me to shake, something I have never seen her do with anyone else including other women. For the first time, Dad, she thanked me by shaking my hand and then, without saying a word, went up to her room.

Oh Dad, I have so much more to tell you about the bustling life in Beirut. Today, our French teacher took us to the Palais du Pins to attend the inauguration ceremony. You must have heard that the French president, Jacques Chirac, has returned to Beirut to inaugurate the Palais du Pins as the new site of the French Embassy. Apparently, President Chirac was in Beirut in 1996 and promised that he would come back to inaugurate the palace once reconstruction was completed. Well, our French teacher, Monsieur de Gaulle, is a personal friend of Chirac and was given special permission to attend the ceremony with his class. Oh, you should have seen the pomp and security around the palace, but after a good search, they let us all in as if we were important dignitaries and seated us near the front. The Lebanese President, Elias Hrawi, was there with the Speaker of the House, Nabih Birri, and the Prime Minister, Rafik Hariri. After the inauguration, President Chirac shook hands with Monsieur de Gaulle who introduced him to every one of us students. One by one, we all shook the President's hand, a rare happening indeed, almost as rare as my shaking the hand of Güzide the other day.

And now, Dad, the moment of truth has come. The real reason I wrote this letter was to ask if you would let me spend my senior year here and graduate from the AUB. If you would, I could save my return ticket and use it to come home next summer instead of this June. I have already checked with a travel agent, a cousin of Fatima, who indicated that I would not be penalized for delaying my return till next year.

When I shared these plans with Grandma, she was thrilled and said that she will pray for me to have my wish. She is so religious, Dad, and goes to church whenever she faces a crisis. The last time I visited her in Tripoli, she showed me some of your pictures when you were a kid. When I asked her if you were mischievous growing up, she nodded, shook her head, smiled, and said: *"He was mainly quiet and spent a lot of time reading. Sure, occasionally, he misbehaved, but he never hurt my feelings, not even once, not even with one harsh word."* She had tears in her eyes as she spoke. Dad, you really should pay her a visit. You are her only child, and sometimes, I feel that you are her entire world.

I am not supposed to tell you this because she swore me to secrecy, but she did indicate that it made no sense to her that, on the one hand, you are afraid to visit Lebanon, but on the other, you allow your own son to visit your homeland with no worry or fear. *"Could he possibly love himself more than he loves you, his very own son? I doubt it. That is not the way I raised him. I have always loved him more than I have loved myself, and he knows it."*

Dad, I feel trapped between you and Grandma, and I don't know what to say to her to ease her grief. I tried to tell her that I am your representative, that you sent me in your stead, and that you allowed me to come here because you loved her and loved Lebanon. It didn't work. You know how she answered? She said: *"It is not a sacrifice for a father to send his son to a far-away college. Your father is not God, and you are not Jesus Christ. No, your father is saving his eyes. He does not want to see the face of Lebanon deformed with scars from the war. He does not want to hear an explosion, listen to gunfire, or look at the destruction of the human spirit. He does not want to face soldiers at checkpoints. He does not want to be humiliated by airport security. He does not want to see what happens to poor little countries that cannot defend their own sovereignties. Your dad wants to deny his roots because they are rotten and because he has started new roots elsewhere. Does he think that there is any virtue in turning one's face away from evil or ignorance? Does he think it brave to run away instead of face problems, especially problems that have no solutions? Does he think that suffering stops if one refuses to see it? Did Jesus seek peace and prosperity, or did he spend his time with the thieves and the poor? Jesus never ran away from ugliness; he faced it with his healing faith. Whatever happened to your dad's faith?"*

Oh Dad, I am so sorry to tell you all this, but I felt I had to because I could see how disillusioned Grandma was. And that's not all; there is more, and I have to tell it. After she said what she said, she got up and slowly walked to the bookshelf where she pulled out your book, *Loves and Lamentations of a Life Watcher*, opened it to the poem *Fatherland*, and began to read aloud with her back to me. While reading, I noticed that she was not looking at the book in her hand. Indeed, she was looking at your medical-school-graduation-picture, which caused me to suspect that she was reciting the poem from memory. I wasn't sure however, till after the first stanza when she closed the book with a snap, and in the same temperamental tone, continued to recite with her eyes still focused on your picture:

"Fatherland, oh Fatherland
If only I could hold your hand
And stand upon your shore
Behold your hoary mountains
Dive into the sea and snore
With mystifying grace
Implore the endless waves
To wash your ancient face.

Fatherland, before I gray, I will be back
I will be back one misty autumn day
To hug your loving dirt against my chest
And plant a garden on your ruddy breast
Loiter together in the timid afternoon
Until the sun begins to blush before the moon."

When she finished reading, she put the book back on the shelf, sat beside me, held my hand, and said: *"How can he write something so passionate but behave so dispassionately? I did not raise your father to be duplicitous!"* When I left, she told me to be careful and gave me a kiss. I think she knew that I was going to tell you everything because the last thing she said to me was, *"Don't forget to write to your dad. He needs your letters more than you will ever know."*

The first thing I did when I got back to my room was to look up the word duplicitous, which brought to mind a line from *My Fair Lady*: *"Her English is too good he said, which clearly indicates that she is foreign."*

Speaking of writing, you will be happy to know that I am writing poems again. The funny ones I read to Tariq and Güzide, but the serious ones I only read to Güzide because Tariq does not like wasting time on serious poetry. The last poem I wrote was serious; I finished it today after we returned from the French Embassy inauguration. It says what I feel about touching hands, and how intimate is the sense of touch in comparison to all the other senses, and how quickly it penetrates the human spirit with its piercing emotions:

> *"Sometimes we see and understand*
> *Sometimes we don't*
> *Sometimes we smell, we taste*
> *We hear, we read,*
> *And understand or don't...*
>
> *But, hand in hand*
> *We see and hear*
> *And taste and smell our very souls*
> *And dance to heartbeats and to sighs*
> *And apprehend that hands have eyes*
> *Eyes like stars that wink and spark*
> *And bring light to the dark."*

I read it to Güzide this afternoon, thinking that she would like it. Well, she obviously didn't because she became quiet and hid her hands behind her back. Then, after a long pause, she asked me if I had read the *Little Prince (Le Petit Prince* by Antoine de Saint-Exupéry).

I said good-bye, went straight to the library, checked the book out, and read it in its original French edition. It is all about seeing and understanding things beyond the ordinary levels of obvious reality. The fox said it best: *"One doesn't see well except with the heart. The essentials are invisible to the eyes."* So, she put me in my proper place and showed me that I was not the first one to discover this truth. But, she didn't have to point it out to me in such a condescending way. I feel intimidated by people like her who can say so much by saying so little.

Sometimes, when I finish reading to her, she goes: *"Humm, what do you think this really means?"* Then, before I have a chance to answer, she stops me with: *"Please don't interpret the obvious; find a more interesting meaning, something even the writer hadn't thought of."* But, when in return I ask her to share with me her own interpretations, she says to me that personal interpretations are private matters that shouldn't be revealed.

Anymore, I don't know if I like or dislike this dimple-chinned Kirk of a Turk. Excuse my flighty puns Dad, but sometimes I think that Tariq and I should switch our *"blind"* dates. Oh, it feels so good to vent. Thanks for listening, Dad. You know that I don't mean any of this. In fact, I think that I like her a bit too much because she always challenges and intrigues me.

Please Dad, forgive my anger and give my love to Mom, Ghassan, Frida, and all my friends. Call me when you've had time to think about my proposal to graduate from the AUB, and let me know what your decision is. I wish there was enough work in Beirut for students like me because I could pitch in and help you out. But, as you know, there is no work for students here because the poor locals need the work much more than we do. I've even thought about asking Grandma for help, but I won't unless you think that it is OK to do so.

Dad, there is one more thing on my mind that I need to share with you. It has to do with Um Al-Huda. I hear so much about her from Fatima, who obviously reveres her. But when I'm alone with Tariq, he makes fun of both Um Al-Huda and his mother. He thinks that his mother has gone berserk with her faith in this saint. He argues that it is one thing to have faith in God or the Prophet (meaning Muhammad), but to hang all your faith on one saint may actually offend God. He even thinks that his mother is not right in the head because she thinks of Um Al-Huda as her personal friend and talks to her as if she were her classmate. And what frightens him most about that relationship is that his mother actually consults Um Al-Huda before she makes any important life decision.

I don't know what to say when he talks like that and so I remain silent. There was one time, however, when I stood up to him and said that Grandma does the same thing but instead of praying to Um Al-Huda, she prays to the Virgin Mary. He laughed and said that praying to God's wife is not any better than praying to a woman's shrine. When I explained that the Virgin Mary is the mother of Christ and not the wife of God, he laughed again and said: *"If Christ is the son of God and the Virgin Mary is Christ's mother, then she must also be God's wife because only God can cause a virgin to become pregnant and since God doesn't sin, then He would have had to marry her before he impregnated her."*

I don't know what to do with Tariq. He is a wonderful friend, but he makes fun of things that should be held sacred. I am not sure if he means what he says or if he just likes to shock me. He doesn't act that way around his mother or his friends. He only talks like this with me. I wonder why? Let me know if you can think of an explanation.

And Dad, you're going to be proud of my grades when you see them. The AUB will mail them to you when they are out. I am going to study very hard for finals. Please, let me graduate from your Alma Mater.

Thank you for all you do, and I will understand if you need me to return home after finals.

I love you,

Nadir

Forty

(En Passant)

(Oklahoma City – Saturday, July 4, 1998)

Dear Fatima,

It has taken me four months to answer your blithe letter not because I lack the time or inclination but rather because I am in the swirls of an emotional tornado that stirs red dust into my soul and blurs my already myopic insight. So far, I have managed to respond with smiles to all the frowns that furrow my days, but in my struggle for light, I have exhausted my alacrity. I try not to waste time—which is my personal definition of life—because without awareness of time, fleeting time, life loses her vibrant colors and languishes into brown inertia. I especially try not to waste life on death because that would be a most sinful futility.

I try to be cheerful, but to no avail; I feel like a morning sun barred behind tenebrous clouds. I try but my woe is Norma, my dying Norma, dying—but not as we are all dying, while still clinging to life—no, unlike us, Norma is wasting away without struggle, like a fleeting fragrance blowing in the breeze, fading unaware, relinquishing life without remorse, going all too gently *into that good night,* while I—sitting by her side—*rage, rage against the dying of the light.* Oh, how it echoes in my heart, that villanelle by Dylan Thomas.

No, I will not waste life on death, Fatima; instead, I will learn from it because it is a mighty life force, great teacher of the living, exhumer of buried emotions, provoker of imaginations, inseminator of thoughts, creator of myths, tamer of rebellious spirits, key holder of the last life door:

"Of life, I am a restless, wandering breath
Romantic, final, intimate, like death
Why do I shed my leaves in spring and waste
My ancient wine upon this heedless earth?"

How much more can a man take and remain sane? Not long ago Norma used to respond when I read poetry to her, smiling with oblivious amazement like a blind child listening to music. Now, I read and stop, stop and read, hoping for a mere twitch, an occasional blink, a meager change of aspect, but instead, I get nothing, nothing at all, not even a frown. The diver has gone too deep into the sea, and all the bubbles have ceased.

I do not know if I should summon the boys now or if I should wait until her lungs begin to rattle. I do not know if I should call the priest to her bedside and confess to him, confess that I have tried to un-love you by loving her, confess that I have failed on both love fronts.

What is this love, Fatima? Is it a transfixion, a glorified obsession, a numen, or is it a life-warping epiphany? Why do we love so deeply and fall so steeply? Why is it so bitterly hard to climb out of love's deep well? Sitting by Norma, night after night, I have pondered the mystery of love and wondered if we are born with pre-programmed inclinations, tendencies, and traits, which lead us by the heart to where love's idealization lurks unforeseen? Somewhere, in the archaic recesses of our minds, love is wired to the idealization of beauty, for it is most difficult for us to love the unbeautiful, unless we beautify it with love.

"Familiar faces
Let us not pretend…
Though life may decimate and send
Our unsuspecting souls across
Uncharted times and unfamiliar places,
Wherever we are loved we end."

I have become bent, stooped with pondering these questions, and have found only one word that deciphered all these mysteries for me. Beauty. Yes, beauty is my answer; it is the only rational explanation for a force so long-suffering, so irrational as love. Think about it, and it will come to you. No one can love ugliness, but we all love beauty. Therefore, love must come first; it comes in order to beautify; otherwise, how can a parent love a deformed child? How can soul mates be attracted to one another without the eyes of love?

Indeed, love is the maker of beauty for without love nothing seems beautiful. Is a hunter half-eaten by a tiger a beautiful sight? Indeed it is, but only to the tigers because they love raw flesh and blood. Is a tiger, shot and skinned, a beautiful sight? Yes, but only to the hunter who loves the glory of a kill. Fatima, it is love that defines beauty. I could not love Norma because I could not see how beautiful she was. I have been programmed to love you, and I have spent half my life struggling against my programmers. How can a programmed mind ever be free? Would you like to read my longing poem, the one I wrote not to you but to my programmers? Would it bore you to read a long, soul-searching poem written whilst I sat by Norma's side, written in the silence of solitude—for she hardly ever makes her presence known—written by the resigned capitulation of denial, by the dread of swelling guilt, by the pain of a life half lived; written with the charcoal of my captive soul, charred trying to escape her destiny.

I have grown doleful with death, gray with guilt, weary with worry, sleepless with sorrow, fickle with fear, and tearful with remorse. Hear my credo Fatima, and try to understand, that like Pablo Neruda, my love has two lives, one to love you when I do not love you, and one to love you when I do. If you will not understand my dichotomy, I fear that you will not like what I am about to say to my programmers. In my December 1997 letter, I sent you two stanzas from this poem; now I send you the entire confessional work, which I have titled, *Hurried Race*.

I pray that this poetic plea will reach my Lord, the Force that constituted me, the Spirit that has the power to transmute my programs and give me the freedom to choose with my cultivated mind, rather than with my archaic brain and its inchoate passions:

"Before the stars were hatched and planets
        laid
I was a mere idea, un-conceived, un-made
Un-trampled by the noisy train of years
A tranquil breath without an atmosphere
Buoyant, in silent, solitude of space.

My hurried programmers,
They did not worry much
Here you are, they said
Here you are, but we will own your head
Though you may think that you can think
And feel that you can feel
And believe that you believe,
What you will see will all be seen too late
And you will call coincidence your fate.

I rub my eyes and beg a color hither never
        seen
No shades of white that rainbow on my screen
A stardust color, bare before my eyes
Deep, penetrating, panoramic, wise
Adrift aloft my tumbling time and space
A cosmic breath, a smile without a face.

They did not worry much,
My programmers
Here you are, they said
Our givens have been etched within your head
Your inter-given spaces filled with lead;
Go then and live the wishes we had wished to
live
Fruit of a native tree is never free
Submit to all the circuits we designed
And all the ramifying webs that link your
        mind

To ancient roots beneath your conscious state
Come now, what use is useless struggle?
Come, recline, capitulate
Coincidence, your maker, is your fate.

My hurried programmers,
Could you not have left a fallow space
A lot, unseeded, I could call my own
A spot, which I could garden all alone
And grow forbidden fruits in colors never seen
To feed these famished questions quickening
in my soul?

My very programmers,
Here you are, they said
This land, your country, is your holy bread
And this religion is your spirit's wine
And you will hold our myths divine
And in our schools you'll incubate your mind
Until our language will become your breath
And with it you will think until your death.

Comply, and do not sigh or you will choke
These burning questions float a murky smoke
A dusky smoke that smogs the air;
You will not ask, what if I were
By fate's coincidence, what if I were
By earth's roulette, what if I were
At random elsewhere sown and grown?
What if I called some other time my own?
What ships would dock upon my shore?
What tides would drag upon my ocean floor?

Where are my wings?
Have I become what I was hatched to be,
A wingless bird perched on an ancient tree,
Poised high enough to fall
But never high enough to see?"

With you, Fatima, I feel the most pain when I am the most honest. Forgive my excogitations; better times or worse might come our way, but now we must await the scrolling verdicts of our fate. I have more to tell you, but not tonight.

Frida has gone out with her friends and has just returned. I need to spend some time with her. Being stoic, she hides her grief all too well for her own good. But she likes tea. It helps her talk. I am going to turn off Norma's lights and invite her to tea. She will say, let us have it in my room. I will say, no, let us have it in my office. We will probably settle for the kitchen because it is on neutral ground.

(Sunday, July 5, 1998)

Good morning, Fatima. Frida and I talked till midnight, in the kitchen, of course. We talked about the Fourth of July parade, which she watched with her friends yesterday morning—about the freedom and human rights we enjoy in this country—about the two tornados that hit Oklahoma City three weeks ago—about President Clinton's visit to China last month—about the electrifying speech he gave to students at Peking University last Monday in which he said that no country could prosper or find political stability in the twenty-first century without embracing human rights and individual freedom—and about the fact that even while the President was still in China, serious human rights violations continued unabashed.

We discussed Nadir's decision to graduate from the AUB, his fascination with Beirut, his tacit attachment to Güzide, and how much we miss him. We talked about Frida's plans to go to the University of Kansas when she graduates in two years. Frida had a lot to say about sundry topics, but she never mentioned her mother, nor once inquired about her. In fact, she has not been in her mother's room for over a week now. Of course, I did not bring up that topic and left her to her peaceful denial, which she must need to guard her inner peace.

Ghassan calls once a week and asks if everyone is OK. He does not ask specifically about his mother, and again, I do not bring up the topic but merely say that I have talked to Nadir and that all of us are fine. My children have no frame of reference. They have no other friends whose mothers, while still in their forties, are dying of dementia.

Norma will turn forty-six this year. Although it is a Tuesday, I am seriously considering asking the boys to come home on the sixth of October so that we can all be together for her birthday. At least, one day this year, we need to sit down together as a family, reminisce about Norma, and celebrate her life as a dedicated mother and wife.

Nadir wrote to me a very emotional letter about my mother. I know that her life dream is that I visit her before she dies. However, I cannot leave Norma, not even for a day. How cynical is fate? All those who love Norma have tacitly left her, including the children, her parents, and her friends. No one comes to visit her anymore. No one wants to be with a brain-dead woman. The only ones who remain by her side are those who could not love her, the hired help and me.

These days, Robert Frost's lines from *Home Burial*, the lines I paraphrased for you in my December 1997 letter, haunt me again and again as I realize how alone Norma is and will forever be. Frost had it right when he said that from the time one falls ill till the time one dies, one is alone and dies more alone...and although friends pretend to suffer, their attention is really focused on life and the living instead of death and the dying.

Perhaps, Norma and I have had one emotion in common throughout our long marriage; we have both felt alone, desperately alone, especially when we were together. And now, united by dying instead of living, both she and I feel the most alone we have ever felt.

Please keep an eye on Nadir. Do you think that he is falling in love with his blind Turkish friend? As you know, he has a soft spot for the underprivileged and the challenged. His friends and teachers have unanimously agreed that Nadir suffers from the *"Messiah Syndrome"* because he likes to spend most of his time with those who need to be saved.

When he calls, and without even realizing it, Nadir seems to talk to me about Güzide more than he talks about anyone or anything else, although *en passant*, he occasionally remembers to send a perfunctory greeting to his mother just before he hangs up.

With love,

John

Forty-One

(The Cough)

(Damascus – Sunday, September 13, 1998)

Dear John,

I took Little John back to Fatima this afternoon and decided to spend the night in Damascus because I have a meeting tomorrow at the Damascus Hilton. Tensions are discernable on the faces in the Hilton lobby. You must have heard about the Turkish Prime Minister's two-day visit to Israel followed by a visit to Arafat last Wednesday. Well, the Syrians criticized both visits because they are already alarmed at the growing military ties between Israel and Turkey. In retaliation, Yilmaz responded to the Syrian criticism by accusing Damascus of supporting Kurdish terrorists inside Turkey.

Of course, they are both guilty of terrorism, Turkey for brutally suppressing the Kurdish quest for independence, Syria for providing training and support to militant Kurds, and both Syria and Turkey for violating the human rights of citizens with illegal political arrests and torture. Anyway, the atmosphere is polluted with worry, and I would have preferred to return to Beirut were it not for my early morning meeting.

What frightens me even more is the fact that I am meeting with a Kurdish reporter who uses the pseudonym of Idrees. He has written a book about Kurdistan, a big book full of photographs and stories revealing Turkish and Iraqi atrocities that have killed over 30,000 Kurds. He wants me to edit his photographs, render them publication ready, and help him find a publisher for his book in Beirut. He refuses to enter Lebanon for fear that

Israeli agents might abduct him and deliver him to the Turkish authorities. This tells me that he is paid and supported by the Syrian Secret Service to produce anti-Turkish propaganda. I am not sure that I should take on the project, but he has promised a $10,000 advance and an equal sum at completion, money that I need since medical care has become so expensive in Lebanon.

Oh John, I have so much to tell that I dare not tell you. Please then, allow me to digress a bit. He wants to call his book *The Kurdish Crucifixion* in order to appeal to the European Christian sympathies. Of course, he also wants me to find an editor who could translate and produce the book in English. When I asked him—during one of our telephone conversations—why he did not want an Arabic edition, he laughed and said that the book would be wasted on Arabic readers because they already know about the Kurdish massacres.

To tell you the truth, I was worried about Güzide's feelings and even about Little John's feelings because books, unlike their authors, have staying power that transcends generations. So yesterday—when Nadir, Tariq, Güzide, and Shamira were having their weekly lunch at my place— I told Güzide about the offer and asked if it would hurt her national feelings if I were to help produce the book. Nadir fidgeted, and the table grew silent awaiting Güzide's reply. She paused awhile and then, with a firm voice, explained that she was just as ashamed of the Turkish government's treatment of the Kurds as she was of the Kurdish use of violence in their attempt to gain independence.

Then, as an afterthought, she added that the same applies to Israel and the Palestinians. *"I, as a Turkish citizen, accept the blame and the shame for the anti-human rights brutalities practiced in Turkey, but I have not met many Israelis or Palestinians who were willing to do the same."* Nadir, who was relieved to hear Güzide's answer, asked if she would be willing to help the editor should the editor have problems with translation. She answered by saying that she would do whatever she could to expose human rights violations regardless of personal or national feelings.

She sounded just like you, John. In fact, I have heard similar words come out of your very own mouth on several occasions—words, which I must admit, have always motivated me into action. So, after the kids left, I decided to get over my fears and made up my mind to meet with Idrees on Monday morning and take on the project.

Now John, I need some medical advice. You remember my cigarette cough and how long it has been bothering me? Well, Tariq, Nadir, and the two girls all prevailed on me to see a lung specialist at the AUB, Dr. Hubaiter, which I did. He remembered you as a medical student and asked me to give you his best. Your name came up during the conversation but not because of something I said—no, not at all. It came up because, to my astonishment, Tariq and Nadir walked into the waiting room right behind the doctor.

Apparently, they were trying to find his office when they ran into him in the hall and, without knowing whom he was, happened to ask him for directions. He smiled and playfully ushered them to follow him in. When, after introducing myself, I angrily asked what were they doing there, they confessed with shameless adolescent giggles—and right in front of the doctor—that they had placed a $5 bet on me! Apparently, Tariq had wagered that I would not show up for my appointment, whereas Nadir had wagered that I would. I cannot believe what these two boys are capable of; they seem to have a surprise for me each time I turn around.

Well, when the laughter finally died down and I was able to properly introduce them, Dr. Hubaiter was the one who asked Nadir if he was your son. He said that the resemblance was striking and then, looking straight at me, added: *"I remember when you and John were dating; the two of you were quite an item then."* At that point, Nadir blushed and promptly took his leave snatching the $5 bill from Tariq's hand as he dashed away. In response, Tariq let out a high-pitched laugh and, without troubling to excuse himself, chased after Nadir. Oh, how embarrassing.

I know that I have not yet told you what the doctor said; I have deliberately digressed because truth is an embarrassing game. But now, let's return to my cough, and please don't be alarmed by what I'm about to reveal. Dr. Hubaiter examined me, took a chest x-ray in his office, and then showed me that I have a small shadow on my left lung, a shadow that he needed to investigate further with bronchoscopy and a CAT-scan.

Having no health insurance, which is typical of most Lebanese nowadays, I asked him about the projected costs. He said that the bronchoscopist usually charges about $850, the biopsies usually cost about $400, the CAT-scan another $800, and the hospital usually charges $250 for the use of its outpatient surgical facility. Then he said that if I should need surgery, it could cost up to $12,000 more.

I must have looked terrified when he mentioned surgery because he quickly put his arm around my tense shoulders and with a kind reassuring voice added that I did not need to worry about that part until the initial investigation was completed. I held back my tears and told him that I would call him when I acquire the money to pay for the investigation. I am hoping that Idrees will hand me the promised $10,000 when he gives me the manuscript tomorrow. I am most eager to finish with this medical mess especially since my cough is becoming more embarrassing, and I am becoming more frightened. Indeed, I should have brought a sleeping pill for tonight because hotels give me insomnia.

Now, I have a few things to say about your famous letter in which you love me but wish to un- love me. You said that your love has two lives, one with which you love me when you do, and another with which you love me when you don't? John, this may be poetic, but it is also confusing. Your head is in the clouds again, speaking words that I don't understand. What do you mean by this nonsense? Should I hope or should I resign myself to a life without you? Just tell me in plain words, and please, don't answer me in verse.

Perhaps, we shouldn't be talking about such things now. Between your Norma and my left lung shadow we have plenty to worry about besides our feelings for one another. Let's remain calm and try to get through one obstacle at a time. Let's keep our heads together. Oh, what was that Kipling poem you used to quote so often? Remember? It was *IF*, and you quoted it to me at the Beirut Airport just before you abandoned me and left for the States twenty-eight years ago:

> *"If you can keep your head when all about you*
> *Are losing theirs and blaming it on you."*

I have never understood how you could love me so strongly and leave me so willfully? Indeed, I still don't understand, so please, do not further confuse me with your philosophical poetry. I know that I have said too much; please forgive me. This heavy Damascus air is bothering my lungs and getting to my head.

On a more pleasant note, Little John's second birthday was an event to remember. Even Kamal sent us a birthday card from Silwan, Kardakan, with $10 in it. I guess he is still in Kurdistan suppressing insurgent Kurds. I invited the entire family and all my friends who had children of similar ages. Little John played happily with all the kids until Güzide walked in. From that point on, he clung to her and wouldn't leave her. When it was time to sing Happy Birthday and blow out the two candles, she was the one who had to lift him up into his highchair because he refused to let me do it.

When I complained to Fatima that he always cries bitter tears when Güzide leaves us and that I did not understand why he has taken to her so strongly, she answered with a most peaceful smile on her face, *"Do not protest Mother Nature's ways; there must be a spiritual bond between their souls, a bond which we are unable to see because it has not been revealed to us. God has prewritten their lives, and they must live them accordingly. Don't try to understand the beauty of love; just let it permeate you, and praise God's wisdom in all things."*

Speaking of love, I think that Nadir and Güzide, after much reluctance, have fallen in love. They spend all their free time together, but unlike a regular couple, I have never seen them hold hands, not even underneath my table. Tariq says that Nadir has never seen Güzide's face and that the only time he touches her is when he takes her back to her dorm and she thanks him by shaking his hand. According to Tariq, they have a true platonic love, a love that involves their souls but not their bodies.

He and Nadir often talk about such issues but never when I am around. Before I left Beirut this morning, Tariq told me that Nadir is planning a surprise birthday party for Güzide sometime next month. When I suggested that it should not be difficult to surprise Güzide, he retaliated by saying that her blind sense of observation is stronger than the eyes of most students, that her insight is keener than teachers twice her age, and that her brain can decipher hints that most of us don't even notice.

Apparently, Güzide is becoming quite a legend among students. In each of her classes, she learns the names and seating arrangements of all her classmates and quickly befriends them. She greets fellow students by name whenever she passes them and even before she hears their voices. She can tell who they are from the sound of their footsteps, their body odors, and their lotions or perfumes. Fatima says that Güzide has been blessed with blindness because Allah has a very special plan for her, a plan she could not fulfill if she were sighted.

I can tell you more, but I am sure that Nadir has already filled you in. Forgive me darling; I am babbling again because I am scared. I think that I shall go down to the bar for a drink and a smoke. Perhaps, after a glass of wine and a cigarette or two, I will be able to go to sleep. There is a pianist in the lobby who is playing songs by Um Kulthoom. I have never heard a piano rendition of Um Kulthoom before. Nevertheless, it sounds good and as familiar as Arabic words written with English letters.

Tomorrow will be a better day; my heart tells me so. I shall tell you more about my meeting with Idrees after I return to Beirut.

Please take care of yourself. You have to stay healthy, especially now that both of your women are sick.

Love,

Fatima

(Beirut – Monday, September 14, 1998)

Life is never easy, but sometimes it is too bitter to swallow. I waited for Idrees in the hotel lobby two long hours; he did not show up nor did he call. He must have needed the money more than I did. There were two men sitting in the coffee shop who, while pretending to read the official Syrian daily newspaper, *Al Baath*, seemed to be waiting too. They did not leave their positions until I walked out. They followed me to my car and drove behind me through the Damascus traffic until I arrived at Um Al-Huda's shrine. Thank God they did not follow me into the shrine; instead, they stayed in their car and waited for me while I prayed.

I told Um Al-Huda that I was scared, that I had bad feelings about my lung condition, that I was worried about Little John if something should happen to me, and worried about borrowing money and not being able to pay it back. I prayed till noon then got up and returned to Beirut. The two men escorted me to the Lebanese borders and then turned back. May God help Idrees; when they find him, no one will ever see him again...

On the way back to Beirut, I decided to ask Jamal for the money when he returns from Australia. As I told you earlier, Mary, Jamal, and Jamie all went to Australia so that Mary's parents could see their five-year old granddaughter—the Australian born granddaughter whom they had not seen since Mary brought her to Kuwait three years ago. They also wanted to celebrate their third wedding anniversary at the place where they had first met.

They should be back next week to spend a few days with us and to see Imad and Ramzi before they return to Kuwait. I am sure that Mary and Jamie will stay with me while Jamal goes up to Brummana to be with his two boys. As you recall, Laila still refuses to allow Mary and Jamie into her parent's home where she and the children still live. What a shame.

Please, pray for me, John. Pray that all will go well next week. I am going to ask Güzide to pray for me too, because her faith is strong. I have not told Fatima yet, but I will have to tell her if I should find out that I need surgery because she will have to keep Little John while I recover. Indeed, I may ask her to come take care of both of us, here at our home, not only because we both feel closer to her than to my mother, but also because she is physically stronger than my frail mother who just turned seventy.

In the meantime, try not to worry too much. There is nothing any of us can do to change the course of events. Everything is predestined in Islam and, as Omar Khayyam says,

> *"The moving finger writes, and having writ*
> *Moves on, nor all thy piety and wit*
> *Shall lure it back to cancel half a line,*
> *Nor all thy tears, wash out a word of it."*

All my love,

Fatima

Forty-Two

(Sayings And Quotes)

(Beirut – Saturday, October 24, 1998)

Dear Dad,

Normally, we would have spent Saturday afternoon at Fatima's lunch table having good foods and meaningful discussions. Normally, Güzide and I would have taken a long afternoon walk along the Corniche accompanied by Tariq and Shamira. Normally, Grandma would have invited me to Tripoli to accompany her to church on Sunday after which she would have served me fresh fish for lunch. Normally, today would have been a regular Beirut day. But unfortunately, Fatima is in the AUB hospital recovering from surgery, and we have spent our time pacing the halls. For lunch, the four of us went to the hospital cafeteria and spoke of nothing meaningful. We spoke just to fill in the silence with empty words.

After lunch, Güzide wanted to visit the site of the U.S. Marine compound at the Beirut Airport where fifteen years ago, on October 23, 1983, 241 marines were killed by a powerful truck bomb. When I asked her (with all possible politeness) what can she possibly see if I were to take her there, she answered in her usual direct manner that what she needed to see, she will be able to see with my eyes instead of hers. Then, when I asked her why is she so intent on visiting such a tragic place, she said that she has great compassion for all those killed during the month of October and followed her strange answer with the following lines, which she said came from Eliot's *Prufrock*:

> *"Oh, do not ask, what is it*
> *Let us go and make our visit."*

After such a response, I knew not to ask her more questions but hoped that she would tell me in due time what is the significance of all this.

Tariq and Shamira stayed with Fatima, and we took a taxi to the site where there was nothing to be seen except remnants of twisted steel and broken concrete. We stood there for the longest time while I described the scene to her in great detail. Then, out of her purse, she pulled a small prayer rug, placed it on the ground, knelt on it, and prayed facing the rubble instead of Mecca.

I felt ashamed because I, the American, did not kneel down to pray while a Muslim woman from Turkey internalized the tragedy enough to visit the site as though she were a pilgrim. When she was through, she wanted to walk all the way back instead of taking a cab. I informed her that it would take us at least two hours to walk back from the site to her dorm. She seemed pleased and said, *"Good, I need the time because I have a lot to say."*

First, she asked me to tell her about our Oklahoma get-together for Mother's forty-sixth birthday, a topic I had deliberately avoided since I returned to Beirut two weeks ago. I hate talking about my sick mother and then having to answer questions full of curiosity and pretense. In fact, her probing into my family affairs made me raise my voice to her for the first time ever.

After a few minutes of silence, she calmly said that it would be better for both of us to begin sharing painful emotions because not doing so would cause us to drift apart. I remained stubbornly silent until we reached the seashore road and began our long walk along the Corniche back toward the AUB campus. When she heard the sea waves and could smell the sea air, she said that she was feeling tired and wondered if there were a bench in the vicinity. It wasn't long before we reached Al Roucheh and found an empty bench facing the giant rocks that rise out of the sea like mammoths.

After sitting there awhile, she asked me why did I avoid mentioning my recent visit to Oklahoma and wondered what was I afraid of. When I told her that she's not my therapist, she said that we should be each other's therapists. At that point, I blew up again and reminded her that I had already told her a lot about my family, whereas, she had told me nothing about hers, nothing at all. For the second time since we had met, she was at a loss for words and began to shed silent tears, which I could see only when they dripped from underneath her veil onto her panting chest.

Of course, I pretended not to notice and began distracting her with the details of Mom's birthday and how Ghassan and I were hesitant about coming home, but what a wonderful experience it turned out to be. I told her how we were able to mix tears with laughter and share memories about Mom and each other. Then I told her that we spent all our together times in Mom's bedroom instead of the living room, that although Mom remained expressionless, we all believed that she could hear us, that we surprised each other when we raised our voices in unison to sing her happy birthday, and that we laughed when together we blew out her forty-six candles.

I told her all of this hoping that it would help her stop crying and to reinforce the pretense that I had not noticed her tears. When I finished though, she began to sob audibly, reached for my hand and clasped it with both of hers, something she had never done before. Then, just as quickly, she pulled herself back together, released my hand, and said that it was her turn now to tell me things she had never told a soul. To follow is my own paraphrasing of her very long confession, a most revealing confession which I will summarize, using her own words:

"Nadir, although I missed you while you were gone, I was rather relieved that you went back home for your mother's birthday because that interfered with your plans to give me a surprise birthday party at my own dorm. I realized that you were up to something when you found out from my student ID that your mother and I shared the same birthday and I became quite upset when, after you left, Tariq informed me of your sneaky intentions.

Well, for future reference, please remember that I

never celebrate October 6th because it's a very sad day for me. As a matter of fact, I dread the entire month of October because bad things tend to happen, such as the senseless killing of 241 U.S. marines by a truck bomb. Already, this October, Fatima has had surgery, was told that she has lung cancer, and that she will need chemotherapy as soon as she recovers. When I tried to tell Fatima that she should avoid having surgery in October, that I knew in my heart that in October bad things tend to happen, and that it would be better to postpone the surgery until November, she wouldn't listen.

Last October, my grandmother, the one who actually raised me, died a slow, painful death from heart failure. My grandfather, may God keep him healthy and well, is the only family member alive, and he's not in good health."

At that point she fell silent then started speaking of the sea breeze and the sound of waves as though she were dreading what other things she was about to reveal. I said nothing and waited for her to resume when she felt ready. A sesame-bread vendor passed by, and I bought a *"ka'ak"* loaf from him, which he punctured and filled with red sumac. It shocks me that the same sumac, which we call poison sumac in the U.S., is used here to spice so many delicious foods!

When her silence became too prolonged, I broke it by asking why was she raised by her grandparents instead of her parents. She clenched her fists and said that her mom died on her third birthday. When I asked her how, she said that she was run over by a speeding car in Cairo on the same day that Egypt's Sadat was assassinated, which was October 6, 1981. When I inquired what were they doing in Cairo, she said that they were forced to live there by her grandfather because her mom had gotten pregnant with her, out of wedlock, and it would have brought shame to the family name for her mother to give birth in Istanbul to an illegitimate child.

Then I asked her about her dad, and she said that she had never met him although she knows that he is alive because her grandmother told her so just before she died last October. Before then, and for as long as she could remember, both grandparents told her that her dad, a Turkish military spy, had died in a car accident in Cyprus on the same day he found out that her mother was pregnant. She was also told that her mom, who was teaching school in Cyprus at the time, had kept the true identity of her dead lover to herself and took it with her to the grave.

When I asked if she knew her dad's name, she said that the only one who could have possibly known his real name was her mom, and went on to explain that military spies use multiple pseudonyms, sometimes a different name for each contact. She presumed that her mom, if she had known the real name of her dad, would have kept it to herself as a well-guarded secret and would have used a pseudonym to refer to her dad in discussions with her parents.

Her grandfather still thinks that he knows the true identity of her dad, but he really doesn't; he just knows one of his pseudonyms, Mahmoud Ali. But her grandmother confessed to her before she died that her dad was a respectable officer in the Turkish army and that he had maintained contact with her mom during the three years when Güzide and her mom lived in Egypt. Her grandma stayed with them in Cairo for a whole year after Güzide was born, after which she visited them several times a year and always flew to Cairo for Güzide's birthdays. She said that they had a nice apartment, that her mom taught Turkish at Cairo University, and that her dad used to call every Friday, and when her grandmother would answer the phone, he would always introduce himself as Mahmoud Ali and ask to speak to Latife, which was her mom's name.

Her mom, her dad, and her grandmother were all in favor of marriage, but her grandfather wouldn't allow it because he did not want his daughter to marry "a sly, seductive spy who had gotten her pregnant out of wedlock."

It so happened that her grandmother was visiting

the day the accident happened. Her grandfather decided, against her grandmother's pleadings, to have Latife interred in Cairo because a funeral in Istanbul would have drawn attention to the shameful family situation. She was buried the next day, a Wednesday, and when Güzide's dad made his usual call on the following Friday, her grandmother told him what had happened. He began to scream and wanted to come see Güzide, but her grandmother, after a prolonged discussion, informed him that it would be in Güzide's best interests if he would not try to contact them from that point on. When her dad protested with disbelief her grandmother's request, she explained to him that contacting them in Istanbul would cause problems. It would anger the grandfather, threaten the family peace, and perhaps cause Güzide to be deprived of her inheritance, which she would direly need given her blindness. Her father sobbed like a child, agreed to leave them alone, and for the past eighteen years has kept his word.

After packing their things, her grandmother brought Güzide back to Istanbul against her grandfather's wishes and raised her in the same family mansion where her own mom, an only child, was raised. Apparently, her grandfather is a rich businessman who comes from an influential family and his name is Fevzi Istanbullu. One would never know it, Dad, but Güzide Istanbullu is a very rich lady and the sole heir to her grandfather's huge estate.

When we resumed our walk, we held hands. Yes, for the first time ever, we walked together in Beirut—a blond American man and a veiled Muslim woman—holding hands. We felt so close after our mutual confessions and talked more as we walked. She told me that she would like to find her father but that, without knowing his real name, she would not know how to begin. When I asked if her powerful grandfather might have mellowed down enough to help her find her dad, she said that she was reluctant to approach him with this delicate matter because she is not supposed to know that her dad is still alive. She then added that, given his already poor health, it might upset him enough to hasten his death should he find out that his own wife had betrayed him to Güzide by divulging his secret just before she died.

At her dorm, she kissed my hand and I kissed hers. How about that for a first kiss? Then, before she got into the elevator, she asked me not to tell her story to anyone, especially to those who knew her, because that would cause them to treat her differently. I promised, but I also understood that it was not wrong of me to tell you because you do not know her and because you are the only one who could possibly understand why I'm so taken with her. I had to tell someone Dad, and you're the only one I could tell. Ghassan, Frida, and my friends would make fun of me if they were to find out that I have feelings for a blind Turkish girl whose face I have never seen.

After leaving Güzide, I went back to Fatima's room where I spent the rest of the evening with Tariq. While Fatima was being very brave and making light of her situation, Tariq was feeling very frightened about the possibility of losing his mother. We had long talks as we paced the halls and commiserated because both of our moms were now in danger. We tried to console each other by telling jokes and making fun of people and things, especially when we were in Fatima's room. This seemed to cheer her up and make her laugh—in spite of the fact that she tried to resist laughter because it hurt her chest.

But Fatima no longer looks good, Dad. Sometimes, I avoid looking at her because she reminds me too much of how Mom looks. How can this be happening to us? This new reality has damaged my vision of life. The other day, Fatima asked Tariq to leave the room and close the door behind him. After he did, she handed me a letter, told me to hand it to you the next time I see you, and asked me not to mention a word about it to Tariq. She also made me promise that I would not open it, not even if you should beg me to, and that I would not mail it to you, not even if you were to insist that I do.

She had big tears in her eyes when she handed me the letter. Then, quite specifically, she asked me to hide it in my suitcase so that it would always be in my possession when I travel. When I told her that I might not see you till after graduation next July, she smiled and said that it would be much safer to wait until then. I had no idea what she meant by that remark nor did I understand why she didn't want me to mail the letter. Nevertheless, I smiled back and pretended to understand, avoiding further discussion.

It wasn't long before Tariq knocked at the door, poked his head in, and asked Fatima if she were ready for visitors. She quickly tidied up her hair, wiped her tears off, and said, *"Visitors, now? It's almost bedtime!"* Tariq smiled and told her not to worry, that there was only one visitor, someone she would be delighted to see. *"Well, tell me who, tell me who before you let her in."* With a wry smile, Tariq let the visitor in, a handsome man in his early fifties with a dark mustache. When Fatima saw him, she let out a feeble scream, which caused the poor man to freeze in the middle of the room. Tariq motioned for me to follow him; then he closed the door leaving the two alone.

I followed Tariq into the hall, down the elevator, and out of the hospital. On the way back to the dorm, he told me that the man was Kamal, a Turkish officer, his mother's former lover, and Little John's biological father. When I asked him how did Kamal find out that Fatima was in the hospital, he laughed and said that Kamal knows everything about all of us because he is a professional spy. He then confessed to me that Kamal and he had stayed in touch ever since his mom and Kamal broke up, that his mother isn't aware of their secret relationship, and that he was the one who asked Kamal to come because he knew that it would please his mother.

That day, we talked till midnight in a sidewalk café on Bliss Street. He told me their entire story from Cyprus to Kuwait to Beirut, and seemed happy that Kamal, after a long absence, finally came back to visit. When I asked him how long would Kamal stay, he laughed and said that he was flying back at midnight because he was needed at his post in Kurdistan due to escalating Kurdish riots.

He also told me that he had arranged for Fatima to bring Little John and come take care of his mom after she is discharged. I never would have thought that Tariq was capable of such delicate, undercover arrangements because he is never serious about anything. In fact, I was pleasantly surprised to see this side of him. I guess things will never be the same again. We used to look forward to our weekend lunches at Fatima's home. Given how frail she has become, it is going to take her a long time before she can host another lunch.

Perhaps, next weekend I will take Güzide to Tripoli to meet Grandma and have lunch with her. I wonder how Grandma would feel about Güzide. Would she invite her to go to church with us and light a candle for her grandfather? What would people say when a blind, veiled, Muslim-woman walks into the church with Grandma and me on her sides? I doubt that Güzide would mind attending church with us; she believes that *"God couldn't favor one place of worship over another and that the holiest places of worship are those where hearts hear God's calling."*

I have learned a lot from Güzide; she seems to have a personal quotation for each and every situation. As a matter of fact, I'm starting to sound just like her and often find myself quoting her just as others quote famous literary figures. The last quote of hers which made an impression on me was: *"People are more afraid of people than of anything else."*

So far, October has been a sad month, as Güzide predicted. But, Dad, you have taught us to insist on joy in spite of life's tragedies. I'm trying my best, but it is so difficult to be cheerful in the face of illness and death. Tariq is much better at this than I am, and I've learned a lot from him too. I loved his latest saying, *"Sadness is surrender while joy is victory."* I am no longer sure who is the wiser, Güzide the serious, or Tariq the clown. When I'm with Tariq, I become playful, and when with Güzide, I become solemn. But when I'm alone, I become myself

and find great relief in being just me. Here's my latest
limerick, composed in the solitude of my room, inspired by
one of your favorite sayings:

> *"When smiles and tears unite*
> *It might be day or night*
> *We either choose to see or else be blind;*
>
> *The night with tears is bright*
> *The day with smiles is light*
> *Insist on joy, insist and you shall find."*

Goodnight Dad. Please take care of yourself and
tell Mom that I love her. Tell her loud and clear even if you
think that she can't hear. Thanks to Güzide, I've come
to believe that *"all that's said is somehow heard, even by
those who cannot hear; and all that's visible is somehow
seen, even by those who cannot see."*

I love you,

Nadir

Forty-Three

(The Will)

(Beirut – Saturday, January 2, 1999)

Dear John,

Although this is the beginning of another year, it is also the last year of this millennium, the last year for me, and this may also be my last letter to you—so a Happy New Year darling, and I hope your Christmas was warm and kind as was our holy Ramadan which wrapped around Christmas this year.

Unlike other years, however, this year's end was not celebrated with Champagne under the 4500 year-old cedar tree, amidst the white smiles of towering mountains. Little John, Tariq, Nadir, Güzide, and Shamira were all here with me when the New Year midnighted at my humble flat two days ago. You'll be happy to know that throughout our festive evening I did not cough once nor even had the urge to clear my throat. If nothing else, the surgery did cure my chronic nasty cough, my *trademark bark* that announced my presence wherever I went.

I really thought that you would telephone me after Nadir gave you my unfavorable health reports. But instead, you seemed more comfortable sending me your best wishes with Nadir's weekly calls. It's too late for regrets anyway, and time is shorter than it has ever been for me. I have resisted writing to you ever since I left the hospital, but I can no longer delay because I am getting weaker and soon the day will come when I shall be too weak to write.

I spend my days at home with Little John by my side while Fatima nurses us both during the week and goes back to her family and home on weekends. What a guardian angel she is. Praise God who created us and put us together. You know that Fatima is a holy name, for it is the name of Prophet Mohammad's daughter who became the wife of Imam Ali and the mother of Al Hassan and Al Hussein.

Before I left the hospital, I had a candid discussion with Dr. Hubaiter and simply asked him what would he do if he had my incurable lung cancer. He became restless and tried to avoid the answer by saying that the surgeon was able to remove the lobe that had the cancer. But when I pressed him about all the positive lymph nodes they found, he conceded that, in retrospect, removing the cancerous lobe was not a good idea because it is not expected to improve the outcome.

When I asked him what was the expected outcome, he evaded the answer and discoursed on chemotherapy and radiation therapy as palliative options. When I asked him if palliative meant just for comfort and not for cure, he nodded keeping his gaze to the floor. Then, I pressed him on and said, *"So, what would you do if you were me?"* He said, *"It depends on so many things."* *"It depends,"* I quickly interrupted him, *"but that's John's favorite phrase"* and we both laughed. (It was good comic relief, you must admit.)

Then, I phrased the question differently by asking, *"Would I be a fool not to take chemotherapy or radiation therapy?"* He said with his gaze still on the floor, *"No, I think you would be wise because the side effects ruin the quality of the little life you have left."* *"And how much do I have left?"* I whispered. He answered me with a cliché, *"Life is in God's hands."*

I was determined not to go home like a blind fool and so I pressed him further by saying, *"God knows the exact time but doctors know the approximate time. Do I measure my remaining life in days, weeks, months, or years?"* He smiled at my persistence and said, *"Not in years, my lady,"* and that was enough for me. I went home content, repeating your words, the words from your last letter, *"I will not waste life on death, Fatima; instead, I will learn from it because it is a mighty life force, great teacher of the living, exhumer of buried emotions, provoker of imaginations, inseminator of thoughts, creator of myths, tamer of rebellious spirits, key holder of the last life door."*

I am not sad anymore, and that is why I am able to write to you. I know that all will be taken care of because Um Al-Huda said so. So far, I have been blessed with much good fortune. Kamal came to visit me in the hospital and promised that he would take care of Little John. Moreover, he has been sending me $1000 a month ever since his brief, four-hour visit. I now understand what Fatima meant when she told me a year ago that Kamal would take care of Little John when Little John would need him. I also understand what she meant when she explained earlier this year that my first seven prayers to Um Al-Huda covered our twenty-eight years apart, a prayer for each four years, and that the eighth prayer meant that you would see me in the next four years. Well, Fatima is never wrong because she speaks for Um Al-Huda. So, get yourself ready darling; you are coming for a visit, even if you don't think so.

Tariq is acting wild these days. He visits me after classes every afternoon and tries to cheer me up by telling me all the dirty jokes he has heard that day. When I see that he is about to tell a joke, I hold my chest with both hands and beg him not to start because laughter still causes me great pain. He tells me the jokes anyway and seems to get a kick out of my painful laughter. When Nadir comes with him, it gets even wilder because the two compete in clowning for me as if I were a sick child. I think they enjoy taking care of me for a change, and of course, I am glad to let them do it.

One day, after a particularly wild session, I happened to ask Güzide if the two of them clowned as much when they are elsewhere. She replied evasively by saying that they no longer clown around her. After she said that, it occurred to me that laughter was their adolescent way of lashing out against the world and their manly way of shedding tears when around me.

Ah, the many faces and disguises of fear. Fear, my darling, is a great mimicker. It may come to the grand masquerade ball of life costumed with laughter or with tears, masked with revenge or hate, camouflaged with seriousness or folly, supplicant with worship or meek with submission, defiant with armor or rebellious with rage. But, once you have dwelt in the caverns of fear, you recognize the chameleon regardless of color or garb. The kids are afraid, John, and so am I. Fatima, on the other hand, seems resigned and unperturbed—confident in her belief that all will be well after I am gone. I wish I had a mustard seed of her faith because faith is the best antidote to fear.

But where does love fit into all of this? What will happen to my love for Tariq and Little John? What will happen to my love for you, a love that I have nurtured for over thirty years? Will love crumble with my ashes or will it re-inseminate other souls? Will you still be able to feel my love when I am no longer? Why is love the only emotion that drives the arts? Why is it that emotions unaccompanied by the tunes of love remain unsung? Indeed, it's love that reaches out to our souls and gives life its significance. I agree with you that love is what defines beauty, and I agree with Gandhi that wherever there is love, there is life. So then, what happens to love after life is no more? Tell me John; will you still feel my love after I leave?

When I asked Fatima this bitter question, this burning question that has focused my attention like a magnifying lens under the sun, she smiled in her usual, pacifying way and went into the kitchen without saying a word. She emerged a while later with a cup of tea and set it in my lap. *"The Prophet exempts the sick from fasting,"* she said as she sat by my side, held my hand, and continued. *"Ramadan is a holy month, and I am a fasting woman; truth, and only truth can come out of my mouth. Love never dies because love is God in us. When we die, love goes wherever we will it to go. You can will your love exactly like you will your worldly assets. All you have to do is pray and ask God to bestow your love on someone else. At the moment of death, love relocates and forever changes the chosen soul. Dying during the holy month of*

Ramadan is especially blessed because the chosen soul not only receives your love; it also receives your faith as love inseminates the chosen soul with God."

While Fatima and I sat in silence holding hands, Little John crawled in bed with me and fell asleep without saying a word, as if something in him understood the solemnity of the moment.

When Fatima turned off the lights, I held Little John's hand and began to pray. I willed to Kamal my love for Little John because that would bind them to each other and may even soften Gulnar's heart into accepting Little John into her Istanbul family. Then, I willed to you my love for Tariq and the reason for that is explained in the letter that Nadir is to hand you the next time you see each other. Then, I willed to Ms. Settembrini my love for you—after that, a serene peace came over me and I was able to fall asleep. I woke up with the early morning Adan calling the faithful to prayer, *"Allahu Akbar, Hayyou Alassalat."* Like God's face, the sea was calm, and I was a joyful woman ready for my new life in all those I have willed my love to.

John, please do not get upset with me, and do not resist my will for it has now become the will of God. I know you too well, more than you care to know yourself—you need to be in love, otherwise your soul lies fallow, unseeded with joy, incapable of sprouting tender, green poems. Moreover, do not target Ms. Settembrini with your ignoble wrath; give each other time, and you will see how love will come naturally to bridge your gaps and fill in your echoing vacuums. Re-invite her to your poetry gatherings; all she needs is a kind sign, a gentle gesture, and a soothing touch to wipe off your last scratch.

As for your dying wife, I willed her my faith, which will relocate into her as soon as I'm gone. The idea came to me when one day, I asked Fatima what was faith? She did not have to go to the kitchen to prepare tea before she answered. She just smiled into my eyes and whispered, *"Faith is the love of God; if you love God enough, all your fears would turn to joys."* I was startled by her answer, but at the same time, I was overjoyed because it meant that my peace and joy at facing my own death were a form of love, the love of God within my soul. It was then that I decided to will my love of God to Norma, because the faith it brings would help her have a joyful death, and will give you and your children enough peace to take the place of anguish in your hearts.

There is one more thing that I need to say. I have carried a burdensome secret for many years and have kept it far away from you for reasons that will become obvious when you find out. My intentions were never to tell a soul, especially you, but I changed my mind when I found out that I was dying. After much soul searching, I decided to save my secret by handing it to you. You are under no obligation to keep my secret alive, and I would understand if you were to decide to take it with you to your grave.

While agonizing over what to do with my secret, and without revealing any details, I asked Fatima's opinion. She said something that made me wonder if she already knew. She said that she sees my secret as an eager fruit tree. *"Trees are God's gifts,"* she said, *"and it would be wrong to kill a tree or prevent it from bearing fruit. Hand it to John, instead; he will know how to take care of it."* That was all she needed to say and all I needed to ask.

I saw the wisdom of her vision as soon as she revealed it to me, and it helped me make up my mind to hand my fruit tree to you, perhaps under your care it might bear sweet fruits for all to taste.

I am too tired to say any more. You will know what to do when you read the letter. Please write quickly, if you can spare the time. I would love to read your last letter as you have read mine. And please, do send me pictures of Frida, Ghassan, and Ghassan's family. I feel a strange urge to see them before I take leave.

John, think of me each time you grant or receive a smile and remember me with joy.

I love you,

Fatima

Forty-Four

(Valentine's)

(Oklahoma City – Sunday, February 14, 1999)

Dear Fatima,

I went to the store today to buy groceries. They are selling flowers for twice the price because it's Valentine's Day. I saw more men queuing at the cashier stands, last-minute men ill at ease with flowers, rugged men uncomfortable with whispering pinks and gossiping reds, men paying hard-earned money to evince love in ways too effeminate for their masculine natures.

Valentine's Day comes every year to rekindle gratitude for loves that have sustained us, loves without which we would have blown away like tumbleweeds and snagged on fences far from where we were uprooted by the winds of fate. Fatima, I am the tumbleweed that blew over the Atlantic twenty-nine years ago and grayed on life's barbed-wire fence awaiting spring. Still, I bought flowers because, as Whitman says, *"earth smiles with flowers"* and flowers smile for those of us who have lost their gleam. I bought two bunches, and when I walked into the house, Frida asked me with a wry grin, *"Are they both for me?"*

We laughed as we embraced, and then I told her that one bunch is for her mother and one for a sick patient in a far away hospital. She took the red roses, arranged them in a vase, and placed them by her mother's side. I arranged the pink roses, took them to Frida's bedroom, and placed them in the window light, facing east. Can you smell their sweet, whispering scent?

Although I get your news from Nadir, telephone calls echo with cold distance that dulls emotions. When I call him, he relates to me the sundry details of his life with Güzide, leaving you unmentioned until the moment I ask about you. That question always tails with an eerie silence that wags between us until his feeble voice returns the perfunctory answer, *"She's doing OK."* I dread that weekly call because it leaves me weak, enfeebled by a situation that I cannot mitigate. I remember Paul Valéry's sagacious saying, *"A difficulty is a light; an un-surmountable difficulty is a sun."* I neither feel the heat nor see the rays; where is that sun, Fatima?

Your last letter drowned into my soul like an anchor, pinning me down, tethering me to a weight I cannot pull. It made me feel as though I were—like Eliot's *J. Alfred Prufrock*—sprawling on a pin, wriggling on the wall, unable to spit out all the butt-ends of my days and ways. I am pinned to Norma and tethered to Fatima, and both of you are leaving ahead of me—or should I not presume?

Your personal will of love, your final gift to me, my soul's rightful inheritance, has razed my apathy to the ground. This last testament of yours leaves me seeds to plant in my hope garden, seeds that will bear fruits, fruits that I shall dispatch into the future as your ambassadors of good will. You entrust Tariq to me, entrust me to Mrs. Settembrini, announce that love never dies, that it trans-locates from one soul to another, and that it is God's immortal spark within us. Oh, my dear Fatima, I wish I had your indomitable faith; I wish I could experience for one moment what you infinitely feel; I wish I could befriend God as you and my mother have.

My views on life and death are not as serene as yours. I see life as an accident that sprouted out of death, an ephemeral flower that blossomed in mutiny out of earth's inanimate crust, a glorious aria that burst out of eternal silence, a voice in the wilderness that sang out of a fire-cold space, a sardonic laugh that roared like a war out of universal peace, the memory of memories that chronicled history upon the cave walls of oblivious time.

I see death as the eternal cradle of life, the solemn keeper of spirits rebellious, the guardian of ineffable mysteries, the resting place of faith and love, the fertile soil of imagination, and the quietude of eternity in whose shade sleeps God.

Perhaps, you and I see the same things but in different lights and say the same things but in different tongues. Perhaps I will learn from you to see heaven as the eighth dimension, an infinite dimension that gleams above space, outside time, beyond life, behind death, and aloft imagination—a dimension emanating solely from the sublime fragrances of faith.

Fatima, I will not say good-bye because life belongs to no one but to itself, because it sings the future with voices from its past, because it is the glorious torch of humanity, a brilliant torch that those finishing, hand over to those starting and those ending, to those beginning. I shall carry your torch, Fatima, and hand it to my children who will hand it to theirs, and theirs, and theirs... until the relay race ends at the feet of God.

And although I yearn to see you, I am unable to entrust Norma's care to anyone else except Ghassan or Nathan, but neither of them is here. Nevertheless, I shall see your flame in every season—when Winter hands its burning firewood to Spring, when Spring hands its blushing blossoms to Summer, when Summer hands its burning torch to Autumn, and when Autumn hands its crimson leaves to winter.

I will not say good-bye, Fatima, because I have learned faith from you, the faith that repudiates death—and because I have learned love from you, the love that transcends time, the love that is life, all of life, life in its inscrutable entirety. Instead, I will think of you as my communion wine, the ageless wine that leaves its holy spirits in me long after it is gone.

Can you feel my insides quickening with you? Can you sense me burning within your soul? Do you see me in Nadir's astonished eyes when they look at you and say, young once but forever in love? Can you look up at your two blossoming branches, Tariq and Little John, and hear the singing nests among their leaves? You will always be the stem that feeds these fragrant branches, which feed the blossoms that hold the singing nests, the nests that hold life, the life that flies away when wings are strong, flies away into the future, never to return.

You will always be a part of me, Fatima. Let us never say good-bye; let us just hold on to our souls and hope they lead us to where spirits and time intersect at the cross, the cross of the eighth dimension, the cross of heaven.

We are the products of our times, and our times are the products of their preceding times, and their preceding times are the products of their preceding times, and this goes on until the beginning of time. Indeed, we are the cosmic fruits of the entire Universe from its very inception until its present state. Indeed, you and I could not have existed, if during the past 13.7 billion years, one atom had gone awry and disturbed the intricate universal order that had produced us.

Let us cling, my love. Let us cling without the feeblest comprehension of what eternity might bring. Let us cling by the sheer might of faith, the faith that your Fatima defined as *"the love of God in us."* Let us cling then; let us cling for the love of God; let us cling because, as Saint Augustine said, *"If you can love God enough, you can do no wrong."*

> *"And when the breeze and trees will die*
> *And when the singing birds will fly*
> *And when the clouds depart the sky*
> *When none will care nor wonder why*
> *When naught is left but you and I*
> *Love, still, will visit us and bring*
> *A hug of dreams upon her wing*
> *And smiles and sighs and everything*
> *Because we cling."*

Sleep lightly and dream of life, of children, of weddings, and of grandchildren. Dream of date-laden oases, of sun-shaded gardens, and of crimson songs that rise out of eve-blushed horizons. Dream of long peace and blithe harmony, which transcend the noisy chaos of life to reunite gracefully with the vast orderly universe.

Sleep joyfully and rest fearlessly for there are no wars among the many kingdoms of sleep and the armless clock of heaven keeps no time and makes no chime; it merely plays subliminal music for souls taking their due repose.

In spite of your turmoil and tumult, you have arrived at the gates of peace whose open arms are eager to embrace you. Seven centuries ago, Meister Eckhart preached that one attains peace to the extent that one attains God and that any soul at peace has God in it to the extent that it has peace.

Sleep in God then, for God's sleep is forever joyful. One day, I, the East-born pilgrim bearing pink roses, shall awaken you with a love-scented poem, a mighty prayer whose vespers reunite the reality of imagination and the imagination of reality.

I love you always,

John

Forty-Five

(Valentine's)

(Oklahoma City – Sunday, February 14, 1999)

Dear Nadir,

Your last letter pulled the veil off my eyes, a veil unlike Güzide's, a veil that protected darkness by prohibiting light. You spoke of Güzide with tender joy, and I received your news with heart-felt delight. I did not realize, however, that I could sprout feelings in absentia for someone that I did not know until I came to love Güzide through your warm renditions of her. From that precept, I simply reasoned that if I have come to love her through you, then you must love her too. Hence, with Valentine's being the day of love declarations, I ask you not to euphemize your feelings any longer nor gossamer them with a veil of camouflaged expressions. I love you always and will always love those whom love chooses for you.

You must have heard that President Clinton was almost impeached and that in his state-of-the-union address he refused to redress the delicate issues that nearly caused his downfall. I am certain that, as an American abroad, you must have tasted the bitter cynicisms of anti-American sentiments among the student body at the AUB and the Arab World at large. Do not be surprised because, even in Oklahoma, I have also heard opinions of equally sinister auras. I say all that not to deepen the wound we both feel but to assuage it with the balsam of sharing.

Disparagements expose the souls' undergarments of both, the disparager and the disparaged. Noble souls, on the other hand, do not take pleasure in the downfalls of others, especially those held to higher standards. Let us ease our pains in private solitude and nurse our wounds unseen—like a father who greets the world with a smile even though his daughter might have been raped, or his wife swept away by the waves of an affair, or his child fallen prey to drug addiction or the HIV virus.

Something about media and public ruthlessness carries within it the stench of cruelty and the seeds of cultural decay. Regardless of offenses committed, trespassing upon another human's dignity diminishes one's own. There is a tight rope between propriety and the exposing of ugly truths, a rope that will readily snap if not tempered by compassion. A hanging is a private punishment, not a public spectacle, and compassion for the fallen and for those perceived to be lesser than we are is what Christianity is all about. Keep your head high, son, and remember that those uncaught are not better than those who are caught. *"He who is without sin let him cast the first stone,"* is as meaningful today as it has ever been because human nature has not grown wiser with time.

Since you have left, Mom has gotten slowly weaker and more withdrawn. Her cardiovascular condition seems stable, but she is unaware of her surroundings and unable to take nourishment unless I put it into her mouth. My help and I keep her fresh and clean like a rose garden. I read your letters to her, and I know that they affect her because she breathes faster and faster while I read and releases doleful sighs when I end. She no longer reacts, however, when I read poetry to her, which leads me to think that she prefers your voice to that of the great poets, an honor that you must cherish, especially at your young age.

Nadir, please continue to write and always write in your beautiful longhand; writing e-mails lacks the artful touch and the emotional bouquet of handwritten letters. Moreover, I would not be able to present them to your mother as handcrafted gifts from her son abroad.

Frida is now driving. I bought her a used car, which she will surely wreck and, by so doing, will hopefully learn to be more careful with her next one. She is starting to help me take care of Mom by sharing shifts; she stays with Mom from the time our help leaves until I return home from the hospital. I prepare dinner, and we eat it in Mom's room. Then, after we take care of the dishes, she leaves and I stay with Mom for the rest of the evening. Mom's illness has matured Frida faster than necessary for a seventeen-year-old girl and has rendered the difference between her classmates and herself rather evident.

We often talk about Güzide and you during dinner. Like her older brother, she can hardly wait to go away to college and meet with her own adventures. Once, during one of our daily dinner conversations, I asked her what would become of her boyfriend of two years after she moves away to college. She blushed and, following an awkward pause, said that they are not serious enough to be possessive of one another. Then, as an afterthought, she mumbled that they planned to see each other when they came home for vacations. It is at times like these that I miss Mom's participation the most. Such conversations always make daughters and dads feel most uncomfortable with each other.

There is a most delicate matter that I need to explore with you now, a matter that must be handled with extreme gentleness. Your last letter unwittingly deciphered a twenty-one year-old, arcane, unrequited love that you and I have the responsibility to resurrect from its dead repose. Please do sit down if you are standing, for this concerns you as much as it concerns Güzide.

A long time ago, when Fatima was in Cyprus, and Kamal was jailed, I wrote and asked her to go visit Kamal's wife on the Turkish side of the island. After visiting Gulnar, she wrote to me a most informative letter in which she related to me a story that not even Tariq knows, a story about Kamal's premarital affair with a Turkish schoolteacher who became pregnant out of wedlock and bore him a blind daughter whom he has never seen. The daughter was born on October 6, 1978 in Cairo. Three years later, while still in Cairo, the mother was killed by a speeding car. It happened on the daughter's third birthday, the very same day that Egypt's Sadat was assassinated—

October 6, 1981. Nadir, do I need to tell you more...?

The dimple on Güzide's chin (the dimple that reminded you of Kirk Douglas and caused you, when you became annoyed with her, to call her Kirk of a Turk) and the dimple on Little John's chin, both came from the same father, Kamal, who by Fatima's description, also has a dimpled chin. Physiognomy aside, congenital blindness runs through Kamal's family line, and Fatima knows it. That Kamal is Güzide's father is a most certain assertion. That he be united with Güzide is imperative given that he was denied his fatherly rights ever since her birth. That their love for one another be ignited is as crucial as setting dormant wood to living flame in order to guard a naked infant against the bitter cold. That they be brought together, in spite of formidable obstacles, in order to complete their life circles, is God's divine wish for us to accomplish.

Think how tedious the Lord's work had been, how meticulously exacting, and how many billion genetic, environmental, and circumstantial coincidences it took to bring them together. Think of yourself as God's tool, and you will surmise that it is now your solemn responsibility to facilitate this heaven-ordained union.

Please be careful in choosing your steps so that no one will falter or break a heart. Work with Tariq and Fatima, prepare your strategy, let your execution be compassionate and kind, and when your work is done, leave father and daughter alone to catch up on twenty-one years of estrangement, twenty-one years forever lost.

As for Fatima, do not worry about overburdening her last days. The joy she will receive from smelling the freshly sprouted love-blossoms between Güzide and Kamal will ease her leave-taking and give her life a fresh, magical meaning.

You might remind her that she was the one chosen by the muses to be love's conductor, for without our adolescent love, Fatima and I would not have stayed in touch with letters all these years nor would she have received you, my ambassador son, into her life and introduced you to her beloved Tariq.

Without her love for Kamal, Little John would not have been born nor would she have learned about Kamal's blind daughter.

Without her love for writing, she would not have related to me Güzide's birth story and, in turn, I could not have revealed it to you and entrusted you with the responsibility of bringing father and daughter together and reuniting their severed lives.

Without Fatima's hospitable love for the group, Güzide would not have met Little John nor would she have experienced the mystery of this sudden love-bond that united Little John with his sister when neither of them realized that they were descended from the same father.

Indeed, without Fatima's love for all of us, you would not have met and could not have loved Güzide—and without her love for Um Al-Huda, her faith wouldn't have redirected all of our lives toward each other and wouldn't have lead us all toward this solemn denouement.

Nadir, go to work with my fatherly blessings; you have a most joyful mission to accomplish. I have my own ideas on how you should proceed, but I will keep them to myself because you are the omniscient man on site, the catalyst in a formidable human reaction that is about to take place, and you, alone, should decide on how to give this blithe love compound its long-awaited renaissance.

Nevertheless, let me leave you with these thoughts. Your mind is a womb, my son, filled with the potentials of life. However, a womb un-inseminated with new ideas is doomed to remain infertile. New ideas come from without, from nature, from other people, and not from within as our hubris would lead us to believe. Let your intercourse with new ideas be both humble and selective lest you be infested with the wrong idea and give birth to a blighted child that would burden the rest of your life.

Inculcation, contamination, and pollution of innocent minds with indelible, archaic, or separatist ideas are social evils that fragment humanity into violent clubs and cruel clans. Be circumspect in allowing separatist ideas admission into your hitherto tidy brain, but also be daring and fearless in giving humanitarian ideas access into your discriminating soul.

I say all this because there is time, and yet, there is no time. I say it because your judgment is good, and yet, your judgment is poor—because, at times, you are rational and at times, irrational—because you are of the democratic, human rights-upholding West but also of the autocratic, violent, dogmatic East. Filter your ideas with your rational mind; quarantine them until you prove them sane, humane, peace loving, worthy of your philanthropic soul, and not separatist or inimical. Understand but pity violence, for it is a regression toward misanthropic animalism, and never grant it admission into your heart, not even as a last resort. Your last resort should always be Christ; understanding, forgiveness, sacrifice, loving indiscriminately, letting go, and moving on are the attributes of a noble soul.

Nothing worthwhile ever happens without passion, for passion is the mother of courage, father of effort, and mighty enthraller of reason. I pray that all your passions continue to originate from the grace of God, from the canons of His divine spark within your soul, and not from the zoonotic needs of your mundane nature. A reckless foolishness abides in youth, fueled by impatience, un-yielding to reason, and un-tempered by wisdom. Season this fire within you with the love of humanity, and you will do no harm to others or yourself.

And when asked if you are a Christian or an American, or a man, reply by saying that you are a human being from planet earth who happened to be born male, to a Christian family, in America. Always let your human identity supplant your birthright identities for that is the shortest road to humanitarianism. Indeed, it is almost demeaning to become known by what you have been given instead of what you have chosen, on your own, as your life's calling.

We miss you here, but you are more needed where you are. You will have to graduate without me in the cheering audience because I cannot leave your mother, not even for a few days, not even for you. But, on graduation day, I shall cheer you from the other side of earth, from your mother's room, and in your heart, you will hear our proud applause.

Give my love to Güzide, Tariq, Little John, Kamal, and the two Fatimas.

I love you,

Dad

Forty-Six

(Leave-taking)

(Beirut - Saturday, March 13, 1999)
<Tariqraci@hotmail.com>

Dear Dr. John,

It has been a long time since I have written even though sending e-mails has become easier and the laptop you sent me still works well. Nadir has become the brother I never had, and we have done a lot of talking lately due to Mom's illness. There are some things that are hard for me to talk about with Nadir, mainly because I like to show him my funny, strong side instead of my weak side.

The other day, he caught me crying and we talked till midnight, but he could not answer many of my questions. He advised me to write to you but not to use the e-mail because you prefer handwritten letters. He said that e-mails are too fast and do not allow the writer the time to think. I know that he is right, but this letter is urgent, and I don't want to send it by airmail. Besides, I need the spell checker and the grammar checker because my English is not so good yet. So I'm sorry to send you this e-mail, but I also need quick answers, and I'm sure you'll understand.

What did you mean with what you said about Mom in your letter to Nadir? You said to him not to worry about overburdening her last days and that the joy she will receive will ease her leave-taking and give her life a fresh, magical meaning. What did you mean by leave-taking? Please don't be like her doctor. Please be honest and tell me the truth.

Dr. John, I need to know if my mother is going to be OK. She tells me that she will be fine, but she keeps getting sicker. The doctor comes to visit her at home and says to me that she is doing better than expected. When I ask him if she is going to be fine and if she will be able to return to work, he gives me a hug and says *inshallah*, if God wishes. I am not medical, but I am smart, and they are not telling me the truth. Please tell me what is going on and if Mom is going to get well or not. You know that if something should happen to her, we would all be in trouble. I cannot imagine life without Mom. Dad and I get along fine, and he pays my college expenses, but he is not my emotional friend like Mom is. I know that I will be lost without her.

Nadir got your letter explaining that Kamal is Güzide's father. He called me as soon as he read it and told me that there is something I need to read. I came to his dorm, and he handed me your letter. I wish I had your English. We read it over and over so many times until we understood what you meant about everything. Then we spent the next week planning how to get Kamal and Güzide together without shocking them. Finally, we decided that we should tell Kamal first and so I called him and told him the whole story. He began to cry like a child, and laugh, and cry again and again. He said that he is going to come next weekend and asked that we should all meet him at the airport, meaning Güzide too. He said that Nadir and I should go immediately to Güzide's dorm and tell her together so that she would have time to prepare her mind. We called her and went to her dorm as soon as I said good-bye to Kamal.

She received us in the community room, but it was full of students, and we did not think it was the right place to tell her about Kamal. Instead, we pretended that we wanted to take her for a walk, and she became suspicious because it was windy and rainy. Finally, we convinced her to take us up to her room, something she had never done before. Then we told her that there was a letter she needed to hear so she sat on her bed and became silent as if she knew that something serious was coming. Nadir first apologized to her for not keeping her secret to himself as he had promised her. Then he said that she would understand why as soon as she heard the letter. She said nothing and remained still, thinking that we were bringing her bad news from home. Then Nadir pulled himself together and started reading your letter very slowly. When she heard you tell Nadir not to conceal his love for her, she became restless and started to sit and stand trying to find a comfortable position, and her hands began to shake and Nadir turned pale. When Nadir finished the whole letter, she became motionless and so did we. We were all afraid to move and afraid to speak. Then, after a long wait, she surprised the heck out of both of us.

She took off her veil. She did, and threw it on the bed, and let us look at her face for the longest time. Except for her eyes, which are small and closed, she is beautiful, and I could see that this pleased Nadir because he blushed and lost his pale face. Then she asked us with a shaken voice if she resembled her father. We both said yes, because the resemblance was obvious. Then she asked if her father had a dimpled chin, and we both said yes at the same time.

Then she asked Nadir to sit by her on the bed, held his hand, put her head on his shoulder, and began to cry but very quietly. Then Nadir put his arm around her and pulled her to him, and they started to cry. At that point, I knew that I was no longer needed, and so I left them alone and went straight to Mom with your letter in my hand and I gave it to her. She said that she had just received a beautiful letter from you, but she was not sure that it was proper of her to read Nadir's letter. I said that Nadir was OK with it and so she began to read and shake her head. Then she gave me back the letter and asked me if I had already called Kamal. Then she told me to call Güzide and have Nadir bring her over because she wanted to talk to her alone and to see her face without a veil.

I called and found them still in her room and so I told Nadir to bring Güzide and come over. They were happy to come, and when they arrived, Little John paused a while as if he did not recognize Güzide without her veil. Then, he let out an eerie scream and ran to her. It was so touching because she lifted him up and kissed him again and again saying, hello little brother, hello darling, hello my love.

Mom asked Güzide to sit on her bed and asked us both to leave them alone and not return until she called me on my cell phone. Nadir and I went out to dinner and then went to the library to study. When Mom called me, it was almost ten at night, which was good because Güzide had until eleven before she had to return to her dorm. I don't know what she and Mom talked about, but it must have been good because Güzide seemed peaceful when we took her back. The only thing she said on the way back was that Mom wanted us to pick up Kamal and come straight from the airport to her apartment, and that she was going to cook a meal for all of us, just like the old days. I didn't think that she had the energy to entertain us like she used to, but knowing Mom, she will probably surprise us all.

We are all anxious now because Kamal arrives next Saturday at noon. Güzide had Nadir take her to the hairdresser because she wanted to look good for her dad and was not going to wear her veil when she meets him. She seems like a different person. She even had Nadir go with her to choose a nice dress. We have never seen her in a dress before. She always wears black pants, a black top, a black veil, and also wears a black coat when it is cold. Even her shoes and socks are black.

Nadir also seems like a different person. He has a strange gleam in his eyes and has become totally absentminded. At times, when I talk to him or ask him a question, I find him unaware as if in outer space. I have to repeat what I say so often now that I wonder if he has become deaf. Can love make one really deaf? I have been in love several times, but I do not recall ever becoming hard of hearing! On the other hand, I have never fallen as deeply in love as Nadir and Güzide have. You should see them together; they are like a pair of spring birds singing to the air, singing for no reason and for no occasion.

Dr. John, I know how much you hate e-mails, but I cannot wait for your handwritten letters because they take too long to arrive. Please write soon and tell me what you meant by what you wrote about Mom. I can take it if you can tell it. I just need to know. Somehow, I think that Nadir knows and Mom knows and even Güzide knows and I am the only one who is still ignorant. I feel that everyone is trying to protect me, especially my mother's family and friends. They all seem to be so interested in me all of a sudden and go out of their way to be kind and supportive. I have never been treated that well before because no one likes the fact that I am homosexual and, on account of that, they usually avoid me.

Please write soon, and thank you very much for loving Mom and for being kind to me and for sending us Nadir.

With all my love,

Tariq

Forty-Seven

(Acquiescence)

(Oklahoma City - Sunday, March 14, 1999)
<**Johnkhoury@hotmail.com**>

My Dear Tariq,

Laden with light and unprepared for darkness, you bring me to prayer with your fervent eagerness to apprehend in youth what is naturally relegated to age. Hence, before I share my truths, I need to wash your eyes with the smiles and tears that sun and storm the annals of human history. Only then would you see that we own nothing but our thoughts and feelings and that everything else is on loan.

Loans are aids to life and not substitutes. Indeed, loans are debts to be paid back, paid back not with grief, but with joy and gratitude instead. What life has loaned us awhile—our bodies and our sensory world—what life has granted us that we may become what we have become, are but loans ephemeral, to be recalled whenever they come due. What we do not have to return, the immortal sparks within us—our feelings and our thoughts—are ours to give, and they will continue to live in others long after we are recalled. Indeed—we are only what we think and what we feel—the rest of us, and the rest of the world surrounding us, do not belong to us.

> *"I placed my life in savings at the bank*
> *I spend it wisely and I always thank*
> *My Banker, though he gives no interest*
> *Nor does he tell me how much I have left."*

I wrote these lines when I was your age, but with each year they acquire deeper significance. Wisdom that resides in our unconscious mind unfurls its more brilliant colors as we gray. Without God's mysteries, there is no faith, and without God's loans, there is no life. Let us water the garden of life with gratitude and rejoice in our unending harvest of thoughts and feelings that will continue long after summer browns the garden and winter renders it white.

Who is not dying, my dear Tariq? Is not everything living, also dying? Is not every living creature due home at curfew time. Your mother is not dying alone; we are all dying with her, and if she must precede us then we all must follow. Death is not an incident, a black mole on snow-cheeked time. It is the beginning of all life, for life always blossoms out of the inanimate and always returns to it as the seasonal garden grows and returns to soil. Indeed, everything living has risen from the dead and everyone alive is a Lazarus, for death is the alpha and the omega of life. Therefore, let us not begrudge our return to earth; rather, let us be grateful for our resurrection.

Think of your mother as an everlasting bouquet of thoughts and feelings that aromatize your soul and the souls of all whom she has touched. Think of her as a living spirit that whispers memories into your heart. Think of her as the light from a star that travels light years to brighten up your darkest moments, long after the star is extinguished. Think of her as a continuum from soil-to-spirit and from spirit-to-soil, a continuum that infused you with life, and a continuum that orbits into the future by encircling the past.

Death is naught but a shortsighted human creation. No one really dies, my dear Tariq—we are merely transformed from one form to another, translated from one page to another, phoenixed from one age to another, arranged and rearranged but never lost to nature or to God.

If you do not know this stanza from Wordsworth's *Ode on Intimations of Immortality,* please learn it by heart because it will help your gift of faith put things into proper perspective.

"Though nothing can bring back the hour
Of splendor in the grass, of glory in the flower;
We will grieve not, rather find
Strength in what remains behind;
In the primal sympathy
Which having been must ever be;
In the soothing thoughts that spring
Out of human suffering;
In the faith that looks through death,
In the years that bring the philosophic mind."

Like death is the cradle of life, life is the sun of death from which it rises, shines, and then sets only to rise again. And because life is motion, and nothing in motion is dead, then nothing in this entire cosmos is dead; indeed, every speck is animated by purposeful motion, and no atom is still.

Your mother, my dear Tariq, is taking leave to go back home to her cradle. She is taking leave a few cosmic seconds before we do, but soon we shall all follow. What are a few cosmic seconds but a sigh that separates our homecomings?

Celebrate her life before she leaves the sky; claim the bouquet of thoughts and feelings your soul is heir to when she sets; rejoice at the horizon's blush with all that your soul has inherited; and then await in the peaceful quietude of night, the coming of sunrise:

"I watch the birth, far at the edge of earth,
A gladdened shimmering without a cry—
And then the flapping, golden clouds of mirth
Before the fireball redeems the sky."

Memory is the garden in which our thoughts and feelings thrive—the richer the soil, the more glorious the blooms, and the sweeter the fruits. Those who take leave of us give us the task of watering their garden, suffusing it with light, keeping it green, visiting it with seasons, and fertilizing it with dreams:

"At splendid morns like these, I find your eyes
In quiet clouds that lash upon the skies,
In vast awakenings that reunite
The depths of darkness and the laughs of
light."

The fear of death is the lack of faith, the fear of loss is the lack of faith, and the fear of adversity is the lack of faith. Indeed, fear is naught but the lack of courage, and courage is naught but the smile of faith within our souls.

"The mighty kindness of the morning sun
The Maker's daily gift for everyone
A giving love, conditionless and free
Is for the frightened, ruthless world to see."

I pray that you understand from all this that you should celebrate your mother at all times and not tether your celebration to the certainty of her presence among us. I pray that you will not lament her transmutation from one realm to another. Rather, cheer her translation with joy for she is about to graduate out of this physical world into the metaphysical.

Taking leave is not taking life away but rather giving back a life put to excellent use. Out of her life so many other lives have been inseminated and are growing lovely blooms that will continue to frolic with the seasons.

"Leaving is giving
Rain leaves the clouds
Rivers, the snow
Light, the sun
Seeds, the soil
Birth, the womb
Thoughts, the mouth
Tunes, the harp
Poems, the heart."

Think of your mother as a seasonal flower, a high-spirited gleam whose beauty lingers beyond the seasons.

> *"Flowers are free*
> *To bloom*
> *To beautify*
> *To die*
> *Birds leave the nest*
> *To seize the sky*
> *High spirits flap*
> *Their dreams and fly."*

My dear Tariq, let your mother leave in peace that she may leave peace behind. Do not cling for that would bring pain to her leave taking. Release her with joy for she is transitioning to realms intangible. Celebrate her pioneer spirit and novel homesteading for she is forerunning to where we will all follow and the only distance between us is meager time.

I have learned happiness from fools, joy from the wise, courage from faith, and acquiescence from nature. I have learned nothing from those who are morose, evasive, or fearful. Indeed, I have learned nothing but worry from those who nurture negative perceptions about life. Remember what the great poet Ghalib said:

> *"The heart is an embarrassment to the chest*
> *if it's not on fire."*

In his last letter to me, Nadir quoted you with admiration. He quoted your saying:

> *"Sadness is surrender and joy is victory."*

Do you remember saying that to him or was it an impromptu aphorism that escaped your unconscious mind, an aphorism that you have already relinquished?

Insist on joy in all things—the joy that comes from gratitude to life, in spite of all its floods and droughts. There is not a better calling for anyone's life than joy.

With all my love,

John

Forty-Eight

(Denouement)

(Tripoli - Saturday, April 24, 1999)

Dear Dad,

I've wanted to write, but too much has happened to distract me. I don't know where to begin so I guess I'll start with Kamal's visit.

Oh Dad, it was both beautiful and emotionally exhausting. Saturday, March 20th was a day to remember. We had made arrangements with Güzide that Tariq and I would pick her up from her dorm at eleven and take her by taxi to the airport. This would have given us plenty of time to get there before Kamal's airplane, which was scheduled to arrive at noon. She woke me up at seven that Saturday morning and insisted that we leave an hour earlier just in case traffic problems delayed us. I called Tariq, and we were at her dorm at ten.

She was waiting for us in the lobby wearing her new dress and her new, bouncy short hair. For the first time ever, she was not wearing anything black. Moreover, she was not even wearing her veil, which made her face look unnaturally pale. Tariq did not recognize her at first and looked through her for a veiled woman in black. Then, when he saw me walk up to her, he followed me with a sheepish look on his face and gazed at her with disbelief because he had never seen her dressed like a modern woman before.

To further play on his embarrassment, I introduced her to him as Miss Güzide Kamal Turkuman instead of Miss Güzide Istanbullu. While she seemed rather pleased to be introduced for the first time by her father's surname,

Tariq fumbled for words, and all he could come up with was a hoarse *"tsharrafna,"* which I translated to Güzide as *"we are honored,"* and then we all burst into laughter. On the way to the taxi, Tariq kept pinching me while gazing at her with utmost admiration, pantomiming his astonishment, and mouthing in Arabic, *"You son of a dog, she's beautiful!"*

In the taxi, we were silent until we passed by the U.S. Marine site. At that very moment, Güzide asked if the U.S. Marine Site was on our left. Both Tariq and I were shocked at her precision and asked how on earth did she know? She said that she knew it because her heart started to pound and she felt sick at her stomach. Nothing was said after that until we arrived at the airport and discovered that no one was allowed into the airport except ticketed passengers.

The waiting area was out in the open with no cover. While we waited, it started to rain, and we had no umbrellas. We took refuge under the awning at the airport entrance, as did all the other welcoming parties, and it quickly became crowded. Güzide was quiet but kept rearranging her hair and asking us repeatedly if she still looked all right. We reassured her by saying that she looked beautiful and kept her busy with idle conversation until we heard the announcement that the Turkish Airlines from Istanbul had landed.

Güzide did not have to wait to hear the announcement in English. She could tell from the words *"Al Khutut al Jawiyah al Turkiyah min İstanbul"* that her father's airplane had landed. Without saying a word, she turned pale, and sweat covered her face. While we waited in silence, we noticed that the crowd was moving toward the airport exit, which did not have an awning to protect the welcomers from the rain. But by then the rain had turned into a fine mist, which most of the welcoming parties did not seem to mind. When I asked Güzide if she would mind waiting in the rain, she put her hand to her hair and said that she did not want to get it wet.

We agreed that I would stay with Güzide under the awning and that Tariq would go to the exit gate and wait for Kamal with the rest of the welcoming crowd. Güzide got more and more nervous by the minute and asked me a hundred times if I could see her dad. It took a long time for the passengers to clear customs, but finally, I could see Tariq rush toward Kamal, give him a big hug, and then point us to him.

When I told Güzide that her father was gazing in our direction, she held my hand and began to shiver. But when I told her that they were hurrying toward us, that her dad could already see us, and that he had a huge smile on his face, she squeezed my hand with amazing strength and did not say another word until Kamal and Tariq stood facing us. During this most solemn moment that seemed to last forever, I guided her arm to her father's shoulder and delivered my hand from her grip. They both stood motionless, breathing into each other's faces, until Tariq put his arms around their waists and pushed them into an embrace. They clasped each other like magnets, mumbled a few words in Turkish, and began to cry. At that point, Tariq grabbed hold of Kamal's suitcase, and we moved away leaving them alone in what must have been the longest embrace that either of them had ever had.

Then, holding hands, they walked farther away from us and sat on a stone bench near the edge of the awning. There they talked for the longest time and were oblivious to their surroundings. Tariq and I waited patiently while father and daughter got acquainted. We could see Güzide hold her father's head with both hands and move them with amazed curiosity over his hair, forehead, eyes, nose, mustache, and mouth as if she were deciphering his features to her heart. When she got to his chin, she put her finger in his little dimple, then in hers, then in his again, and began to laugh. Here, Tariq seized the moment and, at the top of his voice, called for a taxi.

Tariq sat in front and guided the taxi to Fatima's home while Güzide sat between Kamal and me in the back. Kamal's English was poor compared to his French—but because Güzide and Tariq spoke no French, and Tariq and I spoke no Turkish—he was forced to communicate with us in English, escaping into French whenever his English failed him. At such points during the conversation, I would translate his French into Arabic for Tariq's sake while Kamal would translate it into Turkish for Güzide's sake. The taxi driver, hearing Turkish, English, French, and Arabic all spoken interchangeably, seemed both intrigued and entertained. Then, when he couldn't contain his curiosity any longer, he asked how on earth did we all happen to meet in the same place at the same time and followed it with, *"Subhan Allah, the United Nations is having a meeting in Abu Habib's taxi."*

When we arrived at Fatima's home, we all became quiet while Kamal paid the taxi. Then, with Kamal holding Güzide's arm and Tariq carrying Kamal's suitcase, we all went upstairs without saying a word, and I rang the bell. We could hear whispers and footsteps, and then the door opened. There stood Fatima, too frail to carry Little John, but carrying him anyway, and wavering under his weight, welcoming us with a faint smile and a hoarse hello. Immediately, I took Little John out of her arms, gave him to Güzide, and we all followed her into the living room and watched her collapse on the sofa exhausted and panting for breath. Quietly, Tariq went into Fatima's bedroom, returned with the long oxygen cord, looped it around her ears, and put the nasal prongs into her nostrils. It took her a few minutes before she could speak again.

I felt most proud of Tariq because he led the conversation in English and kept everyone laughing. Then he and I brought out the food, which the other Fatima had prepared before she left for the weekend, and we all ate in the living room. Kamal looked keenly at me while I cut Güzide's food and prepared her plate so she could eat without spilling. Then, Tariq took Fatima to her bedroom because she was starting to fall asleep as we ate. When we finished, I helped Tariq with the dishes while Kamal and Güzide sat on the sofa, whispering in Turkish. Little John, who sat next to Güzide during the meal, fell asleep on her lap while she stroked his back. Then, after we had Turkish coffee, we excused ourselves leaving Tariq with Little John and Fatima. As we walked back to Güzide's dorm, Kamal held Güzide's arm while I led the way carrying Kamal's suitcase.

Güzide took Kamal up to her room, and I waited in the lobby. Then, after a while, Kamal came down alone and asked me to take him to a nearby hotel. On the way, and quite unexpectedly, he asked me in French if I loved his daughter. I was lost for words, and while I collected my thoughts, he followed his question with, *"Güzide is in love with you. I asked her the same question when I was in her room and she too refused to answer."* We walked in silence after that until we reached Hamra Hotel and he checked in. Then, he told me that he was going to take a short nap after which he wanted to take Güzide and me to dinner. We agreed to come to his hotel at seven, and I went back to Güzide's dorm because we had a lot to talk about.

You see, Dad, until we received your letter, Güzide and I had not confessed our love to one another, but we both understood that we were in love and had even discussed our future plans after graduation. She said that she was going to go back to Istanbul to live with her grandpa because he is ill and alone and needs her company. I said that I was going to return to Oklahoma for the summer and be with you and Mom after which I would start job hunting. When I asked her if I could visit her in Istanbul, she said that her granddad wouldn't like it and may not allow it because he is very conservative and very traditional in his thinking. Even writing would be difficult while she lived with her granddad because she would need someone to read my letters to her, and she knew of no one she could trust with our secret. As for phone calls, she didn't like the idea of talking to me behind her grandpa's back. We were both at a loss as to what we should do with our lives and were hoping that Kamal would help us with these decisions.

When I got to her dorm, I called her from the lobby and asked her if we could go for a walk and talk. She said no because she felt tired and, instead, asked me to come up to her room. As I walked in, her roommate walked out and left us all alone. We sat on her bed and held hands without saying much. Each of us was afraid to start a conversation that would lead us to say things that we had never said to each other before. Finally, after a long silence, she turned toward me, held my face with both her hands, and asked me to kiss her. She whispered that she had never kissed a man before and did not know how to kiss. After we kissed once, we began to talk and could not stop talking as if the kiss had actually loosened up our lips.

Dad, I am so sorry to be telling you all this all at once, but it all happened so quickly and took us both by surprise. At dinner with Kamal, I asked him for Güzide's hand in both English and French, as we had agreed. He seemed very pleased and blessed us both. Then he asked us where we intended to live, and I said wherever I could get a job. He asked me if I would mind working in Istanbul at the Ministry of Exterior as a liaison American reporter who would translate Turkish reports into English and e-mail them to the U.S. Embassy. When I said that I did not speak Turkish, he looked at Güzide and said that, since Turkish is now written with Latin letters, Güzide could be my interpreter and my Turkish teacher all at the same time.

I clutched Güzide's hand and asked her what would her grandpa do if we were to get married without his permission. She blushed and said that he would not like it, especially that I am Christian, but that if she had enough time with him she could soften his heart. She also said that her grandpa loved her far too much to interfere with her future and her happiness.

Then Kamal asked me if I wanted children and how did I expect Güzide be able to raise a child. At that point, Güzide blushed and intervened by saying that she would have to hire a housekeeper anyway because we would need help with Little John. At this revelation, both Kamal and I looked at each other and almost simultaneously exclaimed, *"Little John!"*

Güzide remained calm and very seriously said that she had promised Fatima that she would take care of her little brother and keep him with her until he is grown. When I asked her how would her granddad feel about

Little John, she answered with carefree confidence that he would be delighted to have a young boy sit in his lap and brighten up his big old house. Then she followed her prediction with, *"Grandfather has never refused me anything. When I return home after graduation, we will talk and I will tell him about my father, my brother, and about you Nadir. Of course, he will get upset at first, then he will accept my reality and learn to love the three new men in my life. He will even be happy for me and will stop worrying about what will happen to me after he is gone. I believe that, given enough time, my newfound life will bring him joy and sweeten his sick years with hope."* After saying all this in English, Güzide turned to her dad and said it all again in Turkish, which seemed to relieve Kamal and bring a smile of gratitude to his face.

Now Dad, please don't get upset, and try to understand that I have come to love Güzide so much that I couldn't bear to live without her, and she has come to love Little John and me so much that she couldn't bear to live without us. Little John is a wonderful boy, and I have come to love him too, and he will brighten up our lives if we raise him together. But according to the Lebanese law, we cannot adopt Little John unless we are married.

And since I am Christian and Güzide is Muslim, we decided to fly to Cyprus for a civil marriage and to do it promptly enough for Fatima to sign the adoption papers while she still can. She had a CAT scan a few weeks ago, which showed that the lung cancer had gone to her brain, and was the cause of her bad headaches and unsteady gait. Her doctor put her on cortisone to reduce her brain swelling and told Tariq that she had very little time left. So Dad, we had to move fast, and I failed to ask your advice or your permission because I was overwhelmed and hurried, and because unlike Güzide, I am incapable of being thoughtful when under pressure.

Dad, its my turn now to ask you to sit down. Please sit down, Dad. We really, really did it on Saturday, March 27th. Both Kamal and Tariq flew with us to Cyprus where we got married and returned to Beirut the same day. We then went straight to Fatima, and she signed the adoption papers. Now, Güzide and I have become instant parents, and you have become Little John's grandfather.

We celebrated our first Easter together as a married couple on Sunday, April 11 because this year, the Orthodox Easter came one week after the Catholic Easter. We went together to the early morning mass at St. Michael's Orthodox Church near the AUB, and we prayed for peace, love, and forgiveness. Güzide has not worn her veil since we got married because she now considers herself to be half Muslim and half Christian, and in turn, I consider myself half Christian and half Muslim. This religious duality is so much more fun because we will get to celebrate the holy days of both religions from now on. We also decided to raise our children as bi-religious so that they would feel free to move between East and West without hang-ups. We have, all of a sudden, become an eclectic family, which must surely please you and make you feel proud.

After Tariq shared with us your touching letter to him, Güzide and I spent many hours analyzing what you had said. Consequently, Güzide and I have adopted your motto to insist on joy, and we will uphold this as our marital ideology, because as you said to Tariq, *"there is no better calling for anyone's life than joy."*

Güzide was the one who pointed out to me that if we were to insist on joy, we could never be destructive, cruel, evil, unforgiving, unloving, untruthful, angry, vengeful, jealous, treacherous, dishonest, unfaithful, inpatient, resentful, unjust, possessive, or punitive because none of the negative human traits can coexist with joy. I wouldn't have gotten so much out of your seemingly simple imperative without Güzide's deep analysis. Thank you Dad, for giving us this precious pearl to be the guiding light of our lives.

I am writing to you from Tripoli because Güzide and I came to visit Grandma. She was so excited and happy for us that she insisted we spend the night at her home. Tomorrow she has invited the entire family for lunch so we can meet them after we return from church. And yes, Dad, tomorrow, Güzide and I are going with Grandma to Sunday church to light candles for all our loved ones.

Grandma told Güzide that her own father was blind from birth, that he was self-taught, and that he became a great Arabic linguist and teacher who earned a good enough income to marry and raise her as an only child. Her story gave Güzide great encouragement, and the two bonded instantly after Grandma's story. Now, Güzide has a grandmother again. Dad, it's three in the morning, and I am too excited to sleep. Please forgive me, and don't rise from your seat yet; I still have so much more to tell you.

Before we got married, Güzide called her grandpa, told him the whole story, and asked for his permission. He roared back at her saying that she can ask her own father for permission because he was not about to bless this marriage. He further added that he could never allow an American Christian boy to sleep with his Muslim granddaughter under his very own roof, and ended the conversation with a threat that he would disinherit Güzide if she were to go through with the marriage. Güzide cried, told him that she loved him, and said good-bye. Please Dad, don't blame me, but after seeing how Güzide's conversation ended, I made my decision not to tell you till after the fact and to tell you by letter, not by phone.

After the marriage, Güzide sent her grandpa pictures of us in Cyprus, and pictures of us in Fatima's room with Kamal and Little John by her side. She mailed the package overnight with a long letter and called him again three days later. When he heard her voice, he began to cry, told her that he loved her, that he was sorry for what he had said, that he considered Little John and me to be his new children, that he wanted us to live with him when we first move to Istanbul, and that Kamal would be welcome to visit us anytime he wished.

Dad, I know that all of this has happened too fast, but Güzide and I still want to ask for your blessings when we come to see Mom and you after graduation. We hope to arrive in Oklahoma City at the end of May and stay with you for a month before we move to Istanbul. I want Güzide to meet Ghassan, Frida, and all my friends. They will all love her and so will you because she is a remarkable woman.

Tariq is so happy for us and plans to visit us in Istanbul many times a year. When we come to Beirut, we can stay with him because he plans to keep his mother's flat. I feel so much love for him that I can't imagine my life without him. After all, he is Little John's brother, which makes him my adopted brother. I no longer think of him as my friend but as my third brother, my Muslim brother, my brother by love, my brother by marriage, and my brother by friendship.

As for Fatima, she is being most brave and always has a smile for us when we visit. I don't think that she will last much longer, though. She stays in her bed most of the time now, but when we visit her, she always asks about you, wants to know all your news, and always asks me not to forget to give you her letter the next time I see you. In fact, she was the one who urged me to write this letter and insisted that I send it to you overnight by DHL so you would not have to wait another two weeks to find out. When I said that I could call and tell you on the phone, she shook her head and whispered, *"I know your father too well. Send him a long letter. It will give him time to come to terms with all your happenings. He needs time to think it over with his big brain. Your father does not like to think things over quickly."*

Well Dad, here it is. Now you know everything. Please read this long letter to Mom, and please be happy for us. We cannot wait to see you at the end of May. Please tell Ghassan, Frida, and my friends the good news.

We all love you,

Güzide, Little John, and Nadir

Forty-Nine

(West Is East)

(Oklahoma City - Saturday, May 1, 1999)

Dear Güzide, Nadir, and Little John,

Your news spurred my heart into a gallop in the direction of youth. I saw the joy in your eyes as you vouchsafed your lives to one another, joy unmatched and unsurpassable, for love can grant no greater gift than joy.

I sense your excitement at having nurtured to full fruition a love that was seeded as a selfless gift, watered with openness, fertilized with friendship, blossomed with passion, and ripened with God's sun.

You have been chosen because you were cast by holy coincidence to find and spark love in one another, love from the first touch. I shall forever think of you as the intercontinental smile that strung a rainbow of joy between life's north and south poles and forged an embrace of peace out of the inimical arms of East and West.

From this other side of earth, I bless your covenant with love, anoint it with hope, and suspend it with prayers in a sublime realm that hovers above this raucous world and its cruel realities.

Your flames warmed my cold, stiff fingers and moved me to dedicate this poem to you. I pray that you read it to one another each time you falter or take one another for granted. Burnish it with daily gratitude so that oblivion will never fade its lines out of your memory.

"Earth was formed four and a half billion
years ago
It took the crust one billion years to cool
enough for life to begin
Single life cells appeared three and a half
billion years ago
Organisms appeared five hundred and seventy
million years ago
Humankind appeared two hundred and fifty
thousand years ago...

My love,
It took two continents, two hundred and fifty
thousand years
And several billion genetic, environmental,
and circumstantial coincidences to
bring us together;
See how tedious the Lord's work had been
How meticulously exacting
All for one couple to fall in love
And for that love to blossom into worship...

Praise Him, my love, and thank Him with all
your joys
For He has manipulated the entire creation for
the two of us;

Four and a half billion years
I have waited for you."

I read your letter to Mom, and she smiled. Do you
know how long it has been since your mother last smiled?
Your blithe news, my dear children, brought an end to her
expressionless drought. I am now sure that your mother
can hear, can understand, and can express her emotions
with her face. How much gratitude we owe you, how much
joy, and how much renaissance.

I gave your letter to Frida without saying a word and
watched her while she read it. Her expressions journeyed
among curiosity, suspense, solemnness, delight, laughter,

and sighs. Then, when she put the letter down, she looked at me with a knowing frown and eyes moist with responsibility and exclaimed, *"I'm now an aunt. Cool."* Then, without saying another word, she got up, patted me on the shoulder, and retired to her room.

When I called Ghassan and told him the news, he grew silent and then asked me if I were kidding. Instead of going back and forth, I faxed the letter to him and waited. When after two hours he did not call me back, I called him again. Carla said that when he finished reading the letter, he gave it to her and took off in his car. She promised that she would ask him to call me when he returned. I waited till midnight and then went to sleep.

The following morning, he woke me up at six and wanted to know what I thought. We talked for an hour, and I managed to put all his fears to rest. When I asked him where did he go last night and when did he return home, he laughed and said that he went to his office and tried to call you at your dorm. When he did not find you, he took a long drive, thought things over, came back home with a bouquet of flowers, gave it to Tamara, and said, *"Congratulations, you now have a younger cousin, and his name is Little John."* Tamara seemed a bit confused and then she asked: *"Do we have to call grandpa John, Big John from now on?"*

Thanks to you both, lightning and thunder have stormed my mind lately and significant happenings have undermined some of my native thoughts. Thanks to you, I find that my grip has loosened and no longer clings to beliefs that I had held intransigent. Thanks to you, I find that change has sprouted out of my stagnant realities and is growing colorful blossoms in my winter garden. Thanks to you, I find that time has rendered my high, inflexible branches fruit laden and ready for picking. Thanks to you, I now fear that if I do not sway with my mental storms, my fruits will remain unreachable until my branches break. Indeed, and thanks to both of you, I fear that if I do not visit Fatima, Tariq, Little John, my mother, and my homeland, I will never be able to put to rest the beckoning cries throughout my restless void.

But I cannot leave your mother unattended, not even for a few days. I cannot leave her because she needs dedicated, exacting care. I cannot leave her because, in her silent quietude, she would realize that I am no longer by her side and that would frighten her. I cannot leave her in anyone else's custody but yours, Nadir, because you are the only one who has kept her smiling. Would Güzide mind if I were to leave you both with Mom while I journey to Lebanon to pay my respects to loves that have shaped and sustained me, loves whose longevity I have taken for granted, loves that may not be with us much longer?

Love, my dear children, is the taproot of humanity, and I can no longer let distance continue to weaken its sap. The words of Edna St. Vincent Millay have given me the resolve I needed: *"Yet many a man is making friends with death...for lack of love alone."*

My plan is to have a reception for you a few days after you arrive, and then leave you with Mom for a week while I make my visit. If this is acceptable to both of you, please e-mail me your itinerary so that I can plan mine.

Tell Fatima not to loosen her grip. Tell her to hang on by a smile. Tell Tariq that I will be meeting him soon. Tell my mother that I will stay with her in Tripoli and take her to church on Sunday. Tell her that after thirty years of roaming, the river has found its way to the sea. And tell Little John that Grandpa John is coming to hold him close to his heart.

I owe a lot to you, Nadir, but I owe a lot more to Güzide because she is the magnet that brought our scattered filaments together and the quiet tree that shaded us all with peace. Your union is an antithesis to the atavistic dogma that East and West can never meet. In fact, the distinction between East and West shows a platitude of imagination because as earth rotates, there is a continuum that rises and sets as East becomes West and West becomes East. Around earth's round table, no knight sits at the helm and upon this globe there is no fore-and-aft.

The main thing that separates humanity is ignorance. Only the enlightened few can see that borders are ephemeral, seams, artificial, and the atmosphere is God's handmade quilt that keeps us all warm.

I cannot wait to see your mother's smile when she hears your voices in her room. I wouldn't be surprised if she comes out of her coma for the two of you, awakens to exchange love embraces with both of you, and orbits back to us from the outer spaces of dementia because her son and his bride have come to pay her a visit. Miracles happen all the time, and if we are willing to notice, we can recognize them everywhere and in everything. Please hurry home; our entire world awaits your coming.

You should receive this letter in two days because I am sending it by DHL. Don't forget to bring Fatima's letter with you. It must contain information that she wishes to pass on to me before she departs.

I love you all,

Dad

Fifty

(Fatima's Letter)

(Beirut – Saturday, October 17, 1998)

My Dear John,

I am writing this letter two days before my operation. I'm going to be admitted tomorrow afternoon, and my surgery is scheduled for Monday morning. The chest surgeon, Dr. Abbas, has an excellent reputation and seems very kind and reassuring. But in spite of all assurances, I feel afraid. I feel that I will never recover after they remove half of my left lung. I feel that this surgery, which seems inevitable now, will mark the beginning of my dying days.

If I do not survive my surgery, Dr. Abbas will give this letter to Nadir and ask him to hand it to you when he sees you next. I do not want it mailed because letters have a way of getting lost, and I need to be certain that this letter will reach your eyes.

Yesterday, as usual, I took Little John to Fatima. She met me with a smile that belied her melancholy. She even spoke slowly and enunciated as if I were deaf. We had lunch together, and she told me to pass by the shrine and speak my peace to Um Al-Huda. When I seemed puzzled, she repeated the phrase, *"Go make your peace with Um Al-Huda,"* then quietly added, *"This may be your last visit to her."*

I said good-bye to Little John, who was playing unconcerned, and went to the shrine. I prayed and listened again and again hoping for a whisper or a sign. I was met with silence, which caused me great anguish. As I left the shrine, a vendor offered me a cool jallab drink with pine nuts floating on top. I drank it slowly as I looked around at all the faithful in the square feeding groups of white pigeons. By the time I finished my drink and was ready to give it back to the vendor, a pigeon landed on my wrist and started to eat the pine nuts in the bottom of the cup. The vendor seemed amused and asked me why didn't I like pine nuts. I said that, on the contrary, I liked them a lot and that I often used them in my cooking. He then asked me why did I leave them to the pigeon if I liked them, and added that most of the faithful eat the pine nuts off the top because they have healing powers. When I heard him say that, I shooed the pigeon off my wrist and tried to salvage at least one nut, but I was too late; all the nuts were gone.

On the way back to Beirut, I became convinced that I was going to die, but I was at peace with my knowing. I enjoyed meditating, thinking about us, and how life with all its powerful temptations had failed to separate our hearts. It was then that I decided to tell you the truth, a truth I had protected you from, a truth I presumed would have devastated your peaceful mind and creative spirit.

In my heart, I know that when you read this letter I will be on my deathbed, but I will refuse to die until I hear your voice reassuring me that what I withheld from you all these years—what I am about to tell you now—will not cause you undue harm or hardship. Only then will I be able to die with gratitude for all that life has offered us.

John, remember when you flew to meet me in Paris early in December of 1976 after having been away from me for six long years? We had to fabricate excuses because both of us had gotten married by then, were unhappy, confused, and starved for one another. After only three days together you returned to Oklahoma with resolve never to talk to me or see me again, and the only form of communication you allowed me was handwritten letters, which you often took months to answer. Well, you were not the only one who felt guilty after that escapade, nor the only one who was disillusioned at our inability to shake off an old, far- away love. I shared your guilt and your disillusionment, but also shared something far more important than these remorseful feelings.

What I shared agonized inside of me for nine

months, and then Tariq was born. You should see how much he resembles you, walks like you, acts like you, and even talks like you. People think that he and Nadir are brothers because they look so much alike. Surely you must have wondered why did they bond with one another so quickly and so effortlessly. I asked myself the same question when Little John and Güzide similarly bonded. Do you think that siblings recognize each other, even though they do not know that they are blood relatives?

Ahmad has asked me many a time if Tariq was his son, and I have always answered with a definite yes. No one knows, John, no one but I because the truth would have complicated both our lives. Forgive me, darling, and pray for my peaceful transition for I have sinned against you by not telling you when I should have.

My love, you need tell no one. You may choose to take our secret with you to the grave, and life will go on, undisturbed, like nothing has happened. I, on the other hand, felt compelled to hand my secret to you before I took leave, because I knew that it would help keep our love alive in your heart.

Now that you know that we have a son together, we will continue to love long after we are gone, because our son will carry our love in his heart and hand it down to others, who will hand it down to others, and on and on...

Good-bye John. Good-bye my darling. I will never say, good-bye my love, because love never dies.

I love you,

Fatima

Epilogue

My father, may God rest his soul, held Fatima's hand while she took her last breath. Before she died, she asked him to take his letters back to the U.S. and hide them next to hers. I wouldn't have known to look for them were it not for Tariq, who was with her when she gave the bundle of letters to Dad, neatly tied with a yellow ribbon.

Dad returned home a changed man. He seemed inconsolably lonesome and would spend hours in Mom's room reading to her. Güzide and I could not spend much time in Oklahoma because we had to return to take care of Little John. It was Fatima's wish that Little John stay with the other Fatima until we returned. Tariq went to Syria and brought him back home the day we arrived, and we all stayed together at Fatima's flat while we packed and got ready to relocate to Istanbul.

Dad called us almost daily and promised to visit us when we had our own home. When mother died at the end of that summer, he called us crying. We left Little John with Güzide's grandfather and flew back to Oklahoma, but after the funeral, we could not spend much time with Dad because I was needed at my job at the Turkish Ministry of Exterior.

When Frida left for college, Dad remained alone in our big house and for a while became a recluse. Then, in the spring of 2000, when his grief had died down, he returned to Lebanon to see Grandma and Tariq. He would spend his nights and mornings at Grandma's home in Tripoli, and his afternoons and evenings with Tariq in Beirut. After Lebanon, he spent a week with us at our new home in Istanbul. Güzide, who seemed less worried about him than the rest of us, said to me when he left, *"Your dad is now ready to live again."*

He returned to Lebanon in the spring of 2001 and spent a month with Grandma and Tariq. This time, when he came to Istanbul, he brought children's Arabic books with him from which he read many stories to Little John. He loved taking Little John to the park and teaching him Arabic and was upset with us because we were speaking mainly Turkish and English at home. He said that Little John should grow up trilingual, and that if I did not speak more Arabic with him, he would soon forget his native tongue. That was the last time we saw Dad.

We received the news from my brother Ghassan, the day after 9/11. He said that Dad had taken Mrs. Settembrini to New York for a few days and was supposed to return to work on Wednesday, September 12. When he didn't show up or call, his nurse became suspicious and telephoned Ghassan in Boston. We waited like the rest of the families until they were declared dead by the authorities. Neither Mrs. Settembrini's family nor ours have any idea what they were doing near the World Trade Center at the time the airplanes hit, but knowing dad, he would have rushed to offer medical help and might have been struck down when the second tower was hit.

After the funeral, I looked through his papers and found the letters. Only then did I realize that Tariq was my half brother. I took the letters back with me and called Tariq. He came to Istanbul and brought with him the few letters that Dad had written him. We spent an entire month reading them together, and when we finished, we felt more filled with brotherly love than ever before.

The letters stayed with me until last year. In the meantime, Tariq picked up his mother's trade and became a freelance photographer. The last time he visited us, he told me that he wanted to publish the letters. I was worried lest the letters should certainly offend his father and perhaps other family members and friends. He said that he would change the names, places, dates, happenings, and countries in such a way as to make it impossible for anyone to put the facts back together, and indeed he did.

He and I have edited several drafts, and I am most pleased with this final manuscript, which should go to print soon.

Nadir Khoury

(Istanbul – Monday, March 19, 2007)

The End